THE SUNLIT STAGE

THE SUNLIT STAGE

SIMONETTA WENKERT

BLOOMSBURY

First published in Great Britain in 2004

This paperback edition published 2005

Copyright © 2004 by Simonetta Wenkert

The moral right of the author has been asserted

Bloomsbury Publishing Plc, 38 Soho Square, London W1D 3HB

A CIP catalogue record for this book
is available from the British Library

ISBN 0 7475 7291 7
9780747572916

10 9 8 7 6 5 4 3 2 1

Typeset by Hewer Text Ltd, Edinburgh

All papers used by Bloomsbury Publishing are natural,
recyclable products made from wood grown in
well-managed forests. The manufacturing processes conform
to the environmental regulations of the country of origin.

Printed in Great Britain by Clays Ltd, St Ives plc

www.bloomsbury.com/simonettawenkert

For Avi

1

A PERFECT DAY

It was a stone house on a hill overlooking an orchard: 'La Camillina', it was called. A path sloped through some olive groves down towards the track where they had left the car, a white Fiat 127 which Ennio had borrowed for the day. From the kitchen window you could see the red-tiled roofs of the nearest village, and beyond that, a shimmering line of sea. It said '*Ingegner* Marelli' on the buzzer of the intercom. The key was hidden inside a wood-burning oven by a grove of hazel trees.

On the way to the house they stopped at the village to buy food for the day: half a loaf of *casareccio* bread dusted with some kind of grainy flour which felt almost like semolina, ham, cheese, some yoghurt in a glass jar and a bunch of black grapes. When they arrived at the house they found a basket of figs by the front door and a demi-john of wine in a plastic mesh holder: a gift from Tommaso who had the farm at the end of the track.

In the kitchen Julia unwrapped the cheese and *prosciutto* from their waxed paper packets, laying them out on the plates she found on a shelf above the sink. Some were chipped; on others the glaze had cracked to a silvery mosaic pattern like fish-scales. She put the figs into a bowl with the grapes. Every now and then she caught glimpses of her breasts and arms beneath the low-cut neck of the new Indian dress she had bought at the market in Porta Portese, and the sight of her skin, brown and gleaming as though it had been sprayed with particles of life-giving oil, made her smile slyly to herself. She wished everybody in England could see her moving around that farmhouse kitchen: confidently, swiftly, as though at last in her true habitat.

It was a special day for many reasons, not least because they were getting out of Rome for the day. And Ennio had gone to the trouble of borrowing his friend Massimo's car – and he was finally taking her to somewhere that belonged to him (if not in name, then in spirit), unlike all those anonymous student houses he divided his time between. And that had to mean something in the general graph of their relationship.

'Are we going to eat, or what?' said Ennio. He was standing barefoot at the table, pouring the wine through a funnel into an empty Sprite bottle. There was a special Italian word for transferring a liquid – oil or water or wine – from a large container to a smaller one: *travasare*, that was it . . . The golden hairs on his arms caught the light from the window: like many of his friends he had a small home-made tattoo above the wrist, yin and yang in a circle. In the distance they heard the snarl of a tractor, then a door slamming and a woman's voice calling *Tommaso, Tommaso* . . . A breeze blew in through the window: it was cooler up in the hills. Julia desired Ennio so much she could scarcely bear to look at him; all she could think about was brushing the tip of her tongue in the exact centre of the tattoo. She averted her eyes, embarrassed by the nakedness of her desire: perhaps after lunch she would sit at the table and try to sketch the view from the window.

They sat at the table like lovers in a painting, and Ennio handed Julia the plate.

'You first,' she said.

'Don't be English. Take what you want.'

Obediently, she picked up a slice of *prosciutto* with her fork and took a fig from the bowl. She had never eaten fresh figs before coming to Italy, let alone with ham. She knew you were meant to peel them, but she loved biting through the dry skin with its plump, viscous underbelly. The seeds were as fragile as husks.

'Who's *Ingegner* Marelli?' she asked, remembering by chance the name on the buzzer.

'An engineer who doesn't exist. And even if he does exist, he doesn't own this house.'

'Who does own it then?' Julia knew she sounded pedantic – English, Ennio would say. Why should it matter who owned the house?

Ennio tore off a piece of bread and gave her half. He looked at her – really looked at her – as though her face had swum unexpectedly into focus. His eyes were hard, calculating, as though he didn't like what he saw. He had Sicilian eyes, the dark irises partly concealed by heavy lids. He looked at her as though the light had gone out on the afternoon. As though, she thought later, everything else that day – the almost unbearable excitement of waiting for him on the wall outside her flat; the smile on his face when he saw her new dress; choosing the food in the village, laying it out on the cracked plates – as though through all that pleasure she had been dancing with a ghost-lover.

'Does anyone own anything? Do I own you? Does anyone really think he can say: this house belongs to me, therefore I have the right to keep you outside my gates? Only a capitalist and a Fascist would, that's who.' He smiled as if he realised he had been too harsh with her, and gently stroked her face. He had laughter-lines around his eyes which curled upwards like a cat's whiskers. 'If you must know, some of the *compagni* bought it as a cooperative a couple of years ago from Tommaso. We've gradually installed electricity and running water; last summer we built the brick fireplace and put in the upstairs bathroom. Is that enough for your analytical Anglo-Saxon mind to chew over?'

Her heart twisted with joy; she loved it when he teased her. 'Yes. No.' (It was never enough.) 'Who looks after the fields?'

Once again the room was flooded with light. 'Tommaso and his daughter give us a hand with the vineyard and the olive groves. The wine you're drinking is from last year's harvest. The rest we do when we can get down here.'

After lunch, they went into one of the upstairs bedrooms to rest. There was a mattress laid out on the floor covered with a surprisingly homely-looking sheet: mustard and orange tulips on a pale yellow background, the kind of sheet a housewife might buy at the market in Piazza Vittorio. The shutters were half-closed with the catch dangling loosely in the middle so that a bar of light seemed to be suspended in the darkness. The air vibrated with heat and the sound of crickets. Julia slowly lifted her dress above her head, letting the wispy cotton shimmer up her spine. It smelt of inky dye and sweat; she hadn't washed it yet. She hung it on the catch of the shutters, so that the afternoon sun shone through it, illuminating a patch of wall above the mattress like the reflection from a stained glass window: red, amber, purple.

Ennio lay on his stomach fiddling with the knobs of a transistor radio which stood on the floor beside the bed: she heard a snatch of a Lucio Battisti song, '*I Giardini di Marzo*', it was called, 'The Gardens in March'. It had an almost unbearably nostalgic refrain . . . '*Che anno é? Che giorno é?*' the day and year lost in an eerie present, that querulous, pleading voice: '*Questo é il tempo di vivere con te*'. It reminded her of the junkies who wandered wraith-like at dusk, along the dusty paths of the gardens at the Colle Oppio. The Hill of Opiates . . . She lay down on the bed beside him, smelling the faintly stale smell of the pillowcase. It was a familiar smell, like the tram she caught early in the morning on the way to the university – a mixture of saliva and mothballs. Unwashed teeth, tongues furred with oily coffee. Everything in the house was like that: tidy but not really clean: the chipped

4

plates faintly sticky to the touch, the floor swept but not perfectly so that it felt gritty beneath their feet. Yet in all the squats and student houses Ennio had taken her to, never once had she seen the almost voluptuous squalor she associated with university flats in Bristol. No matter how anti-bourgeois the *compagni* professed to be, they still all sat down together for their meals, and there was always someone who got up to wash the dishes straight after. Usually one of the men, who said he had a sexist past to be forgiven. Most of the girls claimed they couldn't cook.

Without turning away from the radio, Ennio slipped his hand around her waist, feeling for the hollow of her spine with his thumb. He slid the blade of his palm downwards, driving a slow path between her buttocks as though buying time before he reached the core of her desire: *Questo é il tempo di vivere con te* . . . It was always a gradual disengagement from the outside world – the headline from *Lotta Continua* left open on the table, the *compagno* to be called from the public telephone beneath the stairs of a bar, the pile of leaflets to distribute – so that invariably it was with a sense of surprise that Ennio discovered himself aroused. Which made his abandon all the more exquisite to Julia: each time he entered her it was with the full shock of his personality. Yet he never said he loved her.

Afterwards they slept. When Julia awoke, the space beside her on the mattress was empty. For a moment she felt confused; she had been dreaming of London. It was a winter's evening; she was standing as a child on the bridge at the Ha'penny Steps holding her father's hand as they watched a barge glide along the bend in the canal. *Nebulae*, it was called. She waved as it approached the bridge, then ran to the railings opposite to watch it emerge from beneath them. She turned to her father to tell him something, but even before the words came out she knew he had gone: she was all alone on the bridge with a foolish smile on her lips like a child in a story book. The radio was still on: she heard the pips of the *giornaleradio*, then a brisk woman's voice reading the head-lines: an armoury on the River Tevere had been attacked and looted by a group of left-wing terrorists; Parliament was holding an emergency session to debate a temporary ban on all demonstrations. There was still no word from the group holding the Milanese industrialist, Ettore Labate. Julia wondered if Ennio had heard the news; obscurely, she knew he already had. She stood up and walked over to the window. She opened the shutters and looked out across the hills: beyond the orchard towards the track she heard a car engine hacking to life – had someone been up to the house? She saw Ennio walking between the fruit trees with one hand in his pocket; his head was bent, and in the other hand he was holding what looked like a scrap of paper which he glanced at from time to time. By the gate, a young girl stood watching him. Quickly, Julia closed the shutters, and sat back down on the mattress.

It was gone five; the sun had lost some of its earlier intensity and no longer burned through the fabric of her Indian dress like the light through a stained glass window. She could feel a delicious stickiness between her thighs, which soon she would go to the bathroom to rinse. Or perhaps wouldn't. She thought of Ennio's hands pressing hers tightly behind his back, too proud to say 'hold me', although his heart was exploding in his chest, as though to batter its way through his ribs and hers, and each time that image came into her mind a small shock vibrated in her like the wave following an orgasm.

Still naked, she walked out of the room and stood for a moment on the landing, listening; the house was silent. Then, in a spirit of pure mischief, as she would later acknowledge to herself, looking for trouble, no more, no less, as though all that swoony desire needed a harder edge to it, she opened the door of what seemed to be a lumber room. The shutters were tightly closed and the room was dark. She switched on the light and looked around, at the same time listening out for Ennio, without admitting to herself that was what she was doing.

Piled in one corner were several sacks of cement, while beside them, propped up against the wall, were some pre-fabricated panels, the kind used by plasterers. Obviously there were skilled workmen amongst the *compagni*. A peculiar sensation overcame her; she felt as though she had unlocked the door of Bluebeard's room – not that Ennio had forbidden her from exploring the house. It was more of a transferred feeling, as though that room contained the answer to every one of Ennio's unexplained absences – the forged identity card she found in his wallet together with a dog-eared *santino* of S. Giuseppe, the stolen moped, the keys to the flat of a *compagno* 'who was away'. There were rolls of what looked like fibre-glass on the floor – '*lana di vetro*' it said on the packaging – and on a table by the window stood an old-fashioned IBM banding machine. It reminded her of the worksheets her geography teacher, Miss Phillips, used to hand out: maps of China in violet ink, blurred yet precise, like the tattoo on Ennio's wrist. The machine was still warm.

Julia placed a hand on her belly, the other on one breast: it felt full, the nipple darker than usual. She switched off the light and closed the door behind her.

Ennio was sitting at the kitchen table amidst the remains of their lunch. He smiled when she walked in: she had washed her face and slicked her hair behind her ears. The room was dim and smelt of coffee. She sat down beside him and he poured her a coffee from the small, two-cup *caffettiera*. He kissed her and touched her wet hair: 'Drink up, we'll be leaving soon.'

An immense melancholy overtook her at the thought of leaving La Camillina, that intimacy which in Rome dissipated itself in lectures, catching up with coursework from Bristol, the cleaning rota in the shared flat. Besides, she never knew when she would see Ennio: she had no way of contacting him, and he never called her. He thought relationships were bourgeois.

7

Weeks would pass; she would go and see English films at the Pasquino cinema in Trastevere, or take a book to the gardens in Villa Ada, imagining to herself that all she had to do was raise her eyes from the page and he would be standing by the fountain, his otter's head glinting in the sunlight. Then, just as she had given up all hope, she would come out of the language laboratory with her students and find him waiting for her on the steps of the English faculty. He never looked pleased to see her; it was as though he carried the cares of the world on his shoulders – as though she and their non-relationship were just more of those cares. Once they made love on the grass beneath the plane trees at the Villa Borghese; another time it was raining and they took the *metropolitana* to Ostia to meet a *compagno* in an empty beach hut. The *compagno* never showed up, and all afternoon they lay on the gritty cement floor of the hut amongst last summer's towels and swimming costumes which smelt of seaweed and Ambre Solaire.

Their last hour at La Camillina passed as though in a dream. Julia sat by the window watching the sky flare from blue to gold to pink, the colours of the landscape glowing weirdly – a false dawn, as though the day were her friend, determined to try any ruse to delay the onset of darkness. By contrast, the shadows in the room grew deeper. She reached inside her bag and took out the small artist's notebook she had bought in the *cartoleria* in Via dei Serpenti. On its pages she had sketched all the places where she had sat waiting for Ennio: the view from her room opposite the Colosseum, a group of gypsy children playing by a fountain near the Ghetto, the flower-sellers in Campo de' Fiori, so that each picture was infused with a kind of melancholy optimism. There was always one figure that might or might not have been him, an enigmatic cartoon Ennio with a rolled-up newspaper in his pocket. Until she had drawn that figure her picture was never complete. Sometimes when they made love she would find herself unexpectedly transported back to one of those scenes, as though they were connected by an invisible network of emotions – a secret map of the heart.

As she sketched, Ennio swept the floor and ran a hosepipe out into the orchard to water the fruit trees. He rinsed the plates under the tap and packed the remainder of the loaf and the packets of ham and cheese into Tommaso's basket: 'We'll leave them for him on the way down to the road.'

She drew the scene framed by shutters: afterwards, she wondered if she already knew that one day she might need to remind herself of how she had stood at an upstairs window watching him walk through the orchard. The sketch grew more complex: she added the demi-john of wine in the plastic basket (though strictly speaking the porch was neither visible from where she sat, nor in proportion to the rest of the drawing) and the Fiat 127 which was parked beyond the olive groves. Now it was Julia who was buying time: a kind of mad punctiliousness overtook her, as though she had to get in every single detail of their day – anything to put off the moment when they would have to leave. She sensed Ennio watching her from the sink; deliberately she drew a figure walking through the trees, sleek head bent, a scrap of paper in one hand. Just so he knew what she knew. And to make the picture complete.

He came to the window and they kissed: lovers in a painting. 'I love you,' said Ennio. *Questo é il tempo di vivere con te* . . . She hadn't meant to tell him. Not yet. 'I'm pregnant,' she said. He took her hands. She never saw his face as he spoke: 'Leave. Go back to England. I can't see you again.'

2

CARUSO TALKS

The first time I interviewed Ennio Caruso was back in July 1980.

At the time he was awaiting trial in the maximum-security prison, L'Asinara, situated on an island opposite Sardinia's fashionable Costa Smeralda; it was eventually closed down after a massive prisoners' revolt in 1981. Through his lawyer, Edoardo Casimirri, I submitted a list of questions which first had to be approved by the prison authorities, mainly concerning the Tonino Valpreda affair and relations between the Sinistra Armata inmates and their companions on the outside. All sorts of theories were flying around in those days, mostly claiming the kidnapping had been entirely masterminded from within L'Asinara by the so-called *nucleo storico*; some even hinted at a right-wing plot to discredit the new Coalition Government. Not that I had any intentions of going down the conspiracy road: quite enough ink – then and now – has been spilt on such theories, a peculiarly Italian obssesion among journalists of my generation.

My then editor at *La Nazione* also suggested a few personal questions like 'What would you say to the families of your victims?', and another one along the lines of 'Would you do anything differently if you had the chance?' Not that we expected Caruso to reply: the SA were famously unemotional in all their releases, and refused to see individual loss of life –

theirs or the other side's – as anything other than the price to pay for armed struggle. The only exception to that was the leaflet they distributed when Natalia Pinto was shot dead by *carabinieri* during a night raid on a safe-house near Genova. A week later, journalists were allowed in to photograph the room where she had been killed; the flat had been cleaned yet there were streaks of blood reaching all the way up to the ceiling. In their release, the SA spoke of her 'life and death which no revolutionary will ever forget'. In surprisingly over-blown language (after all, it was written by Dall'Oglio who was her lover at the time) it ended with the words: 'Natalia: from the soil where your blood fell, a flower will bloom, and this flower of liberty will be tended by Sinistra Armata until Victory is ours! May a thousand arms reach out for your gun!' About a week later I received a typewritten document in the post, two or three sheets of airmail paper, with a covering note from Casimirri's office.

In his answers, not only did Caruso, as I expected, ignore all the personal questions, but he also refused to comment on relations between the internal and external factions of Sinistra Armata. During the Valpreda affair, I later discovered, he had received sackloads of mail, begging Caruso and the other SA inmates to put pressure on their outside counterparts to spare the hostage's life. Anonymous letters appealing to his 'intellectual honesty', letters from entire religious orders, letters from left-wing sympathisers. A whole Elementary class wrote begging for Valpreda's release; even the Pope made his famous address in the Osservatore Romano directed to the 'Men of Sinister Armata', whom he begged 'on his knees' to free the hostage 'without conditions'. To this day Caruso maintains the kidnappers acted autonomously; that after his arrest he and the other members of the *nucleo storico* lost control of the leadership of Sinistra Armata, that the 'attack on the heart of the State' was not – and could never have been – orchestrated from behind bars. Yet at the same time, out of a mixture of loyalty or stubbornness, he never went down the path of *pentimento*. Not in public, at least, and not then.

But I'm getting ahead of myself: during the Valpreda affair and the first big SA trial which was taking place more or less concurrently in Turin, Caruso and the others demonstrated the kind of inflexible Marxist–Leninist mindset which most Italians found so difficult to comprehend. And which frankly terrified them. I don't think anyone will easily forget the sight of those prisoners in their metal cage on the day Valpreda's body was found in a red Renault near the Party headquarters in Piazza del Gesù: there was sand in his pockets and his clothes had been sprayed with sea water to make it look as though he had been held hostage somewhere near the coast. When the judge asked Caruso if he had anything to say *which was pertinent to the trial*, I think you would have heard a pin drop. Staring straight ahead, he replied: 'The death of an enemy of the people is the greatest act of humanity in a class war.' He was scarcely allowed to finish: four *carabinieri* entered the cage and hauled him bodily out of the courtroom.

The answers typed in response to my questionnaire were couched in the kind of abstruse, left-wing jargon which characterised all of Sinistra Armata's releases, littered with terms like 'Imperialist Multi-Nationalist State', 'the blood of the proletariat' and 'filthy Fascist regime'. *La Nazione* published it, regardless, in a special midweek edition if I remember correctly, as those days anything on the SA, and Caruso in particular, was guaranteed to boost circulation. Recent events at La Camillina had gripped the public imagination in an almost unprecedented way; the mysterious human drama unfolding behind the by now all too familiar political one had turned Caruso into a kind of Everyman figure – a cardboard cut-out terrorist whom Italians, if not able to understand, felt able – at least in part – to identify with.

The years passed; I went to work for the news agency ANSA in their London office, then was offered the position editing *La*

Nazione in 1992. We returned to Rome, and a few years into the job, I received a letter from Edoardo Casimirri. Not that I had ever really lost touch with him or his client; during the hunger strike at Nuoro in the winter of 1985, I sent Caruso and his fellow-strikers a message of support. Their demands were more than reasonable: visits without bulletproof glass, the chance to cook in their cells, social intercourse between inmates – in other words, the abolition of Article 90. I remember at ANSA our colleagues in Rome sent us a picture of Caruso which was circulating illegally among press circles: he weighed 48 kilos and looked like Holger Meins, the first hunger-strike victim of the German Rote Armee Fraktion. Much later on, when he and I were collaborating on his memoirs from the Rome prison, Rebibbia, he explained why he and the others had decided on the hunger strike.

'We were locked in our cells for twenty-three hours out of twenty-four: I kept going over and over again in my mind everything we had been through in Sinistra Armata. After the Valpreda affair it was obvious that the organisation was crumbling: each week a new *pentito* would emerge from the woodwork who seemed to have been in the SA just long enough to pick up the address of a safe-house and the names of one or two members to sell to the *carabinieri*. The final straw, for me at least, was when they killed those two security guards during a bank robbery in Rapallo *just to publish the names of suspected informers in their leaflet*. That's what things had come to: human life in exchange for publicity. At first I tried to speak to the others about my doubts: mostly to Dall'Oglio as he and I went back years: we joined the Rome cell together, and went underground more or less at the same time. He didn't want to know: all he could do was spout jargon at me – our jargon of Sinistra Armata – which was the only way we knew how to communicate. We were like addicts, addicted to an ideology which was worse than heroin. As I lay in my cell I thought of all those years of violence – ten whole years of bloodshed for what? So that two security guards could be killed for the sake of a propaganda leaflet? When I was transferred to Nuoro I stayed in bed for almost a month. I couldn't bear to be within earshot of a political discussion. All I could think about was death: my death. I began to see why to our German *compagni* in the Rote Armee Fraktion suicide seemed the only way forward. And yet I couldn't bring myself to do it – to give the politicians the satisfaction of using my death as a headstone to the armed struggle. That's why I settled for a hunger strike. It was as though my body was the last thing I owned, and I wasn't going to hand it away on a plate. It was mine, and I was going to devour it myself, bit by bit.'

It was all over for Sinistra Armata by 2000, when I received the letter from Casimirri requesting my collaboration in the writing of Caruso's memoirs. Apart from Dall'Oglio, and a couple of other die-hards – the so-called *irreducibili* – most of the other once-active members of Sinistra Armata had turned their back on the armed struggle. A few had done so unequivocally in return for freedom and the life-long disgust of their fellow *compagni*, some even making a living out of denouncing their past. Many of these found solace in the arms of the Catholic Church, and became active in cooperatives and communities helping drug addicts and ex-prisoners overcome the difficulties associated with their reintegration into society. A few developed promising careers in the media.

To obtain an interview with Caruso, I had to apply for permission from the Ministry of Justice. This was granted in dribs and drabs, and even briefly revoked during the third Valpreda trial, so that in the end I made around fifteen visits to Rebibbia spread out over a period of about four months. The result was thirty hours of tape, based on a list of questions which I superimposed retrospectively to add form and clarity to the material. Caruso was adamant about this: his account of

Sinistra Armata had to be entirely accessible, especially to the younger generation who had not lived through those years.

On my first visit to Rebibbia, one of the prison governors showed me a register with Caruso's release date: spring, 2042. It was 2000 and, like me, he was forty-three years old. At the time, that coincidence seemed chilling, significant.

The man sitting waiting for me at the table in the lawyer's room was both like and unlike what I had imagined him to be. As a journalist, I had become immune to the *frisson* of seeing a famous person in the flesh – that peculiar combination of excitement and anticlimax which all those years in the House of Commons as ANSA's London correspondent had entirely cured me of. And yet I confess I couldn't take my eyes off him. Maybe it was because we were of the same generation – had participated in the same student demonstrations in the seventies – and before he went underground, probably listened and danced, and even fucked, to the same music: Battiato, Lucio Dalla, Battisti, de André. As teenagers, we probably even had the same black and red poster of Che Guevara on our bedroom walls.

It was as though I was looking at a younger version of myself: as though in spite of the prison regime which had taken its toll on his health, both mental and physical, a kind of light burned in him which in me had long been extinguished. And yet there was an unnerving lack of expression in his dark eyes, almost as though that passion were a mask. I had seen that look on the face of IRA prisoners; the inner man consumed by fanaticism, so that in the end there was no inner man left. Just that harsh light, with no shadows. His hair was streaked with white, and his skin had that kind of monochrome pallor all prisoners share, as though his complexion were no longer receptive to the changing seasons or the temperature outside the prison walls and had taken on the very colour and texture of those walls. He was wearing a flannel tartan shirt open at the neck and a grey cardigan. As he smoked, I noticed a small homemade-looking tattoo on one wrist.

The guard left us, and for a moment there was silence. Then Caruso spoke: 'Thank you for coming,' he said. 'I can think of better places to spend a Sunday afternoon.'

I thought of my wife taking our nieces to watch the marionettes on the Gianicolo; afterwards we always went to Fassi's for an ice cream with my wife's parents. 'I'm used to it,' I lied. Usually Sundays were sacred in our family. Later, I realised I had lied instinctively – guiltily almost, as though in some way I wanted to erect a barrier between everything that made my life outside different from – better, I suppose, than – his. (As though we both understood that everything that was pleasurable and rewarding in my life was only possible because all those years ago he had made his choices and I had made mine.) I wondered what it was that had made him cross that threshold into violence: that point where so many, myself included, turned away and retreated into the safety of home, university, friends. I suddenly felt awkward and fat in my expensive weekend clothes: suede Tod's moccasins, Viyella shirt, Murphy and Nye cords. I wondered where Caruso's cardigan came from, whether his mother had chosen it for him from her local STANDA store. Somewhere I'd read that in all those years she'd never missed a visit, travelling up and down the country as they moved him from one high-security prison to another. She was a *portiera* in a block of flats in Rome.

'You're probably wondering why. Why now? Why at all, for that matter?' He picked up the soft-pack of MS from the table and shook out a cigarette. His face looked pinched in the yellow flare of the wax *cerino*; he was incredibly thin still, with cheekbones like scimitars. I wondered whether his health had ever fully recovered from the hunger strike back in '85.

'I must say I was surprised; I never expected you of all people to write your memoirs. To be honest, I thought you'd take your story to the grave with you.'

For a moment I bitterly regretted my words; I thought of the ledger and that terrible date: 2042. Assuming he lived that long, he'd be over eighty years old when they released him. To hide my awkwardness I looked around the interview room; it was quite comfortable, with swivelling office chairs upholstered in synthetic blue hessian and a De Chirico print on the wall. A shaft of light from the small barred window above my head shone directly on to his hands which were crossed on the table, illuminating them like a Dürer still life. There was a faint rumble of traffic from the Lungotevere: I wondered if the sound was a torment to him.

'Don't worry, I'm used to it.' He must have read my mind. 'The worst is when you're being transported from one prison to another in a security van and you get those flashes of everyday life through the window: a newspaper kiosk, a man and woman on a *motorino*, someone crossing the square with a bunch of flowers. Everyone going about their daily business without knowing that you're sitting in there in handcuffs trying to smoke a cigarette with two hands. You'd give anything to freeze one of those images for a moment just to get your bearings.'

His directness had a liberating effect on me; there was no longer any point in trying to be tactful – to do so would only be an insult. I looked at his hand with the bony wrist as he ground the cigarette into an ashtray: 'Birra Peroni' it said in cheerful red and blue letters along the rim. I felt better, as though my hard-nosed journalist's persona had just been restored to me. A part of my brain began to formulate an introduction to his story; I could already see our joint names on the dust-jacket. 'So why, Caruso? Why do we get to know now?'

Unexpectedly, he smiled, and I noticed faint laughter-lines around his eyes. His face was so gaunt you didn't notice them at first. Then his expression grew sombre: 'I have to tell my side of the story – not for myself, nor for you, nor for the great Italian public.'

'You haven't answered my question,' I said mockingly.

'Why now?' I was beginning to enjoy myself. I could picture the pre-publication exclusive I'd run in the magazine: on the cover 'CARUSO TALKS', in stark red capitals, with a picture of the prisoner in his woolly cardigan alongside that famous police shot of him in a balaclava during the shootout at La Camillina, almost erotic in its violence . . .

'Because I'm dying,' he replied softly. I felt my bowels contract; my hands grew clammy and the back of my neck burned as though I'd been whipped with a hot flannel. 'I have leukaemia. Cancer of the blood – quite a poetically satisfying disease, if you consider all the blood that's been spilt. I could live a year if I'm lucky – less if I'm not.' He looked at me almost tenderly, and the depth that had been missing now shone through his beautiful dark eyes. I sat before him at the table, my mouth too dry to speak, desperately trying to collect myself before meeting his gaze. 'The point is this –' and he broke off, deliberately waiting for – willing – me to look up. 'Before I die I have to tell my story. For the sake of my daughter. Somewhere, you see, I have a daughter. And one day she'll need to know why.'

3

MELODY

Melody took her cup to the butler's sink and stood by the window looking out on to the canal. A pair of spiteful-looking, black-browed swans drifted dreamily across the water, cutting a V-shaped path through the twigs and rubbish floating on the surface. She rinsed the cup and propped it to dry on the window sill, then remained for a moment watching a heron standing motionless on the towpath. Its feathers looked as though they were powdered with ash, a stone bird – the last creature you'd imagine was alive. Slowly, the traffic from the Harrow Road receded, until she had that familiar sensation of being surrounded by water, almost as though she were living on the canal rather than beside it. That's what had drawn Hugh to the studio all those years ago: that sense of an industrialised nature winding its way stubbornly and secretively through the Paddington streets, a world of towpaths and narrowboats, which not long afterwards became the *Houseboat* children's books. Not that either of them could have ever imagined just how sucessful those books would become: only the other day, the children's librarian down at Queen's Park was telling her that they'd never gone out of favour with children, no matter how many fashions came and went. They even kept a signed first edition of *The Lock-keeper's Daughter* in a glass cabinet by the entrance, as though Hugh were a genuine local hero.

It was 4.30, time for the news on Radio Italia. With Lotte gone, it had become even more important to maintain these rituals – as though listening to the Italian news and keeping abreast of Italian politics was a way of entering into the reality of Lotte being in Rome. Besides, it was a reminder of more innocent times: as soon as Lotte came home from school, she would leave her bag upstairs in the flat, fling her uniform on the bed, then sit in the armchair by the fire as Melody made tea and toast in the little kitchen behind the shop. How proud she was after a couple of years at Italian Saturday school when she began to understand the programmes in Italian; once when she was about fourteen they even went to a Radio Italia New Year's party at the studios in Clerkenwell. That was one thing you couldn't fault her for, thought Melody: by the time Casimirri's letter arrived, Lotte was as prepared as she could ever be – without even knowing she was.

More than anything, though, keeping up the old rituals was Melody's way of hanging on to the present. She was almost seventy years old now, and her days alone in the shop had become a vast, uncharted journey into the past. Every morning, as she let herself in, lit the gas fire and sat on her chair by the window, she could feel her surroundings growing blurred, and a kind of excitement overtook her – a delicious, dreamlike anticipation not unlike the beginning of a real journey – at the thought of all the places and sensations amongst which her mind might wander that day. If it weren't for Lotte she would have succumbed entirely: heaven knows, she could easily afford to close the shop and get by on Hugh's royalties.

Already, many years before, she had let go of the sexual, sensual side of her nature, although before he died Hugh had begged her to remarry. Mostly for herself, but also for Julia. The last two weeks of his life had an intense, almost hallucinatory intimacy that since then she had only known when Lotte was a baby. That lovely Indian doctor on Elgin Avenue persuaded Hugh to hoard his morphine tablets till the end, so that the sudden respite from pain gave him a burst of vigour that almost convinced them he would live. The three of them more or less moved into the studio as Hugh wanted to leave them a visual record of the life they had shared – rather as he had done in the early years of their marriage. There were eight pictures in all, most of them drawn from the old black leather sofa which became Hugh's daybed: little intimate sketches in pink *gouache* of Julia sprawled out on the floor with her schoolbooks, or blowing bubbles by the window overlooking the canal. Melody's favourite was the one of Julia in the tin bath by the fire, hair tied up in a comical topknot; Lotte looked uncannily similar at that age. How much fun they'd had; they made pancakes in the middle of the night, and spent hours pasting photographs with little handwritten captions into scrapbooks which Melody kept in a tartan suitcase under the bed. After Hugh's death, she converted the studio into a shop and began selling second-hand furniture and fittings. Architectural salvage, they called it these days. She'd always been clever at finding things, and before Hugh got ill she had a stall on the Portobello Road. The shop worked out well with Julia's school hours, and after a while their life reacquired a shape, albeit an altered one.

It had always been a mystery to her what became of her sexuality, as though with Hugh's death a light had been quietly dimmed. At forty years old she felt like one of those southern Italian widows with gnarled hands and black clothes, who, no matter how hard you tried, you could never imagine them as brides. No man who looked at her would ever again think of sex or love or tenderness. She was a surface which would never again reflect light. As a girl, she blossomed late and unexpectedly; she'd been sinewy and flat-chested before it was fashionable to be so, though Lotte used to tease her that these days she would have made it on to the cover of *Vogue*. Apparently *jolie-laide* was the name for it. It was after she met

Hugh that her appearance began to change; she lost that hard, two-dimensional look – a kind of inbred, unexpressed sensuality – and her face grew rounder and softer-looking. Motherhood suited her too, although with Julia's death (even now, twenty years later, it was too improbable to state squarely, even to herself) she reverted to a kind of bleached, washed-out version of her younger self.

Julia's death . . . it was like the tolling of a bell sounding the journey's end, the only reality which could not be incorporated into daydreams; it made her ashamed even to try. She could feel herself returning to her surroundings: the shop was dark and chill; she had forgotten to switch on the lights. For a moment she felt suspended between two worlds, a quivering image frozen on to a TV screen. Without moving, she sat in the armchair in the dark shop, hands folded on her lap, listening to the grinding of lorries on the Harrow Road. She was such an improbable survivor, you see: nothing, but nothing, could have prepared her for outliving both her husband and her child.

It was so greedy, she thought, clinging on to life like that.

This time, change had arrived by letter.

As soon as Melody saw the Italian postmark and her name and address typed on an expensive envelope, she realised at once it could not be from Luciana. It was too official-looking; besides, Luciana only wrote on Lotte's birthday, and always enclosed a sovereign in a felt pouch, embossed in gold letters with the name of a jeweller's in Corso d'Italia, which had to be collected from the sorting office in White City.

Lotte had been at David's when the letter arrived. As she picked it up from the mat, Melody had the absolute certainty that her life was to be devastated once more. Fascinated, she watched her arm with Hugh's large Omega watch on her wrist as though it were the actual instrument of that change, as though in some way she had been forewarned, and was still in time to resist it. Without opening it, she could slide the envelope back under the door . . . And yet she had longed for this moment, too, knowing she would never have made the break on her own. She held the envelope in her hand, and an image came into her mind of the words, seeping greyly through the paper as though they were alive, into a landscape which would never look the same again. She would lose Lotte, it was inevitable. The pain of that made her catch her breath, as though she'd been punched. And yet she had the presence of mind to smile at the postman through the glass door, and even remembered to twist the shop sign around to 'Open'. Still smiling, she stood for a while by the door with the letter clasped to her chest, as though determined to savour as intensely as possible the last few moments of her old life. A kind, wintry sun shone through the shop window, warming her forehead and cheeks. Briefly, she closed her eyes, basking in the orange light she imagined babies in the womb felt long before they could see. Then, without thinking, she picked up her coat from the washstand she was restoring out on the balcony, and after turning the sign back to 'Closed', she locked the door and walked out of the shop towards the canal.

The towpath was Melody's back garden; over the years she grew to recognise the flowers that grew along the banks of the canal – yellow flags, catkins, foxgloves – and had spent countless hours, first with Julia, then with Lotte, waiting to feed the ducks, and the black moorhens with their pretty enamelled beaks and metallic call which sounded like the clang of a blacksmith's hammer. Even the graffiti were familiar: Lotte's favourite was the cow with a halo on a wall near the Meanwhile Gardens: 'Moooooo,' said the speech-bubble. She walked towards Sainsbury's, under the red iron bridge at Virgin with its hanging baskets of flowers, until she reached the bend in the canal by the cemetery. There she sat down on a bench and took out the letter.

There were three sheets in all, written in loopy Italian handwriting.

Dear Signora Melody,

I am writing to you on behalf of my client, Ennio Caruso. As you are no doubt aware, he is currently serving a life sentence in Rome's Rebibbia prison for acts of terrorism committed while he was a member of Sinistra Armata. Unlike many of his *compagni*, he has not renounced his past in return for an early release date; nor, until recently, has he deemed it necessary to explain or justify his actions.

My client has known for several years of the existence of a child, Lotte, who was formally adopted by you, her maternal grandmother, after her mother's tragic death in 1979. Until now he has depended for news of his daughter on his own mother, Luciana, whom he knows to be in regular contact with you in London. Like you, both Luciana Caruso and my client have preferred to keep the circumstances of Lotte's birth a secret from her; they feel she has more chance of living a normal life without being burdened with events from the past. This has been at immense personal cost to both.

Recently, however, my client has been diagnosed with myelogenous leukaemia, and has been told he is unlikely to live longer than six months. At present he is being treated as an outpatient by Professor Castoldi at Rome University's teaching hospital, the Policlinico. His illness has prompted him to leave written testament of his experiences in Sinistra Armata, and he is currently working on his memoirs with the well-known political journalist, Pietro Scala, editor of the current affairs weekly, *La Nazione*. He has also expressed a desire to meet his daughter at least once before he dies. My client has asked his mother, Luciana Caruso, on several occasions to inform you of his illness so that you may break the news of his existence to Lotte in the way you deem best. This request has been consistently refused. As you have probably learnt in your dealings with Luciana, she is a simple woman who has dealt courageously with a tragic fate, never failing in her duty to her only son. It is with a heavy heart that Ennio has been forced to go against his mother's wishes in this case, but his desire to see his daughter before he dies is overpowering: his life in prison holds few other consolations . . .

They had put her in a kind of playpen in the hall, a *box*, she remembered they called it; at the time it seemed a strangely appropriate name, like somewhere you might deposit an unwanted object. The *box* had sloping net sides, like the walls of an aviary, and a padded border covered in pastel-coloured vinyl. She lay there, fed and washed, but with her face turned to the wall, lifeless as one of the babies discovered in Romanian orphanages when Ceaucescu fell. A long shadow seemed to lie over her: a child who was a child only because biologically it knew no better. They'd pierced her ears, and on her chubby wrist she wore a tiny identity bracelet; poignantly, there was no name engraved on the tag.

They were all in black, Melody remembered, the flat was swarming with women dressed in black, though in truth (and the thought shivered through her hysterically) she was the only real mourner there. She longed to share the joke with someone – ached to – but the only candidate was the embassy translator who sat on the sofa in the darkened *salone*, legs crossed effeminately in his oxblood loafers, while in the *box* in the hallway the child lay silent.

Not that she had needed the translator; her Italian was good enough, even in those days. For several years she and Hugh had gone to the same village in Puglia for their holidays, and when Julia was a baby Melody had taken a couple of Italian courses at night school. Maybe that explained why all those years later Julia would choose to read Italian at university. Yet

Melody and Luciana understood each other from the start in a way that went beyond culture or language. She must have only been in her early forties, quite a good-looking woman in that overgroomed Italian way, though her face now was bare of make-up and there was something repulsive in the way the roots glistened springy and black against the vivid gold of her hair. All those years later Melody could still smell the animal smell of that hair, like some kind of hormonal flare-up of grief.

At a certain point one of the women in black – Luciana's aunt Concetta – brought a tray of coffee in little gold-rimmed cups. The embassy man – what was his name, Julian? Julius? – downed his hurriedly and wiped the corner of his mouth with his handkerchief. He looked like a bogus professor in his little glasses and tweed jacket. Idly, Melody wondered whether he was gay, whether he found his pleasures in the cobbled alleyways around the Colosseum. At once she felt suffused by shame; he and the other embassy staff had been kind to her. And yet beneath that kindness she sensed a kind of prurience, as though Julia's death would be discussed for years to come in the modern English bar at Porta Pia. She could feel Luciana and the aunts watching them from the kitchen doorway, almost as though she and the translator were two exotic creatures who had blundered in from the street, and who, if unacknowledged, might just as easily disappear. She could almost sense them wishing for them to be gone – for their two worlds never to have collided. In some primitive area of her brain, she was even ashamed of Julia's death. She thought: they see me as unlucky, cursed – a woman who managed to lose both her husband and child . . . It was a tiny caretaker's flat on the first floor of a neo-classical building near Villa Torlonia; Luciana spent her days in a glass-fronted cubicle behind the old-fashioned cage lift. She took in ironing and mending from some of the tenants.

The first few times she went to the flat, Melody barely acknowledged the child; she was haunted by the almost surreal violence into which she had been born. It was as though each time she gazed into the *box* she was made to confront her daughter's killer; for nine months the baby had festered like a growth in Julia's womb – taking, taking, never giving, until in the end there was no life left to give . . . The first time Luciana held her out to her, Melody recoiled; all she could see was that dark head, ripping like a bullet through her daughter's body . . .

Time and time again, when she looked back on those days, she would ask herself from which hidden reserves she found the strength – not even the strength, the *obedience*, for want of a better word – to walk day after day through those embassy gates at Porta Pia, and sit in a room overlooking a fountain reading coroners' reports and lurid press clippings bound together in a red folder marked HMSO. Every morning, she would leave the *pensione* at eight before the sun grew too hot, and stop for an *espresso* in the same bar on the corner of Via Cavour: Bar Jolly, it was called. Now, she felt tenderness at the thought of that angular middle-aged Englishwoman in her sleeveless cotton blouse and skirt standing alone at the marble counter. She remembered everything about that bar: the signed photograph of a football team above the bottles of brightly coloured syrup, the chink of cups which were flung into the sink as though they were made of tin, yet mysteriously never broke, the unmistakable aroma of coffee and boiled milk, mingled with the smell of bleach from the newly washed floor. Across the years, she longed for someone to have comforted her. *Shame on you, childless bitch* . . . grief turned her ugly, made her round on herself with a viciousness which frightened her sometimes. It was the hoarse, dirty-talking voice of the witch she'd always known herself to be – only grown bolder now, fattened up on all that bad luck . . . *So you thought you'd play housewives and mummies, did you . . .?* The young barman had a kind face; she liked to imagine Julia stopping there for coffee when she went to visit the basilica of Santa Maria Maggiore. Perhaps she was hoping he'd make the connection, ask her what had become of her pretty daughter.

One morning at Stazione Termini, while she was waiting for the bus to the embassy, she saw a crowd of people gathered by an ambulance. She went to look; it was ghoulish, but she couldn't help herself. Sidling through the gaps in the crowd, she saw a one-legged man in a dirty red T-shirt writhing in the gutter, his crutches flung to one side, while a bored-looking *carabiniere*, too fastidious to pick him up, stood beside him, tapping his sword on the pavement. Like an overturned insect, the man was trying to hoist himself up on strong, brown hands; his face was intelligent, outraged. Patches of sweat on his armpits flared out like bloodstains. Then the ambulance doors were flung open, and two paramedics snapped open a collapsible stretcher on to the pavement. They put on rubber gloves and hoisted the struggling man onto the stretcher. A young gypsy boy ineffectually held out the crutches. The sheets on the stretcher were crisp and ironed; for a moment Melody longed to be taken away in the ambulance in his place. In spite of the heat, the desire to lie cocooned in those sheets was so overpowering it made her feel faint. Long after the crowd had dispersed, she stood there, unwilling to board her bus. She wondered what would happen if she simply remained in the station, sleeping on a cardboard sheet laid out on the marble floor alongside all the other homeless people, washing her face each morning at the drinking fountain in Piazza del Cinquecento, until her hair grew matted, her clothes grimy, and she finally began to look like a woman who had lost her only daughter. And all through her own fault. She had let Julia slip through her fingers – worse, through her open hands. . . That night, when she returned to the *pensione*, she dreamt of being wrapped in a tarpaulin and dropped from a high building; the pain on impact was exquisite, briefly numbing her grief.

*   *   *

28

The aunt had taken the translator to the door; they heard the whine of the lift, then the click of the downstairs *portone*. Luciana lit a cigarette and turned to Melody:

'You keep her', she said. She had dark, Sicilian eyes, Ennio's eyes. 'You keep her' she repeated. 'Take her back to England. That child will have no life here in Italy. You don't understand about Ennio; I daren't show my face outside this building. I haven't even been to buy a loaf of bread since he was arrested.'

She was an ordinary woman – the ordinary mother of an ordinary son. Like Melody, she was a widow. She wondered whether Julia and Ennio, both only children, had ever thrilled at those coincidences, believing their love was ordained.

'When he was about seventeen, Ennio started staying out late. He joined *Lotta Continua*, and took part in sit-ins and demonstrations at his school. He was held back a year in the last year of Elementary, even though he was a bright boy and his teachers had high hopes for him. When he was younger he wanted to be a marine biologist; his favourite programmes on the television were those Jacques Cousteau documentaries, and for his birthday one year he asked for a subscription to the *National Geographic* magazine.' For a moment her face looked bitter, yet it was the muted bitterness of hopes which had never risen too high: how easily her features slid into those deep-set lines. Luciana picked up a bottle from the sideboard, poured a few drops of milk on to the inside of her arm, then shook it to dissolve the biscuit she had crumbled inside. 'Biscotti Plasmon,' it said on the orange box; they sold them in Garcia's on the Portobello Road, Melody thought inconsequentially.

'You have no idea what it was like; every week there'd be another one of those crazy strikes. Then they became more violent; shop windows were smashed, and they started tossing Molotov cocktails around like firecrackers at New Year. I knew Ennio was involved: I found a bottle of sulphuric acid in his drawer.' She walked over to the *box* in the hallway and picked up the baby, unemotionally, as if she were picking up a stack of books. She returned to the sofa and settled her in the crook of her arm. Melody watched as the baby gulped greedily at the teat of the bottle. Her heart raced, and for a moment she felt – yes, actually *felt* – Julia's gums on her nipple, that delicious, fatalistic ache as the milk prickled along the hidden ducts in her breasts.

'It was all to do with his father, I suppose. He was a tax officer in the Guardia di Finanza; he was posted to the village near Ragusa where I grew up. We were never married, though before he left, he did give me a ring to wear: he told me it was his mother's, though later I found out he bought it in a pawnshop in Trapani.' She held out her hand, momentarily interrupting the feeding child, as though she needed to prove the existence of the ring, as though all those years later the shame still burned. 'When I found out I was pregnant, the local noble family took me in as a chambermaid. Then Ennio was born, and when he was four or five, the old Contessa del Leonforte found me a place as a caretaker in the building in Rome where the family owned a flat. For many years she took an interest in Ennio; his father rarely visited, and never sent any money. He married a widow from Abruzzo the year after we left for Rome. They never had children: Ennio was his only son. He died when Ennio was eight. Ennio never forgave me for accepting charity from the Contessa; he hated the rich, and was ashamed we depended on them. All I can say is it's a good thing she never lived to see this day, what with everything she and her family did for us. Then, while all this political nonsense was going on, Ennio's call-up papers arrived; he was to be sent to a base near Turin. To be honest, it was a relief; I thought the Army might straighten out some of his crackpot ideas, teach him which way the world really goes round. He left for Turin – in a suit and tie, for once – with his pockets stuffed full of money; all his uncles came up from Sicily to see him off at the station. Then three days later, the *carabinieri* came knocking at my door; he'd never even showed up at the base.'

'What about Julia?' Melody whispered. 'Did she know where he was?'

'I've no idea; he only brought her here the once . . . it was around Eastertime, a few months after he disappeared. He turns up one night with this girl in a poncho: I didn't know at the time that she was English – or that she was pregnant, for that matter – but there was something about her which I suppose you would say looked foreign. When I went out to empty the rubbish, I found them hiding by the tradesmen's entrance to the flats. He didn't let himself in, even though he still had the key – by that time the police were looking for him, and he didn't dare show his face at the door. Anyway, he knew like always I'd check the back of the building before turning in.'

For a moment they were silent, and the only sound was the rhythmic clicking of the baby's palate as she sucked on the teat. But Melody knew Luciana had seen her daughter one more time after that first meeting; they told her so at the embassy. It was at La Camillina: she was lying in a pool of blood on the kitchen floor . . . And then, unexpectedly, Luciana smiled:

'He met her at Rizzoli's on Via Tomacelli, you know. In all those years she was the only girl he brought home.'

For a moment Melody felt suffused by resentment – as though there, with the shared grandchild in her arms, Luciana were the sole guardian of her daughter's past. She too had known about that meeting in the bookshop – how Ennio took her to Santa Maria in Trastevere to see the restored frescoes. It was one of the last letters Julia ever wrote home. A few months later, she'd received a postcard from Venice showing a church called San Lazzaro degli Armeni. On the back, Julia had written: 'I have to be by myself for a while. Please don't write or call the flat in Rome. I'm OK – I just need time and space. If you care, you won't ask why.'

And so Melody didn't ask why: she let her daughter go – as requested, she neither wrote nor telephoned for five long months – and in doing so, lost Julia. Put like that, it seemed absurd. Because it *was* absurd; the truth, of course, was that she had begun to lose Julia many, many years before.

After Hugh's death, Melody had sold the house in Brook Green and moved into the flat above his studio. Everything about those melancholy Paddington streets reminded her of Hugh. Besides, he was buried at the cemetery in Kensal Green, and on summer evenings she and Julia would walk along the canal to leave flowers or pictures at his grave. Once, Julia brought him an avocado plant she had grown in Science, another time, a lumpy clay ashtray.

Right from the start, there was something almost freakish about Julia's childhood. The first nine years of her life seemed to be concentrated into a single, quivering epiphany, as though on some level they had always known it couldn't last. She had an ordinary parallel life, too – Montessori nursery, the playground in Ravenscourt Park, Mr Whippy ice cream from the van on Shepherd's Bush Green – yet, to Melody at least, their three lives appeared to be illuminated as though they were the first family. She was forever creating tableaux in her head: 'Mother and Father Push Child on Swing' or 'Father and Child Fly Kite on Parliament Hill' . . . And while she took a kind of surprised pleasure in watching Julia flourish, motherhood and family life were inextricably bound to her love for Hugh. Put baldly, she ceased to be a mother the day Hugh died. That beam of sensuality which illuminated every corner of their lives – the breakfast table on a winter's morning, Julia's toybox propped open beneath the studio window, the piles of freshly ironed nappies – that all grew dark when Hugh died. She had never much longed for children in an abstract sense: in no way had Hugh been a vehicle for her maternal instincts. Sometimes, even when Julia was tiny and at her most endearingly helpless, Melody would ask herself whom she would save first in a shipwreck: her husband or her child? She would torment herself with an image of the baby lying asleep in the cabin of a ship, lingering over each tender detail, the half-open mouth with the milk blister on the top lip, the little clenched fist, looking so out of proportion to the heavy head. And no matter how many times she told herself that the exquisite abandon of a child's sleep was only possible because of the strength of a mother's love, that it was a pact, an ancestral pact, she would still save Hugh. Every time. She was a freak; and longed not to be.

Now, she wondered how much of that Julia had understood at the time, whether to a nine-year-old child, the day they buried her father was the day she lost both her parents. Melody had never stopped loving her – if anything, the bond became even fiercer. Yet sometimes, as they sat eating their supper in the kitchen while Julia watched *John Craven's Newsround* on the black and white TV set, they seemed like the last two stragglers of some fantastic adventure – bound not so much by blood as by the memory of a lost past.

'He killed her, you know,' said Luciana. 'Whichever way you look at it, Ennio was responsible for your daughter's death. By the time that girl at the farm telephoned me she'd been in labour for forty-eight hours – for two whole days those animals let her suffer like a dog!' she spat.

Melody felt faint. Forty-eight hours in labour . . . forty-eight hours during which she, her mother – her guardian and protector – had woken up in her flat in London and, untroubled by even the mildest twinge of maternal foreboding, had made coffee and read the newspaper, and even (she burned with shame at this) closed the shop early to visit a garden centre . . . a garden centre. She was at Clifton Nurseries choosing herbs for the balcony, while her daughter's life ebbed away on a kitchen floor . . . Rosemary, thyme, borage and sage which the witch-woman would plant that evening in an old enamel sink, then never water again . . . *sticks for my eyes, dry earth in my mouth* . . . She turned away, embarrassed at her tears. Did Julia cry out for her mother, she wondered; and at once came the answer, the truly unbearable certainty: of course Julia hadn't cried out for her. And why should she have? When even as a little girl it was always her father she turned to for comfort.

An image came into her mind of the night Julia was born. In those days it was rare for fathers to be present, but Hugh had somehow managed to wheedle his way into the labour room. All the beds in the ward were occupied – the nurses joked it was because of the full moon – and after they had both been cleaned up, Melody was given a private room. An amenity bed, they called it in those days. It was nearing dawn, and she sat up in bed trying to breastfeed Julia, suddenly shy in front of Hugh. He was sitting by the window drinking a cup of tea from a light green cup and saucer he had brought from the canteen; his face was tired but happy, as though fatherhood were the most natural state in the world. A sketchbook lay open on his lap: the page was blank. Reaching inside her nightdress, she cupped her right breast: it had the unexpected, lolling weight of a bag of sand. She held it to the light: the nipple was gnarled, engorged, the tip studded with tiny seeds of milk. She brushed it on Julia's cheek, as the nurse had told her to do, until she turned her face and opened her mouth like a baby bird: it was that simple. As she sucked, Melody felt her womb contract, as though deep inside her all the blades of a penknife had sprung open at once. She looked down at the crown of her baby's head, and for a moment, the whorls of hair looked like the rings of a tree – as though her destiny were already mapped out in code. So clear, if only one could read the signs . . . Now it was too much to bear – too much to think that the destiny she had been so anxious to divine on the first morning of her daughter's life was this: to live for twenty years. To give birth on a kitchen floor. To die alone.

And still they called it the gift of life.

You should have smothered her there and then, said the witch.

Melody never consciously decided to hide Lotte's past; there hadn't been time to formulate a strategy. Besides, she hadn't given her word to Luciana before she left, nor had Luciana asked: there was no point – they both knew that once she got to London it would be entirely up to her.

The first time anyone asked outright was during a rainstorm in Queen's Park. 'Grandmother and Grandaughter Shelter in Bandstand after Grandmother Fails to Consult Weather Forecast,' thought Melody bleakly, while Lotte slept on in Julia's old Silver Cross pram. She'd been tempted to buy another – in fact Luciana wanted to get her a fancy pram as a leaving gift from La Cicogna on Via Gregorio VII before they left for London, but it seemed ridiculous to spend all that money when there was a perfectly good pram in the attic. Julia's Rolls, Hugh used to call it. Later, when Lotte was sitting up, she'd buy one of those stripy nylon Maclaren buggies all the mothers seemed to have these days.

Gazing ahead, Melody saw a woman running across the park with a jacket wrapped tightly around her enormous stomach, zig-zagging comically from side to side as though trying to keep her bump dry. It was only as she drew nearer that Melody realised the bulge was a baby in a sling. The woman smiled apologetically, as though conscious of invading the silence of the bandstand, then sat down on the bench beside her. Her coat smelt of sodden wool, the sleeves gauzy with drops. For a moment, neither said a word as they both stared ahead at the rain. Then a febrile tremor ran through Melody; she felt like an impostor – a grotesque guardian for the child sleeping in the pram beside her. Perhaps it was because she was no longer menstruating, cut out of that cycle of birth and new beginnings, that her role felt almost obscene. Who was she to play mother again, considering the success she'd made first time round? *Take her*, Luciana had said, *take her; she'll have no life here in this country* . . . And what kind of a life was she supposed to have in England, where, even bearing in mind national reserve, she was bound to attract unceasing attention in the charge of a fifty-year-old grandmother? How well she already knew that scenario, played out in a far more respectable key when Julia was a child: the trips to the cemetery on Father's Day, the careless mockery of other children (without taking into consideration teachers who, wilfully, it seemed, would forget Julia's background and ask what job Daddy did), the lopped-off family scenes at Christmas. And now, with Lotte, a weirder, crueller variant on this theme.

When Hugh died, she remembered the grief felt as though some giant, primeval figure had crashed through the floorboards of their house, casting its shadow over everything, and against which each one of their actions had to be measured. In the beginning, they were forever tripping up against it in the dark; but over the years they grew accustomed to its brooding presence, until finally the grief became their familiar – rather like the Roman pillar she once saw propping up the roof of a house in Rome's medieval Ghetto.

Now, she asked herself, how could Julia's blighted story ever turn into their familiar? How could Lotte hope to have anything remotely resembling an ordinary life once it was known how she came into the world? She was aware, peripherally, that the woman beside her had unstrapped the baby and was attaching it to the breast. The baby sighed and grunted as it rooted for the nipple, and the woman laughed self-consciously. 'Do you breastfeed?' she asked. Startled, Melody scanned the woman's expression for signs of mockery.

But there were none: she had a pleasant face with rosy cheeks and a blue and white striped hat pulled down over her ears. She sounded foreign – northern European, Scandinavian maybe.

'I breastfed my own child . . . once,' Melody replied slowly, cautiously. Her heart beat wildly: she had stage-fright – worse, like an actor who knows his lines ring false. She grasped the chrome handle of the pram; the palms of her hands felt slippery, as though they had been smeared with oil: palm oil, she thought absurdly. 'This is my granddaughter,' she added, swallowing the furry ball of saliva at the back of her throat. She probably thinks I'm a kidnapper, thought Melody, one of those childless women who steal babies from shopping centres.

'Your daughter is lucky to have this help,' the woman replied conversationally. 'In Holland I have nobody to take my baby for me. My father is not interested in small children, and my husband's family lives here in England. We are visiting for a holiday – tomorrow we return to Amsterdam.'

Later, Melody would ask herself over and over again what it was about the woman that made her confide in her. Was it that direct, easy way she had of talking? Or the fact that she was communicating in another language so that each word sounded as though it had been rinsed in cold water until the meaning was pristine? Probably more than anything, though, what swung it for her was that the woman was leaving, those magic words: 'tomorrow we return to Amsterdam' . . .

'My daughter is dead,' said Melody, staring into the strange woman's face. 'She died in labour, alone, in a farmhouse in Italy. Her boyfriend left her to die because he was a terrorist on the run. The police caught him a few weeks later. He's in a top-security prison now, awaiting trial.'

She enunciated each word clearly, as though branding her story on the stranger's consciousness, forcing her to share it, so that never again would she be able to visit Queen's Park, or even think of Queen's Park, without remembering a grey-haired woman sheltering from the rain. She expected the shutters to come down on that rosy face, imagined the woman making her excuses and walking aross the park to one of those comfortable red-brick houses where her in-laws probably lived.

'Would you like to come for a coffee?' she said instead. 'I think the rain has ceased now.'

Which is how Melody found herself in the white-painted panelled café drinking tea with a stranger while Lotte slept on in the pram beneath the window. She was called Petra, she said; she met her husband while she was doing a language course in Brighton. He was her teacher: two years later, when she was twenty-four, they married, and he got a job teaching Corporate English in Amsterdam.

'How old is your child?' asked Melody, gratefully aware that Petra was smoothing the edges of the scene, so that should she have a change of heart, and decide not to confide another word, they could finish their tea and part like two strangers who had passed the time of day during a rainstorm. Or perhaps she just thought she was mad, and was humouring her. *And I am mad*, thought Melody, *but unfortunately not mad enough to lie down on this linoleum and empty that tea-urn over my face . . .*

'Three months,' replied Petra, and she glanced down at the top of her baby's head in her jacket with a kind of helpless pride. 'And how old is . . .?'

'Lotte.' (Like Julia's first doll, named after Hugh's Aunt Lotte, who left him the money to buy the studio.)

'How old is Lotte?'

'Lotte is nearly five months. But she's only been here in England for four days. We flew back from Rome on Saturday.'

'She's beautiful,' said Petra, glancing towards the pram. And then at Melody. 'She looks like you.'

'She looks like her father, actually. The terrorist. Not that I ever met him. But I saw his photographs. In the newspapers, mostly, but also at his mother's house.'

Luciana had pulled them out of a bureau drawer, furtively, glancing over her shoulder at the shuttered windows, as though afraid someone might see her mourning a boy in those photographs who no longer existed. Melody remembered how some of the pictures were still in their silver frames, imagining that well-groomed woman with the animal-smelling hair sweeping them off one of those lace-covered occasional tables on the night she returned from the farmhouse . . . There was one she remembered in particular, a class photograph taken during a spring pageant at the religious school where the Contessa sent Ennio. The nuns had dressed the boys in effeminate costumes, with long white socks and plimsolls, and what looked like cardboard flowers pinned on to their shirtfronts. How acquiescent those children appeared, thought Melody, all of them looking out on the world with the same expression of childish, well-fed sensuality borne of sun and olive oil and afternoon siestas in dark city flats . . . All, that is, except Ennio. There were shadows beneath his eyes, and something preternaturally dark and glittering in his expression which managed to transcend even the cardboard tulip pinned on to his shirt.

'My problem', said Melody, looking over towards the pram, 'is that I don't know how much I should tell Lotte about her story. Or anyone else, for that matter.'

'What does her Italian grandmother say?'

'Luciana thinks that she and Ennio should be erased from our lives. According to her, I should tell Lotte that my daughter, her mother – Julia, that is –' *Come on, said the witch-woman, spit it out,* 'that Julia died in childbirth in Italy. That she had a mystery boyfriend I knew nothing about, and that the first I heard about anything was when the British Embassy in Rome contacted me to say she was dead, and that her baby was being cared for by nuns.'

Petra stirred her coffee thoughtfully. 'Perhaps Luciana is right. At least for now. If you think her father will be in prison for his acts of terror, and she will be unable to see him for many years, why give her this shadow over her childhood? The loss of the mother will be painful, but not a pain she will know as fresh. I can tell you this because I lost my mother when I was a baby.'

'How did she die?'

Petra's face twisted into a kind of sly grimace; then, un-expectedly, her eyes filled with tears. 'She didn't die: she left me when I was three months old. She was an Englishwoman who didn't take to life in Holland. Or to being a mother, I suppose.'

'Did you ever see her?'

'The first time was when I came to Brighton for my language course. I chose Brighton because I knew she was living nearby. But she was not happy to see me: she had married an English-man, and they had two other children, a boy and a girl. They owned a guesthouse in Hove. She did not want to be reminded of the old life in Holland.'

'But she agreed to see you?'

'She agreed to see me, but in secret. We spent the afternoon in a café on the pier among all the tourists: she hoped no one she knew would see us there. She made me understand that she did not want me to enter her new life. She never told my half-brother and sister about our meeting – only her husband, and that was when I had already left. Not long after I returned to Holland she changed her telephone number, so that I would not call her again – now it was only possible to communicate by letter. This is why I believe you should not tell Lotte her true story. If she cannot have contact or meetings with her father, why must she spend her childhood dreaming about something which maybe she will never have? To a small child, prison is no different from death.'

'And how are things now with your mother?'

'I saw her one more time. In the hospital: she died of cancer two years ago. Her new husband wrote to me but I did not arrive in time to say goodbye. Do you see, Melody? You are not alone. Everybody has their unhappiness . . . and also their secrets.'

That meeting in the park changed everything. For a start, it put a frame around Julia's death, gave it shape and a new perspective. When Hugh died things were different: in some way, his illness had prepared her, however unwillingly, for the inevitable; besides, there was always a familiar nine-year-old child to take care of – packed lunches to prepare, the shop to run, Hugh's publishers to deal with. So that even when their life became defined by his death, it was still an essentially familiar life which had been blighted by fate.

Nothing, but nothing, however, could have prepared her for Julia's death – for an unknown baby, her granddaughter, for heaven's sake – to move into Julia's bedroom overlooking the canal. For many years Julia's possessions would lie untouched, so that Lotte's toys stood on the shelves beside her mother's Leonard Cohen records, her books on Italian art history, Yeats's poems, her A-level notes. In that random way in which strangers often touch our lives, the meeting in the park with Petra provided a blueprint for the next twenty years. Melody decided there and then that nobody else would ever know about Ennio and Luciana and Julia's last hours of agony in the farmhouse. Not that there were all that many people who would be interested: after Hugh's death, Melody found friendship an irrelevance She would rather suffer the whispers of acquaintances (just what kind of a mother could she have been if her daughter chose to give birth like that in secret? And the answer? *No mother at all!*) than let that violence seep into their lives. She made it a point of honour that she would never confide in anyone again – ever. She told the same story with the same embellishments (the name of the hospital, the nuns who had looked after Lotte while the adoption came through, the cemetery near Viterbo where Julia was buried) and never once deviated from that story. She put everything to do with Lotte's birth into her old boarding-school trunk: the photographs from *Il Messaggero* and *La Repubblica* of Ennio and his co-members of Sinistra Armata standing trial in a giant metal cage, Julia's Rome sketchbook, the adoption papers, the identity bracelet with no name. A bloodstained Indian dress.

For a truthful woman, deceit came surprisingly easily to Melody. We all have secrets, Petra had said, and with those words she became initiated into a friendly conspiracy of deceivers whose parallel existence she had scarcely even guessed at. She was so straight she'd spent a lifetime knocking into her own sharp corners. Many years later, she would be reminded of that sense of surprise when Lotte picked up headlice at primary school. For an entire weekend she hugged the dreadful truth to herself, not daring to mention it to the nurse at the surgery, until Monday afternoon arrived and she blurted it out to one of the mothers at the school gate. 'Oh yes, we've all had it,' the woman laughed, and suddenly everyone had their lice stories to tell, like Resistance fighters who only drop their guard once they know the new arrival is one of theirs.

Besides, there was so much to do with a small child that Melody rarely had the luxury of examining her feelings about playing God to Lotte's past. She couldn't remember Julia's first years being so tiring, but then she'd been twenty years younger and for those days Hugh had been an unusually involved father. She was a good baby – too good, really, and accustomed to lying for hours in the same spot. She even had an incipient bald patch on the back of her head from spending so much time on her back. There was something watchful about her, an uncanny reserve which Melody found unsettling. Luciana had looked after her well – she was clean, her skin was soft, and she came with a little *corredino* of woollen vests, socks and tiny cardigans with mother-of-pearl buttons. She even had a set of embroidered cotton shifts with ribbon ties which were supposed to be worn under the vests. And yet in five months she had never been taken out of the flat in Via Tancredi – at least not in daylight. Once, one of the aunts bundled her into a taxi in the dead of night to visit a paediatrician, a distant relative of the Contessa, at the Fate-benefratelli hospital on the Isola Tiberina for her first vaccinations; another time Ennio's lawyer, Edoardo Casimirri, brought her wrapped up in a blanket to the police barracks in the Quartiere Trieste, where Ennio was being held . . .

In the months before the trial, Luciana too never went out in daylight: the aunts took it in turns to sit in the glass-fronted caretaker's office and do the shopping at the market in Via Catania. Not that the neighbours didn't guess what was going on, but nobody had the courage to ring the bell of Luciana's flat and demand to see the baby. There was one woman, an old friend of the dead Contessa – what was her name now . . . La Guerrini, that was it – who opened the door of her flat each time she heard the lift descending from the first floor. She was the widow of one of Mussolini's henchmen, one of the architects of the Republic of Salò, and Luciana said her flat was full of treasures looted from Italian Jews. On one of Melody's first visits, when she was leaving the building, the door of La Guerrini's flat opened a fraction, and a tiny figure peered out from the gloom. She was dressed in a belted, navy blue linen suit, and her face was coated in thick powder, while her grey hair was set in neat, symmetrical waves. She wore startlingly bright lipstick.

Melody felt faint; she could sense the heat throbbing beyond the glass *portone*, and the *pensione* in Via Cavour was still a bus journey away. All she could think about was getting back to her room to weep; the walls were so thin, she would turn on both taps and the bathroom extractor to muffle the sound of her sobs.

'I know who you are,' said La Guerrini hoarsely, searching her face with bright, inquisitive eyes. 'I saw your daughter once. She was a beautiful girl, and they made a lovely couple, whatever foolishness they were up to.' She cocked her head to one side. 'He was already a fugitive then – by rights I should have called the police when I saw them lurking behind the dustbins. But I didn't, and you know why? Because Ennio was a good boy: he used to carry my shopping in for me, and it was he who told me that that shark of the *amministratore* was cheating me over the condominium bills. But you must take that baby far away from here. And when all this has died down, and she grows up and comes back to find her father, you tell her to visit me, La Guerrini. If I'm still alive, I'll tell her who Ennio was.'

And just as suddenly as it had opened, the door clicked shut and Melody heard the bolts grinding back into place.

There was a space at the back of the shop, a kind of raised daïs, where Hugh had his drawing boards set up. Now Melody used it to store the larger mantelpieces and bathroom fittings she was just beginning to sell. Until Lotte started nursery, that space became her world. She learned to stand, pulling herself up on the bars of the window which overlooked the canal, and spent hours watching the ducks and swans gliding along the water: in time she grew to recognise the pop-pop of a narrowboat's Bolinder engine long before it appeared beneath the bridge at the Ha'penny Steps.

At first, Lotte seemed to shrink from physical contact: she stared unsmilingly as Melody held out her arms to pick her out of the tin bath; and even when she was lying on her lap feeding, she flinched if Melody ran her finger along her cheek. The witch fattening up Hansel, Melody thought sadly.

She remembered how pliant Julia had been – as though there was no space, no situation, which could not be accommodated to their two forms. She and Hugh used to take her to restaurants and even the theatre in the evenings; and when Julia was tired, she would simply lay her head on one of their two laps and sleep until it was time to go home.

In the beginning, Melody put Lotte to sleep in a cot by her bed. She would lie there quite still until Melody left the room, then she would begin to cry, a harsh whimpering which sounded so prematurely defeated – so *knowing*, almost – that she couldn't bear to hear it. It was as though with each cry she was reminding Melody of how that afternoon in Rome she had looked down into the *box* and seen her daughter's killer. She knew that Luciana had made it her business not to get attached to Lotte, as though she could never forget the circumstances of her birth enough to love her as her own flesh and blood. Either that or, more likely, she knew that one day she would lose her, and was steeling herself in advance against that loss.

One night, after about a month, Melody took her into her bed. It was around four in the morning, and the traffic on the Harrow Road was almost silent. Melody woke with a start to the sound of Lotte's cry. Her lips were dry, her heart racing, as though someone had scratched the very fabric of her sleep; even in repose her whole being was coiled in anticipation of that sound. She reached over the bars of the cot and picked the baby up. The little body felt stiff and unyielding, as though beneath the towelling babygro it were encased in a metal brace; she held her in her arms, watching the car headlights unfurl across the ceiling, while Lotte twisted her neck to one side as though desperate to escape. Never in her life had she felt more alone: a black widow, a serial mourner, crouching in the sludge at the bottom of a disused well . . . 'Help me, Julia,' she whispered. 'Help me.' Then the miracle occurred: the baby's body grew languid, and her head seemed to slide of its own accord on to Melody's shoulder. Afraid to move, she stood by the window, feeling the warm thin breath fluttering on her neck. Then she placed Lotte on the bed, and gently pulling up the blanket, she crept into the space beside her.

The pleasure of waking up to that little rosy face on the pillow next to hers was indescribable: sometimes, Lotte would already be awake, rubbing her cheek on the velvet border of the blanket, or inspecting her fingers in the light. Often, they would sleep face to face on their pillows like a pair of knights on a tomb, and in the morning Melody would wake to find Lotte staring solemnly at her with her round Malteser eyes. Gradually the physical barriers began to break down, as though during the night their bodies created the intimacy to carry them through the daylight hours.

After that night, Melody never again felt like an impostor: the aching tenderness she felt for Lotte, while not exactly maternal (it had an element of astonished gratitude), nevertheless gave her the strength to be mother, father and grandmother to Lotte. Throughout her childhood, not once did she feel she had to compensate for happier times: Lotte had never known anything apart from the dark flat overlooking the canal, the angular grandmother with her thatch of white hair, their mornings in the brass bed.

THE LEAD YEARS

My story is your story.

Turn the pages of your old family albums: you'll see our faces there.

Wouldn't it be cosy to pretend that we came from nowhere, that the armed struggle happened in a vacuum? That we were just a blip in the miracle of Italy's post-war eonomic recovery – a bunch of degenerates and losers who decided to take the law into their own hands. That we began killing, and found it to our taste. That we became addicted to violence.

Many of us did, there's no denying it. And yet a whole generation was prepared to lock horns with a State whose politicians were hand in glove with the corruption which runs so deep in our Italian society. Here in Italy, the post-war generation found it easier to ignore the lessons learned by Fascism, and concentrated on using the kind of dirty tricks rarely seen outside Latin America to silence the protests of the young. Some of these died with heroin in their veins, others took up arms and tried to fight the State on their terms. Many of us ended up here in prison: for the sake of our beliefs, we gave up our families, our friendships, our careers. Look how many of the so-called 'children of '68' ended up in the media, the arts, the universities, some even in Parliament – the respectable, goody-goody Left which took great pains to distance itself from the armed struggle whilst ready to reap the benefits of the hornets' nest we raised.

Few of us today still believe that we were right; only the die-hard *irreducibili* would claim that armed struggle was the only way to break society's impasse. Yet neither is it enough simply to say sorry: abjuration is a long echo which hides more than it reveals. The only way for all Italians to transcend the bloody 'Lead Years' is through open debate; yes, we'll say *why* we were wrong, but only if at the same time we examine the mistakes everyone made in those years – the politicians, the police, the judiciary, the bosses at Fiat, at Pirelli, at Siemens who infiltrated the unions with their right-wing spies.

This is why, after eighteen years of silence, I have agreed to collaborate with the journalist Pietro Scala. When you have been a public hate figure for as long as I have, you learn to single out the decent journalists – the ones prepared to give you a fair trial: no judge or jury can hold a candle to the vindictivenes, not to mention plain inventiveness, of journalists who found us guilty of just about every violent crime perpetrated in Italy since 1968. Among those I include the ones who doorstepped my elderly mother and almost got her evicted from the flats where she is caretaker, the ones who tracked down childhood 'friends' ready to swear I had been a precocious sadist and torturer since infancy, the ones who went down to Sicily and dragged my family's honour into the mud by raking up the story of my birth. There's no need to mention them by name: they know who they are. *La Nazione* is about the only publication I can think of which didn't treat my arrest with the same primitive glee shown by the public the day Mussolini and Clara Petacci's bodies were found strung upside down from a filling station roof in Milan's Piazzale Loreto. Over the years Pietro Scala has shown a journalistic integrity which some of his colleagues would do well to emulate. *La Nazione* was the first publication to start asking questions about the involvement of the secret services in the

Fascist massacre at Piazza Fontana, the first to highlight the appalling conditions at the high-security prisons – and the first to ask whether, perhaps, after twenty-five years, the time has come to offer an amnesty to all political prisoners of the armed struggle.

Only then, once our demons have been set free, can we tell ourselves that we have really moved on.

Ennio Caruso
Rebibbia, September 2000

Tape #1: May 2000

Caruso, let's start at the beginning. Where were you born?

I was born on 17 November 1957, at a Catholic maternity hospital for unmarried mothers in Trapani, Sicily: at the time, I believe it was one of the few institutions of its kind in Italy. My mother, Luciana Caruso, was only seventeen years old when she discovered she was pregnant. The nuns at Santa Corona took her in from the sixth month of her confinement, and she stayed there until I was ready to be weaned, about four or five months after my birth. After that she returned with me to her village near Ragusa.

What about your father?

My father was a tax official with the Guardia di Finanza. He was twenty-five years older than my mother. In him, she probably saw a father-figure, as her own father had died when she was a small child. They fell in love and he promised to marry her once she turned eighteen. But then she became pregnant; and the very week she told him about the baby, he travelled all the way to the Ministry in Rome to ask in person for a transfer – the further away from Sicily, the better. He was a typical Italian *mammone*, incapable of making even the tiniest decision without consulting his mother. Who wasn't going to have her beloved only son marrying a Sicilian village girl. At first he was given a temporary posting in Palermo, but by the time my mother returned from the hospital with me, he had already been sent to a town somewhere in Piemonte.

How did your mother cope with being an unmarried mother in Sicily?

My mother was – and is – a courageous woman. Like me, she has never known what you might call an ordinary life, a life – for want of a better word – without shame. The day they buried her father, she became known in her village as the orphan; then, when she began seeing my father, that turned into the harlot; after I was born, she was the *ragazza madre*, and finally, for the last twenty years, in the eyes of all Italy, she has been the begetter of a terrorist. Aged seventeen, not only did she choose to carry her baby full-term (against the wishes of her brothers, who were also her guardians), but once I was born, she resisted all attempts to have me adopted by the nuns at Santa Corona. Soon after we returned to Ragusa, we went to live in a cottage in the grounds of a castle which belonged to the local noble family, i Conti del Leonforte, who had taken my mother in as a chambermaid when she discovered she was pregnant. We stayed there until I was five, then the family found my mother a job as a caretaker in a building in Rome where they owned a flat.

Was yours a happy childhood?

Yes and no. For about three months in the year I was ecstatically happy. The day school finished, my mother would put me on the train at Stazione Termini with a suitcase, a tin of sandwiches, and five thousand lire sewn into the lining of my shorts, and after a two-and-a-half-hour journey, my uncle Mimmo would meet me at Naples. There, we'd board the ferry to Ragusa. I can honestly say that each time I set foot in Sicily, it was as though my real life were beginning again – as though nine months of every year were just an interruption of that life. I spent the summer sponge-diving off the Sicilian coast and helping my uncles in the small plot of land they leased from the Leonforte family. My mother would join us towards the end of August, when the *amministratore* decided the tenants of the flats could spare her. As soon as it was time to return to Rome, I would begin sleepwalking; once they found me standing by an upstairs window, another time I was sitting in the dark by the front door, which fortunately for me was bolted. Each time I awoke, I had no recollection whatsoever of leaving my bed.

What about the other nine months of the year?

How can I put it? There was a photograph hanging in the living room of our flat in Rome which, even as a child, I could sense was absolutely emblematic of our station in life. Who knows whether it is still there: objects break, get thrown away, replaced, yet in the egotistical mind of a prisoner, everything in the outside world remains as he left it . . .

Tell me about the photograph.

It was an old black and white photograph, taken long before I was born: if I remember rightly, the date was 1946–7, not long after the end of the Second World War. On first sight, it looks like a bucolic country scene: it's a summer's day, and in the corner of the picture you can just make out a trestle-table laid out with food under a makeshift awning.

There are eight or nine men in the picture, one row standing at the back, another sitting cross-legged on the ground. In the middle of the front row is an enormous barrel, and sitting on this barrel is my grandfather. To the left of him, standing, is my great-uncle Lello with a guitar. All the men are wearing open-necked shirts, some with handkerchiefs knotted around their necks; most have handlebar moustaches.

The picture was taken at a sanctuary to the Madonna on a hilltop, about three kilometres above the village. Every year, at the end of the harvest, the Leonforte family would lay on a spread for their workers, which was taken up by horse and cart to the spot with the awning.

So much for what you see. As always, what you don't see is the real picture. Due to the War, there were no horses left in the village capable of carrying a seventy-kilo barrel of wine up a hill. So, on the orders of the Contessa, my grandfather carried the barrel up on his shoulders because he had the reputation of being the village strongman – and also because, according to my uncles, the Contessa was sexually attracted to him. To humiliate her husband, the Conte, she made him follow my grandfather and the barrel on foot up the hill, and when they reached the top, just to really rub his nose in it, she had him take that photograph, with my grandfather occupying pride of place in the middle. But the Conte had the last laugh: the very next day my grandfather suffered a massive coronary and died – his heart had literally burst from the strain.

What bearing did that story have on your life in Rome?

A young family was orphaned thanks to the caprices of a spoilt noblewoman. For a start, it made us even more depen-dent on the Leonforte family than we would have been in feudal Sicily. You could argue the Contessa did a good deed by taking in a pregnant village girl – but why was my mother searching for a father-figure in the first place? I grew up having to thank them for every crust of bread I ate; once we moved to the flat in Rome I was expected to help the tenants carry in their shopping and summon the lift for them like a bell-boy. I was never allowed to play in the courtyard or bring friends home in case one of the tenants complained to the *amministratore* and my mother lost the flat. And what a flat! Our entire living space would have fitted comfortably into the servants' quarters of any of the other apartments in that building. When the police came in with a search warrant after Emilio Riva was kidnapped, they demanded to see my room. My mother opened the sofa bed in the sitting room and pulled out a drawer: 'This is all Ennio has,' she told them.

Was there any one episode you can think of that led you to become a terrorist?

More than the one episode, it was a series of episodes, like the invisible clicks of a mechanism before it springs into action. My generation – our generation, if you like – grew up in an atmosphere of violence. When that bomb went off during an anti-Fascist demonstration in Catanzaro, I remember all the little right-wing *fascistelli* in my school saying the communists had it coming to them. Those were the days, you remember, when you could get arrested for doodling the Red Brigade's five-pointed star on a paper tablecloth in a bar. But on a personal level, then yes, there probably is one episode in my childhood that stands out.

Describe it.

It was around Eastertime, just before I reached puberty – how old would that make me? Eleven? Twelve? One afternoon my mother bakes this Sicilian Easter cake called *cuddura di pasqua*, and she asks me to bring it upstairs to the horny Contessa. Not that she'd have been particularly horny any more: she must have been in her eighties by then, and a widow – the Conte had died several years previously from some venereal disease he picked up in Abyssinia. So, anyway, up I go with this cake covered in a tea-towel and knock at the door, and the Contessa herself opens it. I hand over the cake, and she says, 'Would you like a slice, *caro*?' in such a tone of voice, that there and then I swore to myself I'd make her pay for that *caro* – her, and all the others like her.

You were born a Scorpio, a sign not renowned for its forgiving qualities. Would you agree?

Over the years, several experts in astrology – women, mostly – have sent me my personal horoscope here in prison. And yes, on that basis, I probably would agree. On the day I was born, the Sun and Mars were in Scorpio: Mars being the planet of war, this would explain my vengeful nature. My moon falls in Cancer, which my astrologists tell me is characterised by stubbornness and pride.

Can you give an example of these traits?

I suppose one example regards my relationship with my father. At a certain point in our lives, he reappeared. Or rather, a balding middle-aged man with a civil servant's briefcase would occasionally show up to take me for a walk in the park. Afterwards, if I was lucky, he would buy me a revolting lemon *spremuta* in a bar, 'because Vitamin C is good for growing boys'. I'm talking five or six times at the most; yet so much tension surrounded these visits that I remember each occasion clearly. I couldn't have been more than seven years old the last time I saw him; this time we went to a bar in the Pincio; and after the obligatory *spremuta*, we walked down to Piazza del Popolo, where we saw a Christian Democrat politician coming out of the church of Santa Maria dé Miracoli. It could have been Fanfani or Taviani, or even Cossiga for that matter – in the end all shit resembles itself. I can't tell you the effect this meeting had on my father: his whole manner grew servile and febrile, and somehow he managed to elbow his way through the crowd to shake the politician's hand. On the way home, he couldn't stop going on about what a wonderful person the politician was, and how the Christian Democrats would make sure Italy could soon hold her head up high in NATO. Before we reached the flat, we stopped on a bench in some public gardens near Piazza Bologna, and then out of the blue he asked me if I would like to take his name. Don't ask me how, but it was as though the meeting with the politician had finally given him the balls to declare himself – as though by some gross association of ideas, his offering to become my father (or rather my 'protector', as he chose to put it) was a way of giving me a stake in the glowing Christian Democrat future he envisaged. You understand, nobody until then had actually told me the man with the briefcase was my father – at least, not explicitly. And in fact when it came to the crunch, he still couldn't bring himself to use the word '*padre*'. Instinctively, I replied that I was very happy with my mother's name, Caruso, and that I didn't need another. On some level I must have known he was my father; and my refusal to take his name was my way of rejecting him for having first rejected me. That's what I mean by pride. It also left me with a life-long aversion to right-wing politicians. Not long after that episode, he died, and I found out that his wife – an elderly, rich widow from Abruzzo – had never even known of my existence.

The night before he arrived, a friend came to colour her hair.

Itala was a *portiera* in an office block on Viale Ippocrate; she wore low-cut knitted tops and drew kohl half-moons on her forehead where her eyebrows should have been. His mother sat on a chair in the bathroom, an old towel around her shoulders, while Itala prepared the mixture. Cigarette smoke drifted through the flat, mingling with the smell of peroxide, which made his eyes water. He was reading *The Adventures of Sandokan* by Salgari: every now and then snatches of their conversation reached him in the kitchen where he sat at the table overlooking the courtyard.

'. . . a Lucià . . . listen to me, now, will you! Since when did talking to a man ever get you anywhere? If you want him back, you let him dip his biscuit, and watch how he'll come running!'

Itala laughed throatily, and Ennio heard the whistle of her breath as she inhaled. She carried on talking with the cigarette still in her mouth; the words sounded slurred, yet strangely authoritative.

'You get the boy to watch your cubicle; an hour should do the trick, even if you're a bit rusty these days!'

Ennio sat on the tall stool, looking out on to the polished marble floor of the lobby. He was wearing khaki shorts, and dark blue sandals with two eye-shaped holes cut out above the toes. After a few minutes, La Guerrini came out of her flat and rapped on the window with one of her rings: Ennio opened the cubicle door, and she handed over a parcel of ironing for his mother. She was wearing a tiny sailor's jacket with gilt buttons all down the sleeves: with her bright, sharp eyes, she reminded him of the monkey he once saw perched on a gypsy boy's shoulder in Piazza Navona. He looked down at the table: beside her bunch of keys, his mother's crossword magazine lay open beside *The Adventures of Sandokan*. He stared at the picture of Sandokan amongst the pirates until it grew blurred: he was willing La Guerrini to leave before she started asking questions. For a moment, she remained outside the cubicle door with her head cocked to one side; then, taking a hundred-lire coin from her purse, she placed it on the cover of his book: buy yourself something nice, she said, for after he's gone . . .

His mother left him a bottle of pear juice and a brioche in a cellophane packet for *merenda*. He didn't feel like eating or reading; all he could think about was her face as she closed the door of the flat; she was wearing a black housecoat he'd never seen before, with wispy feathers around the neck: her eyes were pleading as she straightened his collar and cupped his face in her hand, making a hammock for his chin with the flesh between her thumb and forefinger. Through the half-open door, he saw his father sitting on the foam divan which doubled as his bed; he'd taken off his jacket and tie, and his legs were open so that his womanish stomach swelled out beneath his tight crocodile skin belt. Between his thighs Ennio saw the bulge of his penis and the seam of his trousers splitting the scrotum in two . . .

Itala was right – in less than an hour, he was done. Ennio heard the whine of the lift, then the cubicle door opened and his father came to call him for their walk. When they returned to the flat, his mother was in her ordinary work overall, and the black housecoat with the feather trimmings was hanging on a hook behind the door.

She never wore it again.

What were your schooldays like, Caruso?

The Contessa, in her wisdom, decided I would benefit from a religious education. So from the ages of six to fourteen I attended a school attached to the parish of Santa Chiara in Via Venti Settembre. My classmates were mainly the offspring of shop-keepers and low-ranking civil servants – aspirational right-wing types like my father – most of whose children were too thick to get along in the State system. Around the time of my first communion, the nuns asked us all to bring in our birth certificates; once it came out that I was illegitimate – a *'figlio di nessuno'*, as the State so quaintly puts it – my nickname became *'bastardino'*. To be honest, I don't think it did me any lasting harm: it taught me to stick up for myself, with my fists, mostly (though I never actually went looking for fights); besides, the model of family life offered by my classmates – fat, pampered children, bullying fathers, sexually frustrated mothers – didn't hold any particular attraction.

Did you do well academically at school?

I got by, with high – or low – enough averages not to get sent down after the end-of-year exams. My schooldays only really got interesting after the Contessa died and my mother sent me to the local State school, Liceo Giulio Cesare, which, unbeknown to her, was one of the most radical high schools in Rome. At last my classmates had more to talk about than the model of their father's latest car and the fifty ways to spot a fake Lacoste polo-shirt. That was 1974, the year the Red Brigade kidnapped Mario Sossi; overnight, Renato Curcio and Alberto Franceschini became our heroes.

How much did your mother know of your extracurricular activities?

I think my mother knew more than she let on. But like all Italian mothers everywhere, she stood by her son and defended me against the accusations of the neighbours. The instinct to cleave – to defer, if you like – to the will of the man of the house was too deeply ingrained in her to renounce, even if the man in question was a seventeen-year-old trainee terrorist. To give you an idea of the extent of her loyalty, the hood I wore for my first bank robbery was sewn by my mother – you don't get more loyal than that. Actually, it's one of my clearest memories of that period: coming back one winter's evening from some demonstration, pumped full of adrenaline, with an iron bar tucked up my jumper, and finding her sewing a black felt hood which I'd told her I needed for a *carnevale* party. I remember it was *carnevale* because there was a plate of *fritelle* dusted with icing sugar on the table where she sat. No matter what she may have suspected, at the end of the day she was just a mother trying to please her son, in the only way she knew how. At the sight of her sitting there by the kitchen window which overlooked the dingy courtyard, I could feel all my excitement evaporating: it was like being faced with everything I wanted to escape from. And yet, in spite of that, the familiarity of that ugly kitchen was almost reassuring – inviting even; I pressed the metal bar against my ribs until it hurt – to remind myself, if you like, of who I was, and of who I could be – anything to stop myself being sucked back into the reality of that life.

How did you make the transition from school sit-ins to bank robberies?

It was a gradual progression, which took place over a period of about three years, and was as much dictated by my own personal circumstances as by external events. You know yourself, what made the Lead Years so extraordinary is that no one of our age was leading a normal life. Everybody was swept up in some kind of insane activity: either killing *carabinieri*, or kidnapping judges or kneecapping newspaper editors – it was just a question of degree. One day you were occupying your school premises, the next you were under a bridge on the ring-road, learning how to fire a gun at a concrete pillar. However cut off I may be today from the outside world – and believe me, prison life means cut off – I just don't think young people nowadays have to make the same choices as we had to back then: Break the law, or not break the law? Fight the system, or go with the system? Kill, or not kill? Whichever way you turned, young people were up to something – even the neo-Fascist prigs from my old convent school were part of the group which burst into a meeting of Lotta Continua and shot dead the speaker, Pino Bianchi. God knows where those half-wits managed to lay their hands on a gun – and more to the point, learn how to use it. The only people who weren't sucked in were the ones who would have been on the outside whatever the case – the losers and the junkies. Had I ever been tempted down that road myself – and quite a few kids from my neighbourhood were – I think I was put off drugs for life by finding the corpse of a heroin addict who had overdosed by the dustbins in the courtyard behind our flats. It was the first dead body I'd ever seen.

As you rightly say, everyone was up to something. But most people, myself included, were happy to remain weekend revolutionaries. When did you realise that this was not going to be enough for you?

These things are hard to quantify; but I suppose a turning point for me came during a demonstration in the city centre. This must have been around 1976, when I was nineteen years old. My friends and I met up in Piazza Venezia and linked up to the procession in Via Cavour. We managed to push our way almost up to the front, when some of the *compagni* ahead of us raised their hands in the sign of a P38. Suddenly, everyone was running and shouting, and a kind of madness was in the air. I broke away from the group, and with a metal bar in my hand, I began running towards the façade of one of the hotels leading up towards Santa Maria Maggiore. I could feel the ground thudding beneath me – each time my feet hit the pavement a bolt of electricity shot through my body and flung me back up into the air. I raised my arm, and in that split second before the bar struck the plate-glass window, everything went quiet and still until there was the most almighty explosion you've ever heard – more like a bomb going off than the sound of breaking glass. The thrill of that was like an orgasm – in fact it was better than an orgasm. You could actually see the glass folding in on itself like a wave in a storm. Then the police charged, and me and my friends legged it up the steps at Salita dei Borgia and hid in the church of San Pietro in Vincoli. I remember an

American tourist there asked me if he could take our picture: we told him we were students from the faculty of engineering.

Why was this event significant?

It was significant because for the first time in my life I felt in control of my destiny. The sense of calm that filled me in that split second before the window broke is something that I can recall to this day. There was something almost Zen-like about that feeling.

How were you recruited into Sinistra Armata Proletaria?

I was recruited by a *sappista* who has never been tried for terrorism; he's done plenty of time for other things, burglary and fraud mostly, but he decided to call it a day with Sinistra Armata when things started to get heavy – just before the Mazzantini kidnapping. For argument's sake let's call him Piero. I had known Piero since the days of Centocelle: he was also part of the same group who organised the big demonstrations in the early seventies. He was a *borgataro*, a slum boy, if you like, from the outskirts of the city, and he was one of the first *clandestini* to be recruited into the Rome cell of Sinistra Armata. He was also famous for being able to lay his hands on anything. You needed a screwdriver or a spanner – Piero would magic one from the pocket of his eskimo jacket. The banding machine at one of the communes would break down, and within hours Piero would have replaced it. Piero and I started hanging around together with Bruno Tronti and Massimo Dall'Oglio, and at a certain point Piero started giving us little jobs to do.

What kind of jobs?

In the beginning it was mostly stealing mopeds. At night, Piero would take us by car to a spot where several mopeds were parked; he would pick one, hotwire the engine in a few seconds, then Massimo and I would drive it like hell to a pre-established meeting place. There, we would leave it, and Piero would drive us to another spot. On a good night, we could pick up three or four *motorini* in this way. Then, from mopeds, we went on to cars. A favourite technique was to wait outside a chemist's, where people would stop for a second to collect a prescription, often leaving their cars double-parked with the engine running. Even better were schools and kindergartens: all it took was a harassed mother to leave her keys in the ignition and the car was ours. The biggest problem was what to do with the cars after we'd got hold of them. They had to be moved every two days, while in the meantime new documents were being prepared by the organisation's printing presses. Do you know how many documents you had to present to get past a roadblock in those days? Eight. Can you believe it – eight separate documents? Usually – and I'm talking about pre-computer days – the safest way to put a stolen car back on the road was to clone the papers of an existing vehicle and driver. You could get the details legally from ACI, the automobile association. Actually, the printing presses were fairly professional for the time: my driving licence was issued by Sinistra Armata, and it passed several police inspections, though somehow I doubt it would today.

What were the cars for?

All sorts, really – except for actually getting from A to B. There were strict rules which applied to moving around the city; everybody in the organisation had to use public transport, and you had to change bus or tram or *metropolitana* several times before reaching your destination. The cars were mostly for bank robberies and hostage-taking, as well as for longer journeys within Italy and abroad.

Why were you going abroad?

I myself wasn't, but higher-ranking *clandestini* would make regular shopping trips to buy weapons. In the early days, they'd got by with the leftovers from the Partisan movement, mostly hand-grenades and machine-guns which were being recycled on the black market in Milan. When this was no longer sufficient, their preferred destinations were Switzerland and Liechtenstein. Switzerland, especially, was particularly attractive to armed organisations. In those days, to buy a gun, all you needed was a wad of cash and an arms licence – which, handily, Sinistra Armata could print themselves. Their favourite weapons were the PPKs used by the German police, which were extremely accurate and almost impossible to get hold of in Italy.

When did you become a clandestino?

Around the middle of 1977. By this time I'd turned into a full-time car and moped thief. In the back of my mind, I always had this feeling that my luck would run out – that my career as a terrorist would be over before it'd even begun. I kept thinking of my uncles in Sicily, and how they'd react if they knew I'd turned into a petty criminal – in their eyes a car thief was no better than a low-life *contrabandiere* hanging around the docks in Palermo. My reasoning was this: I knew I'd be caught one day, so I might as well be caught doing something worthwhile – something which would be seen, if you like, as a declaration of my beliefs. There'd be no point in trying to explain to anyone *after the fact* that I was only stealing cars for the good of the organisation. I wasn't being melodramatic or fanciful about my chances: before becoming *clandestini*, all new recruits were told the same thing by Roberto Scalzone, the then head of Sinistra Armata: in six months, you'll either be dead or in prison.

Didn't it cross your mind at this point to call it a day?

Of course it did – all the time. You know that corny American saying you used to get on posters, usually with a lurid sunrise in the background: 'Today is the first day of the rest of your life'? (which by the way has a significance all of its own when your release date is set at 2042) – well, those words used to go through my head every morning as I lay in bed trying to muster the energy to get up. It was as though a vacuum had opened up in my life and I was floating along inside it: somehow at the end of the day it was easier to go along with it than to resist. Sinistra Armata weren't vindictive, you know – they weren't a cult: I reckon that at any point I could have broken away without having death squads turning up at my door. Yet I didn't do it, and the reason I didn't do it was pride, that and a kind of moral inertia: I couldn't admit to myself, at least not then, that I had made the wrong choices. Besides, what else could I have done with my life? I had spent my life brainwashing myself into thinking that society would never have anything to offer to people like me. I wasn't about to prove myself wrong.

You say that you were just going with the flow, yet something must have prompted you to make the crossover from car thief to full-time terrorist.

I suppose looking back on it there was. What precipitated events – made everything shift up a gear, so to speak – was the arrival of my call-up papers. If there was one thing I was really sure about in all that uncertainty it was that I wasn't going to do my National Service. And the only way to avoid the Army was by going underground – either that, or having well-connected relatives who could procure you an exemption from the Ministry of Health. Becoming a *clandestino* neatly took care of everything.

Was there any kind of 'official' process involved in becoming a clandestino?

The first step was burning your identity card – in public, in front of all the *compagni* from the cell you'd been recruited into. This was seen as a kind of declaration of intent; and as a ceremony, had its origins in a saying of Simon Bolivar, which the first *sappisti* made their own: 'Victory or death'. Burning your papers, if you like, was a way of symbolically burning your bridges behind you, of closing off all the escape routes.

Did this ritualistic bonfire take place before or after your call-up papers arrived?

Quite a bit after – I'm getting ahead of myself. The postcard from the Ministry of Defence came in January or February, though I didn't have to present myself at the base until mid-April. That was the so-called period of grace you got before kissing goodbye to the next two years of your life. Which in a sense I was too by becoming a *clandestino* – though I knew I was fooling myself if I thought I'd be done in two years. So I went along with it and made my preparations.

So for two months you acted as though you were really about to leave for your military service?

Not only did I act as though I was about to go into the Army, a part of me – some tiny residue of would-be conventionality – almost made me believe I really was an only son about to leave for the Front. Which just goes to show that you're never entirely the rebel you think you are. Not that this was as far-fetched as it sounds: in some ways there was more structure and discipline to be found in Sinistra Armata than in any of Italy's armed forces. It was like being in one of those black and white Totò films from the fifties where the hero wanders around the streets he can barely bring himself to leave. Piazza Bologna, of all places! An area I'd hated since the first day my mother and I got off the train at Stazione Termini with our suitcases – an area of dull neo-classical squares and blocks of flats from the Fascist years – boxy homes for the Duce's heroes – narrow brick façades pocked with bullet-holes from the last days of the War . . . And yet in those few weeks in Rome, I lived our neighbourhood more intensely than I had done in all our years in Piazza Bologna, noticing things I'd never noticed before . . .

. . . like the indoor market at Via Catania, early in the morning with the light streaming in through the vaulted glass ceiling, or La Casina Fiorita in the middle of the square where old ladies sat beneath the plane trees in the spring sunshine, drinking syrup of almonds at wrought-iron tables . . . One day, his mother took him to the Jewish quarter around Piazza Vittorio to be fitted for a suit; she said his father used to buy his clothes at L'Uomo Elegante in the days before all those foreigners took over and the area became like Little Arabia . . . He stood on the marble floor in his socks, arms raised to the sides, while the tailor measured the jacket. Deft hands burrowed like voles beneath the lining of the sleeves, miraculously never touching the flesh beneath, as though the hands and the cloth were dancing. He shut his eyes and felt a harsh cactus of sweat bloom beneath his armpits. It was a *sahariana* suit, with six pockets and a belted waist – all the rage those days – in expensive, khaki-coloured wool: not long after, he would wear it to meet the landlord the day he rented his first flat as a *sappista*.

The shop was cool and dark with faded plaster rosettes on the ceiling; beyond the curve of the *fumée* window he watched Africans, Chinese, Indians moving through the market like figures on a brightly lit stage. Luciana sat on a gilt armchair, upholstered in faded red velvet, her handbag on her lap, ankles crossed delicately to one side, watching her son, murmuring to the tailor about the old days when a woman could still walk around the neighbourhood unaccompanied. He knew she cherished the intimacy of the situation, her restless son still for once, not rushing anywhere dangerous, not angry with her or the world, handsome in his new suit . . . She watched him hungrily, scanning his figure again and again as though she could never gaze enough at a son who had been lost to her for years, averting her eyes only from the tattoo on his wrist . . . Ever since the call-up papers arrived, she had been telling people about her '*figlio militare*', as though he'd already done his time in the Army and come back with his head straightened out – as though this were a new son, one to be proud of.

Before he left, he went to the barber's in Via Salaria: his hair hadn't been cut that short since he was a boy. As he walked through the door of the flat, tears filled Luciana's eyes and she kissed him – she couldn't help herself, even though for years they had barely touched. His uncles came up from Sicily to see him off; they carried his bags and pinched his cheeks with their calloused fingers, slipping 10,000-lire bills into the pockets of his *sahariana*. His mother left a parcel of sandwiches and a cake on the seat beside him 'for the long journey ahead'. He waved to them as the train drew out of the platform, then remained standing by the window with his back to the carriage. Ugly red apartment blocks drifted past: warehouses, billboards and, in a field of lumpy ploughed earth, a show-bathroom mounted in a glass box. He heard the clang-clang-clang of the warning bell as the train approached a level-crossing: two figures on bicycles stood waiting beside a disused signal box; a skull and crossbones was painted on to the wall, along with the words: '*Pericolo di Morte*' in dripping yellow letters. Then the train sped on, past abandoned farm-houses, an INTERSPAR supermarket, and a gypsy encampment with gleaming trailers and half-naked children playing amidst the rubbish . . . a city fraying at the edge of the tracks.

At the next station, Civitavecchia, he got off and caught the 14.33 back to Rome.

Tape #2: June 2000

So, Caruso, if you didn't go to the Army, where did you go?

I took the train back to Rome, and spent the night in a *pensione* near Stazione Termini. All I had on me was an overnight bag which had been left for me in a locker at the station. This contained a change of clothes, some money, and a gun – a Mauser 7.65 – which I carried around with me until the day I was arrested.

What did you do with your suitcases from home?

I left them in the locker at the station, and they were disposed of later by another *sappista*.

How could you check into a pensione *if you had burnt your ID card? Besides, weren't you a bit suspicious-looking turning up with just an overnight bag?*

I told them at the *pensione* that I was a travelling salesman for an insurance company, which would explain my lack of luggage; also, when I checked in, I left them my new ID card, in the name of a certain Roberto Ferrero, which had been issued to me when my old one was destroyed. Even so, I made sure to leave the *pensione* by six a.m., as I knew the tourist police came to collect guests' details every morning around seven. Roberto Ferrero, by the way, was a real person, not some invented character, so even if they had checked up I would have been all right – for a while, at least.

How did you end up with this person's ID card?

Pretty much the same way we used to clone car licences. One afternoon, before I left for the Army, Piero and I saw a young man coming out of Pepys Bar in Piazza Barberini, who we both thought looked quite like me: medium height, slim build, dark colouring. He got into a red Fiat Panda, and while he was starting the engine, Piero took down the number plate and had it checked at ACI. Once he had all the owner's details, I was issued with a Sinistra Armata car licence and ID card, both in the name of Roberto Ferrero. By one of those weird coincidences, I had actually stolen a red Panda from a school in EUR in my car-thieving days, and a few months later was given back the keys of the very same car to use for a job. That meant that for a while there were two Roberto Ferreros going around with the same papers and the same car.

How did you spend your first evening in Rome as a clandestino?

I went to a *trattoria* near the Colosseum, called 'Da Nerone', where, if I'm not mistaken, I had a plate of home-made *ravioli agli spinaci*, and a quarter of a litre of house white. I was probably only about three kilometres from my house as the crow flies, and yet I felt as though I had crossed the sea to a new continent.

In which sense?

In every sense. For a start, I felt about ten years older. Sitting there drinking my *digestivo* amongst all the tourists on that warm spring evening, this platter of fruit in front of me – (all overhanging grapes and big rosy apples like a Caravaggio still-life) – the Colosseum and the Roman Forum floodlit in the background, I felt like a foreigner in my own city – like a foreigner in my own life, come to that. I was in a state of total limbo, as though for a few hours I could be anybody I liked: it's pathetic to think of it now – in fact I'm almost too embarassed to tell you – but I got talking to these German students on the table next to mine, and when they asked me what I did, I told them I was a marine biologist working for the Ministry of the Environment. How's that for wishful thinking? It goes to show you that becoming a terrorist at the age of twenty is as much about a search for identity as anything else. The students were celebrating something – I forget what, probably the completion of a doctorate – and they invited me to join them for a drink. For a moment I was tempted – after all, Roberto Ferrero the marine biologist wouldn't have hesitated – but then I happened to brush the bulge of the Mauser hidden beneath my jacket with my elbow, and it was as though I had literally been transposed to a different place. Everything around me looked dark and sinister: that fat man in a waistcoat with a napkin tied around his neck, his snout in a plate of *tagliatelle*, was probably working undercover for the anti-terrorist squad; the elderly waiter in his shiny jacket was surely in somebody or other's pay, and even the German students had to be members of some crack secret service division assigned to infiltrate European armed organisations. And that, of course, was the whole point of carrying a gun: more than for self-defence (after all, by the time you needed to use it, chances were it was already going to be too late), it was to make sure that at all times you felt different, apart, from everyone else. Which might seem like a contradiction, as in fact our strength, if you like, as urban guerrillas was precisely the opposite: we were ordinary people who knew how to live amongst ordinary people. In order to survive, you had to be aware of changing currents in society – clothes, food, fashions – everything from politics to the latest Umberto Tozzi summer hit – so as not to draw attention to yourself. But those things meant nothing to us: we were like ghosts, watching other people's lives unfolding around us. And just in case we forgot, the gun was there to remind us . . .

When was the first time you used your gun?

Probably about three or four weeks later, during a bank raid near Genoa.

What were you doing in Genoa?

I was ordered to go to Genoa almost immediately after that evening in the *trattoria*: For obvious reasons, it was too risky to remain in Rome. In fact when I did eventually telephone my mother, she told me that the police had turned up with a search warrant only three days after my departure. Which goes to show I must have been on some kind of register of suspected terrorists long before I became a *clandestino*. Not that this was particularly significant, as anyone who had ever taken part in a school sit-in probably ended up on that list.

Where did you stay in Genoa?

I was given instructions to rent a flat off Via Prè. In the 'Lead Years' this was quite a tricky business, as any kind of suspicious behaviour could get the anti-terrorist squad on your back. I remember a safe-house in Milan got busted just because the tenants had a habit of settling their utility bills *too promptly*! The flat in Via Prè was ideal, as it had no *portiera* (and I know from first-hand experience how much a *portiera* gets to know about the lives of the tenants), it was on the first floor – handy for getaways in case of a raid – and was in a quiet residential street with no bus stops, shop windows for lingering over, or benches where a busybody might observe us from behind his newspaper. In the beginning I couldn't get used to having all that space to myself: bedroom, bathroom, sitting room-cum-dining room, and a kitchen which for some weird reason was situated in the hall. Bear in mind I didn't even have a room to myself in the glorified broom-cupboard my mother and I called home. I still remember the second-hand furniture we bought at the flea market down by the docks: a wardrobe, a bookshelf, three folding beds, a camping stove and a light blue formica table with four chairs.

How long did you live in the flat in Via Prè?

On and off for about six months.

Did anyone else live there with you?

Not officially, in the sense that the landlords never found out, although Dall'Oglio and Tronti were there virtually that whole time. There was also a period when a *sappista* from Bologna called Corrado Villa was staying with us; he came home one evening and found a film crew from Rai Due outside his front door; someone had tipped off the police and the Base had been discovered. Luckily it was dark, and he was able to slip away without any of the neighbours recognising him. As this was the second time he'd been busted, we used to call him the *iettatore*. I don't know whether he really did bring bad luck, poor guy, but every time he walked into the room we used to scratch our balls, just in case. I remember Massimo even slept with a bunch of chillies under his pillow. We had to keep a constant eye on our behaviour to make sure nothing that we did would arouse suspicion in our neighbours. As far as they were concerned, I was a young insurance salesman who went out to work every morning with his briefcase, and who occasionally travelled around the country on business. If and when I had a visitor, they would never enter the apartment with me: they would wait at the corner of the street, while I went up first, checked that everything was in order, then gave them the OK signal from the window. This was just one of the hundreds of rules which governed life in a base.

Give some other examples.

For a start, the base was only known to the people who lived there: this way, any *sappista* who was caught would have that much less to give away during an interrogation – and we all know what methods the police were using to prise information out of us during the Lead Years. You were also given the address of at least one other safe-house which could be used in an emergency – and which, like your real name, was known only to you. You also had to keep a constant eye on what was happening outside: anybody walking up and down the street, a boarded-up building which could be used for police surveillance, or even seemingly innocuous details like a certain kind of short aerial to be found on all police cars, even unmarked ones. Otherwise, you tried to live as normal a life as possible within the limits of a strict eight o'clock curfew: shopping at the supermarket, the occasional matinee at the Rialto – I remember I saw Scorsese's *Raging Bull* there four afternoons in a row – preparing supper in the evenings with your *compagni*. In that period I discovered, to my surprise, that I'd learned how to cook several dishes simply by observing my mother, although, disappointingly, they never tasted how I remembered. Once I had a craving for stuffed tomatoes, but I couldn't remember whether you were meant to put the rice in raw or cooked: the temptation to call my mother was almost unbearable.

Did you ever find out?

Years later, when I was already here at Rebibbia, she brought me a tray of stuffed tomatoes which I shared with my cell-mates – along with the recipe, which sadly I haven't had the opportunity to try out.

And was the answer cooked or raw?

Neither. You brown the rice in a *soffritto* until the grains turn transparent, add it to the pulp which you scoop out from the tomatoes, then spoon the whole lot back into the skins with mountains of chopped basil and parsley.

Apart from enjoying culinary moments, what else were you up to?

Learning how to rob a bank, mostly. Along with burning your ID card, this was the other main rite of passage to becoming a *clandestino* – as well as still being the organisation's preferred method of fundraising. In some ways we were quite puritanical; while other organisations had a thriving trade in antiquities (mostly bits of statues robbed from churches which they'd flog to dealers in Milan), we considered these methods to be sub-proletariat, *mafiosi*, even. Obviously, there was a lot to be gained out of a kidnapping – both financially and in terms of image – but the risks and the outlay were proportionately higher. Leaving aside logistics – finding and adapting a house, tailing your subject, preparing to take him hostage – the simple act of choosing your man could take weeks. In pre-computer, pre-photocopier days, this meant leafing through back issues of newspapers and copying out any relevant articles *by hand*. You begin to see why, to a small organisation like ours, robbing a bank seemed, if not easier, at least less labour-intensive.

So tell me, Caruso, how do you rob a bank?

How do you rob a bank? Well, to begin with, you choose your branch. Obviously, anywhere in or around the centre of a city is risky. Almost all the armed organisations operating during the Lead Years came to this conclusion. The best banks were provincial ones – Banca di San Gimignano, Banca dell' Agricoltura, Cassa di Risparmio – situated in small towns or villages, or even the so-called '*città dormitorie*' – those developments of commuter flats which were beginning to mushroom up around all major cities. Once you've chosen your target, the next step is to get to know the lie of the land. Here's where you have to be careful, especially in a small town, where any newcomer tends to stick out like a sore thumb. There's a limit to the number of times you can pass as a day-tripper without drawing attention to yourself. Compared to some of the larger armed organisations, our bank raids probably tended to be better rehearsed – more choreographed, if you like. I was reading recently that towards the middle of the seventies, the Red Brigade got so blasé about their raids that Franceschini even did one without a gun – or rather without taking it out of his pocket – just to see if the words 'Hands up, this is a raid!' were enough to scare the cashier into handing over the money.

And were they?

Apparently yes, although he was the first to admit that it didn't really count, as he had three armed *compagni* covering his back.

Who showed you the ropes?

A semi-*clandestino* who had been recruited from one of the unions at Lancia. He was a really nice guy, older than us, in his late forties I suppose, originally from Calabria. He joined Sinistra Armata for a number of reasons – partly because he'd been dumped on by the bosses at Lancia, but also because he had personal problems of his own. He'd had a heart attack a few years previously, then a nervous breakdown, and was off sick for a few months. When he returned to the factory, he'd lost his position as foreman and was made to work as a kind of glorified messenger boy, delivering invoices and stuff on a bicycle. He was consumed by bitterness at having been tossed aside by management like a piece of old scrap metal. To make matters worse, his wife left him, then he got into arrears with maintenance payments: I think at one point there was even a court order out against him. He had an ulcer; I remember when it flared up, he used to swig Maalox straight from the bottle.

This tended to be quite a common profile amongst members of armed organisations: a definite political commitment, no doubt about it, but with some kind of private hardship which invariably acted as the catalyst. I say this because I know today what I didn't know then – namely, that if I hadn't been the illegitimate son of a *portiera* there's no way I'd be telling you this story from behind bars: at a certain point – much, much earlier on – I'd have been happy to call it a day. There was something, though, about my childhood which in some eerie way was like a microcosm of all the ills of Italian society: living in a relatively well-to-do area like Piazza Bologna, but even as a child, knowing that I would never have a bite of the cherry because of who I was, and because our only benefactors were a pair of decrepit old aristocrats – leaving aside the morality of a system where to get even the humblest job at the post office you needed your political *raccomandazione*.

But to return to our training: 'Gaetano' (you'll see shortly why I don't give his real name) turned out to have a real talent for bank raids – so much so, that in those years Genoa became the organisation's unofficial school for armed robbery. Gaetano was endlessly patient with us: he knew that for all our bravado, Massimo and I weren't hardened criminals, and that for us, the psychological barrier that had to be overcome was far greater than anything we had faced until then. He used to come and call for us in a blue Fiat 500, which was his pride and joy, and drive us out to seaside resorts on the Ligurian Riviera – Sampierdarena, Sori, Recco – and there, sitting at an outside table of a bar, he'd take us through the motions. All in all, I took part in five raids during my time in Genoa: each one was orchestrated by Gaetano. In some ways he was a bit of a loose cannon – impatient not only with his situation in the factory, but also with the local cell of Sinistra Armata. He was forever talking about the Partisans, saying we should stop politicking amongst ourselves and follow their example: I think his dream was to burst into Lancia armed with a machine-gun, and mow down all the bosses.

Then, many years after my arrest, I was sharing a cell in a high-security prison with a member of the Red Brigade who knew him from the Communist Party in Genoa, and he told me what had become of Gaetano: apparently, a few months after our last raid, he'd robbed a security van carrying wages to the factory. In fact, it was a plan he'd suggested to the executive at the time, and the idea had been dismissed as potentially harmful to the proletariat, in that the bosses might have taken advantage of the situation to delay paying the workers' wages. Also, in terms of image, the scope for harm was far greater than if we'd been caught just robbing a bank. So Gaetano did it on his own, using all the expertise he'd picked up in his years as maestro of the bank raid, and after paying off his debts in Genoa, he settled in Brazil, where he married a local girl and opened a pizzeria on the beach in Rio. I have to say, my first reaction when I found out was: good on him. It was thanks to him that I never got caught with my hands in the sack . . .

. . . *think of your mother*, he'd say: *one fine morning, she opens the newspaper and sees a picture of her son in hand-cuffs: is that what you want, Roberto – is it now?* When he got angry, the sweat beaded up beneath his hairline, and he twitched his shoulders as though he were literally trying to shrug the anger down off his back. His lips, caked with Maalox, stood out chalky-mauve against his dark, *meridionale* complexion: it looked as if he was wearing sunblock, the kind used by skiers . . . The appointment was for seven o'clock: the cobbles in the square gleamed in the early-morning mist as Gaetano parked the black Alfetta in a side street behind the bank; Massimo and another *compagno* from Milan waited in the car with the engine running. His mother's *carnevale* hood was folded in his pocket; beneath his jacket the Mauser nestled comfortably against his ribs. He liked the feeling now; he was used to it. They were waiting for the branch to open: *That's the best time to hit them*, he said, *when they're still rubbing the sleep from their eyes – either that, or else, just before the 1.30* pausa *when all they can think about is going home for lunch*. The manager had a mistress in the next village; he visited her on alternate Tuesdays . . . *Hands in the air! This is a raid!* . . . Every afternoon, Ennio sat at the blue formica table, a shaving mirror propped up against the cooker, watching his face as he mouthed those words to the empty flat. *You don't shout*, said Gaetano – *there's no need. You want to reassure them, not frighten them*. It was the first time he had unsheathed his gun, the first time it had left the warmth and intimacy of his body: there was something sexual about aiming the gleaming Mauser at a roomful of thirty, forty terrified faces – hips thrust out, arms extended, two gloved hands on the trigger, the pistol sprouting from his body like a penis or a sword . . . a woman moaned, clasping her hand to her throat: around her neck she wore a showy gold *collier*. Gaetano jumped on to the counter and squatting insolently like a monkey beside the manager, he ground the gun into his face, hooking up the flesh of the cheek as though it were pizza dough: *Come on, lover boy, open the safe*. The man hesitated for a moment, his arms bobbing weakly in the air like a pair of brackets, then slowly he walked towards the safe where a *compagno* stood waiting with the sacks. They were red and white UPIM bags, he remembered; Massimo stole them from the hardware department in the Genoa branch. The cashiers, huddled together behind the Enquiries desk, looked as though they had discovered a primitive kinship which in all those years of working together they'd never acknowledged. Some had takeaway cups of coffee on their desks, still covered with little parchment doilies from the bar next door: 'Bar Centrale' it said in gold letters.

Gaetano turned to the woman whose moans had grown louder. 'We're not after you or your jewels,' he said; his voice through the hood was reassuring, kindly even. When the bags were full, Gaetano jumped down from the counter and, still watched by those forty pairs of eyes, they walked calmly across the sunlit marble floor of the bank towards the rear exit. There, in a side street, the Alfetta was waiting; they drove in silence as far as the turn-off for the Aurelia highway, and got into an orange Citroën Dyane which was parked in a layby, keys ready in the ignition.

Back at the flat they shook the UPIM bags out on to the floor: little bricks of 50,000-lire bills came thudding out, more than a hundred million in all. There was something exciting at the sight of all that money – there for the taking, if you just knew how to ask . . . A spasm of fury shot through him at the thought of his mother working all those years in her glass cubicle: even when she was in her own flat she was still on call, twenty-four hours a day, seven days a week. He doubted whether in her life she had seen even one million lire all in one go.

Later, when the money had been collected, he went downstairs for some air. That supernatural calm, the erotic force of his own will, which had filled him as he stood in the bank pointing the Mauser, cushioned his movements now like an aura: he felt as though he were walking on air.

(And hours later, he still had an erection.)

*   *   *

He entered the station from the rear, mingling with a group of pilgrims who got off the number 64 bus at Termini.

They were travelling with an elderly priest; across their shoulders, they all wore commemorative canvas zip-up bags printed with the name of their church, and a tour operator in Bari. Yellow silk *foulards* were knotted about their necks, whilst their leader's scarf was tied to an umbrella which he carried high above his head like a staff. Most of the pilgrims were short and wiry, prematurely aged, like Southerners of his uncles' generation: the men in suits without ties, the women in print dresses with leather slippers on their feet to relieve their swollen ankles. They were talking and laughing in dialect, carefree as a teenage *commitiva* on an outing, as they passed around a bag of tangerines.

10.25 on the square station clock above the ticket office: beneath the neon lights, a pair of railway policemen with walkie-talkies around their necks stood drinking coffee by the sandwich kiosk: one of them had the *Gazzetta dello Sport* open on the bar in front of him; Ennio recognised it by the pink paper it was printed on. He wasn't worried by the policemen: the ones who'd seen his photo in their files wouldn't be going around in uniform with walkie-talkies. If anything, he had to keep an eye open for young men, his age, in turtle-neck Shetland jumpers and faded jeans worn tight across the hips – the ones with sideburns and two-day stubble on their faces, and black-rimmed left-wing intellectual's glasses à la Gad Lerner.

But he was too tired to worry even about them. He needed to sleep – ached to sleep – but a *couchette* was too dangerous: he was better off amongst the second-class passengers in a compartment. It was only by concentrating on his tiredness, all the physical manifestations of it, that Ennio was able to keep going. He was a mechanism that had been too severely tested: good for nothing now, spent; yet, still, blindly, the instinct to survive drove him on.

He had ten minutes before the Genoa train left; beneath the greenish station lights, he saw *extracomunitari* settling down for the night in the doorways of the closed shops – Africans mainly, with black nylon holdalls they used as pillows. To-morrow morning they would take those holdalls to subways and *gallerie* all around Rome, spreading out the contents on batik-printed cloths they laid out on the pavement: woven friendship bracelets, carved elephants, imitation Louis Vuitton bags and wallets which they bought in wholesale shops around the station. Like him, they risked arrest with each step they took, like him, they inhabited a parallel universe of forged papers, fear, danger. And yet at the end of each day, they were prepared to lie side by side like brothers under the very noses of the policemen whose job it was to arrest them. Because unlike him, they had nothing to hide: their only crime was that they were *extracomunitari*, unwelcome guests. Un-like him, they walked tall, dreamily leaving their mark on a landscape which could never absorb them . . . there was something limpid, trusting, in their fatalism, which made his life appear sordid – even to himself.

At the news stand, he bought a biro and a crossword magazine, *La Settimana Enigmistica*, glancing briefly at the headlines of *Il Messaggero* as he waited for his change: there was nothing on the Rivella kidnapping, but there wouldn't be – the government had ordered a news blackout while his release was being negotiated. The sight of all those newspapers hanging on their pegs oppressed him, and he turned away; he was like a self-diagnosed convalescent – weak, febrile – who had to be kept away from anything that might excite him.

He'd had his fill of the news – making it, reading it, discussing it: he couldn't bear to pick up even a family weekly like *Oggi* or *Gente*, with their chatty articles about actors and *soubrettes* and the latest twist in the saga of Monaco's Grimaldi family. For years now, ever since he could remember, his mother had taken *La Settimana Enigmistica*. She was surprisingly gifted at crosswords, with a quick, sharp mind and an almost scholarly recall of facts. On the marble-topped coffee table by her armchair, she kept a box of sharpened pencils and a well-thumbed grammar book, *L'Uso Corretto dell'Italiano*. The crosswords were almost a subtext to their lives: across the flat, she would call: 'Five across, nine letters – being of two parts . . .' He stood at the bathroom window, looking through the gaps in the pale green venetian blind at the washing strung up between the courtyard walls. Disembodied voices floated through the air, as though the courtyard were a stage. The sharp scent of washing powder mingled with cooking smells emanating from the individual flats: from one window garlic and onion for a *soffritto*, from another, the unmistakable, oily smokiness of peppers held over a naked flame until the skin turned black . . . In each hand he held an identity card: one in the name of Caruso Ennio, the other, Ferrero Roberto – both contained his likeness. *Duplicità* he thought, *being of two parts* . .

Some of the pilgrims were standing by the platform, waiting for the group to reassemble before boarding the train to Bari. A young woman in a blue overall was polishing a small area of marble floor around the kiosk where the policemen stood; beneath the overall she wore rolled-up jeans and bright red cord *espadrillias*. Reaching inside the pocket, she took out an orange and white packet of KIM cigarettes, and putting one to her mouth, she asked the younger policeman for a light. By the flare of the *cerino*, Ennio saw the dark circles beneath her eyes; she was tired – even more tired than he was.

Ennio walked towards the platform; glancing briefly behind him, he boarded the Bari train and walked down the corridor, past a row of dark empty carriages, until he reached the first-class compartment. It was 10.32: he had three minutes before the Genoa train left. He stood for a moment in the corridor, listening to the fitful hum of the engine, then he jumped down on to the other side, and ignoring the '*Vietato Attraversare i Binari*' signs, he crossed the tracks and ran down the underpass towards platform nine. The guard had already blown the whistle as he boarded the train.

Inside the second-class carriage, the passengers were settling down for the night. He took the last empty seat by the window, immediately opening his crossword magazine to avoid making eye contact with any of his fellow-travellers. The carriage lights flickered on and off as the train drew slowly out of the station and Ennio held his breath, forcing his concentration back inwards as the engine picked up speed, resisting the temptation to add his presence to the common pool of intimacy within the carriage. Lulled by the rocking of the train, he closed his eyes: he liked that feeling of cosiness, of belonging – for a moment he could forget he was a terrorist, and pretend he was an ordinary young man catching the night train to Genoa. '*Yes, I work in Genoa for an organisation called Sinistra Armata. You might have heard of us – we rob banks and kidnap rich people to teach them a lesson . . .*' Someone opened a packet of sandwiches; he heard the rustle of greaseproof paper, and smelt the fatty tang of *prosciutto*. By rights he should have been hungry; in a normal world he would be thinking of his supper. He cast his mind back to the last time he had eaten; it was the day before, late afternoon, in that squalid *monolocale*, near the Tuscolana power station. One of the *compagne*, a dark, sullen girl from Milan, made *spaghetti all'amatriciana*: she cooked the food contemptuously, without grace, as though ashamed to be seen in the kitchen. The flat was filthy: clothes heaped in a pile by the door, unwashed plates in the sink, shaggy turd floating in the toilet-bowl.

This was the life he had chosen for himself, an improvised life, a life where second best had become second nature. And yet he had no one to blame but himself – *l'hai voluta la bicicletta? Mò pedala . . .* With those words, he thought of his uncle Mimmo, and unexpectedly an image came into his mind of the first time he tried to ride a bicycle. He must have been eight or nine years old: it was the end of the summer, and his mother was arriving the following day on the *corriere* from Rome. One moment he was fast asleep in his bed, the next, he found himself in his vest and pants, wheeling his uncle's heavy bicycle in the moonlight along the dirt track which led to the communal fields at the edge of the village. He had never ridden a bicycle before; his mother couldn't afford to buy him one and besides, there was nowhere to keep a bicycle in the flat in Rome. As he walked along the path, he felt the stones pricking his bare feet, and yet the pain merely registered in some distant insignificant area of his brain. He stopped by an olive tree and holding on to the trunk for support, hoisted himself up on to the saddle; the leather felt smooth and warm beneath his thighs. He looked at his splayed fingers on the grey bark of the tree: the moment he let go, he was going to fall – it was inevitable, his toes only just grazed the serrated edge of the pedals. And yet it was as though he had no choice in the matter, just as earlier he'd had no choice about leaving his bed. Leaning forward slightly in the saddle, he gripped the rubber handlebar with one hand, and with the other he let go of the tree. Incredibly, he managed to cycle almost to the fields, freefalling slowly along the moonlit path, legs outstretched, rolling around and down to the very edge of the world. Then he fell, landing badly, with the bicycle on top of him. The pain jolted him out of his dreamlike state and he awoke to find his uncle Mimmo carrying him home across the path in his arms.

As the train sped northwards along the tracks, he remembered, across the years, the bitterness of that pain: sitting on the table in his pants and vest, beneath the bare kitchen light bulb, the *mercuriocromo* fizzing along the surface of his wound, redder even than the blood itself; Uncle Mimmo with his back to him, rinsing his hands at the sink beneath the calendar of Padre Pio which hung on the wall above the tap. The monk's eyes seemed to be gazing right through him: hot, sinister. He felt helpless, as though he'd sleepwalked into disaster; the moment of exhilaration on the bicycle before he fell but a distant memory now.

He brushed the Mauser with his elbow, and at once the cosiness of the carriage evaporated, as he knew it would. He closed his eyes, hoping to staunch the panic prickling through him now like bile. For a brief moment his system did shut down, but it was only a simulation of sleep: his head felt hollow as a cardboard box. Whichever way he looked he'd made a mess of things, his existence reduced to eternally crossing and recrossing a muddy field, without a hope of ever reaching his destination. But he hadn't sleepwalked into that field: no, this time he'd gone looking for failure – painstakingly setting things up so that there could be no honourable way out. *Leave*, she said, *come back with me to London – we'll start again* . . . But that was the whole point: even if he ran his life backwards like a film, there was no single episode he could pick out and say: that's where I began to go wrong, let's take things differently from here. It was all wrong, you see, from beginning to end. He was the sum of all his failures: no matter how deep he dug, he couldn't dredge up anything resembling a personality. There was nothing to start again from: all he could do now was follow events to their logical conclusion. The air in the compartment felt stale, used. He got up from his seat, and without disturbing the sleeping passengers, he slid open the carriage door to the corridor. He stood there for a moment, watching his reflection on the window, while beyond the glass, the darkened countryside sped by.

For two days he'd followed her, just like he'd learned to follow his other victims. Both mornings she left her flat in Via del Monte Oppio around eight; he sat and watched her from behind his newspaper on the bench in the gardens where he'd often waited for her before his call-up papers arrived. At night-time the junkies used the gardens for dealing; the balding lawn was littered with syringes and blackened stumps of candles. It seemed incredible to him, now, that he'd ever had the time, the fantasy, if you like, to be a lover – and a poor one at that. Relationships outside the organisation were forbidden: a few *sappisti* broke up with their partners before becoming *clandestini*; most claimed to be uninterested in anyone uninvolved in the armed struggle – they found girls on the outside vapid, bland. Yet still Ennio continued to see Julia, promising himself each time would be the last.

Then came that afternoon at La Camillina. The organisation sent him to the house to run off some leaflets on the banding machine – the first time he had been trusted to carry out such a task on his own. The fact that he brought Julia with him was symptomatic of his frame of mind in those days; if it ever became known he had taken an outsider to a base, his career as a terrorist would have ended before it had begun.

Towards evening, she sat in the dark, her knees drawn up to her chin, as she sketched the view from the kitchen window. She had washed her face, and her hair was slicked behind her ears: she looked more Florentine than English, with a high, pale forehead like Dante's Beatrice. He loved her, there was no denying it any more, even to himself. Emotion reverberated through him as he stood at the kitchen doorway, running the hosepipe down into the sunlit orchard. He watched the long, thick tube of water pulsing upwards on to the dusty soil: he was amazed at himself – literally amazed that such a feeling could have taken root in him. He dropped the hosepipe to the ground and the water drove a furrow sideways through the ground until the earth around the trees grew brown and wet. Then he came to the window, and they kissed. '*I love you*,' said Ennio, and as he spoke, he closed his eyes: he felt slack, at peace, as though whatever it was that drove him – consumed him – in his daily life, had momentarily released its hold. '*I'm pregnant*,' whispered Julia.

And with those words, Ennio finally became a terrorist. If he'd ever had any doubts about abandoning the armed struggle – fantasised about doing his military service, coming out and getting a job – they evaporated the moment she told him her news. He had nothing to give Julia or their child: take the armed struggle out of his life, and what was there left? Nothing. He was defined by a series of negatives: without them he might as well not exist. As night fell, they drove back in silence along the *autostrada* towards Rome; for the entire journey, she sat with her hands on her lap, face turned towards the window. When she turned to say goodbye, her eyes were so puffy from weeping they looked upside down.

For the first few months in Genoa, he was so fine-tuned to his new life as a *clandestino* that he managed to avoid thinking about Julia and the baby. He was almost sure she would have returned to England; occasionally he daydreamed about going to find her once the armed struggle was over. He knew she lived with her mother in London, above a shop overlooking a canal: she said she could sometimes hear seagulls from her bedroom window, on their way to the sea. He would go and visit his child, just as all those years ago his father came to visit him. He would take the child to Carnaby Street and Trafalgar Square, where they would feed the pigeons; and if Julia still wanted him, he might settle in London – get a job somewhere, learn English. In the tiny space in his life left for memory and introspection (the space where he sometimes thought of his mother in her glass cubicle with her mending and her ironing, and wondered what she had said to the neighbours when the *carabinieri* came looking for her '*figlio militare*') he would ask himself how in spite of being a rebel and a revolutionary, he had also managed to remain so true to his own father's ideal of fatherhood . . .

Tape #3: July 2000

Tell me, Caruso, what was Sinistra Armata's definition of a 'moral' kidnapping?

The moral yardstick for our kidnappings, in the beginning at least, derived from what we'd read in the writings of the Tupamaros – elegant, symbolic actions directed against particularly hated figures: the fat cats of politics and industry. More than to punish, the idea was to educate – to force them to listen to the other side of the story for once. Also, we relished the climate of fear and uncertainty the armed struggle was generating: many managing directors began to park their company cars outside the factory for fear we'd set them alight – most, too, became ex-directory.

Which of Sinistra Armata's 'educative' kidnappings were you involved in?

All in all, in my year or so as a *clandestino*, I took part in three kidnappings, each with different aims and results.

Describe them.

The first was in Genoa. The victim, or shall we say target, was Silvio Gadolla, Head of Human Resources (I believe that's the term for it these days) at De Carolis Industries SpA. This was a fairly large, privately owned manufacturer of small parts for industrial engines: production lines, assembly robots – that kind of thing. From our contacts within the factory, we learned that Gadolla was hated by the workers even more than old de Carolis himself.

Why was this?

He was a walking embodiment of the old *padrone* style of management: workers who kept their noses clean were given membership to the local *circolo sportivo* and their children spent every summer at the de Carolis youth camp up in the hills near Finale. The biggest perk of all, though, was that they were entitled to low-(or it could have been even zero-) interest mortgages on houses in a purpose-built de Carolis cooperative just north of Genoa.

How cosy.

Quite. But for the workers who didn't keep their noses clean, things were a little less cosy.

How did you go about planning the kidnapping of Gadolla?

By tailing him night and day. It was a period when in between bank raids there were several *sappisti* knocking around Genoa with time on their hands. We had to cool it for a while with raids in the Liguria area, after a cashier recognized Gaetano one morning and said something along the lines of: 'What – you again? You should have come yesterday when the safe was full!' Our job was to establish how Gadolla spent every moment of his waking life – to walk in his moccasins, as the saying goes. We worked in shifts: I was often on mornings, and for about a week, Gadolla and I had coffee at the same bar near the factory. I used to watch him drinking his *caffelatte al vetro* (which a toadying *barista* always prepared ahead of all the other customers, with a servile '*Ecco dottò*' as he placed the glass on the counter), a Rolex Oyster on his wrist and a gold Mont Blanc pen sticking out of his breast-pocket, as he read the front page of *Secolo XIX*. I wanted to say to him: 'Just imagine, Dottor Gadolla, this time next week it'll be you making the headlines of your paper', but as I couldn't, I got a childish pleasure instead out of making small-talk about the weather or Sampdoria's progress in the Coppa UEFA.

Didn't seeing the 'real' Gadolla, as opposed to the 'symbolic' Gadolla soften your feelings in any way towards him?

Do you want the truth or a lie?

The truth.

In that case, my feelings – assuming I had any in those days – were, if anything, hardened by seeing him in the flesh. Everything about him smacked of self-satisfaction and greed. He took three spoons of sugar in his coffee; and in spite of the '*Ecco dottò*' and the preferential treatment he got from the barman, I never once saw him leave a tip.

Since when have stinginess and a sweet tooth been punishable offences? Besides, they're practically regional characteristics in Genoa. However, to return to Gadolla: how did you manage to keep tabs on him once he was inside his office?

Easy – because, like all jobsworths everywhere, the pen would drop from his fingers on the dot of five-thirty. Then at five thirty-five, he would walk through the factory gates and around the corner to a little tree-lined street where he parked his BMW: he was afraid we'd set it on fire if he left it inside the courtyard, though if he'd had an ounce of common sense, his car would have been the least of his worries. But then you don't expect common sense from middle managers.

The day of the kidnapping, four of us set off in a white Fiat 1100 van: me, Massimo, a member of the Genoa cell called Enzo Berardi, and another *sappista* who now lives in Paris, and whom we'll call Sergio. At about four-thirty, we park the van in the side street and settle down to wait for Gadolla. Only we were stood up! Six o'clock rolls around, and still no sign of him. It was unbelievable – a man as punctual as the proverbial *orologio svizzero*, and he doesn't show up to his own kidnapping! I can joke about it now, but at the time the anti-climax was unbearable. The only sensation comparable to that sour feeling of unspent adrenaline flowing back through your veins was the blue balls you used to get as a teenager after an evening of heavy petting with a girl.

And for which a wank was the only cure – presumably not an option in this case.

It wouldn't have helped. All we could do was turn up the next day at the same time, and pray that Gadolla would show up. We parked the van in the side street and settled down to wait. Enzo was at the wheel, I was next to him, Massimo was in the back, and Sergio was on the pavement pretending to wait for somebody – or rather pretending to be *innocently* waiting for somebody.

Weren't you afraid of drawing attention to yourselves?

Of course we were afraid, and justifiably so. While we were waiting in the van, a woman from the flats opposite had enough time to go out with her net bag, do her shopping, and find us still there on her arrival. Anyone with half a brain in their head would have found our presence odd, to say the least. I know my mother would have: she had an almost supernatural sense of when something was not right. On more than one occasion when I was a boy, she called the police if she saw anyone suspicious hanging around the flats, although once I started hiding crowbars and bottle of Radisol for Molotov cocktails in my drawer, she grew a little more circumspect about bringing the law into her house. This woman, though, looked as though she had no such scruples:

without even bothering to hide it, she began peering out from behind the half-closed shutters of her first-floor flat, staring directly at the van, which was parked right below her window, then up the street as though trying to guess what we were waiting for. Her whole manner was so provocative that it was almost as though she was trying to scare us off her patch by the force of her gaze. And scare us she did: at that point Sergio and Massimo wanted to call it a day, especially Sergio who hadn't yet taken part in anything seriously illegal, and was on the verge of leaving Sinistra Armata anyway. Whilst we were furiously whispering amongst ourselves – still watched over by the busybody at the window – who should saunter around the corner, but Dottor Gadolla himself. There was no need to say a word. Sergio slipped back to his position by the van doors and as soon as Gadolla was level with him, he and Massimo grabbed him by the collar and threw him into the back. They jumped in after him; and even before the door had rattled shut, Enzo was driving at full speed towards the Aurelia National Road.

Where did you take your prisoner?

Enzo carried on for a while along the Aurelia; then at a certain point, he took the turning for Sori and drove to the outskirts of the town, past a small viaduct to a patch of waste ground at the end of a dirt track.

Could you hear any noise coming from the back of the van?

For about the first ten minutes of the journey, all I could hear was the thumping of my own heart – literally. Then, once we were safely out of Genoa, I became aware of an almighty commotion in the back: with the excuse of tying Gadolla up, the other two had taken the opportunity to give him a good hiding. Sergio had an uncle at De Carolis SpA who had recently been made redundant, and I think the hiding was mostly on his behalf.

What state was the prisoner in when you got to your destination?

As soon as we stopped on the wasteland, we put on felt hoods, then Massimo slid open the van door. I wasn't really sure what to expect: to be honest, I thought they'd overdone it a bit with the beating, and I half-expected him to have had a heart attack or something. He was quite porky-looking anyway, and just the type to suffer from angina. They'd trussed him up like a turkey with some kind of silver insulating tape, and he had one of those checked PLO scarves tied around his mouth for a gag. Apart from a split lip, and what looked like the beginnings of a fairly nasty black eye, he didn't look in too bad shape. He was crouching on a pile of old blankets, briefcase on his knees, moaning to himself and trying to reach up to touch his face with one shoulder. Oh, and that's right, I remember now, he'd pissed his pants.

Come on, Caruso, tell me honestly – did you still feel no pity for him?

No I didn't – not then, and not now. I regret most things about the armed struggle, even events that occurred before and after my time as a *clandestino*, but for which I still accept a kind of general responsibility. I refer in particular to the horrific cruelty which marked the end of the Lead Years: the university professors, the newspaper editors, the magistrates who were shot at blank range just because they were part of a hated system – not because of anything they themselves had done. I even feel a degree of responsibility for the Moro kidnapping: I don't think anyone involved in the armed struggle can forget Moro's last letter to his wife, Eleonora, when he knew the end was near: 'What evil will come of all this evil? I embrace you and hold you close to me, my darling Noretta . . .'

And yet you can't bring yourself to feel pity for beating a personnel officer black and blue, just because you disagreed with his firm's internal politics?

No, I can't. Just think about it for a moment – how do you suppose Gadolla got to be head of human resources at De Carolis SpA? Because of his fine eyes, as they say in Rome? Because he had an MBA from Harvard? Because of his skill in interpersonal relations? I don't think so. Gadolla got to where he got because his parents knew a cardinal or a judge or a party member who provided a *raccomandazione* for little Silvio from the first day he stepped out into the world. That meant he showed up to each university exam forearmed with a crib of questions *that he knew he was going to be asked*. And the reason I know all this is because we had a *compagno* who worked in the literature department of the University of Genoa, and who told us how the *raccomandazione* system worked. Then, after Silvio – or should I say Dottor Gadolla, now? – graduates with honours, what does he do to get his place at De Carolis? Win a public *concorso*? Write a brilliant thesis on industrial design? I don't think so. Two months, almost to the day, after his final exam, he gets a position at De Carolis – a position *which has never even been advertised*. And the reason it has never been advertised, is that until that moment it has never existed. It took a bit of gentle tweaking from Gadolla's *raccomandazione* for old de Carolis to realise he needed a new personnel officer.

How long did it take for him to spill the beans about his methods?

A pathetically short time. Enzo started off by telling him we were from Sinistra Armata, and that we wanted him to answer a few questions. In the beginning, I remember he tried to ingratiate himself to us: he said that De Carolis were even trying to set up a plant in the Ukraine – in other words that they understood, and were even sympathetic to, the Communist mentality. It just goes to show you that at the end of the day he honestly didn't have a clue: the workers really were just numbers to him, figures to be squared on a ledger. It was only when we pointed the gun at his temple that his whole demeanour changed. He began to tremble, even though Enzo told him he was in no danger. Then he started telling us about behind-the-scenes strategies at De Carolis: he couldn't stop babbling – he was literally throwing company secrets at us as though his life depended on it. Which he genuinely believed it did: he couldn't see that for us, the gun was a purely symbolic gesture.

What's that supposed to mean?

We were trying to maintain a subtle and, if you like, paradoxical equilibrium: terrorism which avoided the use of those very weapons which defined us as terrorists.

I can see how Gadolla failed to be reassured by your logic. What happened after you pointed the gun at his head?

We hung a placard around his neck, and Sergio took a polaroid photograph of him.

Why the placard? And what did it say?

The placard was probably an unconscious throwback to pictures we'd seen of Fascists taken prisoner by the Partisans at the end of the Second World War. Remember, several of us, especially those who took part in the first wave of terrorism, considered ourselves to be direct descendants of the Partisan movement. Some of the old Partisans thought so too; many begged to join the armed struggle, and failing that, donated Sten machine-guns and rusty hand-grenades which had been lovingly stored in barns and caves up and down the country. There were even Brownings and Lugers removed from Nazi corpses doing the rounds in those days. But to return to the placard: on it we had written a slogan lifted straight from Mao: 'Hit and run. Nothing shall remain unpunished. Strike at one, to educate one hundred.' According to Mao, this was the essence of guerilla warfare: we liked the sound of it, because it made us feel like real soldiers in a real war. We also liked the fear it generated: we wanted managers everywhere to think they had to watch their backs.

What did you do once you'd taken the picture?

We took off the insulating tape (which probably hurt more than the beating), removed the gag and gave him a bottle of Coca-Cola to boost his blood-sugar levels. We tried to clean him up as best as we could – though we couldn't do anything about the soiled trousers – then we left him on the outskirts of Genoa with enough change for the bus in his pocket.

What did you do with the van?

The van was too valuable for us to abandon. We replaced the plates with a set of spares we carried around in the glove compartment, then set about cleaning the inside to remove any traces of fingerprints. Oh – and while we were cleaning, we found Gadolla's gold Rolex behind the front seat – he must have dropped it during the fracas.

What did you do with it?

We took great pride in putting it in the same envelope as the photo and the *comunicato* which we sent to the news agency ANSA. As a proletarian organisation, we were utterly against individual theft, and we wanted to make that clear by returning the watch. Interestingly, when the picture of Gadolla with the gun at his temple made the front pages of both the national and local press, not one paper chose to mention our rather ostentatious honesty. Still, on the whole we were pleased with the outcome of the kidnapping, and our *compagni* inside the factory sent signals of approval.

Tell me about the second kidnapping you were involved in during your year as a clandestino.

This also took place in Liguria. The target was Lanfranco Rivella, heir to Genoa's Rivella ship-building dynasty. Without meaning to offend the Rivella family, who I'm sure don't have particularly fond memories of those days, I have to say that as far as we were concerned, it was Sinistra Armata's most successful kidnapping.

In which sense?

In every sense. For a start, it yielded us almost a billion lire – enough to keep the organisation in funds for well over a year. Plus it looked like being a fairly straightforward job, not to mention providing us with the kind of high-profile media coverage our organisation needed.

I thought you were against individual theft.

We were – in an ideal world. On the other hand, the organisation was growing, and we desperately needed cash.

Besides, Latin American guerilla groups had been kidnapping rich industrialists for years: like us, they'd come to the regrettable conclusion that we weren't living in an ideal world and that if you didn't go out and get the money yourselves, the *padroni* were hardly going to donate it to you.

What made you pick on the Rivella family? Was there any kind of political motivation behind your choice?

The Rivellas are Genoa's first family – I mean that literally. The only comparison I can think of is the Agnelli family in Turin, but somehow what with Genoa being a smaller city, their influence and power seem more far-reaching. The Rivellas are everywhere: aside from the ships, they own Olio Petrarca olive oil, the Hotel Majestic in Rapallo, a private fleet of helicopters, a holiday village, an old people's home – not to mention keeping an unknown number of politicians and clergymen on their payroll. It also turned out that the older Rivella, Guido, apart from being head of Confindustria in the bad old days, had also financed local Fascist organisations after the war. But really that was just icing on the cake: the main reason we chose him was that the Rivellas were rich – so rich, that they had actually taken out an insurance policy with Lloyd's of London against the threat of kidnapping.

What part did you play in the kidnapping?

I had a fairly behind-the-scenes role: partly because I hadn't been a *clandestino* for that long, but also because the executive had another job lined up for me.

What job was that?

I'll come to it later. In the meantime, as with the Gadolla kidnapping, I took my turn in shadowing Lanfranco Rivella, working out his movements to and from the shipyard.

Where did he live?

With the rest of the Rivella clan, in a picture-postcard castle – more like a fiefdom, really – on a hilltop overlooking Genoa: he had a small *dépendance* within the grounds. My other main task was to purchase a house where the prisoner was going to be held. Anywhere inside the city was too risky – likewise a village where nothing is allowed to remain a secret for long. In the end, we settled on the perfect compromise: a development of about two hundred or so family houses on the outskirts of a small town called Chiavari, about seventy miles outside Genoa. What made it an ideal location was that the complex had only just been completed: quite a few of the houses were still unsold, and of the ones that were inhabited, it was fairly unlikely that the occupants had got to know each other well enough to gossip about any new arrivals. To get to it, you turned off the main road into a private road which led to the estate. The house itself was a two-storey villa with its own garage: I paid for it in cash – thirty-two million lire.

What story did you give the owner?

I told him I was – wait for it – a marine biologist working for the Ministry for the Environment. I used another set of cloned documents in a different name which belonged to a *sappista* whose brother had died: somehow his name had got lost in the system, and he was still on the electoral roll. The owner should have been far more vigilant about checking my ID; since the Moro kidnapping, all house sales or rental agreements had to be registered, by law, with the police, but the sight of thirty-two million lire in cash went a long way towards eroding his sense of civic duty.

What did you do after the house was yours?

We set about decorating it, taking advantage of the general confusion to construct Rivella's 'prison'. I was part of the interior design team: our brief was to have the ground floor looking respectable enough to pass muster if a neighbour, or even the postman, dropped by. I remember we bought the furniture in one of those new American-style warehouses which were just beginning to spring up outside city centres, although I imagine they're fairly commonplace now. If I'm not mistaken, we chose two chrome sofas covered in brown corduroy, a dining table and chairs, a large bookcase, a bamboo coffee table and several lamps. Oh yes, and the final touch: a pair of floor-length linen curtains which filled the room with light, but were completely opaque from the outside. I remember we ordered them from a *tappezziere* in Genoa: they cost a small fortune for those days.

What about the cell?

The construction of the cell was left to the most handy *sappisti*, including Piero, mentor of my Rome car-thieving days. In the beginning, the idea was to soundproof the smaller upstairs bedroom, which also had the advantage of looking out towards open countryside, but in the end, we decided against it. Apart from the obvious problem of the window, there was just too much room for the prisoner to move around in. Finally, Piero came up with the idea of erecting a wooden cube inside the bedroom. If I remember rightly, it measured three metres by four, with two and a half metres headroom. They cut sheets of MDF with a De Walt chainsaw, glued them together, then covered the outside of the box with polystyrene ceiling tiles. Then they carpeted the floor, and Piero installed a spotlight with a dimmer switch – a new gizmo which had only just come on the market, and which, knowing Piero, he had been waiting for an excuse to try out.

What did you do for ventilation?

We drilled two holes into the ceiling of the box. In one hole, we inserted an air-conditioning tube which could be attached to a grille in the window, and in the other a fan extractor, the kind used in restaurants, which was connected to the other window. If you switched on the fan, not only could you keep the cell fairly well ventilated, you also created a din which completely blocked out any outside noises.

How did you furnish the cell?

We put a small mattress on the floor, a table, a stool, and in the corner, a chemical toilet, the kind used in caravans.

How did the prisoner take to his new surroundings?

I don't know first hand, as my direct involvement with the Rivella kidnapping ended with the decoration of the house. From what I've heard, he was fairly stoical about the whole business.

How was he taken?

Three individual groups were assigned to the task: the first group was responsible for capturing him, the second for transporting him to the cell, and the third for guarding him there. They got him at eight o'clock in the evening on his way back home. Three *compagni* dressed in overalls from the telephone company, SIP, blocked his car on a bend, hand-cuffed and blindfolded him, then threw him inside a hessian sack. This was harder than it sounds, as although he offered no resistance, he was almost two metres tall and probably weighed nigh on a hundred kilos. They drove his Alfa Romeo to a spot about three hundred yards ahead, where the second group was waiting in a Citroën Ami with the engine running. When they got to the prison, they pulled him out of the sack, and apparently, the first thing he said was, 'Couldn't you have chosen a smaller member of my family?'

Wasn't he frightened?

He must have been, but apparently he never lost his cool. Years later, I read an interview with him in *L'Espresso*, in which he even had a stab at guessing where he had been held. Incredibly, he'd followed each twist and turn of the road as he lay trussed up and gagged in the back of the Ami; then once he was in the cell, he used the sound of the distant trains, together with the fact that the house lay directly beneath a flight path, to gauge its location.

How close was he? And anyway, wasn't the cell meant to be soundproof?

He was pretty close – put it this way, no more than ten kilometres out. To answer your second question, then yes, the cell was meant to be soundproof, but in the end turned out not to be. The polystyrene tiles were too flimsy to insulate properly, while the fan extractor made such a racket, that a neighbour complained, and they could only use it while he was out at work.

What happened once you explained your objectives to the prisoner?

The head of the nucleus told him who they were, and that he would have to pay a tax to finance the revolution. I think they hit him with a ridiculous figure – somewhere in the region of eight billion lire – at which he said forget it, that the family would never cough up. In the end they settled on one and a half billion, although the family managed to whittle it down to just under one. They were an incredibly canny bunch: apparently, when they picked Lanfranco up, he had newspaper lining his shoes, even though it was mid-winter and pouring with rain. That's the *borghesia genovese* for you! Oh, and when his release had already been negotiated, and they handed him back his personal effects prior to his departure, he looked carefully through his wallet and said: 'I'm sorry, but I think one of my luncheon vouchers is missing.'

What were the terms of his release?

The money had to be in old fifty-thousand lire bills with random serial numbers: new notes were too easy to keep track of.

And did everything go smoothly?

Yes and no. The money was delivered safely and taken back to one of Sinistra Armata's safe-houses. It was only when they opened one of the briefcases that the *compagni* realised they'd been framed: the stacks of bills were literally submerged in a fine white powder which clung to your clothes and hair like talc. The powder was virtually invisible to the naked eye, but under an ultraviolet light, anyone who'd come into contact with it glowed like a Christmas tree.

What was it?

In the beginning, some of the more paranoid *compagni* thought the powder was radioactive, and that anyone who touched it would die a lingering death. Then a Sinistra Armata sympathiser with a background in chemistry took a sample off to a lab to be analysed, and informed us that there was a substance to neutralise the powder, but that the simplest solution was just to wash the money. And that's what we did; like in a Laurel and Hardy film, we washed the notes in warm water and *sapone di Marsiglia*, pegged them up to dry in a kind of giant cat's cradle we rigged up over the sink, and finally ironed them one by one between sheets of newspaper. It took us years to recycle that money: because the bills still didn't look perfect, the only way to get rid of them without causing suspicion was to take two or three of them at a time to a bank, and ask the cashier to change them into smaller denominations.

Who do you think put the powder there?

It had to be the Rivella family: either off their own bat, to render the money unusable; or – more likely – on the advice of the police. They probably did it as a provocation, hoping to exasperate us into making some some kind of rash gesture that would get them on our trail. Whatever their motivation, it didn't work: we delayed Rivella's release until we were sure that the money could be used. Then, with the hostage's full cooperation, we disguised him in a hat and moustache, and – as I'm sure you recall – left him on a park bench near Genoa's Stazione Prinicipe.

Out of interest, who delivered the ransom?

Two of Rivella's sisters, one of whom was a lay nun.

And who collected it?

We made them follow a series of precise instructions – two *compagni* on a Vespa tailing them each step of the way, to ensure no one else was tagging along. After a day-long mystery tour of Rome's suburbs, they finally left the two briefcases in a one-way street off the Via Prenestina, near the giant Birra Peroni billboard.

You haven't answered my question. Who collected the ransom?

They needed someone who knew the back streets of the city well enough to stand a chance of getting away if the family or the police sprang a trap; he and Piero were on the Vespa which escorted the car containing the money back to a base in Trastevere. Behind the visor of his helmet, Ennio watched the two briefcases being handed over in the dead-end street behind the Birra Peroni billboard on the Via Prenestina. One of the sisters, the lay nun, looked like Lanfranco, with the same massive build and heavy eyebrows, while the other sister, the one who actually got out of the car, was short and elderly, with white hair swept into a bun. He aimed the Mauser at the back of her neck, at the point where the bun was held up with a tortoiseshell comb. Her hands were shaking as she dropped the cases on to the ground; as they drove off on the Vespa, Ennio turned around to look at them: the older one was leaning against the wall, vomiting into the gutter, while the tall sister crouched beind her, cradling her head in her arms.

He arrived at the gardens towards late afternoon, listening to the choppy rumble of a helicopter circling the city as he climbed the steps leading up to the Colle Oppio from the station. He wasn't due back in Genoa until the following afternoon; for a few hours, a vacuum had opened up in his highly strung *sappista* world, and for now he was content to float along inside it. He stretched his legs, looking at his feet in their Clark's desert boots; he'd been wearing those same boots the last time he saw Julia – he remembered taking them off and leaving them on the porch of La Camillina before entering the house. He wondered what his mother would say if she knew that at that moment, her son was sitting on a bench in a pair of dusty jeans and a sweat-stained shirt; and that, worse still, he was contemplating getting up and pissing behind a tree like an old *barbone*. As the urine thudded on to the ground, Ennio remembered how not so long ago he had stood in the kitchen doorway with a hosepipe in his hand, watching the water throbbing upwards on to the dry earth around the fruit trees. (He didn't dare ask himself what his mother would say if she knew that a few hours earlier he had pointed his gun at a tortoiseshell comb on the back of an old woman's neck; or that he had accompanied a car containing almost a billion lire to a base in Trastevere; or that he was now spying on the flat of an English girl whom he loved, and who was pregnant with a grandchild she would never see . . .

Around seven the courtyard door opened, and Julia's flat-mate, Walter, wheeled his moped out on to the pavement. He was an Austro-Italian from Alto Adige, a tiny homosexual with black teeth and narrow hips, who made a living sublet-ting rooms to foreigners. His name was on the buzzer, top bell on the left: . . . Estler . . . Essler – no Ensslin, that was it . . . Julia said he was a hygiene fanatic, who left instructions in three languages on how to clean the bathroom pinned on the wall. In the evenings he worked for a telemarketing company in Corso Vittorio; once or twice Ennio crossed paths with him in the kitchen as he made coffee for Julia before he left. The courtyard door swung shut, and zipping up his suede bomber-jacket, Walter kick-started the moped and drove down the hill towards Via Labicana. It seemed difficult to remember a time when his and Walter's lives could have entwined: if he looked back over the last few months as a *clandestino*, what struck him most was how monochrome his existence had become, as though bled of all colour or contrast.

He could see Julia moving behind the shutters of the first-floor flat: her desk was under the window, with a view directly on to the Colosseum and the Roman Forum. He remembered when they first met at Rizzoli's, the bookshop on Via Toma-celli, Ennio had asked her where she lived. Julia paused for a moment, as though uncertain whether or not to tell him, and then she smiled slyly: 'If you stand under the sign of the *metropolitana* on Via dei Fori Imperiali and look up, my house is the red-painted building on the corner between the two s's in the word "Colosseo" – you can't miss it.' Ennio had never met an English girl before: until then, the only foreign girls he'd ever had anything to do with were the German *compagne* from the Rote Armee Fraktion who came on a fact-finding mission to Rome – highly politicised women who looked down on the female element of the Italian armed struggle for their subser-vience to men. They were mostly good-looking, with excellent figures, yet with their hairy legs and unironed clothes they seemed contemptuous of their beauty, in a way that no Italian girl could ever bring herself to be.

From the start, Ennio was fascinated by Julia's life; by everything that made it different from his. Before he became a *clandestino*, he would bring her again and again to the regular appointment at Piazza della Chiesa Nuova, where the *compagni* would meet up on the steps of Santa Maria in Vallicella to decide on the evening's film. With Julia at his side he felt like any Italian male who had hit lucky with a tourist girl – he couldn't help it. He was staggered on discovering this trait in himself; which, in spite of his carefully cultivated left-wing internationalism, appeared to have survived intact, like some kind of genetic throwback to his *meridionale* origins. He would ask Julia endless questions about the English diet and climate, and even make half-hearted attempts to pretend in front of the *compagni* that they always conversed in English.

And yet mingled with this was a feeling of irritation: there was something gauche, bookish about her; her shoulders stooped slightly, and beneath her embroidered Indian *kurtas*, she wore sagging grey bras and pants. She said it wasn't her fault if the colours ran, that Walter only allowed them to use the washing machine once a week. His irritation with Julia's housekeeping made him feel provincial, small-minded – like an ordinary Italian *mammone*.

She haunted him in unexpected ways: she never asked for anything, never demanded lover's behaviour from him, yet she gave herself to him as though each time were the first. For five afternoons in a row, they would lie together on her single bed on her return from the university, then for the next five weeks he'd vanish. Each time he waited for her after one of these absences at the English faculty, or at the gardens in the Colle Oppio where he now sat, he would say to himself: This will be the time she turns away from me, says: enough, now, go. But she never did; her face would flush with pleasure, and she would wind a strand of her dark hair behind her ears to hide the expression in her eyes. He'd justify her tolerance by calling it English reserve; it made him feel better about his neglect, made her seem less of a victim. What brought him back, time and time again, was the tenderness of her smile, the memory of her thin white arm, veined with blue, thrown behind her head as she lay on the grass beneath the plane trees in Villa Borghese, the erotic steadiness of her desire, which, obeying only itself, knew no guile, and which could be brought to life by the mere touch of his hand. She was a pool of clear water in a wasteland: she showed him glimpses of who he might have been in another life . . .

He was still in time to leave – no one said he had to disturb that pool once again. If he shut his eyes, he could actually see himself doing the right thing: crossing the cobblestones of San Pietro in Vincoli, running down the steps of the Salita dei Borgia towards Via Cavour, past Santa Maria Maggiore and on to

Piazza del Cinquecento and the station. There, he would board the train for Genoa, and in the morning, he would awake to find himself back inside his orderly *sappista* life. As though to enact the sequence he had played out in his head, make it real, if you like, Ennio got up from the bench and began walking across the grass towards the railings. In his mind's eye, he had become that tiny figure, crossing the park in a diagonal until he reached the gates. The police helicopter was back in the sky; he could hear the blades of the propeller clattering in the dark clouds above the Colosseum. They were looking for something – or somebody. He wondered what the pilot could see from up there in the sky, whether there was anything in his appearance that gave him away as a terrorist. He had a sudden vision of the helicopter swooping down between the columns of the Roman Forum, coming to land on the grassy banks of Circo Massimo, and disgorging a squad of armed policemen, all looking for him . . . Opening the park gate, Ennio walked out on to the street; a few steps later, he found himself outside Julia's flat. '*You can't miss it; mine is the red-painted building on the corner . . .*' He paused for a moment, looking at the row of illuminated names on the intercom panel, which was set into the wall: Fortini, Levati, Pisetta, De Mori, Casaletti, Vesce, Palmieri, Ensslin. Ensslin. Ensslin . . .

He pressed the buzzer and waited.

Swiftly, the train rocked through the night, past unlit stations which were gone in a blur before he had time to make out their names. The corridor was deserted; through the half-open window, a flurry of cool air blew about his forehead and cheeks as he rested his elbows on the metal sash. From the opposite direction he saw the lights of an oncoming train emerging from a tunnel; as it approached, both engines appeared to pick up speed, hurtling towards one another until they were side by side and he could make out the dim blue lights of the sleeping carriages. For a moment, the trains appeared to be heading nowhere, swaying unsteadily on their tracks as though the drivers had called a truce, but it was only an illusion: in a second, they had gone their separate ways with a final gust of wind which left the roof of his mouth dry.

Inside the carriage, the passengers lay abandoned in sleep; one woman was wrapped up in her jacket, while the man beside her had rolled up a pullover to make a cushion for his head. A young soldier lay sprawled on the seat with his arms crossed over his stomach, his Army boots resting on a khaki rucksack at his feet. Only the woman by the far window was awake; she was dressed all in black, with dark knee-high stockings showing beneath her skirt, and a crocheted shawl pulled tight over her shoulders. She was probably only in her early fifties, but everything about her clothes and her posture seemed older. Only her face, in profile, was young-looking, with smooth cheeks illuminated in the blue night light. He could just make out her earrings; heavy-looking gold sleepers which dragged down the lobes. She was staring out of the window as though trying to recognise a familiar landmark; a widow, maybe, returning to her village in Tuscany for Easter. Something about her appearance reminded him of his mother: that sense of the outer person, the clothes, revealing a history in code – a part, but not all, of a life. He couldn't take his eyes off her; hungrily, he watched her reflection in the glass, the ghostly features superimposed on a moving background of hills, and sudden pinpricks of light as the countryside sped by. He thought to himself: because of me, my mother will never again be able to do that, go on a journey, find the tranquillity to sit by the window in a carriage full of sleeping strangers, and let her thoughts roam . . .

Ennio shook his head, shuddering slightly, as though to break a spell. He was so tired, he could barely stand up. He had to hold on tightly to the window sash to stop himself sliding the door open and crawling along the dirty carriage floor until he reached the woman's feet. There he would lay his head on her lap and lulled by the rocking of the train, he would sleep as she stroked his hair and gazed out of the window with her enigmatic eyes.

The train began to slow down; the lights along the track grew more frequent, and he could begin to see apartment blocks, shops, cars as they approached Florence. Hearing a movement behind him, Ennio turned round and looked inside the compartment; the woman had got up and was pulling her suitcase down from the net rack. Gently, without disturbing the sleeping passengers, he slid the carriage door open to let her out. In the corridor, he stood back to let her pass; he wanted her to notice him – find something in him to like. She smiled at him, but distantly: her eyes were scanning the platform as they drew into the station. Looking out of the window, Ennio saw a young man walking alongside the train; he was peering into the compartments, until he caught sight of the woman and waved. Her son, thought Ennio, come to fetch his mother from the station. As the train stopped, the man opened the carriage door and took the suitcase from her hand. Holding out his arm, he helped his mother off the train, and they embraced. A good son, with neatly parted hair and pressed trousers, who got up in the middle of the night to meet his mother's train; Ennio could hardly bear to look at him, such were his feelings of jealousy and hopelessness at the sight of the man's hand hovering protectively beneath the woman's elbow as they made their way down the platform towards the underpass. He thought of aiming the Mauser at the lemon-coloured sweater slung carelessly over his shoulders, imagined the shot cracking beneath the glass ceiling of the station, and that bourgeois *fascistello* slumping face-down on to the marble floor. His presence was a reproach to Ennio, as though the only reason he'd got out of bed that night was to showcase his life: *Look at me*, he seemed to be saying, *look how some people choose to live* . . . But it was worse than that – crueller, more personal. For the son hadn't come alone:

beside the barrier, a little to one side, as though they were saving the best bit for last, there stood a woman, a young girl, with a bundle in her arms: something precious wrapped up tightly in a shawl, which she was holding out towards them . . .

His wife, thought Ennio, with their child.

He was unbearably moved by the fact that she'd stayed.

Not until the courtyard door swung open did he realise how little he'd expected her to be still there. The voice on the intercom sounded faint – subtly different to the voice he remembered, as though Julia had gone away and left an impostor in her place. As he walked up the twisting marble staircase, he thought to himself: you imagine that because you know it's all you deserve, to find her gone . . .

On the second floor the landing light switched off, and he paused for a moment, his hand resting on the chrome bannister, while he waited for his eyes to grow accustomed to the gloom. Through the arched window which looked out on to the courtyard an evening sun glittered opaquely, as though the glass were a backlit screen in a cinema. He heard thunder, and for a moment he felt disoriented: I could be anywhere, he thought, I could be anyone . . . Then his elbow brushed the Mauser, and his heart shuddered with revulsion. A picture flashed into his mind of Lanfranco Rivella lying trussed up in the boot of the Ami, sucking in pitiful gulps of air through the hessian sack . . .

She was waiting for him on the landing. As he turned the last curve of the staircase, the hall light clicked back on, and he saw her standing in the doorway of the flat. She looked thinner, and her hair hung in lank swathes around her neck. She stared at him unsmilingly, with half-open lips that were dry and cracked in the corners. Her face, her skin, were imperceptibly coarsened, as though everything about her manner that was familiar to him, her shy librarian's smile, that bookish English way she had about her, had unravelled down to the essential self: she looked like an animal – how a rape victim must look, thought Ennio; then: *this isn't what she came to Italy for . . .*

'Hello, Ennio,' she said.

He tried to smile. 'You see, I came back.'

She didn't answer. His heart beat furiously, and self-pity stung his eyes: *Look at me, too*, he felt like saying, *look what's happened to me*.

Until then, it had all been so light, so delicate – at least, that was the way he chose to remember it. In Genoa, he would sit at the kitchen table in the flat in Via Prè, and recall their days in Rome like a series of sunlit photographs: her hand brushing against his as they sat in the gardens in Villa Giulia; the light shining through the skirt of her dress as she waited for him on the wall outside her flat, the scholarly precision of her Italian, and the shy way she used *romanaccio* slang words to make him laugh . . . He was different, too: then, he was still somebody's son – he had a house, a name, a life . . . alongside the car thefts and the hours spent learning to shoot beneath the ring-road, there still beat in him the impulse to look for her, to wake up in the morning and think: today I'll wait for her outside the university – something which unconsciously responded to Julia as a lover, from the first time he'd seen her at Rizzoli's.

In the flat in Rome, his mother had a pair of Austrian kissing dolls; two moulded plastic figures in peaked caps and matching red and blue outfits. The moment you placed them opposite each other, they would lurch forwards, puckered lips meeting in a kiss. When he was a boy, the dumb helplessness of that embrace infuriated him: he tried taping over the dolls' mouths to disable the magnets, even painting over the tape with his mother's nail-varnish, but the attraction between the two figures was too strong to overcome . . . He'd never had a girlfriend before Julia, not even a schoolgirl *fidanzatina*. Actually, he'd always despised those teenage betrothals, stifling and formal as any marriage: the sulks, the misunderstandings, the useless geegaws and stuffed toys you had to buy to put those misunderstandings right. Watching her coming down the steps of the English faculty, he would say to himself: *I am not her lover – there is nothing about me to make her or anyone else think otherwise*, deliberately assuming the most slouching, unexpectant pose he could muster, shoulders hunched, hands stuffed deep inside his pockets, as though being a non-lover were a recognizable attitude. And yet he couldn't help it: the moment he saw her, something in him surrendered, lightened up, and he ceased to be the brooding misfit Ennio he'd got used to dragging around with him like a ball and chain. Somehow, against all odds, he had found his mate, his complement: he had about as much choice in the matter as one of those Austrian kissing dolls . . . Walking down the street with her, his gaze would be drawn to the double shadow cast on the pavement by their two bodies, all extremities connected like the row of identical linked figures his uncle would cut out of a piece of folded newspaper. Every trivial thing they did together – buying buttons in the *merceria* in Via dei Serpenti, waiting in line at the *questura* to renew her permit, filling up her tin water-canteen at a fountain – was marked by this sense of connectedness. He would buy her a coffee in the bar opposite the university, annoyed that she drank *cappuccino* in the afternoons like all the other tourists, yet he would look at their two cups standing side by side on the counter, and in spite of himself his heart would quicken. But that connection was gone now, and bereft, they stared at each other – wizened old strangers.

'You'd better come in.'

She shut the door, and Ennio followed her into the flat, through the hallway with its fading dark blue silk wallpaper, lit by a single pair of tiny wall lamps with fringed orange shades, mounted on either side of a gilt mirror. A bronze urn filled with plastic flowers stood on a pedestal by Walter's room; through the half-open door Ennio caught a glimpse of an unmade bed, a low velvet armchair with curved legs standing beneath the window. He felt as though he were in a dream landscape, familiar yet at the same time unreal, as though he were Sandokan in the British ambassador's residence in Malaysia. As they reached Julia's door, he felt unconsciously with his foot for the loose tile on the threshold to remind himself that he knew that house – that he'd been there before, in another life . . .

Inside her room, the shutters were closed and the air felt stale, used. She sat on the bed with her legs tucked beneath her, her back resting against the wall. A poster hung above her head which he hadn't seen before: Borromini's drawings at the Palazzo degli Esposizioni in Via Nazionale. She was wearing some kind of peasant skirt embedded with tiny mirrors; the tassles at the bottom had come loose, dangling down in a strip from the hem. He couldn't see her belly: her hands were crossed protectively on her lap. He heard the faint sound of a radio from another room and he recognised the song: it was 'Life on Mars' by David Bowie.

Ennio sat down on the chair beneath the desk. 'So why did you stay?'

'What do you mean, why did I stay? What kind of a question is that?'

Again Ennio had the peculiar sensation of time telescoping forwards, as though in the months he'd been away, they'd jumped through sixty stages of intimacy till they got to the very bones of their relationship. Never once had he heard Julia express herself with such vehemence. She'd always seemed so passive, so innured to loss; she said her father died when she was nine, and that she didn't believe in the permanence of relationships. But that didn't stop her loving him. (Nor did it stop him from riding for free in the slipstream of that love . . .) Treacherously, he thought: if only she'd shown some of that fury before, I might never have left.

'You could have gone back to London; you have your mother there, your home.'

'You mean I have nobody here? Is that what you're trying to say?'

'No, that's not what I'm trying to say. What I mean is that your year in Rome is almost up, and that nothing is preventing you going home early.'

'So that you won't be tempted to drop by again? So that you can get on with being a criminal?'

Ennio was silent. He shouldn't have come; his being there wouldn't change or solve anything. Whatever came to pass between them in that room, he would still leave for Genoa: he knew that from the start. Ever since he could remember, he'd always had a thing about following events through to their conclusion, whatever the consequences – or maybe even because of the consequences. When he was a boy, he used to fill the bathroom sink with water; then he would take his mother's leather-covered travel clock from her bedside table and set the alarm for two minutes. As soon as the second-hand reached the twelve o'clock position, he would dunk his head into the water and begin counting. At first the sensation was a delicious one; similar to that breath of cool air in his face when he opened the refrigerator door on a summer's day. He liked the unusual feeling, too, of cold water on his eyeballs and his hairline and deep inside his ears. But soon, a slow prickle of panic would set in: his heartbeat would begin to accelerate, his hands would tingle and his head would fill with blood as though it were about to explode. His bowels would turn to water, and he would clench the taps with both hands to stop himself soiling his trousers. Sometimes, it was a near thing: this time, his mother was going to get back from the shops and find her son drowned in the bathroom sink . . . And yet he couldn't do it: he physically couldn't emerge from the water until he heard the muffled trill of the alarm, and the two minutes were up. He would rather have drowned –

'Why did you come here, now, Ennio? To see if I'd turn you away this time? Or to tell me to get rid of the baby?'

'I don't know myself why I came . . . but it wasn't to tell you to get rid of it.' Outside, he heard sirens from the direction of Via dei Fori Imperiali, while in the background the helicopter continued to circle above the Colosseum.

The corners of her mouth trembled and she gave a kind of inward snort that sounded like a sob. Then her eyes filled with tears, and the last of her hard-girl persona dissolved before his eyes.

'Ennio, I know what you've been up to, I'm not stupid. Or rather, I can guess: I saw that room at the house with the banding machine and all those building materials. I also happen to teach at the university, and you'd be surprised what my conversation students tell me. But I don't care – I don't care about any of it.' Uncrossing her hands from her lap, she smoothed her T-shirt over her belly. For the first time he saw the bump, that mysterious swelling, and in spite of himself, he felt a pang of excitement – hope, even. 'This is what matters now . . . don't you see?'

'How many months is it?'

'Seven, maybe seven and a half.'

He had no right to ask, but he did, anyway. 'Have you seen a doctor?'

For a moment a shadow crossed her face and the corners of her mouth twitched downwards again, only this time it was with a resolve which for a moment made her look almost cruel. He regretted his question: what right did he have now to enquire about her wellbeing, or the wellbeing of a child he had abandoned virtually since conception?

'No, I haven't seen a doctor; I'm a foreigner – remember? It's not so easy for an English girl just to turn up at her local USL and demand to see a GP.'

'So how do you know the baby's all right . . . or even that you really are pregnant, for that matter?'

'Ennio, I am capable of going to a chemist's and buying a pregnancy test – *fin lì, ciarrivo pure io, sai.*'

In spite of himself, Ennio's heart leapt: he loved it when she spoke slang. For a moment their eyes met and they smiled at each other shyly: they were on familiar territory now. Emboldened, he went on: 'How can you be so sure how many months it is, if you haven't been to a doctor?' His mother had told him she carried on menstruating well into her pregnancy.

'Because I went to the British Council library and got out some books. They tell you step by step which stage the baby should be at, and you work it out yourself.'

'What about you . . . are you all right?' They heard the suppressed growl of thunder – one clap, then another, then the sound of raindrops drumming like pebbles on the car rooftops below. Through the half-closed shutters he felt a breath of moist air on his neck, and smelled the dusty smell of rain on city streets, imagining the first ragged spots of water on the dry pavements. Her room felt like a spaceship: a tiny lamplit haven cut loose from the sirens and the storm, the dangerous world throbbing outside her window . . .

'Why ask, Ennio, when already you know the answer? Anyway, so long as the baby's all right, that's all that matters now.' Resting her hand on her belly, she gave a start, then her eyes grew distant, inward-looking, and her lips parted slightly.

'Is it moving?' he whispered.

'Feel for yourself.'

Ennio got up from the window and walked over towards the bed. He sat down beside her, and without looking at him, Julia picked up his wrist and placed his hand, palm downwards, on her skirt. Her belly felt hard, distended, as though it had been pumped up full of air. Then she lifted up her T-shirt, and he saw the skin had a faint pattern on it, a paisley network of tiny capilliaries and veins. Pulling down the elastic of her skirt, she showed him her belly button: it had literally popped out of its socket, while running down below it to the crotch was a dark red line, raised like a keloid scar.

'What's that?' asked Ennio, fascinated.

Without replying, she took his forefinger and ran it down the line: to his surprise it wasn't a scar at all, but felt more like a groove, wide enough for the tip of his finger to fit into.

'So what is it?'

'It's my abdominal muscles – see, they've separated from the strain of carrying the baby. I shouldn't have bunked off so many PE lessons.'

Just as he was getting used to this improbable idea, without warning her stomach heaved to one side like a sackful of kittens, and a small knob sprouted beneath the palm of his hand. Now, what was that . . . ?

'It's the baby's foot', said Julia, grinning. 'Now if you're fast enough, you can even grab the heel between your thumb and forefinger.'

Pregnancy had turned her into a magician – that stomach of hers was a box of tricks. No wonder they called it *'lo stato interessante'*. Neurotically, he racked his brains for more puns: *'gravidanza'* . . . from *'grave'*, as in: *'Figlio mio, questa volta l'hai fatta grave'* . . .

Julia slipped her hand into his; he held it to his heart, shutting his eyes for a moment to try to block out the competing anxieties threatening to engulf him – the baby, Rivella, his mother's voice: '. . . *questa volta l'hai fatta grave* . . .' If he concentrated hard enough, the touch of her skin was sufficient to transport him, at least for now, back to a place and time where he could forget everything . . . Then she kissed him: her mouth tasted of iron filings, as though her gums or her lips were bleeding. Even her hair smelt different: when he ran his fingers through it, her scalp felt oily. He buried his face in her neck; then reaching inside his shirt, he pulled out the Mauser and without looking, stretched out his arm and placed it on top of a book on the bedside table behind him.

'What's that?'

'Don't look. It's my gun – but it's not loaded,' he lied. The disgusting thing, the really disgusting thing, he thought later, wasn't the lie: at the end of the day, what did it matter if it were loaded or not? No, the point was that it took the touch of his gun, and not Julia's lips, to revive his senses. Or rather a combination of the two: for all his self-pity and fatalism, at the end of the day he was just a *coglione* – an impotent *coglione* who got off on the drama of those gestures: the urban guerrilla who lays down his arms before kissing the girl . . .

Amazingly, Julia didn't look, at least not then. She didn't get the chance to: within seconds, Ennio had pulled her T-shirt over her head and taken her into his arms.

'What happened to your grey bra?' he said, running his hands over her ribs. In spite of the protruding belly, she was thinner than he remembered.

'It doesn't fit any more: my breasts have grown.'

It was true: they were engorged, warm and hard as sunlit marble. Her nipples were two bronze discs: no, darker than bronze, two circles of oxblood leather, with thick protruding teats.

'*La mia lupa romana*,' he whispered, taking one of the teats between his lips while he squeezed the other between his fingers. To his surprise, the tip was wet.

'Don't tell me it's milk . . .'

'Not milk. Colostrum. Taste it.'

Ennio licked his fingertip: it tasted sweet, like the *acqua e zucchero* he drank as a boy in Sicily. Before he had the chance to ask what colostrum was, he felt the baby hammer against his chest, and Julia's belly lurched to one side away from him.

'Maybe he thinks I'm stealing his supper.'

'It's not that.'

'What is it then?'

For a moment Julia looked sly, with exactly the same expression in her eyes as that afternoon in Rizzoli's when he asked her where she lived. He could see the blushes literally staining the pallor of her cheeks right up to her ears. 'The baby kicks when its mother's turned on,' she said, looking away from him.

In the weeks, months and years that followed, as Ennio ran through the events of that afternoon – mostly at night-time in his cell, when it was raining, and for a moment he thought he could recall the smell of the raindrops on the dusty pavement outside her room – he regretted never asking Julia on which other occasions the baby had been forced to register its displeasure. Yet it was a memory so complex, composed of so many different sensations and emotions, that it never failed to yield new secrets. It was as though someone – Julia? God? himself? all three? – foreseeing the wasteland his life would become, had provided him with a concentrate of human experience he could return to, time and time again, like a canary in a cage with its block of salted cod.

Later, as he came inside her, he thought to himself: *I am the gardener watering his seed with more seed*, while the baby writhed in fury, and he felt Julia's clitoris bloom beneath his fingers. Then they lay in the dark, side by side, and she whispered, as though she already knew everything: 'This is it now, Ennio: it's all we'll have.'

Almost, but not quite.

That evening they reconfigured, briefly, as a family by the dustbins of his mother's flat. Not that the perfect trio at Florence station would have anything to worry about, thought Ennio, as he watched them disappear together down the steps of the neon-lit underpass. An elderly man in a shabby white tunic was pushing a handcart up and down the empty platform, calling: '*Bibite! Panini! Caffé!*' in a subdued whine, as though anxious not to awake the sleeping passengers, and yet unable to modulate the daytime urgency of his cry. The effect was comical, like a dog howling to the moon *sotto voce*. It reminded him of the weird opening of that Battisti song, '*I Giardini di Marzo*', they heard that afternoon at La Camillina as they lay on the mattress in the upstairs room: '*ll carretto passava / E quell'uomo gridava . . . gelati!*' only instead of shouting the word '*gelati*', Battisti's voice dies down to a whisper.

After they made love, she got up and obediently began to dress by the light of the bedside lamp. Sitting on the edge of the bed, she looked like one of those Dutch nudes, now: hunched, apologetic, like a potato just pulled out of the soil. Her legs were white and thin, bowed slightly, as though unable to bear the burden of all that plenty – the pointed belly, those staring black nipples – while her ribs and spine stuck out as though her body were a chicken carcass, sucked dry by the devouring needs of the foetus. Ashamed of his disgust, Ennio turned away until she was dressed; the atmosphere in the room was cloying, and all he could think about now was getting out of the flat. Together they walked out on to Via del Monte Oppio. It had stopped raining, and the spring air blew in gauzy swathes about their cheeks. He couldn't explain to himself what made him take a detour to his mother's flat in Piazza Bologna: perhaps he was hoping to be arrested there (anything to delay getting on that train to Genoa), or, maybe yet again, he was just acting in character: an Italian male taking his girl home to meet *mamma*, making an honest woman of her, before abandoning her once again to the dogs.

Assuming you'd call it a meeting: Julia hiding by the courtyard wall in her poncho while his mother stood frozen by the open metal *bidone*, a sack of rubbish by her feet. Nobody spoke, then the ground-floor window of La Guerrini's flat rattled open and a light clicked on. With one finger on her lips, his mother signalled for him to leave: how well he knew that movement, the palm of her hand sweeping upwards and out as though to give him an imaginary hiding. The familiarity of the gesture, its association with an irretrievably lost past, brought tears to his eyes . . .

Ennio brushed his cheek, letting his gaze grow unfocused as

he stared ahead down the platform, feeling the engine vibrate through the wall of his chest as the carriage lights winked on and off. There was a sharp smell of urine coming from the direction of the toilets down the other end of the corridor. The station was deserted; the elderly vendor was alone on the platform with his cart. In one of the carriages towards the middle of the train, someone else, like him, was awake and in need of refreshment. He too longed for a drink, but he didn't dare ask: he didn't trust his face or his voice any more not to betray him. Ennio watched the man pour coffee into a cup from his thermos, while a ghostly hand appeared from the open window holding out a note. But before the transaction could be completed, the guard blew the whistle and the train began sliding down the tracks. As the engine picked up speed, the vendor abandoned his cart and began trotting alongside the train, bearing the cup of coffee aloft like a trophy or a rose, until improbably – tenderly, almost – their hands met. Like –

Like lovers, thought Ennio.

5

THROUGH A PEEPHOLE

'So you're back.'

From somewhere in the hall, from behind one of those bolted doors, came the sound of breathing. Luciana had warned her the neighbours would be curious – ravenous, actually, was how she put it.

She put down her shopping bags and felt along the wall for the light-switch.

'It's by the plant-stand,' said the voice.

She pressed the switch, and a neon bar clattered on above the stairwell. Looking about the hallway, she pretended to follow the sound of the voice, although she already knew where it was coming from. Most of the ground floor belonged to La Guerrini; aside from the entrance with its brass plate in the name of 'Commendadore Aldo Guerrini', the two dummy doors beside it were hers; she even had her own separate access to the communal courtyard.

Uncertain whether to answer, she paused for a moment, then picked up her shopping bags. The hallway was filled with the tom-cat scent of basil; a stallholder in the market at Via Catania had slipped a bunch in amongst the tomatoes. The smell was almost overpowering: more like an essential oil than a herb. After all this time, she still hadn't got used to the careless plenty which surrounded her.

Behind the door, she heard more breathing. A person (and a

very tiny one at that, if the height of the peephole was anything to go by) was watching her still, as though she were an actor, the hallway a stage. Luciana said La Guerrini never came out, that a few years back she'd been robbed at knifepoint by a young man posing as a technician from the national electrical company, ENEL. Since then, her only visitors were a Filipina maid who came in twice a week to cook and clean; and, rarely, her only son, a steward with Alitalia.

Lingering for a moment on the stairs, she realised she was delaying going up to Luciana: once the door of the flat closed behind her, she would feel her world literally shrinking down to those four walls, like the walls of the pop-up doll's-house book she used to play with as a child in London. When the book was open, the house would come to life, transcending its flimsy cardboard structure with a series of incredibly detailed interiors; however, the moment she snapped it shut, it became just a book again – flat, two-dimensional. Luciana had no friends, no visitors even. Aside from her brothers in Sicily, the only person who telephoned was an old lady called Itala: she had been a *portiera* once, too, in an office block in Viale Ippocrate, but she was retired now and lived in a *casa di riposo* near Terni.

Unexpectedly, she heard the sound of a bolt grinding open; then another, and finally a chain clattering against the wall.

'But what have I done with my keys?'

How am I supposed to know what you've done with your keys? Look for them, she felt like saying. She was irritated now, as though she had just caught sight of herself from the outside, standing in a shabby hallway with her shopping, at the beck and call of a capricious peephole – a grim snapshot of her new life. She was just on the point of picking up her bags and going upstairs, when the key clicked several times in the lock and the door creaked open.

But that second, the automatic light went off, and the hallway was plunged into darkness. Disoriented, but quite enjoying the protracted drama of the moment, she scanned the space ahead of her, as though her eyes were the beam of a searchlight, waiting for an image, any image – a chair, a picture, a bookshelf (that was the whole point, never quite knowing) – to develop at random before her eyes, just as she used to do as a child after lights-out in her bedroom in London. Then the smell hit her. Not a smell, more like a rank stench of decomposing food, sweat, urine, which hung in the air like a slab of asafoetida. Automatically, she stepped back, sick to the stomach as though she'd been punched, while a line of sweat prickled above her upper lip. Then, before her eyes, a white, kabuki-like mask appeared at shoulder-height behind the door.

'Come in, sharpish, before Luciana sees you.' Before she had a chance to react, a little claw hooked itself on to her arm and reeled her back into the flat, into the very heart of that smell. Then the door slammed behind her.

It was an enormous space, more like a storeroom than a place where a person might live. Everywhere she looked objects lay stacked up against the walls as though waiting to be catalogued: paintings and mirrors in heavy gilt frames, a cabinet of stuffed birds, even a china dinner service laid out on the floor, complete with soup tureen and gravy boat. The room was so full of furniture that it was difficult to imagine negotiating a path to the rest of the apartment: chairs lay piled on top of tables, while on an inlaid rococo sideboard she saw a collection of silver menorahs, lined up in a row beside a pile of folded linen. The shutters were closed and barred, and the only light in the room came from a pair of dusty crystal chandeliers, hanging side by side above an ornate ebony safe.

La Guerrini stood by the door, breathing heavily – panting, almost; she was sweating, and above her kabuki make-up a greasy film spread right up the edges of her hairnet. She was wearing a kind of housecoat, more like an undergarment, which left her sinewy shoulders bare, and a pair of leather mules decorated with a gold horseshoe on each heel.

'Let's have a look at you then.' As she opened her mouth, a poisonous smell shot out from between her gums, like the sludge at the bottom of a forgotten vase of flowers, adding a new component to the general stench which hovered over the flat, and which, surprisingly, she could feel herself almost getting used to. She gazed ahead of her at a triptych of portraits on the wall – a father in skullcap and prayer-shawl, mother, two pretty dark-eyed boys – as the shiny, quilted face loomed nearer and nearer . . .

Then, unexpectedly, she felt a hand on her breast. La Guerrini stood before her with her arm outstretched, expertly squeezing and prodding the flesh like a bra-fitter in a department store, while a new smell of spring onions emanated from the damp cluster of hairs beneath her armpit. The edges of her slip were rimmed with a watermark of sweat. Yet there was something fascinating about the grotesqueness of the situation, even the grosser physical aspects of it, which kept her mute. There was an Italian expression for that attraction – *il gusto . . . il gusto dell'orrido*, that was it. It reminded her of an occasion when, as a child, she got dog-shit on her hand whilst rolling around with her friend amongst the piles of leaves on Parliament Hill. She wiped her hand on the grass, rubbing it hard into the wet ground until all that remained was a kind of tea-coloured film, the mere patina of a smell, but she didn't wash it – not then, in the public toilets on the Heath, nor when they got back to the friend's flat in West Hampstead. Instead, all afternoon, as they sat watching television in the overheated front room, she would take surreptitious sniffs of that lingering musky scent, until she was back on the windblown Heath, amongst the drifts of leaves . . .

'You English girls are all flat-chested,' La Guerrini said at length. Then she looked at her sharply, and her little claw-like hand began to pinch the flesh around her waist. 'You're a fattish one, too. My Aldo used to buy me tins of liquorice from Bar Alemagna to keep me slim; it's an appetite suppressant, d'you know?' Pointing one toe, she thrust her hip forward, lurching stiffly to one side to show off her silhouette. 'But now my son takes care of my figure. He's starving me –'

'Starving you?' She could feel La Guerrini's hand travelling expertly down her waist towards her belly.

'Oh, yes. Him and that Filipina whore, Consuelo. The government put him up to it, d'you know. They're after my treasures: they want me to give them back to the Hebrews. They seem to forget that if it hadn't been for my Aldo the whole lot of them would have perished down the Ardeatine caves. He risked his life for that scum; he even took their possessions into safekeeping when the Racial Laws were passed. And now this is all the thanks he gets . . .'

With a sense of exquisite relief, she thought: *she's mad. I can leave now, before she starts asking questions –*

'She brings me food, and I hide it under the furniture. That'll teach the pair of them to poison a poor old woman. Before you know it, I'll have an army of slit-eyed grandchildren.' Then, without warning, her hand slid downwards, and she pressed her palm firmly on to her belly.

'How many months?'

'I'm sorry?' Heart racing, she began to edge back towards the door, knocking against a child's doll's carriage propped up on a pile of leatherbound books, with *Enciclopaedia Treccani* embossed upon the spine.

'Don't play the *cocotte* with me; I've seen it all in my time. The baby – when's it due?'

She fumbled with the chains and locks on the door, searching frantically for a way out of that flat. Through the peephole, she caught a glimpse of the lobby, a miniature concave world contained within a glass marble: the plant-stand, her shopping bags, the iron cage-lift beneath the stairs. La Guerrini was behind her now, barring her way with an outstretched arm.

She was so close, she could feel her chin digging into her back. The other hand continued to press and knead her stomach. 'He's a good boy,' she whispered, 'but don't you go getting your hopes up. He'll never marry you – never; he's got other fish to fry.'

Defeated by all those locks, she turned around. 'Who won't marry me?'

'Your lover-boy, that's who.'

'He's not my lover-boy,' she said defensively.

'That's what they all say. You won't fool me – I saw the pair of you lurking behind the dustbins. That poncho didn't hide a thing; you should have taken parsley, my girl – kilos of it, before it was too late!'

'I'm sorry?'

'You think I wouldn't recognise him after all these years? Just thank your lucky stars I didn't turn him in.'

'Turn who in?' She genuinely didn't understand, but her incomprehension barely registered, floundering as it did in the wider surrealism of the moment.

La Guerrini unlocked the door, shoving her out of the flat just as vehemently as moments earlier she had dragged her in. 'Ennio – the father of your baby!' she shrieked spitefully up the stairs.

'He's not the father of my baby.' Wearily, she picked up her shopping bags; she was past caring any more who heard. She felt as though she'd just come off a ghost train – a white-knuckle ride in an amusement park.

'So whose father is he then? Winston Churchill's?' La Guerrini grimaced wildly, waggling her head from side to side like a mechanical monkey in acknowledgement of her witticism.

Lotte never thought she'd hear herself say it – at least not yet, she didn't – but the words seemed to slide out on their own.

'Ennio is – was . . . my father.'

6

LOTTE

What Lotte knew (and what she might know if she but chose to ask), were two quite different things – they always had been.

For almost as long as she could remember, she had been told the story of how her beautiful mother set off one day for Italy, and fell in love with an Italian who was to become her father. There, she would die whilst giving birth to her, and without Melody ever discovering the identity of her lover. Lotte accepted this fable in the same way she accepted the mysterious cruelty of Cinderella's sisters, or Rapunzel's father, forced to hand over his newborn daughter to a witch for the sake of a bunch of stolen radishes. This was because Melody, not unintentionally, began to tell Lotte the story of her birth at around the same time she began to read fairy tales to her. And yet, while most children grow to question the existence of, say, Father Christmas, after that no-man's-land phase of complicity, when they know, but (as much for their own sakes, as for their parents'), put off asking, until next year, at least, Lotte never tried to browbeat her grandmother into telling her the truth.

No matter how hard she searched in her memory for the words – the seminal moment when she learnt about her parents – all she could recall was a series of bedtime scenes in her mother's old room overlooking the canal, fuzzy and reassuring as a Shirley Hughes line-drawing: Melody sitting on a scuffed white-painted chair by the bed reading aloud to her, a china night-light with an orange bulb set inside a toadstool grotto, her collection of Smurfs lined up on the shelf.

What she did recall, though, with almost supernatural clarity, was getting chickenpox around the age of eight or nine, and Melody setting up her grandfather's canvas camp bed on the daïs at the back of the shop. There was an old wardrobe beside the window, with an oval mirror set into the door, and during the worst days of her illness, while her temperature soared, Lotte would sit up in bed and stare for hours at her unfamiliar spotty face reflected in the glass, her hair sticking up like a bird's nest on one side of her head. She remembered everything about that mirror: the blotches in the shape of a witch's head and cauldron, the crenellated border, twisted like a silvery candy-striped ribbon, the little glass screws set into the edges of the frame. The longer she stared at her reflection, the more convinced she became that if only the chemistry were right, if only she could perfect the exact degree of focus, the communicating door to the shop would swing open and her mother and father would enter the room.

Every time the bell of the shop shrilled, Lotte thought: this is it: they're here. They would enter the room, hand-in-hand, and her mother would sit on the bed beside her, smoothing down the blanket with her long fingers, her silver Claddagh ring catching the evening sunlight from the window overlooking the canal. She was wearing a maroon tunic with wide sleeves, and an Indian scarf around her neck, just like in the photograph Melody kept in a cork frame beside her bed. Frustratingly, though, her father always remained in the doorway, his face in shadow, so that Lotte could never make out his features.

Hearing Melody's low voice from the shop, she imagined her grandmother explaining to the visitors that she was ill, and how it was a pity about the spots, as everybody always said she was so pretty and the living spit of her mother (though unusual, was almost always what people said). Then the shop door banged shut, and more clearly than if they had been standing before her, Lotte pictured her parents walking back down the Harrow Road, towards the Ha'penny Steps and the canal. 'Next time,' they were murmuring, 'we've waited so long, it's a pity to spoil it when she's ill . . .'

The communicating door swung open, and Melody entered the room with a tray. There was a glass of orange juice for Lotte, in her favourite Scooby Doo cup with the curly straw, and tea in a flowery china cup for her grandmother. Placing the tray on a packing case beside the bed, Melody sat down in the armchair by the popping gas fire. Outside on the Harrow Road there was the grinding sound of a lorry changing gears, then another, and the whine of the number 18 bus stopping outside the shop. Lotte looked at her grandmother sitting in the orange glow of the fringed lamp – really looked at her, as though a window had opened up in the exaggerated world of her fever – and debated asking whether it was true that her parents had come into the shop that day. It could have been the effect of her illness, plunging her into a fantasy world of her own yearnings; yet the image of the two of them was so striking that in the years to come she grew to believe she really had been visited by ghosts.

Later, when everything grew more complicated, she wondered what it was that had made her stay silent that afternoon. It went deeper than the need to preserve the illusion of her parents' apparition, as though the very stability of her life – of both their lives – was at stake. There was something about Melody's face, the way she sat there, kindly, drinking her tea in the armchair, head cocked slightly to one side, that was somehow different, as though she were waiting for Lotte to say something, ask the question that would change their lives for ever. And maybe that was it – Lotte didn't want their lives to change. At least, not yet.

*   *   *

In her primary school, they celebrated Eid and Diwali, as well as Carnival and the Chinese New Year.

Over half the children in her class spoke English as a second language; and only four, had they so wished, could have ticked the box marked 'British white' on a Government census form. One of these children, a girl called Natalie Regan, became Lotte's best friend in Year Two. Every Saturday, Natalie's brothers would take the girls swimming at the Jubilee Sports Centre on Caird Street. One afternoon, as they were standing in the changing room in their pants and vests, Natalie looked at Lotte and said, 'You've got really hairy arms, Lotte. And a hairy back.' Stung, Lotte craned her head to look over her shoulders, but it was only a charade to hide her tears: she already knew it was true. Her legs were hairy too, and no matter how hard she scrubbed her knees and elbows, her skin always looked grimy. Olive, Melody called it fondly as she dried her after her bath. Lotte looked over at Natalie: her ponytail hung over her shoulder in long, straw-coloured rats' tails; while her skin, blotched with mauve leopard spots from the cold, was so white that it was almost the same colour as the changing-room tiles. Lotte felt shocked at the contrast between their two complexions: as they were getting dressed, she kept stealing surreptitious glances at Natalie's freckled thighs, and each time she thought of the fur growing in a shameful V between her shoulder-blades, more tears welled up in her eyes. There was another girl in their class called Hanan, who had a hairy back too, and sideburns which went all the way down to her jaw. Hanan the Man, the boys called her.

'Anyway, I'd rather be hairy – it keeps me warm in the winter,' said Lotte eventually – far too long after the subject had been dropped.

Though in Year Three, Hanan became her best friend.

Lotte must have been nine or ten at the time, and going through a phase of unarticulated rebellion. (Or at least she would have been, had Melody given her anything half-decent to rebel about.) Mostly, she felt aggrieved at the unconventionality of her home life: while she couldn't blame Melody for her lack of parents or siblings, she could – and did – blame her for not buying her the Clark's sandals she yearned after in John Lewis. Her heart thrilled at the sight of those sandals: the latex heel with the gummy bobbled edges, the adjustable straps, the cushioned soles with the word 'Clark's' written in gold, joined up writing. They came in four colours: white, tan, blue and red. To Lotte, those sandals were more than just shoes, they represented a lifestyle – a way of looking at the world, and, more importantly, of determining how the world looked at you. The two children she once saw on a waterbus travelling from Regent's Park Zoo to Little Venice were both wearing those sandals. The girl was sitting on her father's lap, while the boy and his mother were standing on the open part of the canal boat, throwing scraps of bread to the ducks in the water. Lotte liked everything about them: their stripy blue and white tops, their tousled hair, the checked gingham alice-band in the girl's hair.

She had felt a sudden burst of fury at the sight of Melody chatting to her friend Rachel, the ticket-lady with her old-fashioned conductor's leather satchel. Why did she have to wear those big old sunglasses and that polka-dot handkerchief knotted around her neck like a pirate? All her clothes looked as though she'd had them for years – or else, as was mostly the case, that they'd started life belonging to somebody else.

That evening, when they returned from their trip to the Zoo, Lotte reproached Melody by taking out her box of pencils and ostentatiously sketching the perfect family on the boat. She drew with savage intensity, yet no matter how hard she tried, the children's faces came out wrong: instead of frank and engaging, the boy's expression was dull, while the girl looked like Miss Piggy's long-lost sister.

Not long after this episode, she woke up one morning, and

switching on the bedside lamp, found a paper carrier bag at the foot of her bed with the words 'Planit Earth' misspelt on the front. Inside was a parcel wrapped in brown tissue paper. She tore open the paper and stared in disbelief: inside was a pair of unsuitable-looking sandals with leather strings threaded through loops, instead of buckles, and certainly offering no proper width fitting or support. There was no name inside, either, and the stitching down the side was rough and uneven. You couldn't even call them a colour; they looked just like the pine furniture which Melody stripped down on the balcony overlooking the canal, all oily and patchy. Lying back on the pillow she thought of the family on the waterbus with their matching stripy sweaters; and, in spite of herself, she felt two tears trickle down the side of her face and into her ears. (By which time, interestingly, they'd gone cold.)

Melody was already up: Lotte could smell *espresso* and toast, and she heard the sound of footsteps as Melody went down to the shop to collect the newspaper. It was Saturday, and they were supposed to be going to the Lisboa Café on Golborne Road for lunch. Then the telephone rang, and she heard Melody pick it up in the kitchen.

'Oh, Catherine, of course I remember you! . . . Yes, I knew you'd gone abroad . . . fine, yes . . . no – she's ten now, would you believe . . . No, I don't open on Saturday's any more . . . usually we take a walk down to Portobello . . . I'm sure she'd love to meet you . . . one o'clock then, Catherine, outside the Lisboa.'

'Who's Catherine?' asked Lotte accusingly as she came down to the kitchen for breakfast. Melody looked up from her paper and smiled; she hadn't heard Lotte get up. 'Catherine? She was at university with your mummy, they shared a room in halls during their first year in Bristol; a few years ago she came to visit us when you were still a baby.' She got up and planted a kiss on the top of Lotte's head. In spite of herself, Lotte felt better: she could never remain in a bad mood with her grandmother for long. The kitchen was warm and sunny; out on the balcony, zinc window-boxes filled with ornamental cabbages glowed purple and green in the crisp light.

'Thank you for my sandals, they're lovely,' said Lotte stiffly.

'Oh, I'm so glad you like them. They're from a little shop in Kentish Town where many years ago your mummy used to get her clothes. I was so thrilled to find it still there, when I went to Chalk Farm the other day to deliver those chairs, that I couldn't leave without buying something.'

There – she'd said thank you as though she meant it, and they needn't talk any more about the sandals. Lotte licked her finger and collected a skull-cap of toast-crumbs from the tablecloth. Sunlight poured through the stained-glass window above the sink, illuminating the butter in the dish as though it were embedded with jewels. Melody was pouring milk into a triangular blue pan with a wooden handle; she lit the gas, then cut Lotte a thick slice of bread. Putting it on to a plate, she handed her a flat knife to spread the butter by herself. When the milk had boiled, she poured it into a bowl and spooned out the froth from the sides on to the top. Then she added a drop of *espresso* from the burnt nickel pot, and added a large spoon of honey. No one believed Lotte at school when she told them she was allowed to drink coffee. While she had her breakfast, Melody read the paper: it was a new one called the *Independent*.

When she had finished eating, Melody ran her a bath, and Lotte went into her bedroom to choose some clothes. Then she got in, squatting in the shallow water to keep her chest warm as the bath filled up. Holding a finger beneath the running tap, she watched the water bounce unevenly off the tip; then she dipped it below the surface, feeling the pressure thrumming through the barrier of the bath water. It was the strangest sensation, almost like the repulsion of two like magnets, as though, more than a liquid, the water were a glutinous substance, like oil or gelatine. She lay back, lifting out her legs one at a time to examine the hairs in the light. It was mostly on her shins, which was fortunate, as long socks covered the worst of it. But a new and depressing discovery was the hair growing Down There: she'd always had a bit, more like the shadow of hair, which seemed to demarcate where one far-off day she would get it, but now it was as though someone had drawn random biro marks there during the night. She glared at it, as though by the power of her gaze she could force the hair to retreat – absorb it back into her body. Angrily, she scrubbed her legs with Melody's loofah: in Superdrug you could buy a kind of sandpaper mitten to remove unwanted hair – maybe a loofah would have a similar effect. And if it didn't, she could buy one of those gloves with her pocket money, or ask Hanan to. Hanan wasn't scared of anything.

Lotte stayed in the bath until her body turned satisfyingly pink. Before getting out, she emptied her bladder, watching the urine dissolve beneath the water in a puff of amber-coloured smoke. She liked that feeling of being so thoroughly cooked that the sweat broke out on her forehead and upper lip, and she felt dizzy when she stood up. As she dried herself, she wondered what Catherine Smart would be like. She buttoned up the metal buckles of her dungarees and looked at the Greek sandals sitting on her bed, half-wrapped in the brown tissue paper. She thought she might wear them, or at least try them on.

'You're full of beans today,' said Melody fondly, as they turned into the Meanwhile Gardens. A group of Moroccan men wearing kaftans with hoods, and pointy slippers with the backs squashed down, were sitting on a bench smoking strong-smelling cigarettes. A hand-painted sign saying 'Strong Winds! Hold on to Your Buggy!' was planted on the verge of grass above a weed-choked stream. That corner between the canal and the railway line was always colder and windier than anywhere else: sometimes you could see swirls of rubbish spinning up in the air as though dancing in time to secret music. A group of Japanese tourists were standing on a traffic island taking pictures of Trellick Tower: one girl with plaits and a short skirt was kneeling down with her head tilted back, so that the photo would come out looking as if the building was rising up at a slant like Jack's Beanstalk: they learnt that trick in Photography Club at school.

'Where does Catherine Smart live?' asked Lotte. (Perhaps one day she would invite her to stay and let her sleep in the spare room like an adult guest; then in the morning, over breakfast, she would show her pictures of her mummy as a student, looking like Ali McGraw in *Love Story*.)

'Mostly in New Zealand, but she's over here for her brother's wedding.' Well, no overnight visits then; but they could still meet up to see her photos . . .

Turning into Golborne Road, they passed the halal butcher in his gleaming white-tiled shop, standing by the window amidst his potted palm trees, gazing out towards the railway line as though this were the most beautiful view in the world; while inside George's Fish Bar next door, the owner was leaning over the light blue formica counter with his arms folded, the violet light from the electric fly-box reflected off his oily white hair. Further up the road, a goods lorry with Portuguese number plates was parked outside the Lisboa grocery; high up in the cab sat a baby with a dummy in its mouth, holding on to the massive steering wheel with one hand, a torn-off hunk of bread in the other. A tarpaulin had been rolled up all along the length of the lorry, and the driver was standing amongst the cargo, chucking down multi-packs of tins and boxes to a man wearing a maroon-coloured Lisboa overall, who was catching them and stacking them on to the pavement. As they passed, Lotte looked down the open trap-door outside the shop, where another Lisboa assistant was standing with his arms akimbo, looking up at the street, the gold crucifix around his throat gleaming in the semi-darkness of the cellar.

On the other side of the road, Melody stopped to talk to her friend Edwin, who had a stall outside the Spanish hairdresser's. (Lotte knew it was Spanish from the notice in the window which said: '*Hablamos tu idioma*', which Melody said meant 'We speak your language'.) On Monday, Melody and Edwin were going to an auction up North; they had to sort out the details of the journey. While they talked, Lotte waved to Hanan's brother, Hakim, who had a stall selling household goods opposite the mosque.

The suspense was almost unbearable. How could Melody do this to her? For all they knew, Caroline might have already tired of waiting, and decided to leave. (Not that it was likely, as Melody was famously punctual; and indeed it was only ten to.) Sometimes, when she was angry, Lotte could feel her whole body tingling, as though tiny sparks of rage were squirting out of her pituitary gland, flooding through her nervous system, like the electric model of a lactating cow they saw on a school trip to a farm. She turned away, staring ahead at an elderly Rasta standing outside the newsagent's shop. He was leaning against the window, swaying gently from one foot to the other as he drank from a can of Special Brew partially hidden in a brown paper bag. His locks were grey and matted; when he turned round, Lotte saw the hair at the back had knitted together into a kind of giant mono-lock, shiny as sealskin, which looked like one of those rope fenders on the end of a canal boat.

To distract herself from her anger, she forced herself to list the contents of Edwin's stall, as though she were on the *Antiques Roadshow*: four pairs of second-hand men's shoes, a small brass bolt, two door panels, a 1974 *Jinty* Annual, three taps, a Moody Blues album, a metal soapdish with legs, some Rawlplugs in a half-open brown envelope, a pile of rude magazines, a rug . . .

'You must be Lotte,' said a man's voice behind her. Lotte spun around: only it wasn't a man, but a mannish-looking woman wearing a checked shirt over a pair of khaki trousers, her eyes blanked out by teardrop-shaped aviator glasses. 'I'm Catherine Smart', she smiled, lifting up the sunglasses on top of her head like a hairband. Her face was sandy, ordinary, with small eyes and pudgy cheeks. Before Lotte had a chance to react, Melody finally stopped talking to Edwin and turned to hug Catherine.

For a while, Lotte was too surprised to say anything. To be honest, she felt duped; all morning, a tiny irrational part of her brain had been formulating plans and theories, all of which revolved around a completely different Catherine Smart. Her imaginary Catherine had called Melody because she'd suddenly remembered something Julia told her when they shared a room . . . before she died, she wrote to Catherine, revealing the identity of her lover . . . she had a letter for her daughter to be opened on her eleventh birthday . . .

As they walked the short distance to the Lisboa together, Lotte held on to Melody's hand, something she hadn't done for years. She was panic-stricken at the thought of being left alone with Catherine while Melody went inside to get lunch, anticipating her own disappointment at the non-event the encounter was going to be. As they sat at the peeling, wrought-iron tables, Lotte stared down at her sandals, the other disappointment of the day. How could her mother have been friends with somebody so uninteresting? All around her, well-dressed Portuguese families in their Saturday best milled in and out of the café, carrying cream and red boxes of pastries to take home, mingling with the gaunt-looking junkies and dealers who sat a little apart on the pavement.

'You look just like your mother,' said Catherine in her deep voice. Lotte looked up, blushing with pleasure in spite of herself. Every time someone told her she resembled her mother it made her feel secure, grounded, as though without that link she might be absorbed into the hovering dark mystery that was her father and Italy. 'Do you mind if I take a picture of you? I'd like to have one back home as a souvenir.' Lotte shook her head, even though she hated having her photograph taken. Shoving her hands deep into the pockets of her dungarees, she crossed one leg over the other, scowling down at the uneven stitching on her sandals. There was a click, then another click, and the sound of the film automatically rewinding. 'I took two, so I can send you a copy once I get them developed.' While Catherine put the camera back into her rucksack, Lotte swallowed, trying to think of something interesting to ask her, something that might lead to the sign she had been waiting for. It suddenly seemed important to talk to her before Melody returned with the lunch, even though many more years would pass before Lotte began privately to question her grand-mother's version of events, let alone confront her with her doubts.

She took a deep breath, feeling the colour saturating her face and her ears, so that even the nape of her neck felt hot. She meant to say: 'Is there any memory of my mother you would like to share with me?', which sounded grown-up and casual – at least in her head it had. But instead, she looked at Catherine with pleading, tear-filled eyes and whispered, 'Please tell me about Rome.'

The indulgent smile froze on Catherine's lips, and Lotte felt herself sting with shame at her childish behaviour: it was the last thing she had meant to ask – how was Catherine meant to know anything about Italy when she had remained in Bristol during Julia's year abroad? But actually, it was an inspired question, and was to give Lotte an enduring faith in her own instincts. For Catherine paused for a moment, then said, 'Your mother only wrote one letter and one postcard to me while she was in Rome – we weren't that close, even if we did share a room for a year – and unfortunately I no longer have them. If I had known how things were going to work out, I would have made sure to take better care of them.' She craned her thick neck towards the café – to see if Melody was about to reappear with the food? – then turned back and added quickly: 'But I'll tell you one thing: she loved your father, whoever he was, really loved him, and she loved being in Rome.'

Just then Melody returned with the drinks: two glasses of coffee, and a bottle of thick peach juice with a straw for Lotte. Placing them on the table, she returned inside for the food while Catherine took a noisy slurp of her coffee. Lotte wanted to ask more, but there wasn't time as Melody came back with lunch: shaggy yellow croissants, glazed like Chinese buns, and filled with ham and cheese, together with the Lisboa speciality – burnt custard tarts.

Try as she might, every time Lotte thought about Catherine Smart, she could remember nothing else about that Saturday afternoon outside the Lisboa, even though she could recall everything else leading up to their encounter. Had they walked her back to the Tube at Westbourne Park, or did they carry on down Golborne Road towards Portobello? And yet, more than the words 'she really loved your father', what stayed with her was the thought that her mother had loved being in Rome. It offered a sunnier perspective on the tragedy of her own birth, knowing that at some point before she died – before her coming into the world had killed her – Julia had been happy. At least for a while.

When Lotte was sixteen, most of her friends cut out family life. Hanan refused to go back to Morocco for the summer and took to smoking weed behind the playhut in the Meanwhile Gardens. She joined every single after-school club going, to put off returning home in the evening, and while there was nothing about her appearance you could actually call disrespectful, her entire look – scraped-back ponytail, baggy Fruit of the Loom sweatshirt, no makeup – exuded insolence. And sex. She had a mixed-race boyfriend, too, Karl, who worked in Dixons on Kilburn High Road. Her entire life was spent walking a glamorous tight-rope of deceit and danger.

The only way Lotte, on the other hand, felt she could rebel against Melody's gentle and respectful upbringing was by professing an ostentatious interest in everything that lay outside their lives.

'You should ask her more about your dad,' said Hanan one afternoon. They were meant to be decorating the float for the Flamboyan Carnival Club, but Hanan had an appointment with Karl in Queen's Park. By a curious twist of fate, they were sitting drinking Diet Coke in the very same bandstand where, all those years ago, Lotte had lain oblivious in her pram during a rainstorm while Melody poured out her heart to a stranger. It was summer, and Hanan was wearing a strappy vest which showed off her famously hairy arms. (And which would have got her sent packing back to Tangiers on the first available flight if her father had seen her.)

'Ask her what?' said Lotte, rolling up her jeans to the knee. 'Anyway, there's nothing to ask.' (Her heart beat faster, as she remembered Catherine Smart's words: *she loved him . . . and she loved being in Rome . . .*)

'Well, look at it from your nan's point of view. If your only daughter goes off to a foreign country, gets pregnant and dies while she's having the baby, don't you reckon you might at least try to find out who the loser was that done it?'

'She did try to find out,' said Lotte defensively, although, if she was honest, what she was really defending, more than her grandmother's integrity, was her own right to remain ignorant. 'As soon as the embassy contacted her, she went straight to Rome and did everything she could to find out about my mum's life. But there was nothing to find out. When she left for Italy, she and her mum weren't getting on, and apparently she hardly even wrote home. Melody says it was her fault, because ever since my mum's dad – her own husband, if you get me – had died, she had rubbed her nose in what a great family life they'd had till then, and she reckons she didn't do enough to make the best of Julia's childhood after his death. At least, that's why she thinks my mum kept her relationship with my dad a secret: not because she was scared Melody would disapprove, but because she wanted her own big love story to be up there with her mum and dad's'.

'My mum hates my dad – at least that's what she tells us kids. I can't say I blame her neither: now he's saying he wants me and my sister to fast for Ramadan just because my uncle's coming over from Morocco, and he doesn't want the family back home to think he can't control his own kids. That man's an animal; my mum's got a twenty-four-year-old son, and three grandchildren, and now she fucking thinks she might be pregnant again!' Hanan looked at her watch and scanned the park for signs of Karl. 'He's not coming, you know, the bastard.' She grinned: 'Here am I risking being packed off home for an arranged marriage to my forty-five-year-old cousin, and he's probably up Harlesden watching football with his mates. That's men for you, innit . . . Anyway, you know what I'd do if I was you?' She shut her eyes, stretching out her arms above her, the side of her face tilted luxuriously towards the sun. 'Get your nan to take you to Italy. Tell her you want to see where you was born . . . visit all the places your mum used to hang out and stuff.'

'She won't.'

Hanan sat up sharply. 'What d'you mean, she won't?'

'She won't take me to Rome: she won't go back there. When my mum died, and she went to Italy to collect me, Melody says she probably would have killed herself if there hadn't been this baby to take care of. I mean, think what it must be like: burying your daughter – your only daughter – in a foreign country . . . Somehow, she managed to pull herself together, don't ask me how, but she swore to herself that she would never set foot in Italy again. She always said, ever since I was little, that when I was ready she'd pay for me to go to Rome, sort everything out – help me find all the places to do with my mum, tell me where the grave was, but she couldn't take me there herself. In all these years, it's about the only thing she's ever refused me.'

'You're joking, innit?'

Lotte blushed. How spoilt did that make her sound? 'Well . . . *and* she never let me have my ears pierced in Year Two.'

But did she really want to know more, Lotte asked herself for the thousandth time as she stood in the queue at the new Sainsbury's in Ladbroke Grove. No matter how much she and Melody promised themselves they would carry on doing a weekly shop at the market, the novelty of this new superstore proved hard to resist. More than anything, Lotte liked going in the evening, mingling with the smartly dressed people stopping off to buy supper on the way home from work. It was childish, but being able to do her shopping after dark made her feel as though she were living in an exciting non-stop city like New York. She stood at the express checkout, staring idly at the basket in front of hers: one tub of Blueband margarine and a tin of economy chicken soup. The shopping belonged to an elderly woman called Judith whom Lotte had come across several times sitting in an armchair by the fire in Melody's shop. She was a tiny, shabby creature, half tramp, half lady, who winter and summer, wore the same belted raincoat with bare legs and lace-up shoes with the laces missing, her hair scraped into an oily-looking bun off her nut-brown face. Melody said she rarely spoke; once she told her, à propos of nothing, that she had walked along the river to Twickenham to visit some relatives; most days she could be found sitting in the reading room at the library working her way through a pile of newspapers. Once she had paid for her goods, she went to sit on a chair by the Customer Services desk with her drooping, half-empty shopping bag, her toes barely reaching the polished floor. Beneath the harsh lights, her face seemed yellower than usual, jaundiced almost. It seemed incredible to think of that tiny figure negotiating the bewildering wasteland of the car park, floodlit like an all-weather sports facility, just to buy margarine and a tin of soup. And yet to Judith, and people like her, the supermarket was a new place to visit, an interesting landmark on their private map of Paddington.

It was all very well Hanan saying find out the truth, but if there was some terrible secret surrounding her birth, Melody must have had her reasons for hiding it. A coward, that's what you are, she said to herself as she rode back home along the towpath on her bike. Beyond the cemetery walls, a huge orange sun was sliding beneath the headstones, multiplied in tongues of rippling flame along the windows of Kensal House, making it look as though the flats inside were burning. The truth was, she'd probably become addicted to the romance of not knowing who her father was, she thought, as she unlocked the door of the flat. That way, in her imagination, he could be anything she liked: tinker, tailor, soldier, sailor . . . Putting down her rucksack, she hung her bike on the iron hooks above the bannister and walked slowly up the stairs to her room. Melody was at a residential furniture restoration course, and she wasn't due back until Sunday night. Anyway, who was to say that families were such a great thing at the end of the day? She didn't know a single person – not one – who was really happy at home. She walked along the passage to the kitchen and turned on the radio. Melody had left supper on the table for her: lamb sausages from the Lebanese grocer on Fernhead Road, and a tomato salad. Lotte picked at a piece of pitta bread while she waited for the sausages to grill. Look at Hanan: there wasn't one member of her family she was really open or honest or comfortable with. Funnily enough, for all her talk about forcing Melody to tell her about her father, Hanan was the first to envy Lotte the tranquillity of her home life. Melody was a good listener, and more than once, Lotte had returned from school to find one of her friends having a cup of tea and a chat with her at the back of the shop.

The sausages were ready now; she put them on to a plate, and pouring olive oil and salt on to the tomatoes, she sat down to eat. So if her home life was so wonderful, what was missing? More than the daily rub of family life, she missed being part of a bloodline, with traits and foibles handed down from one generation to the next. Whenever she saw families walking together, some unconscious reflex would force her eye to scan each face for linked characteristics, swiftly archiving their features to identify whom had been dealt which. And all that in a single glance. Julia's face she knew off by heart: the high forehead with the Shakespearean widow's peak, the straight dark hair, parted in the middle like a typical seventies beauty, the delicate eyebrows. Her mother took after Hugh's side of the family, though there was something of Melody, too, in the sombre, heavy-lidded eyes. She was such a lovely child: in her room Melody had a series of pink *gouache* drawings of her that Hugh had done before he died; Melody said the one in the tin bath with her hair tied up in a topknot was the spitting image of her at that age. Not that Lotte could see the resemblance herself; there was something about the shape of the head, maybe, and the eyebrows, but otherwise they were entirely different physical types.

As she undressed for bed, Lotte looked at her body in the wardrobe mirror – the very same mirror she had stared at for so many hours during her childhood bout of chickenpox. Once again, she felt that peculiar state of limbo as the familiar contours of her body grew dim and blurred as though she were staring at the body of a stranger – a familiar stranger, like someone she saw every day on the bus, suddenly revealed in all their intimacy. She looked like an Arab girl, she thought, with her curly hair and sturdy thighs. No matter how multicultural her daily life was, the truth of the matter was that Lotte felt like a foreigner in her own country. Being English didn't mean the same thing today as it might once have meant for her mother, or Melody for that matter; but being born to foreign parents, or even mixed-race parents, meant identifying with – or rejecting – an alternative culture. And that was her problem: there was nothing, and nobody, to measure her foreignness against.

After that meeting with Catherine Smart, she had begged Melody to teach her Italian. When Melody realised she was serious, they went to a shop called Grant and Cutler in Soho to buy an Italian book for children. *Impariamo Assieme*, it was called. Inside, there were pictures of schoolchildren, boys and girls in checked smocks with round white collars, and illustrated extracts from Italian poems. She still remembered the first one she and Melody read together: it was called '*Valentino*', by a poet called Pascoli, and went: '*O Valentino, vestito di nuovo / Come le bacche di biancospino . . .*'

Looking back on it, Italian was about the only hobby – assuming you could call it such – that she stuck with. At various stages of her childhood, Lotte took up (and abandoned) guitar, canoeing (one fall into the canal was enough to put her off) and, when she was going through her most respectable, Clark's sandals phase, Girl Guides. She couldn't explain, not even to herself, why she stuck with Italian. She thrilled at the sound of her voice articulating those gentle, musical words, and when Melody was out, she would sit in front of the mirror and whisper: '*Sono una ragazza italiana . . . sono una ragazza italiana.*'

One summer's evening, they were sitting on the roof-terrace stripping down a fireplace Melody had found on a skip in Harlesden. It was painted rust colour, and MDF panels, covered in a design of stencilled urns, had been nailed on to each side of the grate. Melody had a corrugated iron shed on the roof where she kept her materials: wire brushes, paintstripper, razor-blades, gloves. Everything was laid out on a trestle-table, ready to begin. Lotte walked over to the parapet and watched the late-night shoppers walking back down the towpath with their orange and white Sainsbury's bags. Across the canal, the lights of Trellick Tower twinkled like a spaceship in a violet sky. She could hear the scratchy, zig-zagging noise of the wire brush, and the sudden thrilling bass of a stereo from a car parked outside the Caribbean takeaway on the Harrow Road.

'Do you want a go?' asked Melody, holding out the razor-blade: it was the size of a playing card with a worn wooden handle. Lotte sat beside her and began slicing off long slivers of the rust-brown paint like some master *charcutière*. The sight of the clean, bare wood, glistening, so it seemed, with tiny beads of oil, moved her as it always did, and she sighed with pleasure.

'There's an Italian Saturday school Giuseppe's children go to near here,' said Melody without looking up from her work. She was trying to prise off the plywood panels with a screwdriver.

'Where?' asked Lotte.

'Just past the library on Willesden High Road, going towards Harlesden.'

'Who goes to this school?'

Melody looked up. She seemed to know where the question was leading, more or less.

'Italian kids, mostly. Or half-Italian ones.'

'And where am I supposed to fit in?' *Sono una ragazza italiana . . .*'

Melody gave the screwdriver one last wrench and they heard the sound of the plywood splintering. She lifted up the panel; beneath it was a row of Delft tiles, depicting a series of windmills and Dutch cottages, new, clean-looking as the evening sky.

Lotte saw her grandmother look up, as though hoping to catch an expression on her face before it hardened. 'Don't worry, Lotte my love – you'll find your way', she said.

All the Italian stuff hurt – how could it not? – yet Melody went along with it just the same. Sometimes she felt like the guardian of an exiled monarch or Lama, conscientiously preparing Lotte for the day when she would return to Italy to reclaim her heritage. It was always going to be a temporary arrangement, the carefully constructed vacuum in which Lotte had been allowed to grow up. How could it be otherwise? There was an Italian saying: '*Le bugie hanno le gambe corte*' (which roughly translated meant 'Lies have short legs' i.e. that they soon get found out) which Luciana kept repeating to her over and over again in those first days after Julia's death. It was her main argument for getting Lotte out of the country as soon as possible; a belief that were she to remain in Italy, any attempt at concealing her history would be destined to failure. And while Melody could not deny the truth of Luciana's words, she always knew that the same would apply were Lotte to grow up in London: it was just a question of time. Anticipating that day, she went to the Italian school in Willesden, prepared to fight for her granddaughter's right to learn the language of her father. She imagined the school would be full of children like those of Giuseppe the grocer on College Road: traditional, insular. Instead, there were few children of Italian immigrants. In Lotte's class, there were two mixed-race girls, Sara and Jamila, daughters of Italian mothers estranged from their Caribbean partners; Eritrean twin brothers, Angelo and Giulio, and a brother and sister, Alex and Vanessa, children of an Italian mother and a Latvian father. Between them, their wildly mixed parentage was more than enough to take the spotlight off Lotte's own background.

She turned out to have a real gift for Italian; she took the GCSE at fifteen, as a private candidate, and two years later, the A-level at the University of Westminster. It was there that she met and began a relationship with her tutor, a languages lecturer twenty years her senior.

His name was David; he lived in a converted loft opposite the cemetery on Kensal Green, and he had an eight-year-old son, Cal, from a Dutch-Indonesian ex-girlfriend, who came to stay on alternate weekends. At first Lotte seemed happy; he was her first boyfriend, and his age seemed to have spared her some of the fumbling agonies of first love. It also, if Melody was honest, provided her with the nearest thing to a father – or any other kind of male figure, for that matter, which had so conspicuously been lacking in both their lives. David, for his part, seemed enchanted by Lotte; he bought her a Penguin first edition of *Dr Zhivago*, and recorded his favourite Leonard Cohen tracks on to a tape for her. (Lotte didn't have the heart to tell him that her mother had left a boxful of Leonard Cohen LPs in her old bedroom.) He took her to see Italian films at the Italian Institute in Belgravia; her favourite was Fellini's *Amarcord*, which seemed to depict perfectly her ideal of chaotic, earthy, Mediterranean family life.

Whether Lotte loved David or not – well, that was another story. First, she had nothing against which to measure her feelings for him: the only relationship she knew anything about was her grandparents' idyllic-sounding marriage. She didn't love him spiritually, celestially, like Lara loved Zhivago; nor did she think she would have taken the risks Hanan regularly did to be with Karl. She'd already had two abortions: the first time through her GP, the second, only four months later, with the help of one of Karl's cousins who used to be a midwife.

'I love his prick, Lot, I can't help it,' said Hanan, crossing her legs and clasping her knees tightly, as though vowing that this time she would help it. Whenever Hanan talked like that about Karl, Lotte would feel an immense stillness creeping over her, as though she were gazing out on to a snowfilled landscape. Like her Latin blood, her sexuality seemed dormant, a photograph of a flame . . .

Sometimes, she and David would be walking down the street, and she'd find herself locking eyes with a stranger. It didn't matter where they were from – Portugal, the Middle

East, India even – just so long as they had dark eyes and skin, that bluish shadow around the jaw and cheeks which no amount of shaving seemed to eradicate. Occasionally, her stare would be met with raised eyebrows or a half-expectant smile, at which point Lotte would turn away, ashamed at her sluttishness. And yet she couldn't help herself; she felt invisibly connected to these men in a way that went beyond sexual or physical attraction, as though they were blood-brothers – had known each other, shared something, in a previous life.

She and David made an unusual couple; to be honest, she didn't much like how they looked together. This was brought home to her forcibly the afternoon David took her to choose her eighteenth-birthday present at a clothes shop called Poppy overlooking the canal at Ladbroke Grove. Lotte liked going to Poppy because it didn't sell the usual chain-store clothes, give or take the odd detail, to be found on every high street. This phenomenon never ceased to amaze Melody: 'When I was young, we would have died if anyone else turned up at a party wearing the same dress,' she used to say, and each time she heard this Lotte would have the same little flash of surprise thinking of Melody in her paint-stained corduroys ever going to a party, let alone in a dress.

She chose a semi-transparent light green shirt with flowing sleeves that hung over the wrists. In the tiny, purple-painted alcove at the back of the shop, David held the shirt under Lotte's face, and together they turned to the mirror. They looked so incongruous as a couple that for an instant, Lotte recoiled: he towered above her, narrow-hipped, faintly stooping, with a thin white face, while she looked dumpy, swarthy, watchful; as though, she thought, flushing with shame, she would go all warty in middle age with unexpressed sensuality. She waited outside while David paid; she thought she had caught something she didn't like in the assistant's expression.

On the way back to his flat, Lotte was quiet and sulky. As they walked along the Harrow Road, dwarfed by the leaning, moss-covered cemetery wall, she fanned the flames of her bad mood by trying to recall what her and David's reflection in the shop mirror reminded her of. It had something to do with a photograph she had seen in a shop window recently, but the image remained irritatingly out of reach. Then, just as they reached Kensal Green station, she remembered. It was a window display in Supasnaps on Notting Hill Gate, demonstrating a new technique which allowed one photograph to be incorporated into another. There was a large, framed wedding picture on an easel of an Asian couple with the usual blue-sky studio background; and below it, individual portraits of the two subjects. It was only by looking at the single photos that you realized they must have married by proxy – that they might have never even met. While the woman was in her wedding dress and veil in both shots, the groom was originally wearing a flowery, pointy-collared shirt which had been substituted for a tuxedo in their reconstructed wedding portrait. Returning to the main picture, you began to notice how subtly unconvincing it was; two images from different times and different places, not for a moment inhabiting the same reality.

Although in bed, she could, for a moment, believe they did. He took her so swiftly, so cleanly, that she never had time to organise a defence. Afterwards she lay in his arms, her heart beating fiercely. She felt as though she had been wrenched inside out like a skinned hare, bare flesh exposed to the world. 'My exotic little girlfriend', he called her.

Sometimes she believed him; at others, she despised his gullibility and wondered what it would be like to have a Latin man.

'Are you happy?' Melody asked. Lotte knew she was worried – thought she was drifting, and had been since she left school. They were sitting at a table outside the Canalboat Café in Little Venice.

'What do you mean by happy?' She wasn't drifting, anyway; she was working in a wholefood shop in Portobello, and making up her mind whether or not to go to university. She was also about to complete a TEFL course.

'I just thought you could do with a break. Maybe you and David could go away somewhere.' Screwing up her eyes against the sun, Melody put on her Jackie O sunglasses, the ones which had so irritated Lotte when she was a little girl. The sight of them filled her with tenderness now. She looked at her grandmother's hands, fingers locked together on the green-painted wrought-iron table. They were scratched and coarsened, yet strangely harmonious, with a kind of virile strength, even in repose. Between the furrows of the veins, the skin was thin, liverspotted. When had she got so old? Lotte felt guilty; she took her freedom so much for granted – indeed, had been so encouraged to by Melody herself – that she rarely thought of her grandmother's age, or the responsibilities this entailed.

From the window of David's flat, you had a view directly on to the cemetery at Kensal Green. Sometimes she would look over the rows of overgrown headstones and think of her grandfather who was buried there. She had never known him; but without him – without his bloodline – she would not exist. Her mother had spent much of her childhood in that cemetery, leaving gifts at her father's grave; and she supposed one day Melody, too, would be buried beside him. She had always known that when her grandmother died, she would be alone in the world: that most Victorian of figures, a young female orphan. Only of course she probably wasn't a real orphan –

'You should take advantage of some of those charter flights,' Melody was saying, 'go and get some sun. You could go to Cyprus, or even Tunisia or Morocco.'

Never Italy, thought Lotte, never once would she suggest going to Italy . . .

'Actually, David was talking about going to France for Easter. There's some conference going on in Paris he's interested in. Something to do with the thirtieth anniversary of the student uprisings – "Sixty-Eight: Thirty," I think it's called.'

'And would you go with him?' Somehow, Melody managed to control the tremor in her voice . . . 'Le bugie hanno le gambe corte . . .' all those lies, breaking out of their box like a swarm of rank bluebottles . . . Thankfully, though, Lotte was too busy snapping off the edges of her polystyrene cup, piling up the pieces in a lopsided drift, to notice her discomfort. Melody locked her hands tighter together, pressing her thumb down on to the bone until the skin around the knuckle grew white.

'I might, who knows, if nothing better turns up.'

Lotte made her words sound more brittle than they were meant to; again, she felt an obscure desire to wound Melody, to blame her for the hollowness of her existence. Sometimes she felt her relationship with David – her life, really – consisted of sitting in a twilit room, waiting for something to happen. She was smoking too much, too; Hanan had given her a bag of weed for her birthday, and she'd got into the habit of rolling up every evening before going to sleep. She couldn't remember the last time she'd started the day with a clear head. Actually, it wasn't just Paris David was talking about: he'd also suggested driving south to Italy after the conference, but until now they'd never got beyond generalities; she blanked him out whenever he started hassling her about dates. In some ways it would be handy to have him there, there was no denying it, but a part of her recoiled – actually, more than recoiled, throbbed with rage, was more like it – at the thought of him showing her around her own country. Besides which, why should she make the most momentous journey of her life just because it happened to fit in with David's holidays?

They watched a mother duck glide past Browning's Island, her ducklings following her in a messy V-formation. On the table beside them, a group of Italian tourists shrilled with surprise at the sight. '*O, che carine! Dai, fagli la foto!*' Obediently, one of the husbands got up from the table and stood at the edge of the canal to take a photograph. They were two middle-aged couples, all dressed in subdued brown and greens, their clothes looking as though they'd been specially ordered in a catalogue named *English Holidays*. All four of them wore perfectly brushed brown suede shoes with nubbly rubber soles: they were called Tod's – she'd seen pictures of them in magazines. Hanan even had an imitation pair from a shop in Church Street market. In spite of feeling sullen, Lotte couldn't help thrilling at the knowledge that she understood those people and was really one of them, like a native of some far-flung, post-imperial nation, pathetically loyal to a homeland she had never even visited . . .

Melody watched her sadly. She couldn't help thinking she had failed Lotte. Recently, she had felt an oppressive sorrow weighing down on her, a familiar sense of loss which reminded her of the period before Julia left for Italy. She'd stayed in her old room overlooking the canal before catching her flight to Rome; yet looking back on it, Melody could barely recall a single thing about her visit, as though Julia had spent those last days in London flitting tantalisingly beyond her grasp. She did countless loads of washing, running up and down the roof-terrace steps with the white-painted wicker basket they used for laundry; then there was a last-minute panic getting some books she needed for her course from Grant and Cutler. Melody had hoped to do something special on the Sunday – perhaps drive out to Richmond for lunch, or go for a walk on Hampstead Heath, followed by tea in the Austrian *konditorei*. The possibility, like the flickering ghost of an olive branch, had hovered in the air all weekend, yet neither had grasped it. Over the years, she would ask herself: what if they had made a connection that weekend – what if they had parted on a different, more intimate, footing, might Julia have confided in her from Italy, unburdened her heart of some of its troubles? Would her daughter still have travelled that lonely road towards her death? She hadn't even been able to pin her down to a meal together at home; on Sunday morning, Julia announced that she had a few last-minute things to sort out, and she only reappeared late in the afternoon with scarcely enough time to finish her packing. Afterwards, Melody discovered she had spent the morning at the cemetery; when she went herself, a few weeks later, she found a bunch of faded irises and a single rose on Hugh's grave.

Julia left early on the Monday morning; it was still dark outside as they had a last cup of tea together in the kitchen. Melody remembered her daughter sitting at the table in the threadbare kimono which had belonged to Hugh's Aunt Lotte, her slim fingers with the Claddagh ring clasped around her mug. The coral and white patterned silk of the kimono set off her beautiful pale face, the dark hair twisted into a loose plait over one shoulder. She was adamant that she wanted to go to the airport alone, though in the end, she agreed to let Desmond, the owner of the mini-cab firm next door, accompany her to Heathrow. Melody stood and watched from the shop doorway as Desmond loaded her suitcases into the boot; she remembered he was wearing a trilby hat and a T-shirt which said 'Take me to Jamaica'. The Harrow Road was supernaturally quiet, broken only by the diesel grunt of a dustcart as it turned into the Avenues, and the crackle of reggae music from the car speakers. As the sky began to lighten over the canal, they embraced hurriedly, then Julia walked away from her towards the open car. Desmond must have cracked a joke before slamming the door shut – maybe Julia had commented on his T-shirt, and he'd offered to take her with him if he ever made it to Jamaica – because Melody caught sight of her daughter's face a second before they drove off. She was leaning back in her seat, smiling radiantly – the first real smile of the weekend, as though out of her mother's radar, away from the atrophied nostalgia of their shared life, she was finally able to be herself.

Melody never mourned Julia properly, at least not in her twenty-year-old guise. Since Hugh's death she had grieved protractedly – vicariously, even – for everything Julia had lost: the happy father who sat that morning in the hospital room with his light green cup and saucer, the eight pink *gouache* sketches he left behind like a testament to the years he had shared with his daughter, her own self-fulfilling prophecy that the graceful nine-year-old child in those pictures would cease to exist the day she ceased to be so loved. Consciously, or unconsciously, Melody had bound Julia over to a servitude of grief: she would only ever see her daughter in terms of the child who visited the cemetery on Father's Day, making no real effort to rekindle the vitality and promise of those early years.

And when Julia herself died, and her baby daughter, a child she would never know or hold or nourish, took her place in her old bedroom overlooking the canal (like some bizarre trade-off, Melody sometimes thought bleakly – new lamps for old), still she continued to mourn the prelapsarian child of the pictures, never the young woman smiling in the back of the taxi as she set off for the airport.

Now Melody looked at Lotte sitting at the table, arms folded across her chest, her lovely broad face staring stubbornly out towards the water. Even as a small child, her rages, her wilfulness had filled Melody with tenderness. She ached to help her, in the same way she had ached to catch her when she was a toddler learning to walk. She would have to sit on her hands to stop herself from holding out her arms protectively, reluctant to break the hesitant swagger of those first steps.

Lotte didn't love David; there was no fooling him, or her, or anyone else, that she did. She was so consumed by feelings of incompleteness that the usual adolescent self-absorption was in danger of turning into her granddaughter's defining trait.

Lotte was literally incapable of coming out of herself, as though she were still that baby lying in the *box* in the shadows of Luciana's hallway, with the newly pierced ears and the tiny identity bracelet with no name.

She lay on the unmade bed, watching David shuffle through his papers at the long trestle-table beneath the window. The room was in near darkness, lit only by the anglepoise lamp with the shade turned obliquely towards the bare brick wall. The computer thrummed in the background; every now and then the screen would go blank, and without looking up from his papers, David would press a key at random to restart it. He had a photo of his son, Cal, which Lotte had taken, set up as a screensaver; in the picture, Cal was sitting on the edge of the skateboard bowl at the Meanwhile Gardens, fastening his knee-pads with a look of absorption which reminded her of his father. She liked Cal; she'd never imagined an eight-year-old child could be such enjoyable company, and to be honest, she liked watching David be a father to him; it was a side of his personality she found attractive.

Lotte felt like a detail in some grungy fashion spread: a young girl, lying in her underwear in an anonymous loft, rolling a joint on a bed. The first of the evening, to be precise; her TEFL course was finished, and for once she could sleep in in the morning. David wasn't smoking; he was sifting through a sheaf of articles on the student movement photocopied from French, German and Italian newspapers which a colleague in Paris had sent him in preparation for the conference.

As she rolled the joint, she asked herself for the thousandth time whether she loved him. By now it was an idle, redundant question, but thrilling none the less, as though she were holding his life in the balance. Not that David would die if she didn't love him – only the thought made her grin – but there was something irresistibly decadent to be questioning her feelings for him, especially in his presence.

David stretched his arms above his head, linking his fingers into an upside-down arch. He was wearing a white T-shirt, the out-of-shape neckline slung between his shoulder-blades like a saddle so that the top vertebrae stuck out. He yawned noisily: 'This stuff is never-ending. Most of it's in the original, too.'

Lotte squeezed the tip of the joint, letting it swing back and forth until it crackled and grew compact. 'What languages?'

'Mostly French and German. There's some Italian in there, too, somewhere.'

'Let's have a look.'

Too lazy to get up from the bed, she stretched out an arm as David got up from the desk and walked barefoot towards her. He handed her a stack of papers, and switched on the lamp above the bed before returning to the desk. Recently, he too seemed to have been infected by Melody's anxieties; he was forever giving her books and articles to read, and he made a point of only smoking on weekends, as though to reproach her for her idleness.

Slipping a T-shirt over her head, Lotte settled back on the cushions, the joint unlit and forgotten on the bedside table beside her. Afterwards, when it became clearer to her, and to everybody else around her, what exactly it was she had stumbled across, she was glad not to have been stoned: it gave the moment a kind of unrevealed significance she was able to return to later.

It was a print-out from an internet site called 'Gli anni di piombo'. 'Piombo' meant 'lead', 'anni', 'years': in other words, 'The Lead Years'.

'Why is the site called "The Lead Years"?'

Lotte looked up to find David watching her from the desk, as though he had been anticipating her question, hoping for it, even. 'Italians call that period of terrorism "The Lead Years" mainly because of the lead in all the bullets that were fired, but also I guess because people look back on it as a leaden, black period of history.'

'What was so leaden about it?'

'What was so leaden about it? Well, let me see . . .' David swung around on his office chair, bare feet stretched in front of him, so that he was facing her. His voice had slipped into the kind of neutral vernacular he used when he was teaching – a pre-emptive strike against student boredom, Lotte always felt, although in fact he was one of the more popular teachers in the college, and his courses were always oversubscribed. 'It was leaden in the way you could say any society at war with itself is leaden. People lived in fear of being caught in terrorist gunfire, of their children getting mixed up in the *Movimento*. I remember when I first visited Rome on a sixth-form exchange trip towards the end of the seventies – more or less when your mother would have been doing her year abroad – the family I was staying with in the suburb of Monteverde never let their daughter out after dark.'

Just imagine, thought Lotte, *you and my mother might have crossed paths in Rome. Knowing what you know now, you could have told her to make peace with Melody, advised her go back to London to have her child* . . . She pictured David as a clean-shaven, slightly nerdy sixth-former, trying to chat up her beautiful, pregnant mother on the steps of a Roman church: '*Oh – and by the way, chances are in twenty years' time me and that baby of yours will be fucking in a London loft . .* '

'That spring, the Red Brigade had kidnapped Aldo Moro, and the city was swarming with armed *carabinieri*. Even though in those days I knew next to nothing about the political situation in Italy, you could literally feel the menace in the streets: our coach was searched several times, and every second corner seemed to have a roadblock. Things were so bad, our trip was almost cancelled. It's difficult to imagine anything remotely like that happening in England – it really was like living under siege.'

Lotte looked up, startled. Terrorism was one element which

had absolutely not figured in her mental picture of her mother's Rome sojourn. Most of the time she imagined Julia wandering ethereally through the narrow cobbled streets of the eternal city, looking like Dorothea Brooke in her Quakerish grey cloak the moment Will Ladislaw discovers her standing by the statue of Ariadne in the Vatican Museum. 'Why didn't the police arrest all the terrorists, then?' Bereft at the loss of this image, she felt a pang of retroactive fear at the thought of her mother exposed to such dangers. Yet how could she be worrying now about the safety of someone who had died twenty years ago? She had a sudden, comical vision of herself as a foetus, gazing gnomically through the keyhole of her mother's belly-button, the womb awash with adrenaline, as Julia negotiated the war-torn streets.

'It wasn't as simple as all that – not like the IRA bombing campaigns which were strictly territorial, and meant very little to anyone outside Ireland. The armed struggle in Italy was everywhere: whereas in England, only a certain kind of moderately politicised young person goes on CND marches and boycotts Barclays Bank, or demonstrates against the Poll Tax and the introduction of student loans, in those days Italians from all walks of life – students, blue-collar workers, even academics and professionals – joined underground movements plotting to destabilise the Government. There was a huge core of sympathy then for the armed struggle, though probably most would agree now that violence wasn't the best way to rid Italian society of its corrupt politicians.'

'Why should Italian politicians have been more corrupt than any others?' retorted Lotte pettishly; she was bored of his lecturing tone, and obscurely blamed him for ruining her fairy tale about her mother. *You can forget sex tonight, for starters* . . . she thought vulgarly to herself.

As usual, David wouldn't rise to the bait; he was infuriatingly patient with her – so patient, that she sometimes complained he treated her like Cal. 'Maybe at the end of the day they weren't, but it's no coincidence that the three European countries with the strongest "ideological", as opposed to "territorial", armed movements – in otherwords Germany, Italy and Greece – were also those emerging from Fascist dictatorships.'

Lotte was interested, in spite of herself. There was something exciting at the thought of being born into a period of social unrest, like the Troubles in Ireland, or the Bolshevik revolution in Russia. She wondered how she could have remained so ignorant about that period of recent history; and, more importantly, why Melody had never told her about the background to Julia's stay in Rome. Surely she must have been aware of the political situation when she went to Italy to collect her from the convent where she was being cared for? Her not saying anything had to be deliberate – had to mean something . . . Lotte felt her stomach lurch; her hands grew cold, and her heart beat queasily as though she were standing on a ledge looking down through swathes of fog at the invisible ground below. It reminded her of the same disproportionate terror she used to feel during PE lessons at Junior School, when they used to practise walking along a beam which was only about a foot from the ground, and yet the fear of falling off was no different than if the beam had been suspended from the rafters: it was the falling, not the height itself, which frightened her. She glanced down at the papers David had given her: on the first page of the internet sheets was a photocopied article from a newspaper called '*Il Messaggero*'. The headline was '*Sparatoria al Casolare in Abruzzo*' – 'Shoot-out in Abruzzo Farmhouse'. The photograph beneath was of a man in a balaclava firing a gun. He was standing in a sloping field of long grass, aiming up towards what looked like a semi-derelict house. Behind him, you could make out the rear-end of a police car parked in a grove of trees, with the word *CARABINIERI* painted in white along the doors. The gunman was in profile, heels together and knees bent, so that you could follow the Z-shaped curve of his left thigh in the crumpled flared trousers. He was clasping the gun in gloved hands, his arms held straight in front of him at shoulder-height, the sleeves of the jacket riding up so that half the forearm was exposed.

Lotte stared at the picture. It had the raw quality of one of those *Life* magazine photos, like the naked child fleeing a napalm attack in Vietnam or the black corpse swinging from a tree in the midst of a holiday crowd in America's South. You could tell the man wasn't a professional killer – the clothes were all wrong, the jacket unsuited to the firing of a gun, so that it bunched up behind him like a smock, the crumpled trousers those of any peace-loving hippy. Even the way he stood, thighs splayed and heels together, was more glamorous than menacing – erotic, in its very amateurishness. Most of the face was hidden by the balaclava and the hunched shoulder, but just visible were the nose and the deep-set hollow of the eyes.

The call came on a Saturday evening, about six weeks later.

She remembered they'd planned to go to the cinema at Whiteley's in Bayswater – David had booked advance tickets for the late-night showing of *The House of Mirth* – and he was just hunting for the scrap of paper where he'd written down the booking reference number, when the telephone rang. David took the call at his desk, the receiver tucked awkwardly beneath his ear while he continued to search through his papers. Lotte stood in the doorway, trying to gauge from the expression on his face whether it was Pearl, his ex, hoping to dump Cal on them at the last minute. She studied him, wondering whether she'd find him attractive if she'd just walked in off the street ... *bits of him, I suppose, eyes, maybe, forearms ... oh, and he's got nice hands ...* Then David did a curious thing; he shot her a brief, almost sly glance – *so now all of a sudden he's psychic? Seen just how thread-*

bare my feelings are for him? – then deliberately turned his back on her so that he stood facing the window, receiver hitched up to his ear, letting the papers he was holding float down on to the desk and on to the floor. She heard him mutter something like: 'Give us five minutes', and then, without hanging up, he let the receiver fall on to the table.

'OK, let me guess. The babysitter never showed up and Cal needs his supper?'

She heard him sigh, clear his throat a couple of times, then he turned around to face her. Slowly, annoyingly, as though he was enjoying keeping her on tenterhooks, he placed the receiver back on its base.

'It was your grandmother, Lotte. She wants you to go home.'

'Now?' Then, idiotically, 'What about the cinema tickets?'

'Right now. Forget about the tickets. She needs to talk to you.'

'Is she . . . all right?' *One day, God, granted, but please not this day . . .*

'She's fine, Lotte, don't worry. Something's come up – something . . . but anyway, she'll tell you herself. Come, I'll take you home now.'

As she followed him out of the door and down on to the fire escape which led to the car park, a rage took hold of Lotte, so obdurate, so completely formed, that the effect was almost electrifying. She felt like kicking David behind the kneecaps until his legs buckled at the centre like a broken X and he toppled headfirst down the iron steps: *You mean nothing to me, David, nothing, so why don't you step out of the fucking limelight, and stop milking this . . .?* She clung to it for dear life, her fury, pressing her forehead against the cool glass of the rain-spattered window, as they drove the short distance home, her breath coming in little shuddering gasps – *Look I'm breathing in little shuddering gasps* – as though each intake of air had to do battle with the wild drumbeat of her heart, past the cemetery, E. M. Lander, the headstone makers, the bridal shop and the Boys Café, until they reached the shop doorway where Melody stood waiting out on the pavement.

After this, something in Lotte probably snapped. From the moment she entered the flat and saw their two passports sitting on the dining-room table, the moment forked out in two separate directions: the present and a kind of heightened dream-time, neither of them permanent nor recognisable states. She could literally feel herself drifting between the two, as though trapped inside an Expressionist woodcut – a totally animate landscape where every object in that familiar room appeared to be quivering with pathos. She remembered Melody pouring them both a glass of wine – the bottle she recalled perfectly well, even the label with its crimson stripe across the top, and the name of the producers in white letters: 'Grimaldi Giacomo', with an interlocking G and G in a gold crest beneath it. (An Italian wine, coincidentally, a 1997 'Dolcetto d'Alba', from the Maida Vale branch of Oddbins.) Then, formally almost, they sat down in their respective armchairs by the fire, which wasn't lit as it was summer, and Melody switched on the reading lamp above the book-case. Still neither of them had spoken, and for an instant, Lotte debated saying to her grandmother: *Don't tell me – whatever it is, I don't want to hear.*

'Your father's dying, Lotte; we fly to Rome in the morning.'

Across the landing, in the kitchen, she heard the compassionate drone of the fridge, the sympathetic shiver of the clock striking ten.

'You see, he was a terrorist, my darling, for all these years, ever since you were a baby, he's been in prison . . . he and his mother – all of us – felt it was better not to say anything . . .'

A jailbird father and another grandmother: *She's known all this since the day you were born . . .*

It was an apocalyptic feeling, sitting in that armchair

surrounded by the ashes of her childhood, as though there had been a fire, her sawdust life gone up in smoke . . .

At some point she got up and went to her room to pack a case – *Oh, and what do you wear to meet a dying terrorist?* – then, at around three, she lay on her bed, fully dressed, waiting for the mini-cab to take them to Stansted.

Never in her life had Lotte thought herself capable of such facetiousness, of such stunningly misplaced levity. For example, sitting in the cab at some traffic lights just past Euston, she thought: *Good – whatever happens, this gets David out of my hair . . .*

Or, buying *Hello!* at the airport Smith's (*Hello!*? She *never* bought *Hello!*): *Good – I finally get to visit Rome . . .*

Or, checking in at the GO counter (separately from Melody, to make a point): *Do I need another lonely old woman in my life?*

She didn't feel like crying at the thought of her father dying – after all, what was there to cry about? She was hardly going to miss him – but each time she looked across the aisle of the plane at Melody, chin cupped in her hand, steady profile gazing out towards the runway, Lotte's eyes filled with tears. She had betrayed her, lied to her for all those years, but that split second at David's flat when she thought Melody had been taken ill had been the most frightening of her life: *One day, God, granted, but please not this day . . .* Yet still she'd treated her grandmother like dirt; watched her carry her own suitcase down the stairs of the flat and into the cab, the African driver staring at her in appalled reproach as he hurried out of the car to help her. Her father's death – his life – was a machete, hacking through the very trunk of their relationship – a cosh to *beat her, beat her, beat her . . .*

The plane thrust forwards and up, and she thought: *I must have inherited that terrorist gene . . .*

* * *

They landed at dawn, twenty minutes ahead of schedule.

As the wheels bumped along the tarmac, Lotte stared out of the window at rows of squat apartment blocks painted in taupe and ochre and green: little tablets of colour in a child's paintbox, mimicking the drab shades of the surrounding hills. Waiting in line to disembark behind a family of Italian Londoners (mother and father communicating monosyllabically in some kind of dialect, with the occasional English word thrown in, sleepy-looking teenage sons in trainers and nylon Umbro shirts), she felt like saying to the mother of the boys: this is my country, too, you know, as much as yours; until once again the awfulness of what lay ahead washed over her like a sickness. She felt like a criminal, slipping in through the back door – one of those shifty-looking relatives you saw giving interviews on the news, hair crackly with static, voices electronically distorted, who chose to be filmed from behind in the hope of keeping their identity a secret. Then she walked out on to the steps of the plane, felt the dense warm air blowing about her cheeks; and gazing ahead at the bushes of sugary-pink bougainvillea lining the tarmac, her heart gave a sudden flip of joy, and she remembered thinking to herself: *This is my land of opportunity . . .*

The terminal building smelt of coffee and kerosene; it was only six o'clock in the morning, but the atmosphere was surprisingly animated. Walking through customs into the arrivals area was like flicking the switch on one of those old-fashioned Moviolas she once saw on a trip to the Science Museum: dumpy nuns were milling around a group of soldiers in green berets; a sun-tanned man with wavy brilliantined hair, hand on hip, sunglasses resting on the fleshy ridge of his forehead, was leaning against a pillar, smoking; people were shaking hands, clasping one another by the shoulder, and allowing the hand to linger in a way that would never have been comfortable in England. Even the sleepy teenagers on the plane appeared to have come to life in the fizzy air, shedding all traces of their London personas: sheepishly, the older boy was having his cheek pinched by a middle-aged man carrying a clutch bag, while the younger was swinging a pretty toddler up in the air.

As they waited in line for a taxi, Lotte kept stealing surreptitious glances at Melody; once or twice during the flight, she had attempted to strike up a conversation, but each time Lotte had blanked her out without a word. Actually, it was almost surreal, staring right through the contours of that familiar face, now the mask of an enemy. Her grandmother looked old, her features ashy with tiredness, and the white-gloved policeman allocating the taxis had insisted on pushing her up to the front of the queue. There was so much she needed to know, but asking Melody meant setting aside her anger, allowing things to return to a normal footing. Only now there was no normal footing, and there never again would be . . .

Once inside the taxi, Lotte took out the notebook and four-coloured biro she had bought at the airport Smith's; her heart was beating so erratically that her arms and legs felt shot through with wires of numbness. She opened the notebook, hoping to trick her brain into slowing down for a moment. Switching the pen on to green, she wrote at the top of the page: 'SOME QUESTIONS TO ASK A LIAR (my grandmother)' and underlined it twice. Then, turning the pen on to red, she wrote:

I never asked you my father's name, Liar. What is it?
How long has he been ill?
Is he likely to still be alive?

But as she looked at the words on the page, one of those broken circuits in her head temporarily reconnected, the whole gruesome picture flashed before her – *rich man, poor man, beggar man . . . thief* – and the horror of it made her snap the book shut. She stared out of the window; the morning sky was light blue, streaked with wisps of charcoal. Tumbledown shacks with corrugated-iron roofs lined the sides of the road, while up on a hill, the ruins of a broken Roman aqueduct snaked between clumps of pine trees. As they approached the city centre, the traffic began to grow more intense, and the taxi slowed down. Lotte's eyelids grew heavy; she remembered that ever since she was a small child, there was only so much tension and excitement she could take before a kind of waking trance would overcome her. The last thing she recalled seeing – though looking back on it, this now seemed so improbable, that most likely it had to be part of a dream – was an abandoned house, a grove of stubby palm trees, and, down at the edge of the road, a pair of African prostitutes seated on a sofa beneath a half-broken sun umbrella.

7

THE SAFE-HOUSE

1. Silvana

Two weeks later, when Pietro Scala drove her to La Camillina, Lotte stood in a field of long grass, looking up towards the house in the photograph, so that she could see what Ennio saw through the slit of his balaclava as he aimed the Mauser between the trunks of the twisted, ashy trees.

Only the windows were boarded up now, and the front door encased in sheets of corrugated metal whose curling edges rattled in the breeze. A yellow-eyed dog, chained to the trunk of a hazel tree, paced restlessly around the ruins of a brick oven.

It was an autumn day, and the air was filled with the smell of wood smoke. Down on the farm at the end of the track, Tommaso's daughter, Silvana, was making *passata* over an open fire in the courtyard. The jars of tomatoes stood lined up in a blackened, rusty oil drum which had been sliced in half lengthwise and filled with water so that the *passata* cooked in the boiling water, as though in a giant bain-marie. Every now and then Silvana would poke at the fire with a copper tube, rearranging with her bare hands the pennants of flaming, twig-tipped branches.

Lotte watched her from a step by the house. She felt disconnected from the scene, as though she had walked on to the set of a film or a play. In vain, she waited for the emotions, that tremendous explosion of grief and self-knowledge, which she had been preparing for all her life, to flood over her. I am still without a story, she thought, without a past . . . She felt so bitter about Ennio's death, more bitter than she did about any of the choices he had made in his life, that it cast a sullen shadow over everything. Thanks to Melody and her lies, she would never know the expression in her father's eyes, or how his voice had really sounded in conversation. She would never know what food he liked to eat, how he walked, whether he was a good listener – whether their sweat smelled the same. He was all that was 'other' about herself; his death was like the passing of the last inhabitant of some tiny forgotten village, who would take with him to his grave the secrets and memories of an entire community.

Somewhere she remembered reading that firstborn children tended to be of the same stock as their fathers – nature's way, supposedly, of turning men on to the idea of fatherhood. Ennio looked attractive in some of the newspaper photographs, with his sleek dark head, his thin face, and those heavy-lidded eyes which were identical in shape, at least, to her own. There was one picture of him, taken in a courtroom soon after his arrest, in which he was standing in a kind of gigantic metal cage, together with other members of his organisation. He was wearing a light-coloured polo-neck jumper: his face was unshaven, while his long hair reached almost to his shoulders. Like a pack of hunting dogs, the prisoners were chained individually to the bars of the cage, arms held out, wrists placed one on top of the other, with the handcuffs wrapped around them like slave bracelets. And yet, thought Lotte, more than criminals, they looked like a band left-wing intellectuals; most of them wouldn't have looked out of place selling the *Socialist Worker* on the corner of Golborne Road. A couple of the prisoners were actually smiling; a balding, older-looking man had his arms raised in a salute, while another, wearing a collarless shirt buttoned up to the neck and a pair of heavy, Onassis glasses, appeared to be engaged in animated conversation with someone just visible beyond the bars of the cage. In the midst of that group, Ennio stood apart; the loneliness radiating out of him almost palpable, so that the others appeared to be keeping their distance for fear of contagion. There was an expression of despair on his face, as though spread out before his eyes lay the full horror of what was happening – a horror which he alone could comprehend . . .

In the back of her mind she'd always had this fantasy about coming to Italy and having sex with a stranger in a train, and that stranger turning out to be her father. (Another reason she hadn't wanted David tagging along when she first visited Italy.) And while she didn't much mind relinquishing that particular fantasy (which invariably ended in tears once the truth came out), Lotte still felt bereft of everything else associated with it. For twenty years she hadn't been alone on this earth but instead connected to another human being – someone who had brought her into the world – who, probably, over the years had followed her progress from his prison cell, learnt everything there was to know about her, and yet had never expressed a desire to meet her. Put it how you liked (it was for her own good, how could you bring a child into a prison environment, what would her friends at school have said?), he had chosen not to know her. She could blame Melody – and Luciana, for that matter – all she liked, but the truth was that *he had chosen not to know her* . . .

Listening on her Walkman to the eerie interview tapes Pietro Scala had given her was like listening to one of those BBC archive recordings of famous people before the advent of television: the voice vulnerable, yet remote. At times, when Ennio was talking about his early involvement in Sinistra Armata, there was a sardonic, chilling edge to his voice which made it clear why he had never become a *pentito*; while at others, mostly when discussing his mother and his uncles in Sicily, he sounded affectionate, respectful even. During siesta-time, when the streets were empty, she would sit on a bench in the gardens outside Luciana's flat, following the transcripts of the tapes which Pietro Scala was editing for his book, trying to connect the printed words to the constantly mutating voice in her headphones. *I was born on 17 November 1957, at a Catholic maternity hospital for unmarried mothers . . .*

Chickens wandered around the courtyard, pecking at the stony ground, while sheets flapped on the line strung up between the trees to the side of the house. Lotte found Silvana's thick *abruzzese* dialect incomprehensible, and Pietro Scala made no effort to translate. Yet her face was kindly, and there were tears in her eyes when she brought them out coffee and aniseed cake on a tray. Lotte guessed she must only be in her late thirties, if she had been a young girl during the Lead Years, yet her face was as lined as an old woman's: her two front teeth were missing, and her auburn hair was striped down the centre with a skunk's white parting. By an outhouse wall covered in strings of garlic and giant red chillies, an old man in a flat cap and muffler sat propped up on a string chair in a square of sunshine, his gnarled purple hands crossed over the head of a walking stick. He was Silvana's father, Tommaso, the owner of the farm, and the person who had sold La Camillina to the founders of Sinistra Armata back in '78. When she and Pietro Scala arrived, Silvana introduced them, and Lotte had shaken the old man's hand: it felt cold and lifeless as marble, and just as heavy. *How my father's hand would have felt that day, if only I'd touched it . . .*

Looking into his face, she noticed one eye was milky with cataracts, while the other, ringed with folds of black skin, glared malevolently at her as though the entire force of his personality was distilled into that one organ. From time to time she would glance across the courtyard, and catch him staring at her as he leaned over his stick.

Pietro Scala was standing with his back to Lotte, talking to Silvana as she picked up the jars one by one with a pair of long, wooden-handled tongs and stood them to cool in a tray of sand. He was leaning against an olive tree, hands in his pockets, his feet in their English brogues crossed nonchalantly on the grass, like some parody of a country squire. He was like the gatekeeper to her father's memory, she thought, acting as though by virtue of all those hours they had spent together before Ennio's death working on his memoirs from Rebibbia Prison, he was the only person qualified to tell her anything about his life. Luciana couldn't stand him; she said he and his kind had got rich on the back of their family's suffering. And yet when it was discovered that he and Ennio belonged to the same rare blood group, Pietro Scala would visit the hospital three times a week to donate blood; and towards the end, it was he who lobbied the Ministry of Justice to allow Ennio to die at home.

She didn't much like Pietro Scala either, thought Lotte. He was a fat, bourgeois-looking man, with a greedy mouth. His yellowing teeth sloped inwards, like a wolf's fangs, and his breath smelt of nail-polish remover. She caught whiffs of it as they drove down from Rome in his battered Renault 4, stopping for a coffee at an Autogrill on the motorway. She noticed he took three spoons of sugar in his *cappuccino*, and he chose the stickiest, sweetest looking *cornetto* beneath the plastic dome on the counter. When they left, she didn't tell him at first about the trail of icing sugar down the lapel of his tweed jacket, until back in the car, the sight of it began to bother her so much that she blurted it out just as he was overtaking a goods lorry on a bend. But then he ignored her, and she had to put up with the secondary irritation of knowing he didn't care enough about her good opinion to dust himself down.

Like a hippopotamus in a swamp, the man wallowed in self-confidence. And yet no matter how overweight and unattractive he was – especially by the standards of the average overgroomed Italian male – he had the knack of making her feel badly dressed and unfeminine. The first time he came to Luciana's flat, to drop off the transcripts and the tapes, he took one look at her Camper bowling shoes and told her they were *sconcertanti* – unsettling. And when she asked him – defensively – what that was supposed to mean, he grinned his wolfish grin and told her to work it out for herself. Even the way he stood talking to Silvana with his hands in his pockets was arrogant, as though he wanted her to feel he had paid her a compliment that day by turning up at the farm and inter-rupting her work. Lotte knew he was only there for the sake of his book; there was nothing sentimental about his offer to take her to the place of her birth. And while Luciana – and Melody, too, before she left for London – had offered to accompany her to La Camillina, Lotte still felt too raw about recent events to risk having someone close to her witness her turmoil. Besides, her relationship with Melody was still far from healed, and she and Luciana were only just getting acquainted.

Just then, Pietro Scala came over to where she was sitting, and stood before her with his hands in his pockets, blocking the light with his bulk.

'Silvana says she'll take us over to look at the house once the old man's safely back indoors.'

'Why? Isn't he meant to know we're going up there?'

Pietro grinned slyly. 'Put it this way – Tommaso doesn't have the fondest memories of your father and his merry band of *compagni*. You can hardly blame him if you think of the trouble they landed him in.'

'Why, what happened to him?'

Pietro sat down awkwardly beside her, stretching out his fat thighs and crossing his ankles to make it look, she thought, as though he were in the habit of perching on tiny doorsteps.

'What happened to him? I'll tell you what happened to him . . . In 1978, he sold La Camillina to the founder members of

Sinistra Armata for the tidy sum – in those days at least – of sixteen million lire. Of course they didn't tell him they were a fledgling terrorist group; their story was that they were a cooperative of nature-loving schoolteachers looking for a base from which to go hiking in the surrounding countryside. Which sounded plausible enough – in the way that anything can sound plausible if you want it to. He even helped them with the olives and the vineyard, looking after the harvest when they were away. But then during the Mazzantini kidnapping the house got raided by *carabinieri*, and Tommaso ended up having to pay a hefty fine to the tax authorities for not declaring the sale of La Camillina to the Guardia di Finanzia. Of course no one in Italy ever declares anything to the taxman – that's not the point. The point is he was unlucky enough to sell his house to some of the most wanted men in Italy, whose mug-shots just happened to be plastered day and night all over the media.'

'So then he did know they were terrorists?'

'Your guess is as good as mine. The judge decided he must have known – if not at first, then at least towards the end. The fact that old Tommaso had been a Partisan during the war, and voted Communist in local elections, probably didn't help matters either, what with the judge being from an old *abruzzese* Fascist family. He got a suspended sentence and a fine for harbouring fugitives, which, along with the tax fine from the sale of the house, almost ruined him. Then, a few months later, his wife got sick, and Tommaso had to nurse her himself; he had no money left for doctor's fees, and his politics had made him so unpopular in the village that his neighbours more or less left him to it. Not long after, the wife died, and he and Silvana have been alone here ever since.'

Lotte looked across the courtyard: Silvana had picked her father up bodily out of the chair, as though he were a child, and the two of them, one of Tommaso's hands around her neck, the other still clutching the head of the cane, were shuffling towards the house. No words passed between them, not a single smile or gesture, as though for years, father and daughter had been locked in this cycle of weary dependency – as though, thought Lotte, Silvana were caring for an unlovely plant she couldn't bring herself to let wither. Stopping to part the curtain of plastic strips hanging over the doorway, she led him slowly inside the house.

Not long after, she reappeared with a canvas toolbag slung over her shoulder, a ring of keys on a chain in one hand, and in the other, a saucepan of leftover bones and pasta, which Lotte guessed must be for the dog. Lotte got up, spitefully enjoying Pietro Scala's discomfort as he struggled to manoeuvre his bulk off the step. She knew why she was being so petty: it was a way of compensating for the unforeseen emptiness she felt about visiting La Camillina. Silvana smiled at her shyly, patting the toolbar slung over her shoulder. 'The house is locked,' she said, – '*serrata*', hammering an imaginary nail into the air. '*Capisco l'italiano*,' replied Lotte, a little more sharply than she intended. '*Se parla piano, capisco tutto*,' making an effort to soften her tone. She was getting tired of being treated like a stupid foreigner; most Italians she came into contact with, Pietro Scala included, seemed to regard her Englishness as denoting a kind of slowness or, worse still, a cultural brutishness, dating back to the days of the Roman Empire. She had lost track of the number of Italians who had reminded her that the British were still living in huts during the architectural and engineering glory of Ancient Rome. *Yes, yes, yes – we Brits are brutes*, she thought, dully, although the irony of her new-found chippiness about being *English*, of all things, was not lost on her. She was obviously predisposed to being perennially chippy about something, she thought gloomily. The most recent example of this had been that very morning, during the car journey down to Abruzzo, when they stopped at the Autogrill service station and, tucking into his enormous *cornetto*, Pietro Scala asked her whether English people ate fish and chips for breakfast.

He had finally made it off the step now, and the three of them began walking across the courtyard, down a dirt track which led towards La Camillina. As she followed Silvana through a rusting metal gate, Lotte turned around one more time to look at the courtyard; at an upstairs window, she caught sight of the old man, partly concealed by the half-open shutters, watching them, wraith-like, as they crossed the fields towards the house.

'They'd take me dancing on Saturday nights,' said Silvana. 'We'd drive down to Pescara, five or six of us piled into an old Cinquecento, and go to a tourist discotheque near the port. On the way back we'd stop for bread at the all-night baker's; they'd sell it to you hot – so hot, it burnt your fingers – through a little hole in the bakehouse wall.' Silvana picked a stalk of grass and twisted it between her fingers. She was wearing a flowered overall, and a pair of white mules that looked as though they had been moulded from a single piece of rubber. Her feet were surprisingly soft-looking, as small and neat as the Asian women's back in London. On her wrist, she wore a blue and red plastic watch with 'Pasta Barilla' written on the dial. She must have got it with tokens, thought Lotte. Luciana kept hers in a wallet in the kitchen drawer. She was saving them to get an electric Parmesan grater.

'I knew they weren't teachers; right from the start I guessed they were involved in some funny business – even down here in Abruzzo we'd heard about the *Movimento*. Besides, they were forever turning up in term-time, or else arriving late at night and leaving first thing the next morning. But shall I tell you what? I didn't care. I didn't care what they were up to. All I knew is that thanks to them I got to live like a normal teenager for a while. I think they felt sorry for me, stuck up here on my own with my parents. Not that I fancied any of them, mind: they were too hairy and scruffy-looking for my tastes. My type was more clean cut – Umberto Tozzi, or that nice American actor, Robert Wagner – remember him? Your father was handsome, though, *era proprio un bell' uomo*, and he had lovely manners – real old-fashioned *meridionale* manners.'

'What about my mother? Did you ever get to meet her?'

Silvana paused, as Lotte stared ahead at the olive trees. Tears unexpectedly stung her eyes at Silvana's words . . . *he had lovely manners*. She couldn't explain to herself what it was that made her finally feel like crying: a voluptuous melting, the tears coursing like a balm through the parched ducts behind her face . . . It was because there'd never been a real person to mourn, she thought, just that pallid corpse in the neatly ironed tartan shirt and Clark's desert boots, lying with his arms folded on Luciana's bed. Or it could have been that Pietro Scala had gone on ahead, and was standing at the side of the house taking notes (all the while keeping a careful eye on the yellow-eyed dog chained to the oven), or perhaps it was the note of genuine affection in Silvana's voice. Then she realised what it was: she had never heard Ennio described in ordinary terms, as an ordinary person. In Luciana's eyes he would always be the son who, time and time again, had disappointed her (and yet whom she in her turn could never bring herself to forsake); to Pietro Scala he was a misunderstood revolutionary born ahead of his times; while everything Lotte subsequently read about him in the Italian press just seemed to reinforce the image she carried of him in her mind from that first photograph she saw back in David's flat: the iconic seventies urban guerrilla in his flared trousers and balaclava.

For a second, Silvana averted her eyes. Then abruptly she picked up the saucepan of leftovers and began calling to the dog in dialect: '*Rex! Rex! Vein' a chi a magná!*'

The dog lunged at its chain, causing Pietro Scala to leap surprisingly nimbly to one side. Sitting on the stump of an oak tree, Lotte watched as Silvana left the saucepan of food on the churned-up ground beside the dog. From where she sat, she had a direct view inside the oven; the walls were blackened with smoke, and right at the back she could just make out a pile of charred wood. She wondered whether Silvana still used the oven for making bread or pizza; or whether they, the *sappisti*, had found time for such homely pleasures in between their kidnappings and raids. It still gave her a jolt – she couldn't help it – to think her father had led such a violent life, in the same way that back in London, it had given her a frisson of terror when she heard on the news that Kilburn was an IRA stamping ground; or that even closer to home, an Al-Qaeda base had been set up in Beethoven Street, just around the corner from the flat where she grew up. And yet from things Pietro Scala had told her, her father and his *compagni* didn't sound like your average terrorists. After all – and she giggled silently, and inappropriately, to herself at the thought – you could hardly imagine the Real IRA rustling up loaves of soda bread in their spare time.

Silvana was walking back across the orchard now, picking her way between the piles of rotting fruit on the ground – a superabundance of apples, peaches, pears, figs, apricots, and a kind of hard orange plum they called *nespoli*. A sweet, heavy smell hung in the air, part wholesome, part vinegary, which seemed to settle on the very hairs inside her nostrils. On some fruits you could make out the clear outline of a beak, the lacy edges blackened as though they'd been charred. Birds were the ultimate consumers, thought Lotte: one bite, the rest discarded . . .

'Does no one pick all this?' she asked, as Silvana sat down beside her on the stump.

'What for? My father's not allowed fruit because of his diabetes, and why go to all the trouble of bottling it if it's only going to be me eating it? Besides,' she added bitterly, 'the less I come up here, the better it is all round.' For a moment her expression reminded Lotte of Tommaso's: a kind of defeated resentment that made her heart shrivel. Again she felt the tears bubble up behind her eyes, and a wave of self-pity washed over her. She should never have come here without Melody . . .

'I'm sorry,' she blurted out, '*scusami tanto per tutto.*' And yet a voice in her head, detached, maddening as a cartoon icon hovering on the edges of a computer screen, whispered: *You're like one of those self-hating English people – galumphing off to the Third World to apologise for colonialism.*

'It's not your fault,' said Silvana kindly, and she patted Lotte's leg. Her face grew sly, coquettish almost, and she twisted a lock of skunk-coloured hair behind her ears. Picking up the husk of an almond from the ground, she ran her finger along the velvety edges. Then, narrowing her eyes, she gazed up towards the house where Pietro Scala was standing with his back to them talking into a dictaphone. 'He's dead now, so I suppose there's no harm in telling. Only swear to me it stays between you and me. I don't want *lo giornalista* over there poking his nose into my business.' All traces of the *abruzzese* dialect had disappeared now: startled, Lotte thought: *She did it on purpose, back then, to disorient me . . .*

'I swear,' she said. '*Lo giuro.*' Again she was standing on the beam, gazing down at the swirling ground below.

'I had a crush on your father, *una cotta vera e propria.* Roberto was different from all the others –'

'Roberto?'

'Roberto Ferrero – that's what the *compagni* used to call him. No one in the organization used their real names, not even among themselves. You could have knocked me down with a feather when I heard on the *telegiornale* that his real name was Ennio Caruso. Mind you, to me he would always be Roberto – even when I wrote to him in jail, I used to address my letters to "*il mio caro Robbi*". Every week I wrote to him – I never missed a week – and for his birthday, I'd bake him a *pan di Spagna* cake to share amongst his cell-mates.'

'So you knew all along that they were terrorists?'

'You could say that . . .' Again her expression looked sly, and she placed one hand obstinately over her mouth as though to keep the words from leaking out between her fingers. But then she let it fall, palm upwards, to her lap, and her face sagged. 'I would have done anything for him – anything. I begged them to let me join the organization, but they didn't want to upset my father. It was only because he kept his mouth shut all those years that La Camillina never got discovered as a base.'

'So Tommaso knew too?'

Silvana tapped the side of her nose knowingly with a stubby finger. 'Why d'you think I was allowed to go dancing with them in the first place? If any local boy had dared turn up here to ask me out, my father would have greeted him with the barrel of a Lupara aimed right between the eyes.'

'I'm sorry, but I still don't get it. Why should he let you go out dancing with terrorists?'

Silvana sighed impatiently. 'He sympathised with them – *capito*? He was a Partisan during the war, and long after the Armistice, when the Germans were retreating – when most of them had already made it back home – he executed two German soldiers. At point-blank range. They were hiding in the barn of La Camillina: he shot them in the middle of the night as they lay sleeping in some bales of hay. Then he took their guns off them – a Luger and a Browning – and hid them for years down a disused well. He donated them to Sinistra Armata not long after they bought the house. So you see, *figlia mia*, you could say there's always been bloodshed at La Camillina.'

'But if he sympathised with the *sappisti*, why wouldn't he let you join?'

'There's an expression we have in Italian: '*Mogli e buoi dai paesi tuoi*'.

'Wives and . . .?'

'*Buoi*. Big cattle – with horns.' Silvana lowered her head and placed her knuckles on her forehead.

'Oxen. So, "Oxen and wives from your own villages". What's that supposed to mean?'

'It means, *cara mia*, that my father didn't want his daughter marrying or getting involved with strangers. Not that any local boy stood a chance either,' she muttered bitterly, as though to herself.

Lotte looked down at the grass. The soil around the roots of the tree was light brown, with a texture more like sand than earth. Then something red and shiny caught her eye: it looked like the corner of a sweet wrapper partially buried in the earth. She pulled at it and a strip of plastic began to emerge from the ground like a tapeworm. For a moment she thought it was a section of bunting, the kind used in fairs, until she made out the words '*VIETATO PAS*' in cracked, veined letters.

Silvana took it from her and smoothed it over her knee as though straightening out a length of ribbon. ' "*VIETATO PASSARE*", it says. The *carabinieri* sectioned off the house and the orchard, right down to the barn out the back, with metres of this tape while they waited for the forensic team to come down from Rome.' Pausing for a moment, she looked at her watch; then, getting up from the tree stump, she rolled up the strip of tape and slipped it into her overall pocket. 'If you've finished with your questions now, I've got work to do. I'll leave you the tools – you and Perry Mason over there can let yourselves into the house on your own.'

Something in Silvana's tone had hardened, Lotte thought. There was an undercurrent of hostility in her voice which again seemed to be directed against her personally. She feels guilty about something, Lotte thought, and she's defying me to find out what. Her heart beat faster, and once again she was a ten-year-old child, sitting in her dungarees and hated Greek sandals at a wrought-iron table outside the Lisboa Café, looking for the one question to ask Catherine Smart which would tell her everything she needed to know about her mother.

'Silvana,' she said. 'Please. One last question before you go.'

'There's no need,' Silvana replied, *'non c'è bisogno – ti racconto tutto io,'* and she sat back down wearily on the log. The skin around her nostrils had turned pale, yellow almost, while the rest of her face was a mass of ashy wrinkles. Her body swayed forward, and she gripped on to the edge of the trunk with both hands to steady herself. For a moment Lotte thought she was about to pass out, and her mouth turned dry with fear. For one hideous moment she actually saw her lying sprawled in the long grass, her flowery overall riding up her legs so you could see the network of capillaries along the inside of her thigh. Then Silvana composed herself, sucking in deep gulps of air through her missing front teeth, like the wind rattling through a windowless house, and slowly she began to speak. Her voice sounded flat, disengaged almost, as though she were giving evidence in court. Either that, Lotte thought, or else she's already gone over this a million times in her head. 'I knew for months before it happened that they were pre-paring La Camillina for a kidnapping: one night I saw them bring up rolls of fibreglass and these big sheets of plasterboard to the house. My father was waiting for them at the end of the track; he helped them unload the materials, then a couple of hours later I heard them leaving again. The next day, when my father was in Pescara, I went up to La Camillina and had a good nose around upstairs.'

'How did you get in? Didn't they leave the house locked when they were away?'

'They did, but they always left a key hidden in that wood oven over there. That's how my father used to let himself in when he was building the prison.'

'You mean Tommaso built the hostage's cell?' Startled, Lotte looked over towards the house where Pietro Scala was still talking into his dictaphone. *If only you knew the half of what I know*, she thought pettishly. That would teach him to be so precious about his special relationship with Ennio.

There was silence, as though Silvana's story had run its course, as though she'd said all she was going to say, and she began to roll up the strip of bunting into a tight tube. Lotte remembered how as a little girl she used to roll up her bus tickets like that until they were so stiff you could hardly bend them. *She's still not coming out with it*, thought Lotte, *whatever it was that nearly made her faint back then* – until from nowhere, it seemed, came the sound of her voice: 'What about my mother, Silvana, did you ever meet her?'

Even before Silvana had a chance to answer, Lotte knew she'd hit the nail on the head. She could actually sense a change in the quality of air, as though the light, the landscape itself, were mutating; as though everything around her had been thrown into dazzling and cruel focus.

'I saw your mother twice in all. The first time was one day towards the end of September. Roberto – Ennio – drives up in this white Fiat 127 which belonged to another *sappista* they used to call Massimo. I nearly died when I saw him; Roberto hadn't showed his face at La Camillina for weeks, it could have been months, even, and I was beginning to think he'd left the organisation for good. It was the first time, too, he'd been here on his own. Only it turns out he wasn't on his own: a girl gets out of the car wearing one of those Indian dresses made of that flimsy cotton you can see right through. She was dark, with long, straight hair which came down almost to her waist; I could see she was slim, and very pretty, even from where I sat.'

'Where were you sitting to get such a good view?' asked Lotte curiously – anything to blank out from her mind the image of that dress: the same dress, stained now with Julia's blood and hers, which was lying folded, along with the newspaper clippings from Ennio's trial, at the bottom of

Melody's trunk which she brought down from the attic the night before they left for Rome.

'I was on the roof of the smaller outhouse round the back where the rows of chillies are drying; you get a view from there across the orchard, right up to the house. So the two of them disappear together into the kitchen, and after a while, I see the shutters of the upstairs bedroom closing. At this point, I get down from the roof – no need to guess what they're doing up there; the state of the sheets, when I went up later, said it all – and then, after about an hour I hear a car driving along the track which leads off the main road. Roberto must have been expecting whoever it was, because he comes out of the house and, barefoot, he walks up the track to meet him. Upstairs, the shutters are still closed, and there's no sign of the girl. So, I wait for him round the side of the barn, and when I hear the car engine starting up again, I go to meet him by the gate.'

'Was he surprised to see you?'

'Not particularly. I was always lurking around the house when I knew Roberto was there. In fact some of the *compagni* nicknamed me "*la piattola*" – you know, those insects that stick to you and suck your blood? But I knew I didn't have long; at some point she'd be waking up, and I wanted him to read my note before she came down.'

'What note?'

'A note I wrote him – one of many notes I wrote him – since the last time he was at La Camillina.'

'What did it say?' Again, anything not to have to think of her mother lying asleep, satiated, in that shuttered room . . .

Silvana's face twisted with a grimace of pain. 'It doesn't matter now what the note said. To Roberto, I was just the *contadino's* daughter they took dancing on Saturday nights: he probably never even read it. One thing I do remember, though, is that I wrote out all the lyrics of that Umberto Tozzi song, "*Ti Amo*". You know the one: "*Ti amo / Io solo ti amo . . .*"'

Her voice, as she sang, sounded quavering and old-fashioned, virginal almost. But at once her face grew sombre, and her voice returned to the earlier monotone of the courtroom deposition. 'So I handed the envelope over to Roberto, then I watched him walk back through the orchard to the house. When I looked up, I saw your mother had woken up; she'd opened the shutters and was standing by the window, naked. I don't know whether she saw me or not, but she stood there for a long time before going back into the bedroom.'

'What about the second time you saw her?' Never once did Lotte imagine it would hurt like that, her mythically beautiful mother suddenly coming to life before her eyes like the statue of Hermione in *The Winter's Tale* – loved, and in love – the image inevitably coarsened by the raw, animal suffering in Silvana's voice. She could have told her to stop – she almost did – but her story, the telling of it, had a momentum now all of its own. Besides, if she could bear to hear it all in one go, she would never have to see Silvana again. There was something unbearably sad, too, at the thought of this prematurely aged woman with the missing front teeth and the unexpectedly delicate feet, standing as a young girl at the gate, watching her father walking away from her, back to his lover, with the unread note in his hand. *Because if you concentrate on her, you don't have to suffer for your mother . . .*

'By rights I should have been in Ascoli Piceno. The week before they kidnapped Mazzantini, my father sent me there to stay with my aunt and uncle. I knew why he wanted me out of the way – or rather, I guessed – but there was nothing I could do about it. He must have been really desperate to ask such a favour from my aunt; they'd fallen out years back, something to do with my grandfather's will, and even though she was my father's only sister, I'd only met her once or twice in my whole life. Funnily enough, it was my mother, God rest her soul, who kept up ties with her – in secret, of course. She was an orphan herself, and all her life she'd dreamed about having a big family. I remember he sent me loaded down with gifts; two pheasants, some oil, and a whole round of *pecorino*. Only he could have saved himself the bother; the morning after I arrived, one of my cousins suddenly comes down with bacterial meningitis, and my aunt packs me back home on the first train to Pescara. My father wanted me to stay in Ascoli, and catch the meningitis I suppose, but my aunt, bless her, was having none of it. She knew how selfish my father could be, and she wasn't having it.'

'So was my mother – Julia – already at La Camillina when you got back?'

'Not at first. For two or three days the house was as silent as a graveyard. So much so, that I started to think it was uninhabited. I was given strict instructions to keep right away, though once or twice I caught a glimpse of a *compagno* I'd never seen before standing guard at the window. I knew my father was going up there at nights, I used to watch him from my bedroom window, and me and my mother reckoned he was stocking them up with provisions from the larder: bottles of *passata* and tins mostly.'

'Did you know they had a hostage in there?'

'Not for definite, although by this time Mazzantini's kidnapping was all over the news. Though I still didn't make the connection between what I saw on the TV and any funny business down at La Camillina. I should have, if I'd been looking, but that was the whole point – I wasn't looking. Mazzantini was a local man, see, a magistrate from L'Aquila, though to start off with, the *carabinieri* weren't searching for him around here, as they'd picked him up somewhere in Lazio. He came from a family of *ricconi*, that's why they chose him; the *compagni* asked for a ransom of one and a half billion lire, but it was never paid. Then, on about the third or fourth day after my return from Ascoli, I'm sitting out in the yard shelling peas, it's late afternoon, six o'clock, maybe, when out of the corner of my eye I see this figure moving between the two outhouses. I didn't see her face, but I knew straight away it was the same girl.'

'How could you be so sure if you didn't see her face?'

'The dress. She was wearing the same see-through Indian dress as she was that day back in September.'

'Did you follow her?'

'I didn't dare. Remember, I was forbidden from going anywhere near La Camillina. Besides, they weren't playing cowboys and Indians up there; they were armed to the teeth. If she wanted to risk it, that was her business.'

'So then what happened?'

'For the rest of that afternoon, nothing. Everything as normal, at least what counts as normal in our family. Then that evening, we're sitting down to dinner watching the *caroselli* on the TV, me, my father and my mother –'

'What are the *caroselli*?'

'*Caroselli*? They're the programme of adverts they used to show on RAI after the evening news bulletin. Anyway, right in the middle of the transmission we hear this terrible wailing noise like an animal is being tortured. There used to be wolves in the forests around here, and sometimes you'd hear them tearing their prey apart. For a while, no one says anything, then my father gets up, and without a word he leaves the room. Me and my mother look at each other, but we say nothing; we both know where he's gone. While he's away, the noise stops for a while, then it starts again, only louder, and even more blood-curdling, if that's possible. By this time I think both of us realized it wasn't an animal making those sounds; it had to be a human being, most likely a woman.'

'Did you guess it was her? My mother?'

'Not at first. At first I thought it had something to do with the hostage, though in my heart of hearts I knew they hadn't taken a woman. I suppose that's when I finally admitted to myself that I knew they were holding Mazzantini up there. And then the more I thought about it, the more I realised the person making that noise had to be her, the girl I'd seen by the outhouse.'

'What did you think they were doing to her, Silvana? For her to be making all that noise?' *And why didn't you call the police, bitch?*

'To be honest, I thought they were punishing her for coming up here. I suppose I didn't even want to start imagining what could make her howl like that. I'm sorry, but I didn't. Then, after about an hour, my father comes back with a face like thunder. He gets a bottle of *grappa* out of the sideboard in the hall, sits down at the kitchen table, and starts downing shot after shot in one gulp. Me and my mother are careful not to get in his way; when he drinks, he gets violent – that's how I lost these two teeth.' She ran the tip of her tongue experimentally up and down the gap as though she were still not used to it, as though it had only just happened. 'So we're clearing up around him – she's washing, I'm drying, none of us daring to say a word – and all the while, the screaming is getting louder, when out of the blue, he goes: "I told them to shoot the bitch. Put her and her pup out of their misery. Before she brings the *carabinieri* up here with all her caterwauling."'

'That's what he said?'

'The very words, *le parole testuali* – cross my heart and hope to die. Now I knew for a fact they didn't have a dog up there – if they did, wouldn't we be the ones looking after it? – so it had to be a person he was talking about. A woman. And then it all made sense: my hunch was right – it was her, the girl in the Indian dress.'

'So what did you do next?' *While my mother lay there bleeding to death?*

'Nothing. I went to bed, and tried to block out the screams. I hardly slept a wink, and when I got up the next morning, she was carrying on like the day before, only worse, even. It went on like that, all through the next day, right up until that evening.'

'Didn't you feel you should do something?' *Ignorant peasant woman.* 'Call a doctor at least?'

'Of course I did. But I was scared. You have to understand that the moment anyone came up here, anyone in authority, they'd realise we were involved up to our teeth. It was as simple as that: even calling a doctor meant handing my father over to the law.'

So you chose, instead, to let my mother die?

Lotte gazed out towards the house. Pietro Scala had finished talking into his dictaphone; and, with a surprising show of delicacy, was sitting on a concrete block, waiting for them to finish. A long shadow lay across the ground, falling over the yellow-eyed dog as it lay beside him, at peace now, head lolling between its outstretched paws. For a moment she had an impulse to run to him, bury her face in the lapel of his tweed jacket, so as not to hear another word.

'That evening I rang the *pronto soccorso* in Pescara. And the *carabinieri*. It was Ennio who told me to. All of a sudden he shows up in the yard; he was dressed in a suit, I remember, one of those khaki suits they used to call *sahariane*, but it was all crumpled up as though he'd slept in it that night. He was white as a sheet. My father was away – he was filling up our gas bottles down at the village petrol pump – so Ennio must have heard the truck leaving down the road and decided to chance it.'

'And what did he want?'

'He says that his girlfriend's up at the house, her name's Giulia, and that she's lying on the kitchen floor in labour. The baby's stuck, she's got to get to a hospital – he thinks she'll need a Caesarian. He tried to get her to come away with him, but she was too poorly to walk. The other *compagno* won't call a doctor for her, he's scared, and he won't set the hostage free, either. Ennio reckons it's the only way now, the only way out for all of them, but he won't see sense. He says we have to tell the *carabinieri* first before calling the *pronto soccorso* – any doctor going up there unarmed is risking his life.'

'So you did call them? In the end?'

'I did . . . in the end. Though by that time, they were already on their way: they were conducting house-to-house searches in the area, and La Camillina was next on the list. I telephoned your grandmother in Rome, too. Ennio – Roberto – gave me the number before he left. He asked me to make sure Signora Luciana came down at once, and that whatever happened she was to look after the girl and her baby. He left me an envelope full of money, and a sheet of paper declaring he was the father of the child, together with your mother's name, address and date of birth. Apparently she'd turned up without any documents on her.'

'But he didn't hang around to see what happened?'

'There was no point, *figlia mia*, there was no point. He was a wanted man; by that stage they were even showing photographs of him on the news. An informer told the police everything – the only bit they didn't know was the location of the base. You can't blame him for trying to get away. Although, as it turned out, he didn't go far – when all the shooting started, somehow he appeared again from nowhere, and covered his *compagno*'s back as he made his getaway. A police photographer got a shot of him in a balaclava, standing in this very field . . . After that, he disappeared again, and stayed on the run for another three weeks. If he managed to make it out of Italy, to France maybe, or Switzerland, there was a slim chance he could start afresh with the girl and the baby, under a new identity, perhaps. But it wasn't to be – because of me, because I didn't act sooner, it wasn't to be. She died; and I'll have to live with that for the rest of my life . . .'

Lotte sat in silence, staring ahead at the boarded-up windows of the house. They must have threatened her, she thought, tried everything to make her keep quiet. She pictured her mother walking across the courtyard that late afternoon, flitting like a hunted animal between the outhouse walls. *There used to be wolves round here . . . sometimes you'd hear them tearing their prey apart* . . . her mother had walked through the village, past the staring eyes of the villagers, up the hill to the house. Somehow, nine months pregnant (the pathologist's report said she was born full-term), she'd made it to Pescara, desperate to find Ennio, hoping against hope he'd take care of her now – a part of the story left undaubed by the violent stain of Silvana's words. Lotte hugged her knees to her chest: it was all she could think about now, a last image to cling to: that journey from Rome – anything to blank out from her mind, like the boarded windows of the house, her mother's hours of agony on the kitchen floor . . . *I can't go there – I can't – at least not yet* . . . Perhaps, she thought, a stranger had taken pity on her as she stood on the *autostrada* in her Indian dress, driven her to Pescara in the front seat of his car . . .

2. 'Piero'

'I took her as far as Chieti,' said Piero. 'Then I gave her five thousand lire, enough for the journey home, and left her at the bus station in the main square.'

'Why couldn't you take her all the way to Pescara?'

Piero reached inside the pocket of his bomber jacket and took out a soft pack of 'Nazionali'. Jerking it upwards, he pulled out a long, half-smoked butt, and lit it with a gold Ronson lighter. As he inhaled, he held the cigarette between his thumb and forefinger, concealing it inside the palm of his hand as though he'd spent a lifetime smoking in places where it was forbidden.

'I couldn't, could I? Already I'd risked enough by coming as far as Chieti. For all I knew the place could have been swarming with *carabinieri*.'

Piero took a last drag of his cigarette, then ground it into the remains of his pizza. On the table beside them, a pair of

German tourists with rucksacks ordered the *Pasto Completo* advertised on the blackboard outside: pasta or pizza, fruit, coffee and a glass of wine for 15,000 lire – £5 in English money. At the bar, two Somali girls sat drinking bottles of Coke with the restaurant owner; one of them was quite pretty, with a high ponytail and red lipstick, while her friend was dumpy, watchful-looking, with bad skin. In a corner, an old *barbone* wrapped in a grimy skiing jacket dozed and muttered over his empty carafe of wine.

The area around Stazione Termini was teeming with small *trattorie* like 'Lo Spuntino', although this was the first time Lotte had set foot inside one. Luciana warned her over and over again to stay away from the station – 'full of drug addicts and pimps and *extracomunitari*'. When Pietro Scala telephoned to say that someone who knew Lotte's father wanted to speak to her, she was horrified to learn where the rendezvous was to take place. 'Tell him to come here, to Piazza Bologna, if he's got anything to say to you,' she muttered, but via Pietro Scala, the man refused: the meeting was to be at Lo Spuntino, or not at all – and she was to come alone.

At first, Lotte was surprised when Piero introduced himself. She hadn't expected anyone quite so – so . . . low-life, she supposed. He was a tiny man, with coarse dyed hair, dressed in tight-fitting white jeans and a leather bomber-jacket, a red jersey shirt open to the chest. Around his neck he wore a coral horn pendant hanging from a chain, while an effeminate chain-bracelet dangled from his wrist. His hands were square and grimy with tiny, bitten nails; on some fingers only the cuticle remained, embedded like a splinter in the inflamed skin around the tip. Like Ennio, he had a homemade tattoo on his left wrist: a yin and yang in a circle. Luciana said they used to carve those tattoos with a penknife and a bottle of ink; sometimes the wound would get infected, and there'd been cases of blood-poisonings – amputations even.

'Did you know for sure my father would be at La Camillina?'

'No, of course I didn't know. I hadn't seen any of that lot for months before the kidnapping.'

'Had you left Sinistra Armata by then?' As she spoke, Lotte felt herself blush; there she was, shamelessly interviewing him like she was an authority on the armed struggle, when only weeks previously she'd never even heard of Aldo Moro.

Piero glanced furtively around the restaurant, motioning for her to lower her voice. 'Look, *cocca*,' he said impatiently, 'let's get one thing straight: I never was a member of any armed organisation – *chiaro*? I've never been tried for terrorism, and if I've spent any time inside, well, that's water under the bridge, now – *acqua passata*.' Angrily, he straightened the collar of his bomber jacket, yanking down the sleeves in a gesture reminiscent of Latino gang-fights in films, as though literally shrugging off the insult.

'*Perdonami*,' said Lotte, 'I shouldn't have asked.' Was there no limit, she thought, to the number of times she would have to apologise for asking about the past? Although this time, in truth, she should have known better; according to Pietro Scala, 'Piero' (apparently his real name was Mariano Salice) was a small-time crook from a long line of small-time crooks whose second home was Rebibbia Prison. No biographer of the armed struggle had ever succeeded in interviewing him, even though he was reputed to have been one of the first members of the Rome cell of Sinistra Armata.

Pietro Scala told her that not long after Ennio's death, he had begun receiving a series of confusing messages on his voicemail at the newspaper. 'A friend' had some information for him, which he might find interesting – providing he could pay. The calls invariably arrived in the early hours of the morning, when Pietro Scala was never to be found at the newspaper. Then the phone-calls stopped, and a number of scribbled notes in misspelt capitals began to arrive on his desk:

'YOU PAY, I'LL TALK' was one of them, while another simply said: '*IL CANARINO FISCHIA*' 'The canary whistles'. Finally, one evening, 'Piero' stood waiting for him outside the office in Piazza San Silvestro. Pietro Scala recognised him at once – unlike Lotte, he *was* expecting him to be a low-life character – and took him for a coffee at Bar Alemagna in Via del Corso. They talked about the early days of the *Movimento*, and at the end of the meeting, he slipped him two 100,000-lire bills in a napkin. After about the third encounter, none of which yielded anything Pietro Scala didn't already know, 'Piero' demanded to see Lotte – alone.

'How did my mother find you that day?' she asked, hoping to be on safer ground here.

'She didn't find me – I found her. I ran into her not so far from where we're sitting, near the market at Piazza Vittorio. I hadn't seen her for a long time: in the early days, Ennio used to bring her to our meeting place in Piazza della Chiesa Nuova. The *compagni* used to call her "*la signorina inglese*". I remember Ennio thought she was a real *bonacciona*, as they say in Rome, though she was too flat-chested for my tastes: no offence, but I always preferred blonde girls myself – Scandanavian, if you're asking. In my opinion, if you're going to have a dark girl, you might as well go for a proper *mora italiana*.' For a second, an impish grin crossed his features, erasing the deep furrows etched into his face, and making him look at least twenty years younger. His skin was grimy, dotted with open pores into which the dirt appeared to have settled like inkspots, and there was something lean and hungry about his appearance which, together with the re-cycled cigarettes and the *caffè lungo* he ordered after the pizzas – 'it lasts longer, that way' – made Lotte think he was down on his luck.

'What was she doing in Piazza Vittorio?'

'Nothing, so far as I could tell. She'd come out without her money or papers or anything, and she was just wandering the streets. In those days they had the *orario spezzato*, like any decent Christian country still does, and all the shops had the blinds down for lunch. I remember she was wearing these tatty old *espadrillias*, with the rope sole all coming undone, and her hair looked like she hadn't brushed it for weeks. She was so far gone that I thought she was going to dump the baby right there and then in the middle of the square.'

Lotte felt her heart quicken; she hadn't counted on her mother being in such a state when she left Rome. *And you think he's down on his luck . . .* She stared down at the remains of Piero's lunch, the cigarette twisted into the gnawed crust of his pizza, and a wave of nausea overtook her. The *trattoria* smelled of cooking and unwashed napkins, as though the walls with their mock-hessian wallpaper, the plastic red-checked tablecloths, the leatherette *banquettes*, all exuded the same ancient greasy breath. She looked outside at the sunlit street; across the road, there was a clothes shop with a banner saying. '*SALDI*' over the door. Brightly coloured summer dresses hung on a rail on the pavement: *I wouldn't mind trying one of those on*, she thought guiltily . . .

'What did she say when she saw you?'

Piero shifted on his seat and reached inside his jacket for his cigarettes; this time he pulled out a fresh one, tapping it on the table first before lighting it with his gold lighter. As he spoke, he furrowed his brow and lowered his head, deliberately slurring his words, as though the act of first lighting, then smoking, the cigarette were more important than answering her question.

'She throws her arms around my neck, like I'm her long-lost uncle from America, and all the while she's going on about how she'd been out walking the streets since early in the morning, and that she'd lit a candle to the Madonna in every church she passed, and now her prayers had been answered. She's hanging on to my sleeve and begging me to take her to Ennio. She says if I don't take her to him she'll lie down in the square and have her baby right there. I try and tell her I don't know where he is, but she's carrying on so loud now that people are starting to stare. So I bring her over to some gardens and sit her down on a bench –'

'Did you know? Where Ennio was, I mean.'

Piero looked up from his cigarette. '*Cristo buono*, I told you, didn't I? I hadn't seen any of them for months. How was I supposed to know where Ennio was hiding?' He flicked an imaginary speck of ash from his jacket, as though recalling the previous slur on his integrity.

Again Lotte thought: he's lying, and he wants me to find out why. Perhaps just as with Silvana, rage had made her psychic . . .

'But you knew about the kidnapping. About Mazzantini?'

Piero looked at her with slit eyes, the kind of eyes you saw on photographs of Romanian street children, children high on glue sniffed in sewers beneath the city pavements – bright, flat eyes which have seen so much they no longer look capable of expressing any identifiable human emotion.

'Maybe I knew . . . maybe I didn't.'

'But all the same you still agreed to take her to Pescara? To Chieti, I mean.'

'I felt sorry for her, didn't I? Is it a crime now to feel sorry for someone? Besides, Ennio had the terrorist squad on his back –'

'Because of an informer? Because someone grassed on him?'

Piero was silent, and Lotte knew she had found her mark. For a moment, she almost pitied him as he sat slumped against the banquette, chin against his chest, scrubby black hair barely reaching the head-rest, cracking his knuckles one by one as though to splinter the bones.

'Was Ennio your friend? I mean in the early days?'

He looked up. 'I never told them. Not in the beginning. They had me in for robbery. Me and my brother did one of those big villas on the Via Cassia, and we got caught by a security guard on the way out. The police knew us – they knew all our family – and they knew I'd been involved with the *Movimento*. They even had pictures of me with Ennio and the other *compagni* in that piazza where we used to meet up before I became a *clandestino*; then they found my prints on a stolen car used for a bank raid up in Liguria. You have no idea what the *digos* was doing those days to get information; they kept me naked in a cell with a light shining in my face twenty-four hours a day; every time I fell asleep, they woke me up with a rubber truncheon across the balls. Then they started with an electric probe . . . I told them then – I defy anyone not to talk with two thousand volts up their arse – some names, not all of them, and I never said about the farmhouse . . . I signed a confession, without even reading what they'd written: after that they let me go.'

'So you gave my mother a lift? All the way to Pescara, because you felt sorry for her?'

'Not Pescara,' he murmured, 'Chieti. I took her as far as Chieti, to the main square in Chieti. I gave her 5,000 lire for the bus home . . .'

3. The Prisoner

(Extract from an article by Pietro Scala published in *La Nazione*, 23 June 2001, entitled 'Twenty Years On: A Hostage Remembers'.)

Dr Mazzantini, how much do you recall about the actual moment you were kidnapped?

I remember everything, down to the last detail. It might sound strange, but the whole thing turned out to be a life-changing experience for me. I'd been going through a bad patch both in my personal and professional life, and being taken hostage 'jump-started' my energies, gave me back the will, if you like, to overcome my difficulties. They got me in the early afternoon on a country road near one of our warehouses. Some men in green overalls – I thought they were from ENEL, the electricity company – flagged down my BMW on a bend. They'd set up cones about half a kilometre ahead, and even rigged up one of those temporary traffic lights you get during roadworks when the traffic narrows down to one lane. I pulled into a layby, rolled down the window, and that second, one of them pointed a gun at my head. They opened my door, pulled me out and threw me on to the back seat of my car. Then they tied some kind of rough wool scarf over my eyes, and put a pair of handcuffs on to my wrists. Someone else covered me with a blanket and held me down with the weight of his body, sitting on me practically, for the rest of the journey.

How long do you think the journey lasted?

Between half an hour and forty minutes, including a change of vehicle about halfway through.

Who did you think your captors were?

I couldn't make up my mind whether they were the Mafia or a terrorist organisation like the Red Brigade. At that stage I hadn't heard about Sinistra Armata, or any of the other smaller splinter groups.

When did you realise they weren't the Mafia?

I don't think I ever knew for sure, or rather, not until my release. But, strange as it might sound, what made me almost certain I was being held by terrorists was the noise of slippers flapping up and down the stone floor outside my cell. Let me explain: once we got to our destination, they took away my watch and wallet and threw me into this tiny room, two metres long by one and a half metres wide. There was a compressed foam pad on the ground, the kind used for camping, with a filthy cotton blanket folded up on it. In one corner was a bucket for waste. I sat there trembling, until one of them came in and took off my handcuffs; they were too small, and they left raised welts on both wrists. Then the one who brought me in came back with a torch, some paper and a biro, and the draft of a letter they wanted me to copy: a ransom demand for a billion and a half lire. He had a Roman accent, and beneath his balaclava I could see he had dark hair. He was quite olive-skinned, too, and he had one of those ink tattoos on his left wrist. Later I found out he was the one they called Roberto, though of course we now know that wasn't his real name. Then another one, more well-built with longer hair, and dirty, disgusting toenails, came in with some food: water, a carton of UHT milk and some *grissini*. Nothing cooked. And yet I kept hearing the noise of those slippers flip-flapping outside the cell: it had to be a woman, one of the captors. Only much later on, once it was all over, did I discover that the English girl – that poor suffering creature who died – had nothing at all to do with them. But at the time I didn't know that, and I was thinking how I'd read that women in the Mafia were used as cooks during kidnappings, and yet here I was getting only cold food. 'Are you members of a terrorist organisation?' I asked the one with long hair. He told me to fuck off, and ordered me to write the note by the time he returned – if I didn't, I'd have nothing else to eat or drink, and he said they'd put the cuffs and the blindfold back on.

And did you write it?

I did, but I asked to pen another one at the same time, to the Financial Director of the family firm. I said that without his cooperation, my family wouldn't know how to begin trying to raise such a large sum of money. With all due modesty, I'm still exceedingly proud of what I wrote. Basically, it was a series of questions, to which he knew the answer was always 'No': a coded message, a way of saying: 'Don't pay'.

What happened after that?

They left me alone for a good while after that. The cell had no window, and I had no idea whether it was day or night. I must have dropped off for a while, I was exhausted, and sleep was a way of blanking out what was happening to me. Then I woke up with a start to the sound of a woman screaming. Immediately, someone switched on the radio outside the cell – hoping to cover up the noise the woman was making, I suppose – and for the next few hours, on top of the cries, I was forced to listen to a series of back-to-back sermons from Radio Vaticano.

Did it work?

On the contrary, the noise only seemed to intensify. And the harder I listened, the more convinced I became that the screams had nothing to do with a hostage. If it had been a hostage, they would have gagged her long before. Besides, something about the way she was shouting, not the words themselves – I couldn't hear those – but the pitch and the regularity of her cries sounded familiar. My wife had recently given birth to our second daughter at home – it all happened so fast we never made it to the hospital – and I remembered you could have set your watch by the frequency of the contractions. This woman's screams followed a similar pattern: a burst of animal-like howling, then several minutes of silence.

Did you ask your captors what the noise was?

I couldn't – there was no one to ask. Someone was asleep outside the door, I could hear them snoring, but no matter how loud I shouted, he wouldn't wake up. I began to lose all hope then; I couldn't hear any sounds of helicopters or vehicles either, which made me think that the police weren't looking for me in the area. Later, in fact, one of the *carabinieri* told me that at midnight they'd ordered the search to be shifted into the Lazio region, nearer to the spot where I'd been taken.

So how do you think they found you?

A combination of bad luck and bad organisation – on the terrorists' part, needless to say. First, they made the incredibly foolish mistake of abandoning my BMW in a dried-up river-bed on the outskirts of Pescara, where it was discovered by a sharp-eyed refuse collector. It was a new car, undamaged, and therefore unlikely to have been dumped by the owner. Second, another *sappista* had the misfortune to crash his Fiat 132 not far from a *carabinieri* barracks in Silvi Marina. He had nothing to do with the kidnapping: unbeknown to the executive, he was on a secret visit to his girlfriend who lived in the nearby holiday resort of Pineto. So they take him to the station, fingerprint him, and lo and behold he turns out to be on a list of suspected terrorists. Well, those two facts are enough to convince the *digos* to redirect their operations back into Abruzzo, and they begin house-to-house searches in all the surrounding countryside.

What happened when they reached La Camillina?

Two days after the kidnapping, a patrol of *carabinieri* drive up to the house in the late afternoon; of course, I had no idea what time it was – or, for that matter, how long I'd been held hostage, as being a prisoner in that cell was akin to what I imagine lying in a flotation tank must be like: you lose all sense of ordinary time, though I suppose at least you're not paying for the privilege.

Were they expecting to find you there?

Not in the beginning. That's why they only sent two men. At that stage, it was only a routine search, part of a wider operation covering that area. Then, as soon as they get here, one of them, Tenente Adolfo Zuffada, gets a message over his radio saying they've received a call from a woman claiming a hostage was being held at La Camillina, and to bring a doctor and an ambulance. In those days, they didn't have the sophisticated tracking equipment they have now, so it was never discovered where the call originated from.

Out of interest, how did you get to be so well informed about the internal workings of the anti-terrorist squad?

Tenente Zuffada and I have become good friends; we usually meet up once a year on the anniversary of the kidnapping.

When did you first become aware of the raid?

At one point the guard outside the cell wakes up, and comes in with another carton of milk and a loaf of stale bread. I can tell by the state of his toenails that it's the aggressive guard, the one who told me earlier to write the letter. The other one, the one with the tattoo and the Roman accent, seems to have disappeared. I ask him whether the woman having the baby is part of their group, or whether she's a hostage like me, and again he tells me to fuck off. He goes out, and after a while the snoring starts again; in the meantime, the woman's cries seem to be getting closer together; she's in such distress that she's almost lost her voice: later I found out, *pace all'anima sua*, that she'd been in labour for almost forty-eight hours before haemorrhaging to death. How my jailer could sleep through that, and Radio Vaticano, remains a mystery. Then, in the distance, I hear the sound of tyres on a dirt track; afterwards, the *digos* told me it was the local *contadino*, Tommaso, on his way down to the village. For a moment, though, my hopes had soared, until it became obvious that the vehicle was driving away from the house, not towards it. But soon after, I heard another car; and this time it seemed to be getting nearer. Amazingly, the guard outside didn't seem to have heard. I held my breath, hardly daring to make a sound.

How many people did you think were in the house at this point?

I wasn't sure, but obviously I was hoping that the guard outside was on his own. Later, I found out the one with the Roman accent had left – to get help for the girl, perhaps – but then he appears to have had a change of heart and returned to the house. But this was much later on; when the first patrol arrived, the sleeping guard was effectively the only one present.

What happened then? Did the police knock?

They knocked, and I heard a man's voice ask if anyone was there. From within the house, I heard the guard wake up and start cursing to himself in the most unimaginably salty language.

What about the girl?

Strange you should mention her, because at some point – probably between the *contadino*'s truck leaving and the arrival of the *digos* – the cries had stopped. And yet I couldn't hear the sound of any baby. Then when the raid began, even though my senses were so completely attuned to what was happening outside, I was oppressed by this feeling of dread about the girl. Later, I found out she'd managed to deliver the child herself, a truly heroic feat under any circumstances, and to wrap it in her dress before she passed away. Tenente Zuffada told me the little creature was lying there quiet as a mouse on the stone floor, still attached to the cord.

What happened after they knocked?

Still no one answers, then one of the *carabinieri* calls out, '*Ingegner* Marelli! Is anyone there?'

Who was Ingegner *Marelli?*

No one, just a made-up name they had on the bell outside. Finally, my jailer goes to an upstairs window and says, 'Yes, what is it?' The *carabiniere* asks him to step outside, at which point he must have retreated back into the house, and for a minute at least there's silence. Later I found out it was the time it took him to stuff his pockets full of hand grenades. Then I hear the sound of kicking on the front door, and finally, in an aggrieved tone of voice, my jailer says something like: 'All right, come on in if you must.' There's the sound of footsteps down the stairs, the front door opens, and the most almighty bang as he chucks the grenade right into the *carabiniere*'s face. His name was Tenente Gallinari; he lost an arm and his left eye in the attack. Taking advantage of the confusion as the *carabiniere* lay there on the ground screaming in pain, my jailer makes a run for it, throwing another hand grenade in the direction of the parked vehicle where the police reinforcements are hiding. This one hits another *carabiniere*, Tenente Schiavone, who tragically loses his life. The *sappista* manages to get to his own car, his back covered by the Roman one who in the meantime has reappeared, aiming his Mauser towards the *carabinieri*. After that, all hell breaks loose. The police began spraying tear-gas into the house, and I thought I was going to suffocate. I was yelling and yelling, and they're yelling back at me to come out and show my face, only of course I couldn't, because I was still locked in the cell.

What happened when they found you?

Two *carabinieri* burst in, and I swear I thought they were going to kill me: they were that maddened by the carnage outside, and the loss of one of their men. They threw me against the wall in readiness probably to beat the living daylights out of me, until at that moment one of them says: 'Wait a moment – stop – it's Dr Mazzantini!'

Was the one who threw the grenades ever apprehended?

The identity of that *sappista*, the one who got away, was never discovered, although Tenente Zuffada says he's fairly sure he knows who he was. Apparently, these days he's making quite a good living from the university lecture circuit.

Do you think your captors merely saw you as an enemy of the people, a source of ready money to further their cause?

I'm not sure I buy into the *autofinanziamento* story. After all, there were plenty of richer, less well-known figures they could have picked on. But because the name Mazzantini was bound to finish up in the newspapers, they chose me – with the primary aim, I believe, of destabilising the electorate in the week before we were due to go to the polls. Though if you ask me who was pulling the strings . . . well, that's another story. Sometimes, though, I think Italians prefer to blame the entire phenomenon of the Lead Years on the Russians or the Americans, or the Mossad or Colonel Ghadaffi – anything to avoid confronting the deep-rooted *malaise* in their own society. Besides, at the end of the day, what's so shocking about a class war? In many ways, things were clearer then: at least you had ideals, young people prepared to die for a cause. Whereas now it's just Berlusconi, the Mafia, cocaine . . .

4. Tenente Zuffada, Adolfo

(From a preliminary statement taken at L'Aquila Barracks, shortly after the end of the siege at La Camillina.)

'. . . arriving at the farmhouse at approximately 19:00 hours. On first sight, the dwelling appeared to be inhabited: a white Fiat 127 was parked diagonally across the yard, and the two dustbins standing by a brick oven were full to overflowing. Tenente Gallinari parked our vehicle at the side of an orchard which ran down to the dirt track; and, as prearranged, he walked the hundred or so metres to the front door. La Camillina was the last farmhouse to be searched that day, and it was his turn to go to the door – it may sound childish, but taking turns was our way of making our shift go faster. As he rang the bell, I remained behind to note down the number plate of the parked car: Roma 615 8LP. Then I remember reaching in the glove compartment for my sunglasses – it was a bright evening, and the light was bothering my eyes – while in the background I could hear my colleague knocking at the door. With increasing vigour, he was calling out: 'Is anyone there? *Ingegner* Marelli, is anyone there?' (*Ingegner* Marelli being the name on the bell). At this point a face appeared at an upstairs window: a dark, long-haired man in his late twenties. My colleague asks him to step outside and present his papers, at which point the man retreats once again behind the shutters.

It is during this interval that I receive a signal over our radio, but up in the hills the reception is so poor that at first I am unable to comprehend the controller's message. In the time it takes for his words to become audible, I hear the sound of tyres behind me and see two of our unmarked cars from the anti-terrorist division approaching at full speed along the track. At once, the reason for their arrival becomes evident, and I shout to Tenente Gallinari to duck down, but it is too late. The door of the house opens, and I see a male figure on the threshold rip something with his teeth and throw it directly at my colleague . . . After that I am unable to piece together events in their logical sequence . . . forgive me, it was too much . . . Valerio was lying on the ground with his arm turned to mush, blood was pouring out of the wound in his eye . . . it could have been me – it could so easily have been me . . . Then he throws another grenade towards the second of our cars. This time it's fatal, and I can hear shouting and crying from my colleagues. The terrorists both got away on foot, we didn't manage to catch either of them . . . another one had appeared from nowhere, covering his friend's back until he made it to the getaway car parked at the rear of the house. I was part of the group that entered the house at approximately 19:40 hours, once the smoke from the tear-gas had subsided enough to make this possible. Even so, we could hardly breathe; we had to tie wet rags over our faces. Two men were assigned to the upstairs, while myself and a colleague from Rome were told to search the downstairs area. We walked through a kind of porch, used for storing firewood, and into the kitchen which was situated at the front of the house. On first entering the room, my immediate thought was that we'd found the hostage . . . the stone floor was covered in blood, pools and pools of it, running right down to the sink by the window, and there were streaks of blood all over the walls and furniture. It looked like the scene of a massacre, like something from a Dario Argento film where a psychopath goes on the rampage

. . . Then, behind the table, I see a body lying on the floor, completely naked except for a pair of rope sandals: it was the English girl, the girlfriend of one of the terrorists . . . though we didn't know that then: we only found out later, when his mother came to identify the corpse. But at the time I was still convinced we were looking at a murder victim: she had a bundle of rags between her legs as though she'd tried to staunch a wound, yet no matter how obvious it must seem now, I still didn't make the connection with childbirth – I suppose because a baby was the last thing I was expecting to find in that inferno. I thought she'd been stabbed, or shot in the stomach, see: the cord was dangling down, all twisted and grey, still attached to her body . . . like it was the entrails spilling out from a knife-wound. It was only when I bent down to look that I saw a baby lying there wrapped in her dress: the face had been wiped clean, and the skin was all rosy and bright like a doll, or like the images of the *Bambin' Gesù* you see in holy pictures: as though the mother had found the strength to cradle it and nurture it in her arms before she passed away. She was such a pretty girl too, with long dark hair which came all the way down to her waist. The little one was staring at me with these big calm eyes, like it had seen everything . . . I'll never forget those eyes, God help me . . . I'll never forget them for as long as I live . . .'

5. The Scent of Lemons

They filled the cell with their perfume, six lemons in a brown paper bag.

She brought them from her village in Sicily, a journey of nine hours including a ferry crossing and two changes of train. This time she arrived for her monthly visit in slippers, with feet so swollen they no longer fitted into her shoes, her fake wedding ring hanging on a chain around her neck. The lemons were from his uncle's citrus trees which were situated in a communal plot of land at the edge of the village. As a boy, he would help his uncle pick the fruit, standing on a tall ladder which was propped against the tree, a wicker basket hanging like a satchel from his back. A box was always sent to the Leonforte family up at the big house. And at the end of every summer, his mother would bring a bag of those lemons back to the flat in Rome; they would sit in a bowl on the kitchen table overlooking the dingy courtyard. Then, as now, their scent filled him with melancholy and longing.

It was evening, his favourite time of day, and the corridor was filled with the sounds of quiet activity. From some cells you could hear the chink of metal pots as the inmates heated up cans of Siementhal beef and jars of ready-made *sugo* over camping stoves. Down the other end, Panzieri was working on his memoirs which were being serialised in a right-wing paper; to speed him up, the editor had sent him an electric Olivetti typewriter which bleeped just before it reached the end of every line. The televisions were off, and if you listened hard, you could hear the sound of rain pattering on the floodlit courtyard outside. It was autumn, and outside, beyond the high prison wall – a wall so high you couldn't see where it ended, and the sky began – there lay an imaginary landscape of cities, forests, lakes, where the trees bent in the October wind, shedding their leaves in drifts.

In the cell opposite, Diego Esposito, a young Neapolitan, was listening to a cassette of Renzo Arbore's folk songs with the volume turned down. Barechested in a pair of dark-blue nylon tracksuit bottoms, he was kneeling on the floor, hunched over a jigsaw puzzle which was spread out on his bed; through the bars, Ennio saw him hold a piece up to the light, then scratch his head and yawn, clasping his armpits and shuddering until the yawn had subsided. Esposito had infected him with the jigsaw bug now; along with the lemons, Luciana brought him a 5,000 piece Ravensburger puzzle of a marine landscape. She said it reminded her of the *National Geographic* magazines he used to pore over when he was a boy.

The box, still wrapped in its cellophane covering, stood unopened on his table. He would open it that evening, after lights out: if he was lucky, making a start on the edges of the puzzle would help lull him into sleep. All he had left was half a Tavor tablet, and he was saving that for a really bad night. Propped up against the jigsaw box, beside the television set with its shatterproof screen, was a photograph of a young girl: his daughter, Lotte, aged ten. In the picture, she was sitting at a table outside a pavement café: you could just make out the name of it written in joined up red letters on the window behind her: 'Café Lisboa', it was called. She was looking downwards, her features partially hidden by a tomboyish fringe; yet her face, and even the way she sat, shoulders hunched forwards, one leg crossed over the other, was familiar. Heartbreakingly, miraculously familiar. Somewhere, Luciana had found a photograph of him at that age, taken at a spring pageant during his last year at Santa Chiara: if you held them together, they looked like two pictures of the same child. Both photos had only just arrived, together with a letter from Luciana and 50,000 lire, in yesterday's post – coinciding, annoyingly, with her monthly visit, so that for the next few weeks at least there'd be nothing to look forward to. Unless you counted Silvana's weekly love-letter, which, to be honest, a part of him still did look forward to . . . For hours, he'd pored over each tiny detail in the picture – the drill *salopettes* she was wearing, the leather sandals with the criss-cross laces (had his daughter been to Greece, perhaps, for a holiday?), the anonymous faces glimpsed through the window of the café. There was one figure, visible only from the back, in a queue by the counter, but which, based on Luciana's descriptions (together with a hazy recollection he had of another photograph on a shelf in Julia's room), he was almost certain had to be Melody, Lotte's grandmother. A scene, a life he would never be part of; a country he would never visit, a daughter he would never meet . . . If you believed in biology (a belief which, for him at least, never quite withstood the memory of his father, or his 'protector' as he liked to be called, sitting on the foam sofa in the Rome flat, thighs splayed in anticipation beneath his distended stomach) it meant that a part of him was living because of him – *in spite* of him, even – like a plant transported to a distant colony, or like the *piante grasse* which every summer Luciana used to bring up from her brother's garden in Sicily, the roots wrapped in layers of sodden newspaper. Unless Melody had told her, his daughter would know nothing about him or his life – not this miserable excuse for a life, lived behind bars, but of the boy who every summer would travel alone on the train to Naples, face pressed hungrily against the window (in the days before trains, and stations, became nightmare landscapes for him), with 5,000 lire sewn into the pocket of his khaki shorts and a tin of sandwiches on the seat beside him. If he ever had to define a moment when he had been most himself – if someone said to him: find something of your character, your passions, you would like your daughter to have inherited – he would have to go back to the boy of those summers in Sicily. Forget all the rest – the terrorist, the lover, the son, the accumulated failures of his adult life . . . As for his years in prison, they had simply extinguished all remaining traces of that boyhood self.

Right from the start, he'd sought to put a distance between himself and his *compagni* from Sinistra Armata, refusing to contribute to their endless ideological discussions, their bitter wrangling with the executive on the outside. As far as he was concerned, the dream was over: in an effort to survive, to embrace the crushing monotony of his existence, he'd let go of any individuality or drive, becoming seedy, sour, spinsterish even (the offputting tidiness of his cell, the jigsaw puzzles, the laundry, with its concrete troughs, where he washed his clothes, the cup of Lipton tea he drank in the mornings), adapting to the limitations of prison life like a foot adapting to an ill-fitting shoe.

He'd only seen his daughter once, just before Melody took her back to England, not long after his arrest, when he was still being held in those barracks in the *quartiere* Trieste. His cell measured no more than eighty centimetres across by one metre-fifty long: almost the exact dimensions of the box where Mazzantini was kept hostage. One night, his lawyer, Edoardo Casimirri, brought his daughter to him, wrapped in a white woollen blanket: Luciana was still a virtual prisoner in her flat, not daring to venture out for fear of the neighbours. Beneath the harsh neon lights the baby slept on, her thin eyelids, veined with red, fluttering as she dreamt. On her wrist she wore a tiny gold identity bracelet, but there was no name engraved on the tag. He took her in his arms, aware of the hostile curiosity of the guards who watched him behind the reinforced glass window – the same guards who, in another example of grim symmetry, concealed their faces with their jackets each time they entered the cell. He felt like a fake, a prisoner of cliché: the jailbird father meeting his newborn daughter for the first time. On the floor beside Casimirri's chair stood a thermos of formula milk, together with a sterilised bottle and teat, which Luciana had prepared in case the baby woke. But thankfully she slept on, sparing him the gaze of those eyes . . .

He was in a bar in Pescara when he learnt of Julia's death.

For two nights he'd slept rough – one night in an abandoned farmhouse in the hills around La Camillina, the other on a park bench in Silvi Marina – then on the third evening he made his way to a destitutes' hostel in Pescara, run by the Catholic charity, Caritas. There, he cleaned himself up, and using the money he'd managed to stuff into his pocket before his escape, he bought himself a dark blue Fruit of the Loom T-shirt and a pair of Rifle jeans from a *jeanseria* in a side-street behind the main square. Back at the hostel, he bundled his *sahariana* suit

215

into a plastic bag and threw it into the incinerator behind the canteen kitchens.

The bar, down by the port, was empty, aside from a couple of Polish backpackers and an African street trader with the inevitable black holdall at his feet. Ennio ordered a coffee and a *pizzetta* from the glass cabinet near the till and stood by the counter to wait. Later, as the months, then the years passed behind bars, moving from one high-security prison to another, often in the dead of night with scarcely enough warning to bundle his few possessions together into a bag, he would try to recall how he could have felt so lighthearted, so focused – hopeful, even – in those first few days. In part, he felt relieved of a burden, that primarily emotional link to Sinistra Armata: whatever happened, of one thing he was certain: his days as a terrorist were over. This was the main reason why he did not join his *compagno* in the getaway car parked behind the house; and why, until then, he had not contacted the number of a safe-house in Ostia. If he could just make it through the next few weeks, lying low down in Sicily, perhaps, with his uncles – long enough, at any rate, for Julia to recover from the birth and return to England – there was a chance he could join her and the baby there later.

At the height of her agony, as he squatted behind her and held her in his arms, massaging her breasts and back with the olive oil from last year's harvest, as it mingled with the milk ('Not milk, colostrum,' she panted) leaking out in rivulets from her nipples, he felt overwhelmed by tenderness at her courage. Never in his life had he felt such compassion for another human being. Ever since he was a boy, his mother used to call him heartless: *sei senza cuore*, she would say, shaking her head in sorrow when he refused to attend the Contessa's funeral, or weep tears at the news of his father's death, or when he laughed at her concern about the neighbours, to the point where he began to believe she was right: he was heartless. That most basic of human qualities, the capacity to identify with the suffering of others, was lacking in him, or else had been stunted since birth. How else could he have carried out all those atrocities – the raids, the beatings, his abandonment of Julia – without feeling any pity? But now, it was as though, without warning, that coldness and reserve had melted, flinging him abruptly into line with the rest of humanity. Dazed and humbled, he felt her pain as his own – not physically, but mentally, as though in some way he had become the foetus on its journey towards birth. Between contractions, the hostage all but forgotten now, they paced up and down the flagstones of the kitchen floor, planning the life they would have in London with their child. He would go to college to learn English while she finished her degree course via correspondence. Then, once his English was good enough, he could study to be a marine biologist, and they would settle in Canada or Australia, putting a distance between them and the armed struggle.

At first, he tried to reason with Tommaso and the *compagno* from Trieste, the one they called Raffaele. If they would just leave them alone, let Julia deliver the child in peace, he would find a way to get them out of the house before the hostage's release. He felt like someone who had just woken from a long dream: all vestiges of his *sappista* mindset – the discipline, the blind adherence to rules – had disappeared. Or perhaps he had merely exchanged one dream, one delirium, for another. *Let Julia deliver the child*, he said, as though he were superman, or an obstetrician, entirely *au fait* with those medical terms; just as over the years, big words, like *hostage, gun, raid*, had slipped into his everyday *sappista* vocabulary. Taking the cheat's route to family life, skipping all the planning and mutual support leading up to the birth, he felt like a fully fledged husband and father now, ready at last to assume his responsibilities towards Julia and their child. He felt like standing at the window and shouting out to the fields: *Adesso sono un uomo! Sono un vero uomo di famiglia!*

So much for the myth . . . At the end of the day, the truth was altogether more simple – more sordid: once again he'd abandoned Julia, cut free of the ties that should have bound him to her for the rest of their lives. Whatever the circumstances, he'd chosen to hide behind the irrefutable drama of events (*You're dead meat if you stay* . . .) to avoid seeing their story through to its conclusion. No matter that this time it was Julia herself who told him to leave – '*Go, my love, don't let them find you here*' – what kind of man was it who could bring himself to obey her? Who could have left her there, the mother of his unborn child, crouched naked and shivering on the kitchen floor, the bones of her haunches sticking out like those of a skinny dog? He was a *ramollito*, a soft man, and like all *ramolliti*, at the end of the day he didn't know his own mind.

As the barman heated up his *pizzetta* under the grill, Ennio picked up a copy of the Abruzzo edition of *Il Messaggero* from the counter. He shut his eyes, remembering that moonlit night as he wheeled his uncle's heavy bicycle down the path towards the fields, freefalling slowly to the edge of the world. Now, just as then, his rational self was staring at defeat in the face; and yet still he felt no fear . . . Opening his eyes, he looked squarely at the front page; the headline was: '*Sparatoria al Casolare in Abruzzo*', and there, directly beneath it, was a photograph of him in a balaclava and his *sahariana* suit – the same suit his mother had paid for with such a hopeful heart that spring afternoon in L'Uomo Elegante and which at that very moment was burning away in a canteen incinerator. His first thought, shamed by the shambling amateurishness of his pose, the spread thighs, two hands clutched around the Mauser, was: you second-rate bastard. You corny, second-rate bastard. He actually felt himself blush in the same way he blushed that afternoon in the flat in Via del Monte Oppio as he laid his gun on the bedside table before taking Julia into his arms.

'*Ecco a lei*,' murmured the barman as he placed the *pizzetta* on the counter beside him. Ennio looked up, wondering surreally if anything about his appearance connected him to that shaming photograph. He imagined saying to the barman: 'Go on – I'll give you three guesses who that piss-artist in the picture is –'

'What a business,' murmured the man, wiping down the counter with a greying rag. 'What a sorry business . . .' He had an enormous balding head and the kind of damp, *mozzarella*-like complexion you often found in workers in the catering trade. Sucking in the air between his teeth, he placed a cup of *espresso* on the counter, rattling it self-consciously on to its saucer, as though hoping to strike up a conversation. 'Though it's the young girl I feel most sorry for, getting mixed up with those delinquents . . .'

Silvana, he thought, *they've probably gone and arrested poor little Silvana* . . . 'What girl is that then?' Ennio asked casually, flipping the lid of the oval stainless-steel sugar bowl back on to its hinges. A ball of crystallised coffee nestled like a fly amidst the snowy grains. Filling up the long-handled spoon to the brim, he tipped it slowly into his cup, watching the sugar settle, then dissolve, into the gleaming light-brown foam.

Having engaged his interest now, the barman feigned to be busy at the sink, repaying him for his earlier uncommunicativeness by making him wait before answering his question. *That bastard, Tommaso, should never have let her get involved*, thought Ennio, remembering with a pang the squat figure waiting for him by the gate that afternoon with her love-letter. 'There's a picture of her somewhere on another page,' said the man, wiping his hands on the dishcloth which was tucked into the waistband of his apron. Leaning over the counter, he picked up the newspaper, licking his finger with showy efficiency as he turned the pages. He had a plaster all down the side of one hand, the edges brilliant with *mercur-*

iocromio. He must have cut himself, thought Ennio, *or else burnt it on that coffee machine . . .*

'There, that's the one,' said the man, jabbing triumphantly at a photograph towards the bottom of the page. Ennio craned his neck to look, his coffee forgotten beside him on the counter. He saw the shoes first, those tatty rope sandals poking out at right-angles beneath the blanket, and his first thought – a thought willed into being by the sheer, crushing enormity of his despair – was: Why did Silvana borrow her shoes? Why did she borrow those tatty rope sandals? Like a marvellously inventive machine, his brain continued to work at high speed, formulating a series of increasingly illogical questions: What was Silvana doing lying on the kitchen floor of La Camillina? With Julia's rope sandals on her feet? And the blood – where did all that blood come from?

'No one knows who she is yet,' said the man, folding his arms across his chest. Ennio stared at him, feeling the colour drain away to the edges of his face. His bowels twisted, wrung dry like a towel in a mangle, while his heartbeat reverberated through his body as though someone were striking the inside of his breastbone with a hammer: *boom, boom, boom*. Then he thought: *The blanket, they only covered her up to keep her warm . . .*

'She was dead by the time the *digos* and the paramedics forced their way in . . . a haemorrhage, they reckon, though it says here the baby survived.' Ennio heard the chink of coins as the barman dropped a tip from the counter into a glass bowl beside the till. The man was nothing but a *iettatore*, a bearer of evil tidings . . . what could that *mozzarella*-face know about anything, stuck here in this shitty bar? His hands were shaking, but Ennio forced himself to take a sip of his coffee, feeling the sweetness of it restore the blood to his face. She was dead now, and there was no reason for him to keep running. He might just as well turn himself in on the spot . . . give pasty-cheeks here the chance to be a hero. Like a character in a science-fiction movie, he could feel himself physically ageing, the sap draining from his body, leaving him with the face and posture of an old man. He actually brushed his fingers against his cheek, expecting to touch wrinkles, though puzzlingly, his skin felt clammy and smooth. He paid up leaving his *pizzetta* uneaten on the counter, and walked out on to the sunlit pavement.

Down by the port, he found an SIP telephone exchange filled with tourists and *extracomunitari* calling home. It was a long, dark room, with peeling walls, and tiny barred windows set high up near the ceiling. A single neon tube flickered noisily above the clerk's desk while a ceiling fan barely stirred up the soupy air which smelled of breath and old coins. He queued up for tokens behind a group of Chinese sailors, letting an old Moroccan woman in ahead of him, then a couple of East Africans in white robes: he was in no hurry to make his call. Finally, he took his place in an empty booth and for a while he stood there, listening to the babble of voices – Arabic, Chinese, French – floating through the smoke-filled air. The walls were covered in graffiti, numbers mostly, with impossibly long codes, scratched into the plaster and on to the plywood walls of the booth. Slowly, he took out a folded piece of graph paper from his pocket and dialled a number in Ostia. Identifying himself with a few mumbled words, he listened in silence to the voice on the other end, and made a note of an address on the other side of the paper. Beside the name of the street he drew a house, with four windows and a plume of smoke curling upwards into the sky. Long after the call was over, he stood in the cabin with the receiver still at his ear, listening to the voices around him swelling and rising to a raucous crescendo, as though striving to be heard in those far-off lands. He could have stayed there for hours, weeping silently in the dark booth, and still found more tears to cry, but after a while, the clerk got up from his desk and rapped indignantly on the window with his pen.

Back on the street, a wave of nausea overcame him, and he heard himself grunting out loud as he waited to cross the road by some lights.

His arrest, almost three weeks later, came as a relief.

6. 'Raffaele'

(Fragment of an internal report to the executive, discovered beneath a loose floor tile in a base near Genoa, along with a draft of the ransom note, a second-class train ticket to Milan, and two copies of the comic-book, *Mandrake*.)

'. . . as well as showing a total disregard for the basic rules of our Organisation. From this moment onwards, Roberto acted entirely autonomously, thus endangering our lives as well as the success of the operation. From the outset, he refused to send the girl away while she was still able to walk; and when her condition became such that she was no longer able to walk, he absented himself from the base in order to get help for her. Thanks to my constant vigilance, I espied the arrival of the first patrol car from the window of the upstairs room, and was in time to gather important documents and weapons before they knocked at the door. As I stuffed grenades into my pocket, I became aware that more cars were arriving, and that our situation was now desperate. I opened the door and threw the first grenade at the *carabiniere* standing on the threshold. In spite of aiming from such close range the result was only partially satisfactory, in that the Fascist *porco* only lost an arm and an eye. The others scattered, amid much shouting and wailing; and taking advantage of their confusion, I shouted to Roberto to run to the cars which were parked to the rear of the house. Again, he refused to cooperate with my orders; and in order to buy time, I threw another grenade towards the patrol cars. Fortunately, this second grenade was a bull's-eye, eliminating one of their men and injuring two others. I then ran alone towards our vehicles; and after ascertaining that Roberto was indeed not coming, I started the engine and drove along the country roads towards Pescara. Abandoning the car in a layby on the outskirts of the city, I made my way to the station; and there, as instructed, I caught the first train to Rome . . .

7. The Indian Dress

He knelt beside her and wiped her forehead.

The cloth of her dress felt cool and fresh on her face: she could feel the water prickling through her pores as her skin drank the moisture up. She shut her eyes, imagining each drop, magnified, evaporating in a bright little halo of spray.

'*Coraggio, amore mio*,' he whispered, 'the doctor will be here soon.'

He kissed her and touched her wet hair, just as he had done that first afternoon at La Camillina. She smiled at him, remembering the smell of coffee as she'd entered the dark kitchen, and the brilliant evening sky visible through the half-open shutters. He smiled back, but sadly, with tears in his eyes, as though he too was remembering, and he took her hands into his. For a moment, neither of them moved, frozen like ghosts in the past – a past which in itself was merely t' recollection of a different past, so that even then sh always been haunted by memories of other pl emotions, as though they had never really ma mandeer the present for themselves . . . T again, first on her face, then on her bre from the floor. As he walked tow an envelope from the table and s of his jacket.

She heard the front door slam and .

receding along the dirt-track. The room felt empty without him and the silence of the house unnerved her. *Go, my love . . . don't let them find you here . . .* If she listened hard, she could just about make out the hum of the radio from an upstairs room punctuated by the grisly sawing noise of the *compagno*'s snores. She felt alone and frightened with Ennio gone, frightened for herself, and for him, but mostly for their child. Not only had she lost the one presence that kept her on this side of delirium – just, only just – but also the hands which were to have received their child: the same hands which time and time again would pull her back from the precipice by the power of their touch. Frowning with concentration, he would pour oil from the demi-john into his hands and rub it over her breasts and shoulders, down her back to the base of her spine, the pads of his fingers like divining rods, drawing strength from the dark spaces between her bones . . . Then, from nowhere, it seemed, the pain would come calling – crashing down on her, sucking her into a kind of demonic tunnel, where she would thrash around inside the centre of it, until with a word or gesture he would hold out a hand and she would find herself back on the kitchen floor, her arms clasped around his neck, his lips on her forehead . . . *Go, my love . . . don't let them find you here . . .*

She felt thirsty, and the sweat had dried on to her face like a salt-water mask. Turning over on to one side, she grasped the edges of the kitchen table and slowly pulled herself up to her feet. The contractions were shorter, sharper now, more bearable. Slipping on her rope sandals, she picked up her Indian dress which was rolled up on a chair: her lucky dress, her lucky Indian dress . . . Lovingly, she held it against her brow, remembering the delicious fizzing sensation earlier as Ennio d her brow, the moisture penetrating the pores of her ow it merely felt clammy and damp. She laid the dress the table, smoothing out the wrinkles as though she k in her room in Via del Monte Oppio, hanging it out to dry at night after washing it in the basin with the yellow block of *sapone di Marsiglia* she kept in a drawer. The material was so thin that usually it would be dry by morning; if not, she would wear it all the same, shivering slightly as she slipped it over her head.

Ennio was right: she should have returned to London – any fool could have told her that. Even Walter wanted her out of the room by the end of the month; one night he slid a note under her door, saying he wasn't running a hostel for unmarried mothers, that her presence in the flat would attract the wrong sort of tenant. The memory of that letter, the mean, cramped handwriting, brought tears to her eyes; that same afternoon, she'd walked halfway to the travel agent's in Piazza Barberini to book her flight home. But she'd returned empty-handed; she knew her only chance of finding Ennio – or of Ennio finding her – was by staying in Rome. By continuing to frequent the places where he'd always found her: the English faculty (even though, months before, she'd handed in her notice at the university), the balding lawn outside the flats. Every day she wore her Indian dress, remembering his smile of pleasure when he came to collect her in the borrowed Fiat 127, the jewel-like shadows cast on to the bedroom wall at La Camillina as the sun burned through the flimsy material. She'd been wearing the dress the day Piero found her in the market at Piazza Vittorio; it had led her to Ennio, as she always knew it would . . . Naked, she straightened up and, leaning against the table, looked out of the kitchen window towards the orchard. She had to concentrate her mind, she thought, find some cave in her memory to shelter from the next contraction . . . *I never stopped loving you*, she thought, and the words – the steadfastness of her feelings – made her smile through her tears . . . That was where she would shelter, she thought, deep within the folds of their love, like Thumbelina nestled inside the waxy yellow tulip on the cover of her

Ladybird book . . . a dazzling, brilliant love which had burst into bloom after that first kiss outside the church of Santa Maria in Trastevere –

Then, without warning, she felt a massive churning sensation inside her belly, as though she was about to void her bowels. She slumped over the table, panting; then, placing one hand between her legs, she felt the membranes bulging out like a balloon. The urge to push was irresistible; and yet somehow, instinctively, she knew it was too soon. Sweating and mumbling, she slid down to her knees and laid her head on the floor, grasping the legs of the table until the desire to push subsided. But it was unbearable now; and rearing up once more on her knees, she held the baby's head in her hand, feeling the face turn towards her, the glistening caul stretched over its features like a mask. Instinctively, she stuck her fingers through the membrane, hooking it up on to her nails until it ruptured, and in a gush of clear liquid, the baby slithered out between her legs. She held it face downwards over her knees, peeling off the last flaps of the caul from its shoulders, then turned it over to face her. It lay in her hands, still and blue, eyes open wide: a girl. In silence, Julia stared at her face, the round little thighs, marvelling at the unexpected beauty of the cord: pulsating still, veined with silver and gold, like a burnished steel rope . . . The liquid was still pouring out of her body, but it was bright red now, collecting in a widening pool beneath her legs. Still the baby hadn't cried, as though both were grasping at the same feeble thread of life – a restless wind whistling through the room, hovering above them both, uncertain upon whom to settle – as though it could only be one of them . . . Reaching for the dress, she wrapped her daughter in its folds; then, holding on to the wall, she slid carefully on to the wet floor, the baby nestling between her legs.

She closed her eyes; and the sound of cries pierced the room.

8. La Camillina

'Who's *Ingegner* Marelli?' asked Lotte.

Condensation had formed beneath the transparent, plastic bell-tag, and the edges of the letters had bled from black to orange. Pietro Scala paused, and glanced at the name on the buzzer. 'No one', he said briefly, prising off the last wooden board from the doorway with the claw-hammer from Silvana's cloth tool-bag. 'It's just a made-up name, one the *compagni* must have chosen.' For a moment, out of delicacy, perhaps, or fear, neither of them moved; then Lotte reached out and pushed the door. It swung back surprisingly easily on its hinges, and she found herself staring into a dark lobby. A mound of logs, dusty with cobwebs, was piled into a corner, while a row of demi-johns in yellow mesh holders was lined up along the wall. A coil of hosepipe hung from a hook behind the door.

From the threshold, Lotte watched Pietro Scala walk through the passageway and into the kitchen beyond. Her Camper bowling shoes appeared to be screwed down to the linoleum, while her stomach felt as though a gigantic cat's cradle were stretched out inside it, pinning her guts to her ribcage. For a moment she considered turning her back on the house and waiting for him down in the orchard. What material difference, after everything Silvana had just told her, could it make whether she saw the inside of the house or not?

'You've come this far: no point pulling back now,' said Pietro Scala, not unkindly, from the doorway. He held out a pudgy hand and, mortified at her own passiveness, Lotte took it. He led her into the kitchen, and drew out a chair for her from beneath the table. She sank down on to it, thankful not to have to test her strength any further.

The room was dark and cool, and a light breeze, edged with woodsmoke, blew in from the open door. The shutters were barred, inside and out; but when Pietro Scala lifted the catch, the boards on the outside clattered to the ground, as though they had merely been propped up on the window frames. All at once, the evening sun flooded the room, and Lotte averted her eyes from the view outside, concentrating on a small area of flagstones between the table and the window. The last sketch in her mother's notebook – now in a brown envelope at the bottom of her bag – must have been drawn from this window, framed by those very same shutters: if she weren't such a coward, she would take it out and compare the two scenes. But there was something disorienting, nullifying even, about finding herself part of this pre-existing landscape, a landscape which twenty years before had been so significant to her mother that she'd felt the need to sketch it in all that cloying, unrealistic detail – as though, thought Lotte, twenty years too late, she'd stumbled into someone else's idyll, the theme-park of her own birth . . . What was the Italian word for ostrich? *Struzzo* . . . that's what she was: *la ragazza struzzo* . . . She could hear the sounds of cupboards opening and shutting, and a sudden gush of running water from the sink.

'You wouldn't think this house has been uninhabited for twenty years.'

'Why not?'

'Well, for a start, take a look here.'

Reluctantly, she raised her head and turned towards where he stood. A broom stood propped up by the sink and beside that, a plastic bucket with a cloth spread out over the top. 'She must come up here on a regular basis – look, the floor cloth's still damp.'

Lotte got up from her chair and walked over towards the sink; the tap and surrounding tiles gleamed as though they'd been recently polished, and a faint smell of bleach lingered in the air. On the yellowing marble worktop stood a tray covered by a tea-towel; on it was a small *caffettiera*, a tin of Kimbo coffee, a box of matches and a jam-jar filled with sugar. Beside them, two small cups were piled crookedly on to their saucers. *She was expecting us*, thought Lotte; *and after we're gone, she'll walk into this kitchen and check up and see if we made ourselves coffee, like she used to come up here and sniff around in my parents' bed* . . . And yet, to be fair, it was a kindness, too, leaving them coffee like that on a cloth-covered tray . . .

'Why d'you think she comes up here?'

Pietro Scala shrugged his shoulders, as though Silvana's habits were none of his concern, and again Lotte felt a small stab of triumph: *If only, Mr Journalist, if only you knew the half of what I know* . . .

'I'll make coffee if you like,' she said, keen to be doing something practical.

Pietro Scala looked at his watch, a Baume et Mercier which Luciana said was worth fifteen million lire, regularly citing this improbable sum as proof of how he'd got rich on Ennio's story. 'It's a bit late in the day for coffee, but I suppose the one won't hurt, seeing as Silvana's gone to the trouble.'

'What do you mean, it's late?' replied Lotte sharply. Everything in Italy had its proper time and place, she thought: tea was for invalids, dark blue was only to be worn in springtime, oranges were too heavy to digest in the evenings. If you let it get to you, you could drown under the weight of all that *correttezza*.

Pietro Scala didn't answer; taking off his tweed jacket and hanging it on a hook behind the door, he sat down at the table, dragging the chair noisily along the flagstones. His gaze made her feel self-conscious: no doubt there was some rule written in stone about how much coffee you should use, how long it should boil, where the water should come up to in the base of the *caffettiera*. As she set the cups on their saucers, Lotte had a sudden feeling of unreality, as though she had caught a glimpse of herself out of the corner of her eye: nothing, but nothing, in her life up to then could have prepared her for this moment – not just being in Italy, and discovering the identity of her father, but actually coming to the place of her birth, the very room where her mother had lost her life – and yet the only way she could rise to the occasion was by . . . *making coffee*. Setting the cup in front of Pietro Scala, she took hers back to the window, irresistibly drawn by that square of evening sunlight. Recently, she had become frightened of the dark; even the gloom of Luciana's flat oppressed her, and she spent most of her days walking the streets, never returning before the start of the eight o'clock news bulletin on RAI Uno. Luciana said she was like Ennio, always going somewhere, never at peace. She wanted to be alone now; yet at the same time, it was a comfort to her knowing that Pietro Scala was sitting behind her at the table, a solid bulk in the shadows. Later, he would drive her back to Rome in his Renault 4, leaving her outside Luciana's flat in Via Tancredi. Gratitude made her feel almost affectionate towards him; he was less arrogant than she'd thought, less insensitive, and she'd caught an expression of tenderness in his dark eyes as he took the coffee from her, which made it almost appear as though they were brimming. Or perhaps it was merely a trick of the light, a projection of her own *stato d'anima*: if he too was moved by the atmosphere at La Camillina, then, irrationally, this lightened her own burden of grief. At some point she became aware of him getting up from the chair, then she heard the tread of heavy footsteps on the staircase.

Afterwards she couldn't have said with certainty how long he was up there – ten minutes? An hour? – as she sat on the window ledge by the open shutters, the sketchbook on her lap. Never in her life had she felt less of a person, less complete. If someone had walked into the room right then and asked her her name, she would have said, 'Lotte, my name is Lotte,' but it would have meant no more than any other word – 'house', 'table', 'cup' – picked out at random. In her own eyes; she'd become no more substantial than a single sheet of tissue paper in one of those complex window-hangings she used to make as a child, layering the sheets, one on top of the other, so that red turned to orange, then brown, then purple; until the final colour was merely the sum of its parts – disappointingly opaque when held up to the light. Now it was gone – that yearning she'd had all her life to *know the truth*, to start at the beginning, leaving her feeling robbed of the hunger that had become her defining trait. Self-knowledge, instead of making her whole, broke her up into little pieces, dismantling her ego like an old car. There was an Italian word for this oblivion: *annientare*, to make nothing . . .

Her mother had laboured in that room: for two days her parents had fought like heroes to bring her into the world, until eventually each in their different way had given up the struggle . . . And, in the end, all they had to show for that sacrifice was herself: a tissue-paper girl – *disappointingly opaque when held up to the light . . .*

She looked out towards the orchard; smoke from Silvana's fire hung like a pall in the grey sky, while the twisted trunks of the olive trees looked as though they'd been scored on to the hillside in charcoal. Down on the farm, a single light burned from the outhouse window, where Silvana must be carrying in her bottles of *passata*. The room was in shadows; and yet, more than just the drawing-in of day, it was as though an apocalyptic darkness had descended upon the countryside: a gaunt, ashy darkness that deadened all it touched . . . She could make out the outline of the table and chair, and the plastic bucket beneath the sink, and yet it was all inconsolably strange to her, as though she'd fallen by the wayside, lost her place in the world . . .

At some point she became aware of the sound of footsteps, and Pietro Scala entered the room. He walked up to the window where she sat and leaned his arm against the shutters, as though, Atlas-like, he were bearing their weight on his shoulders. He was so close she could smell his body smell: a mixture of laundry starch and cologne, with an undertone of sweat. She turned around, and he held out his arms to her as though she were a child. At first, all she could do was bury her face in the fleshy crease of his armpit, breathing in his odour and warmth like a traveller on a snow-filled plain who throws himself for comfort upon the heaving flank of a buffalo . . . Then, slowly, he took her chin in his hands and raised her face to his: his mouth felt hard and warm and as he pressed his lips to hers, literally breathing the life back into her body, she thought, triumphantly: *I'm kissing my first Italian* . . .

There was no time for questions, no time to make sense of the moment. Deliberately, she took off her clothes: her jeans, her grey short-sleeved jumper, the Camper bowling shoes he found so *unsettling*, until, completely naked, she sat down to wait for him by the window. Bit by bit, his clothes came off too: the enormous trousers whose waistband entirely engulfed the back of the chair, the buckle of his belt knocking twice against the wooden seat, the Viyella shirt, the brogues whose shape had been so deformed by his swollen feet that the toes now pointed upwards like Turkish slippers. When he too was naked, apart from his socks (*there must be some rule about walking barefoot on stone floors*, she thought), he laid down his jacket on the ground and patted the space beside him.

Smiling to herself, Lotte got up from the window and knelt down on the flagstones: there was so much to choose from, such a superabundance of flesh was hers for the taking, that at first she scarcely knew where to begin. The title of a book, *Love of Fat Men*, by Helen Dunmore, kept rippling fantastically through her head. How could she have remained ignorant of such pleasures – why had she never thought of this herself, she wondered, squeezing his hairy breasts in her hands and burying her face in the smooth skin of his neck. His hair grew in a solid hank down the back of his head: dead straight hair, which reminded her of Al Pacino's in *The Godfather*.

Like a lamb gambolling around a pasture, or a sow in a

mud-bath, Lotte continued to explore the delights of his body: the gigantic thighs, each one the girth of her encircling arms, the soft belly with its acres of dark hair, rippling sideways like seagrass, the padding all down his waist and buttocks, as though he was an actor wearing a fat man's costume. *Oh, my Italia, my new-found land . . .*

Rolling on to her side, she slid down the floor and took his penis into her mouth. Hungrily, she sucked him, feeling the leathery weight of his testicles resting on her cheek. He sighed, and grunted, and she felt a shudder run through his body. Looking up, she saw him staring towards the wall; for a moment, he looked like John the Baptist, as though his head had been severed from his body at some moment of extreme sorrow.

'What's the matter?' asked Lotte, crouching down beside him on the floor.

Turning his face towards her, he raised one hand to her cheek and ran his finger down her nose and along her lips. 'Nothing's the matter' he replied; and he took her into his arms, holding her tightly against his chest, as though to muffle her questions with his flesh, like a mother soothing a fractious child at the breast. Then, parting her legs with his knee, he rolled over on to one elbow, careful not to crush her chest with his weight, and slid his penis upwards along the inside of her thighs.

As he entered her, Lotte thought: *He's done this before, learnt the fat man's way to make love . . .*

'So why did you look so sad just a moment ago?'

He thrust harder: 'Because I love you, my little *Inglesina*, that's why.'

'And what's sad about that?' The sensation of him deep inside her, pinning her spine on to the flagstones, made her feel as though she'd regained her old centre of gravity, her old place in the universe. The joy of it, knowing that he loved her too, made her grin in the darkness.

'You're young, you have your whole life ahead of you. I'm a middle-aged man. And I'm married.'

'And what's wrong with that?'

'What's wrong with it? It means that nothing will ever come of this.'

Lotte arched her back, twisting her body towards the window, deliberately putting a space between them, turning his words into a game.

'And why's that?'

Roughly, Pietro Scala turned her back to face him, so that their eyes were level, and she could smell the acetone on his breath: 'Because it's against the natural order of things – do you understand what that means? – *l'ordine naturale delle cose* . . .'

There was no time to ask what he meant – it was too much pleasure now for one fragile system to contain – the busy man tamed at last . . a collar around that thick neck . . . a silken cord dangling from her fingers . . . As Lotte came, the sound of her cries keening through the tree-tops, all the way down to the farm at the end of the track, where Silvana stood in the darkness, warming herself by the embers of her fire, she felt as though she were falling, hurtling head-first through a series of ringed chambers, sloughing off her old self like so many scraps of caul . . .

9. Lotte

The baby lay on the stone floor.

With eyes the colour of slate, she gazed ahead at the edges of the dress which was wrapped around her head and body like a shawl: a pattern of peacocks and elephants, conjoined at the trunk, standing in line beneath a rose-decked canopy. White vernix covered her body, settling into the creases of her bluish, still-curled limbs, and mingling with the stream of blood which continued to pump over her head and shoulders from above. As though to mimic this action, prolonging the subtle exchange of hormones which had kick-started the whole evacuation process, she too bled from her vagina, while beneath her crossed hands, a single drop of milk formed on the tip of each pale nipple.

Chin on her chest, she had descended through the pelvis, each contraction slowing down her heart as the walls of the womb closed in, expelling her from the dark cave which had been her home and her seedbed. And when she emerged with a final shrug of the shoulders, first one, then the other (as though to say: I had no choice in this), her nose was flattened, her cheeks bruised, while the bones of her head had slipped over and under one another, forming ridges on the edge of her skull. Like a candle flickering at a window, a steady pulse beat beneath the fontanelle, and yet still she made no sound . . .

For a while, it was touch and go whether she would breathe – after all, no need to cut her losses as long as the old system still worked. But as the placenta began to peel away from her mother's womb, inexorably closing off the ducts in her heart, she truly no longer had a choice. Beneath the Indian fabric, her tiny chest expanded, her shoulders lifted, and she drew her first shuddering breath: at once, the deflated bags of her lungs filled with air, flooding her bloodstream with oxygen. With each shallow breath, her circulation hotted up like the lights coming on in an amusement arcade, until her cheeks and body began to glow, the greyish limbs turning to pink. Tricked into living, she gave her first cry.

Then, puzzled, she waited.

8

THE NATURAL ORDER OF THINGS

For a while, she toyed with the idea of becoming a bourgeois Italian to please him.

Although she was a late starter, Lotte was hoping that some of this new grandmother's fabulous precision would rub off on her. She would spend hours sitting at the kitchen table, watching Luciana ironing the tenants' laundry which was left in carrier bags emblazoned with unfamiliar shop names (UPIM, La Rinascente, La SMA), outside her cubicle down on the ground floor. Melody, on the other hand, never ironed sheets, or anything else, come to that; many years before, an Irish cleaning lady called Imelda had taught her the trick of stretching out the washing when it was still damp, an approximation of good standards which, thought Lotte spitefully, you could apply to just about every aspect of Melody's housekeeping.

She found it difficult to explain, even to herself, why she found the ironing so desirable – a dormant housewife's gene, perhaps, that had been awakened on meeting Luciana. Part of it, she supposed, was the sheer effort expended upon each sheet: first it was ironed in its entirety, then each fold would be pressed again, first with the heel of her palm, then with the iron, until with a sigh of resignation, as though her hunger for perfection had been satiated, at least temporarily, she would place it on its pile on the table. The inside of Luciana's linen cupboard made the bedding department of John Lewis look scruffy: row upon row of perfectly aligned linen, exuding a homely smell of washing powder and mothballs, mingled with something musty yet utterly familiar, as though inside that cupboard lay a living creature whose breath lay upon every surface and corner of that house. *I probably slept in these sheets when I was a baby*, Lotte thought, and tears sprang to her eyes, partly at the narrowness of Luciana's world (so much artistry and rigour for something no one was ever going to see), but also at a part of her childhood which had been lost to her for all these years . . . Although the contents of the cupboard looked shabby, the sheets in faded browns and yellows, with the occasional acid-coloured rosebud-pattern, the fabric of the towels flattened to the texture of boiled wool, there wasn't a rounded edge or corner in sight. Everything was severe, geometrical, as though still in its original packaging.

A few days had passed since the funeral, and that evening Melody was leaving for London: a taxi had been ordered for 3.30 to take her to the airport. She could have waited to get her sheets – no one said she had to settle in there and then, right under Melody's nose – just as she could have waited before unpacking her few belongings into the section of the wardrobe Luciana had cleared for her, but wounding Melody had become her release, a coping mechanism she clung on to, as though each act of unkindness, every careless word or moment of feigned deafness, went some way towards righting the massive wrong she felt had been done her. Its main purpose, though, was to normalise the surreal kink her life had taken: goading Melody helped her remember who she was, put a lid on the jumble of new experiences, which from one day to the next, it seemed, had been dumped into that familiar, gaping chasm labelled: 'father: unknown'.

'Tell me, Melody, why should I ever believe another word you say?'

'You're right, my darling, I don't blame you for being angry.'

'Why did you do it? How could you possibly think I'd be better off not knowing?'

'I just thought . . . we all thought . . . it wouldn't be fair to give you a start like that in life. It's one thing not having a family –'

'You mean a storybook family? Like you and Hugh?' And, as if that weren't hurtful enough: 'I thought you'd got all that out of your system, Melody, when you ruined my mother's life . . .'

Lotte looked around the bedroom: the ceilings were high, but the room had an oddly truncated feel, with a partition wall bisecting the window overlooking the courtyard. A small picture of the Madonna, carved in shiny wood, hung over Luciana's bed, with a sprig of olive tucked behind the frame. On the bedside table stood a fringed lamp with a dark blue cloth folded over the shade, a Bible, and a copy of her crossword magazine, *La Settimana Enigmistica*. Luciana climbed up a small stepladder and, unlocking the cupboard with a twist of the decorative gilt key, handed her down a pile of bedding: two sheets, a pillowcase, and a total of four towels: bath, face, hands, *bidet*, all decorated with a woven floral border.

Her father had lain on that bed, his hands crossed over the breast of his shirt, the soles of his unworn desert boots still displaying the name of the shop and a round sticker with the number 43. He died a few hours before they arrived: the doctor thought he'd had a small stroke, bled into his brain.

She remembered opening her eyes in the back of the cab, and it feeling no different from being asleep: the gaudiest of waking dreams . . .

She'd followed Melody out of the taxi along a gravel drive-way, and up some stone steps to a pair of double doors. Wisteria climbed up the mustard-coloured wall, overhanging the porch in faded purple clumps, Melody pressed the intercom button marked 'PORTIERA' and instantly the door had clicked open and they'd walked into a dark lobby. Beside the staircase stood an old-fashioned cage lift. Putting down her suitcase, Melody had pulled back the hinged metal gate with both hands, and they'd entered a panelled cube which smelled of beeswax and cigarette smoke. Then the grille had concertina'd back into place, locking them together inside the cage. *Close enough to scratch your eyes (or throw myself into your arms . . .)* As the lift climbed to the first floor, Lotte had stared down the shaft, watching the ground disappearing beneath their feet; she'd felt like slipping her hand through the bars of the cage, dragging her fingertips along the scabby wall, in an attempt to slow things down . . . Then the lift had bumped to a halt on the first floor; they'd walked out on to the landing, and she'd found herself standing before a door, with the name 'CARUSO' engraved on to a brass plate. *Which makes me a Caruso, too*, she remembered thinking.

Melody rang the bell, and an old lady in a housecoat and slippers had appeared in the hallway – *would that be Mrs Caruso? Nonna Caruso?* – and, in silence, as though the moment had been choreographed, the two women embraced. Then Luciana had turned towards Lotte, and clasping her hand over her mouth, she shook her head. '*Se n'é andato*,' she'd whispered, he's gone; and dully, Lotte realised her father was dead.

She'd felt her hands grow clammy as a sudden burst of adrenaline shook her out of her dream-state. Heart pumping, she'd followed Luciana through a long dark passageway to a half-open doorway. The linoleum floor-tiles appeared to be sloping downwards, then back up again: each step had to be cunningly negotiated. It was too raw for her now; every nerve in her body, every ounce of self-love, resisted crossing the threshold of that room. She'd held on to the door-handle, eyes fixed to the ground. *Steady on*, she'd felt like saying to them, *steady on, I'm not used to this kind of thing . . .*

She'd looked at her father lying on the bed while her heart swelled with gratitude at the sweetness of her life until now.

At the last moment, literally as the taxi driver was loading her grandmother's suitcases into the boot, Lotte told Melody she wasn't coming to the airport. Because there was no –

'– no need,' echoed Melody quickly, 'I'll manage fine.' She flashed a half-smile at Lotte, as though to exonerate her in advance from any guilt about breaking her promise, shouldering all the burden of ill-feeling between them as though it was hers, and hers alone. But her complicity and generosity only made it worse.

Mulishly, Lotte stood on the gravel driveway of the flats in a pair of Luciana's old slippers. *She must have known*, she thought, *the moment I left the flat without my shoes*, and a tiny splinter of pity inflamed her heart. Looming behind her was the dreary, airless flat she had chosen to call home (where, out of delicacy, perhaps, Luciana sat chain-smoking her 'Muratti' cigarettes in the sitting room, the volume turned down low on the TV, leaving them alone to say their good-byes), while in a matter of hours Melody would be back in London: unlocking the entrance to the shop, climbing up the dark stairwell where their two bicycles hung on hooks above the bannister, until she reached their front door. The longing to go with her – more than a longing, an almost physical propulsion, as though she were a pile of iron filings being swept towards a magnet, or a figure in a Chagall painting, skimming lopsidedly off-canvas – made her feel faint . . .

Slamming shut the boot, the taxi driver got into his seat and switched on the engine of his cab. '*A segnora – se n'annamo?*' he said impatiently in dialect, leaning out of the rolled-down window and striking the side of the car with the heel of one hand, while with the other, he fiddled with the dial of the radio. She heard a snatch of a Nirvana song, then an advert for a chain of beauty shops called Acqua e Sapone. She could see a pewter disk of St Christopher glued on to the dashboard beside a sticker of Padre Pio, the same monk on the calendar which hung in Luciana's kitchen: she said he was a saint, a miracle-worker. Melody bent down so that her face was level with the window: '*Un momento solo*', she said to the driver. Then, straightening up, she held out both hands to Lotte, pressing her fingers between her rough palms, just as she'd done on the first day of infant school, when she crouched down beside her at the tiny table, holding her clammy hands in hers and blocking her from view until her tears dried and she was able to face the other children. Lotte's heart raced, and a sickening wave of dread washed over her, turning her bowels to water. Even now, she was still in time to change her mind . . .

'Come home when you're ready, my darling,' said Melody, and she kissed her on both cheeks, as she always did – a reflex Italianism (like the *caffèlatte*, the Saturday school in Willesden, Radio Italia playing all day on the light blue Roberts set in the back of the shop), which had been administered, so it seemed to her now, in minute, homeopathic doses, turning her into the Italian-in-waiting of today.

She watched as the taxi driver did a flashy three-point turn in the driveway, sweeping histrionically through the open gates towards Via Tancredi. When the car was no longer in view, and she heard the electronic blinds in the fruit shop across the road rattling shut, and the thump of crockery and glasses on the tablecloths of La Botticella next door, Lotte dragged back the gates, shoring up a fresh semi-circle of gravel on each side before twisting the bolts down deep into the ground, locking herself into the courtyard, into her new life.

He said he'd call, but he didn't.

Or rather, he didn't say he wouldn't, which came to near enough the same thing. And when, three days after their trip to La Camillina, Lotte (*groaning each time she recalled his leathery testicles slapping against her cheek as she lay beside him on the cold stone floor)* still hadn't heard from him, she rang him herself at the magazine. Knowing what Luciana felt about Pietro Scala, she bought a 5,000-lire phone card from the Meeting Bar in Piazza Bologna and dialled his direct line from the wall-mounted orange payphone near the toilets. She got his number from a business card she found in a folder containing Ennio's papers which Luciana had given her to look through.

His secretary sounded as though she'd had her lips siliconed – either that, or she'd recently applied lipstick (or else just finished sucking off her boss under the desk, *but get that idea out of your head right now*) and was talking through her teeth. Lying through them too, thought Lotte furiously, as she waited for the payphone to spit back her card. She'd kept her waiting for a good two minutes, while an annoying monotone robot repeated '*Attendere prego . . . Attendere prego*', before returning and simpering, '*Il Dottor Scala sta in riunione,*' in her ditsy, Playmate's voice. Not much chance that this one wore unsettling bowling shoes around the office . . .

Italian girls, even plain ones, had a knack – more than a knack, a holy vocation – for maximising their assets, thought Lotte as she walked back through the square, watching the children climbing up the grimy iron slide, while Filipina *babysitters* (themselves honorary Italians now, with their alice-bands, their imitation Superga plimsolls and stovepipe trousers worn an inch above the ankles) sat chattering on benches. They all had at least one really good feature, be it hair, figure, or even something as trivial as neatly plucked eyebrows, but you could guarantee that whatever it was, they would find a way of drawing attention to it, while at the same time deflecting scrutiny from any less attractive traits. Luciana said that when she was young, girls were either pretty or not – none of this tricksy, fake *bellezza* you got nowadays. A constant beautification process seemed to be at work – a civic duty all Romans subscribed to – promoting '*il bello*', ensuring that the eye always had something attractive to dwell on: be it the stripy brown and white heart in the centre of a morning *cappuccino*, the checked smocks with Peter Pan collars that Italian schoolchildren wore, turning them all into little cherubs, or the blonde *vigilessa*, perched on her little platform amidst the maelstrom of the Piazza Venezia traffic in her coquettish high heels. Even the really hideously ugly – the no-neck woman with the tree-trunk legs and the cast in one eye, the balding near-midget with his child-size feet – didn't give up: somehow, they were driven by their genes, or their environment, to get up in the morning and, disregarding the irrefutable evidence they saw before them in the mirror, put together the silk necktie, the double-stranded coral necklace, the polished shoes, the Mandarina Duck handbag, for the sake of the common aesthetic. Only the other day, she'd been on the *metropolitana* going towards Piazza di Spagna, when she watched a young girl, sitting beneath an advertisement for Moneygram, literally morph into a beauty before her eyes. She looked like an ordinary student, dressed in a black T-shirt and dark blue jeans, hair tied off her face in a low ponytail. There was nothing at all memorable about her face, a kind of blank regularity of features, perhaps, but that was it. About two stops from Spagna, the train stopped in a tunnel and the entire compartment sighed in unison, exhaling the hot, stale air as the carriage lights flickered on and off. After a few moments, the girl took out a hand-mirror and a small crocheted bag from her rucksack, and began applying make-up. Fascinated, Lotte watched as she dabbed foundation on to her nose and chin, a sweep of blusher on the cheeks, a tiny bit of mascara, and last of all, opaque wine-coloured lipgloss with a thumbprint of white powder in the center – a trick, Lotte remembered reading somewhere, to make the lower lip appear fuller. In less than a minute, her face looked utterly transformed, as though she'd had one of those makeovers advertised in the back pages of women's magazines (the ones which included a professional portrait taken under studio lights, where mousy, librarian types were turned into Cinderellas for the day), but she hadn't finished. Loosening her hair from its ponytail, she rummaged inside her rucksack and pulled out a beautiful embroidered scarf, what here in Italy they called a *foulard*, made of a kind of gauzy peach-coloured viscose material; and without disturbing the man sitting next to her, she swept it casually over one shoulder so that it framed her newly radiant face in a series of perfectly scalloped waves. Speechless with admiration, Lotte watched her. She knew for a fact that she could have spent an entire afternoon trying out ways to wear such a scarf (assuming she been cunning enough to pick such a flattering colour), and she could never have got it to lie like that. As the engine thrummed back to life and the train began to slide along the tracks, she felt furious with Melody, who, along with even the most basic of housekeeping skills, had neglected this vital part of her education.

Back at the flat, Luciana was watching a chat show on one of Berlusconi's private TV channels: it was called *Lui, Lei e L'Altro* – Him, Her and the Other. A kind of Italian Jerry Springer Show, participants were invited on the programme to rake over their infidelities before a studio audience. Mostly, the stories sounded made up, while the protagonists looked and sounded like jobbing actors, and yet Luciana swore it was all true. 'How could you make up a story like that?' was her stock answer, no matter how improbable the tale. The smoke from her cigarette, perched on the edge of an onyx ashtray, coiled towards the half-open shutters, where a faint breeze thrashed it back into the room. Luciana looked up.

'Somebody rang for you when you were out. A man.'

Lotte sat down heavily on the armchair; her heart was beating so fast, she could hardly breathe.

'Did they say who it was?' To hide her agitation, she picked up a copy of Luciana's magazine, *Oggi*, from the coffee table.

'David. From London. He said he would call back later.'

Disappointment flooded through her like bile: David was about the last person in the world she felt like talking to. They had spoken once since the funeral, and even then, after a few minutes, Lotte cut him short, saying she was tired. The truth was, she thought, flicking through the pages of the magazine, David was too English for her; she'd always felt that, but now, since . . . since Pietro –

'Let me tell you, he's a low-life *poco di buono* – and he's old enough to be your father!'

How –

'And it serves you right for going with a married man!' she spat.

Unable to meet Luciana's gaze, Lotte blushed and stared down at her magazine. A whole page was devoted to classified ads for fortune-tellers and tarot-card readers: 'Medea: the Ineffable Gypsy', 'Lucrezia and Her Sensitive Angels,' 'Daniel Leon and His Expert Helpers' . . .

'And there's no fooling anyone now with those crocodile tears!'

Lotte grinned with relief: Luciana was addressing the television, a habit no doubt borne of all those years of living alone. During *La Ruota della Fortuna*, Lotte would hear her haranguing the contestants from the kitchen, calling out: 'Try "R" for Roma!' or 'Now's the time to buy a vowel!' as she prepared the evening meal; while the eight o'clock *telegiornale* on RAI Uno sounded more like a studio debate than a news bulletin, with Luciana heckling the newsreaders as though they were morally accountable for the stories they reported.

Looking up from her magazine, Lotte stared at her grandmother's profile silhouetted against the shutters. Beneath her *fumée* glasses, she had nice features, with soft skin and beautiful grey eyes. And yet there was an air of sadness about her, an absolute lack of vitality, which you could tell wasn't just to do with Ennio's death. Apart from the day of the funeral itself, Lotte had never seen her wear anything other than a sleeveless work pinafore over the drabbest of skirts. And yet she must have cared once about how she looked, made the effort to dress up, look pretty. And she was bitter and judgemental about everybody. Only the other day, she'd surprised Lotte by the savagery of the way she talked about the woman downstairs, La Guerrini: 'That son of hers should lock up the incontinent old bat in a *casa di riposo* and throw away the key! That'll teach her to keep pissing in my hallway!' She'd had a hard life, Melody told her, orphaned at a young age, and deserted by the father of her child when she was just seventeen.

'Do you have any photographs? Of your own family, I mean.'

Luciana looked up. 'You want to see pictures of my family?'

Lotte nodded. For a moment Luciana hesitated, then she took off her *fumée* glasses; she looked like someone who had been jolted awake from an unquiet sleep. Stabbing the air with the remote control, she switched off the TV and walked over to the bureau by the window. She returned with an old Amaretti biscuit tin, and beckoned Lotte to sit beside her. 'Switch on that lamp, please, in the corner.' Obediently, Lotte leaned over and switched it on; day and night, her grandmother's sitting room was bathed in an amber twilight, which the thirty-watt bulb did little to dispel. Her skin, too, looked as though it rarely saw the light of day.

'This is my father,' she said. 'The one sitting on the barrel. To the left of him, holding the guitar, is my uncle Lello.'

It was a black and white photograph in a cracked gilt frame. The men had the bronzed, glamorous beauty of another age: stern expressions, light eyes screwed up against the sun. The caption below, in joined-up letters, read: 'Leonforte, 14 Settembre 1947'.

'Looks always ran in our family, you know; we were blond Sicilians – direct descendants of the Ancient Greeks. When your grandfather was a boy, his nickname in the village was "*Il Tedesco*", the German. Ennio inherited his father's colouring – you too . . .'

'Can I see a picture of your hus– I mean, of Ennio's father?'

Again, Luciana's eyes swam, and she turned her face away towards the window. 'Ennio never understood – about me and his father . . .'

'Never understood what?'

Without answering, Luciana reached inside the tin, and rifling through the contents, pulled out a brown envelope sealed with an elastic band. Opening the envelope, she handed her a small black and white snapshot. It was of a startlingly pretty girl, dressed in a sailor's top, belted tight about the waist, and a wide 1950s-style skirt. Her waving hair was tied off her face with a scarf, gypsy-style; and she was smiling confidently straight into the camera. Beside her, one arm about her waist, stood a balding middle-aged man in shirt-sleeves. He too was looking into the camera, but his expression was sombre, watchful, as though he could see further ahead into the distance than the girl. 'He was the love of my life, you know – I loved him till the day he died . . .'

'What was it that Ennio didn't understand?'

Luciana sighed. 'There're different ways of being in love. Gilberto was weak . . . his mother wanted him to marry well . . . wanted him to have a good career in the Ministry.'

'So you gave up? Just let him go?' She thought of Pietro Scala's head gazing out sadly into the darkness like John the Baptist: *because nothing will ever come of this . . .*

'What could I do? I was just thankful he kept an interest in his son, even though Ennio hated him and refused to take his name. Nobody told him Gilberto was his father; he worked it out for himself. Every time he visited Rome, they would go for a walk in the Pincio; I'd have to push Ennio out of the front door to make him go.' She pulled out another photograph from the tin, a colour one this time, though brown and metallic-looking as though it had been left out in the sun. It showed the same man, now wearing a light-coloured suit, standing beside a small boy carrying a balloon. The boy was wearing a dark, short-sleeved shirt, khaki shorts and sandals with no socks; his arms were folded tightly against his chest, and his thin frame seemed bent by the weight of his father's hand, which was resting, rather pompously, it seemed, on his left shoulder. He was scowling at the camera beneath a heavy fringe. In the background was an old-fashioned carousel, and you could just make out the balloon-seller standing behind a group of palm trees. Lotte looked at it and recognition flooded through her: if she hadn't known better, she could have sworn the child in the picture was herself. Around the age of nine or ten, just before puberty, her hair went dead straight; and for a while, she too wore it with a long fringe.

'Ennio looks – I mean, I look –'

'You resemble him . . . he knew that.'

'How could he know? When he never even met me?' Lotte felt a surge of childish rage boil inside her. She would never forgive either of them – not Luciana, not Melody – for depriving her of a father. How *dare* they decide she was better off not knowing the truth about her birth? And as for Ennio himself, why wait until his deathbed before remembering he had a daughter?

All her life Lotte had this thing about arriving *too late*: born too late to know her grandfather, or her mother, in the days when, along with Melody, they had constituted what you might call a proper family. She and Ennio should have had twenty years to know each other: that was his slot, his allotted time to be a father. And yet, more improbably than the clunking machinations of a Thomas Hardy novel, circumstances would conspire so that all she got of those twenty years were the dregs – the winding-down of that life. It was like arriving at a theatre just as the lights are coming up at the end of a play, and watching the audience emerge flushed and transfigured by what they have seen, and knowing that you will never have the chance to discover what it was that made them feel like that – like the doors of every underground train in the world closing in your face: *If only you'd got here before . . .*

'This picture he kept in his cell. I sent it to him myself.'

She couldn't believe it: it was her! There she was sitting outside the Lisboa Café in Golborne Road wearing her dungarees and hideous Greek sandals (which, come to think of it, weren't that hideous after all), glowering at her own reflection in Catherine Smart's aviator glasses . . . *I took two so I can send you a copy once I get them developed . . .* And the destiny of that copy was to be shuffled about between two deceitful old women, only to end up in some prison cell in Rome, where her father could look at his daughter as often as he pleased, without ever having to trouble himself about meeting her. Lotte felt violated: her image had been exploited without her consent, as though – as though . . . For a moment, she was too angry to speak. It was far too easy to play happy families now that Ennio was dead and everything was respectable and above-board. *Yes, I'm sorry you missed him . . . he passed away just before you arrived . . .* The pair of them – Melody and Luciana – deserved to rot in hell for what they'd done.

'He would have written to you long before, if I hadn't begged him not to. It was the only thing that kept him going, all those years in prison – hearing your news, and hoping one day you'd be able to meet.'

'But not enough to do anything about it?' They were going round in circles, but she didn't care.

'Lotte, *figlia mia*, you don't know what it cost him – what it cost both of us – to let Melody take you away to London. I had nobody here – my only son in prison, my brothers down in Sicily – don't you see what having a granddaughter here would have meant to me?'

'So what stopped you getting in touch?'

Luciana picked her glasses up off the table and placed them back over her eyes. In the dim light of the sitting room, the polaroid lenses darkened and contracted, blanking out her expression like sunglasses. *She hides behind those lenses, thought Lotte, like she hides away in this room, in this flat.* 'They called him *bastardino* at school: he never told me, but I knew. Once the children found out that Ennio was illegitimate, a *figlio di nessuno*, that became his nickname. And the nuns did nothing to stop it. Through no fault of his own, my son had to put up with years of name-calling – and worse. Because of my mistake – not *his* mistake, *my* mistake – Ennio never had the chance . . . he never had a chance to be a normal little boy. I couldn't do that to you, Lotte – maybe I was wrong, maybe in England people care about these things too – but I couldn't let all that happen again.'

At night, sometimes, he would come to her.

She would lie on the sofa-bed in the sitting room, listening to the sounds from the street: a car door slamming, a blind rattling shut, a *motorino* engine stuttering to life in the courtyard down below. In the darkness she could make out the single red eye of the standby light on Luciana's TV, as though the giant set were building up its strength for the next day's marathon. Occasionally, she would hear Luciana getting up to drink or use the bathroom; at night-time, she never flushed the toilet, and in the morning Lotte would find a wad of toilet paper stuck to the inside of the bowl. Such were the intimacies of their life together.

The moment she switched off the light, her first thought was: *watch me – I'll never fall asleep in this bed, never.* But, as her mind lurched, none the less, towards oblivion, there'd be this shortfall in credulity (like the sensation of a foot stepping on to an underground train, and, instead, falling into nothingness) and it was inside this void that everything started to unravel: recent events – somehow bagged up together to create a more or less functioning reality – would break free of their ties and flaunt their strangeness before her: *I am somebody's child now . . . I am the daughter of a terrorist – that man on the news is my father . . . And Luciana, who two weeks ago you didn't even know existed . . . you're living with now like a flatmate . . . and what about Pietro Scala . . . who you fucked on the kitchen floor where your mother met her death . . .?*

This, too, was when she would dream of her father. Sometimes he was the man of her childhood fever, emerging from the shadows of the doorway which led to Melody's shop. 'So *that's* who you are,' she murmured in her dream, '*that's* who you are', repeating the words over again, just for the pleasure of putting a face to that ghost. He would sit down beside her mother on the bed; and lying between them, Lotte would think: *Now we're a family – at last we're a real family . . .* Strands of a kind of silvery substance floated in the air above their heads, binding them together like DNA. She ached to touch them, to communicate her joy to them, but they were so wrapped up in each other that it was as though she had become the ghost now, they the living, and all she could do was watch their reflection in the wardrobe mirror with its crenellated border, the tiny glass screws set into the four corners of the frame . . .

At other times she would dream of the *camposanto* at Viterbo, where, together with a hundred other corpses, her parents were buried side by side in a kind of enormous, marble-fronted chest of drawers. In the dream, she and Luciana were walking down the concrete steps which led to the new, underground part of the cemetery. Wheeling out giant, double-sided aluminium ladders from opposite ends of the sunken courtyard, they climbed up to the top of their ladders until they were standing side by side before the two graves. There, Luciana pulled out a stripy bottle of Siderol from her apron pocket, the same preparation she used to polish the name-plates outside the flats, and began shining the plaque on Ennio's side. 'Here, take this,' she said, handing Lotte a bunch of rotting carnations, while from her bag she pulled out a bundle of tall-stemmed plastic roses which she divided between the two brass urns. Lotte stared at the photograph of Julia in its oval frame: the same picture which stood on Melody's bedside table in London. *You knew all along, didn't you?* she said, addressing the picture. *You knew all along what he was up to, but you cared more about fucking him than saving your own skin and mine.* Her mother looked at her sadly, and she wound a strand of dark hair behind her ear: *You're right to say I knew . . . I did know . . . but I had no choice . . . you see, ours was a love I would have died for . . . Ask your father,* she murmured, *see if he can explain . . .* It was only when Lotte turned to Ennio's photograph that she realised it had gone, and in its place was a likeness of Pietro Scala. She stared at his face, at his unreadable dark eyes, and her heart brimmed with love. 'Don't worry, your father's over there,' said Luciana, pointing towards the wall which separated where they stood from the older part of the cemetery. Looking over the top of the wall, Lotte saw a figure in a balaclava standing amidst the long grass surrounding the headstones; arms held straight out ahead, he was holding a gun in gloved hands, his crumpled jacket riding half-way up his back. She watched him, heels together, thighs splayed, as he aimed the gun towards his own grave. Then a shot rang out; the bullet whined past her ear, and she heard the creak of breaking glass as the frame behind her shattered.

You see, ours was a love I would have died for . . .

A week later, Pietro Scala called.

'You sound out of breath, *Inglesina.*'

'I'm not out of breath, just . . .' (*just crouching on the lino of Luciana's hallway with my hand pressed to my heart . . .*)

'How have you been?'

'OK. You?'

'Busy. We're running a mid-week special on your father.'

'Did your secretary tell you I called?'

'Cinzia mentioned something.'

Between one blow-job and the next . . . 'So why didn't you ring back?'

'Too busy. Anyway, I'm talking to you now, aren't I?'

'Yes . . . why?'

'To arrange a meeting.'

Thank you.

Thank you.

Thank you, Lord, for putting me on this earth . . .

'So where are we going to meet?' *And what am I going to wear? And –*

'Not us. You and someone called Piero; he used to know your father. Says he wants to see you alone.'

Only you shouldn't have bothered, Lord, if this is the best you can do . . .

'Can't I see you as well? After I've seen him?'

'I told you, I'm busy.'

'Not even for a quick coffee? So I can tell you how the meeting went?' *Which is actually called begging* . . .

'No, not even for – oh, all right . . . call me when you've finished, and I'll see what I can do.'

With Ennio's death, Pietro Scala lost the final link to his youthful past, while at the same time it was brought home to him, more forcibly than ever before, what a wishy-washy kind of person he was.

On the one hand, his reputation was going from strength to strength. Suddenly Ennio was hot news: RAI Tre wanted to do a *Bulletins* special on Sinistra Armata to tie in with the recent resurgence in urban terrorism, while a small bidding war for Ennio's memoirs was going on between the major players in the Italian publishing world. Current affairs magazines from as far afield as Germany and the United States were interested in buying the rights to his Rebibbia testimonials, while a persistent (and very pretty) French journalist from *Le Monde* wished to collaborate with him on an *exposé* of the hundred or so ex-members of Italian armed organisations – the so-called 'tourists of terrorism' who were living with impunity in Paris under their real identities.

Yet there was no escaping the almost crushing despair he'd felt since Ennio's death. Those few months doing the interview at Rebibbia had been among the happiest of his life; each time he was buzzed through the electronic door leading to the visitors' section, he felt thirty years younger (and thirty kilos lighter). Towards the end of Ennio's illness, when he grew too weak to continue with his testimonial, Pietro Scala would visit him in the hospital wing of the prison, first stopping by the *ambulatorio* to donate blood; it gave him a deep, irrational joy to know that his blood was helping to keep Ennio alive, however temporarily. Sometimes, when he arrived, the blinds were drawn, and Ennio would sleep for the whole two hours; at others, the prison nurse would prop him up on a couple of cushions, and while he sipped the Santal pineapple juice Pietro brought him through a straw (he was supposed to drink the most calorific juice you could buy; his consultant wanted him to consume at least 1,200 calories a day, and chewing most foods had become too painful) they would discuss Roma's progress in the *campionato*, or how the young Mayor, Rutelli, was planning to turn the *centro storico* into a traffic-free zone. One Sunday evening, when his wife was already in bed, Pietro Scala dug out his vinyl LPs from a box in the garage and made up a compilation tape of Italian music from the 1970s, a kind of soundtrack to the Lead Years. The following morning, he brought the tape with him to Rebibbia, and the two of them spent an agreeable couple of hours discussing the merits of Fossati versus Guccini, or Lolli versus Battisti. There was one song by Battisti, 'I Giardini di Marzo', which Ennio asked to hear again; but after listening to it twice, he turned his face towards the wall, appearing to withdraw into his own thoughts, and, presently, he called in the nurse to draw the blinds.

Once they got on to the subject of regret; by this stage, their discussions were all off-record, and they'd agreed Pietro Scala would no longer even bring the tape-recorder with him. 'Do you remember that questionnaire I sent you through your lawyer back in 1980, asking if you'd do anything differently if you had the chance? How would you answer that today?' Pietro felt comfortable enough now to hazard such a question.

Ennio looked at him, then, placing the glass on the bedside table, careful to avoid the tangle of tubes looping around his drip like the strings of a marionette, he picked up his softpack of MS, and with a scrape of the red BIC lighter, he lit himself a cigarette. The chemotherapy had turned the inside of his mouth into a mass of open sores; as he smoked, white gobs of skin peeled off his lips and stuck on to the filter, which he would fastidiously pick off with his fingers and wipe on a folded handkerchief. Sliding the ashtray nearer to his bed, he replied: 'I'd answer that question with another question. Seeing it's me that's been doing all the talking till now. What would *you* do differently, in *your* life, if you had the chance, Mr Journalist?'

And with those words, the floodgates opened: the cork flew out of the bottle and the evil genie escaped from his lamp, insinuating its presence into all the dusty, best-forgotten corners of Pietro Scala's life. That evening, as he drove back to his home in the Parioli, bouncing over the cobblestones of Piazza Barberini towards the Muro Torto, Ennio's words rattled around inside his head like a marble in a tin. *What would you do differently in your life . . .?* Not that he hadn't put that question to himself, in the past. No, for years it had been a kind of comfortable, unthreatening subtext to his daily existence – the underbelly of his professional success, if you like – a barely articulated yearning for the boy who once dreamed of revolution – who sat on his bed beneath the black and red poster of Che Guevara, doodling the Red Brigade's five-pointed star on the cover of his Latin primer. But one thing was putting that question to himself, within the context of his sterile, everyday life (a life so well insulated from the chill draught of the past that any answer would only ever be theoretical) while Ennio doing it was quite another: Ennio, who *was* that past . . .

He was the middle son of a middle-aged, middle-ranking civil servant. (Now, himself, *nel mezzo del cammin* of his days . . .)

Whilst still a student at Rome's fashionable Liceo Visconti high school, he was sweethearts with a girl called Flavia; she was the prettiest (and richest) girl in the class, the only daughter of a self-made tycoon, proprietor of a chain of upmarket holiday villages on the Costa Smeralda and in the Dolomite mountains. They lived in a brand-new villa on the Via Salaria, surrounded by an electrical fence and guarded by two large alsatians. A few months into their courtship, Flavia's father began inviting Pietro Scala to spend a part of all the main holidays with him and his family: two weeks' skiing in the mountains at Christmas and Easter, the May Day weekend and most of August at one of their Sardinian resorts. Later, to escape the worst of the heat, they would cut short their stay in Sardinia and travel up north to the Dolomites: there, their days were spent walking along the nature trails, between one village and the next, often stopping for lunch at one of the mountain *rifugi*. When it rained, they would stay in the hotel playing cards: a favourite game was *Tresette*. He and Flavia soon got used to making up a four-some with her parents; neither particularly minded not mixing with people nearer their own age. After seventeen summers spent at a shabby *pensione* near Rimini (he and his brothers squashed into a single room that overlooked the yard, a dining room that smelled of drains, tablecloths that were never changed, so that by the end of August they resembled a culinary map of their vacation), Pietro Scala found Flavia's tenor of holiday to be far more to his liking. Indeed, so much to his liking, that he never went away with his family again.

Flavia's father was so rich that during the Lead Years, he hired bodyguards to protect him and his dependants: most mornings, Flavia would be dropped off outside the school by a thug driving a bullet-proof Mercedes. Whilst Pietro Scala quickly grew accustomed to life as Flavia's boyfriend, a part of his soul still throbbed to the wilder beat of revolution: inside his wardrobe door, he stuck a photograph of Renato Curcio and Alberto Franceschini, founders of the Red Brigade; and with the excuse that he needed to study at a classmate's house, he would slip out on Saturday afternoons to attend the highly charged demonstrations organised in the city centre. Thus a pattern was established: a duplicity more of the soul than anything else, which would endure throughout his adult life.

Whilst he would only ever be a weekend revolutionary, he still managed to pack a great deal of fervour into his hatred of the system. Like Ennio, he owned a black felt hood which he wore at demonstrations; and although he never used it, he always brought his father's heavy spanner with him in case of trouble. Interestingly, he and Ennio crossed paths at several of the more violent demonstrations during the late seventies, although, unlike Ennio, Pietro Scala would call it a day at exactly the moment when things started to heat up. (While Ennio was having his Zen moment, watching the plate-glass window of a hotel fold in on itself like a wave in a storm, Pietro Scala was already halfway home on the number 85 bus.)

In the early days, he loved Flavia, or at least he thought he did. In spite of being so pretty, rich and popular, she was actually very unspoilt and kind-hearted. Although she wasn't academic, her father was keen on her completing her studies; and to this end she enrolled at Rome's university, La Sapienza, at the same time as Pietro Scala; he majored in Political Science (the course of choice for any would-be journalist) and Flavia in Economy and Commerce. By the end of his time at university, Pietro Scala's revolutionary flame was all but spent, while his feelings for Flavia had undergone a similar, though less radical, lowering of temperature. The sexual spark between them – never all that ardent, even when they were both teenagers – had more or less gone out by the time he took his final exam.

Giving up his secret life as a rebel had not proved difficult; he was hungry for professional success, and had become increasingly unwilling to waste time on any activities that would divert him from reaching his goals. Flavia, though, was harder to give up. For a start, she was so sweet-tempered that in five years together they had never had so much as a single lover's quarrel, let alone the kind of serious bust-up required to break up with someone. His own family was devoted to her, and while he couldn't swear her parents felt the same about him (sometimes he caught her father watching him with an unfathomable expression in his eyes), they certainly treated him in every respect like a future son-in-law. Leaving Flavia meant divorcing a whole way of life – saying goodbye to everything that made his existence pleasurable and, more importantly, was helping set him up for the future: not just the holidays, but being able to drive around Rome in the latest Alfa, the meals at the best fish restaurants on the coast, membership of the tennis club in the Parioli. All these factors contributed to his standing in the eyes of the world. Besides, Flavia's father was working to procure him a position as unofficial press officer to a Christian Democrat politician friend of his; and while this was theoretically incompatible with his work as a cub reporter on one of Rome's dailies covering the highly unpopular areas of education and drugs, his work at the newspaper barely covered his rent. He wasn't enamoured of the idea of working for a right-wing politician; but, he reasoned with himself, he would never make it in the world of work without a *raccomandazione*. Besides, once he had made a name for himself in his profession, there would be plenty of scope for changing the system from within. Whichever way he looked at it, it seemed perverse to rock the boat now.

Instead, he and Flavia married at the church of Santa Sabina near Circo Massimo; afterwards, four hundred guests were invited to a reception at the Hotel Excelsior in Via Veneto. For a wedding present, the bride's father bought the couple a 350-square-metre apartment in the Parioli; as well as paying for a two-week honeymoon in the Maldives.

In some respects, Pietro Scala remained true to that earlier promise: when he joined *La Nazione*, first as a reporter, then as editor, he made it his business early on to start asking questions about the methods adopted by the Secret Services in the war against terrorism; he was also working in London for the press agency ANSA when Roberto Calvi was found hanging from Blackfriars Bridge, and the reports he sent back made him several enemies within the political establishment. Over the years, *La Nazione* published a number of articles highlighting the appalling conditions in the high-security jails; as well as regularly polling its readers on whether they thought the time was right to offer an amnesty to all political prisoners of the armed struggle.

In contrast to his liberal credentials as a journalist, Pietro's private life was lived within a straitjacket of habits and customs. His clothes were bought in one of three shops: Polidori in Via Frattina, Petilli beneath the colonnades of Piazza Colonna, or Cenci in Via del Seminario. His socks had to be knee-length *filo di Scozia*, and he only ever wore two kinds of shoes: Church's brogues or Tod's driving shoes. The brogues he wore on his wedding day had the soles blacked out by a cobbler: he didn't want to give the guests seated behind the altar anything to comment on. He only ever took coffee in Bar Alemagna, near his office on Piazza San Silvestro, though in the summer months he would often buy an ice-cream after work at the famous Gelateria Giolitti in Vicolo Valdina. He and his wife continued to holiday in Sardinia and the Dolomites, though work commitments meant they had to give up the summer break in the mountains. Sundays followed one of two patterns: lunch with his parents in Monteverde, followed by a stroll on the Gianicolo with his brothers and their families; or lunch with his wife's parents in their villa on the Via Salaria, followed by a stroll in Villa Ada. On the Sundays when they met up with his family, they often took his young nieces to watch the marionettes on the Gianicolo.

He and Flavia had no children of their own. Six years into their marriage, Flavia went to see a gynaecologist to determine whether the problem lay with her. When it was established that everything was functioning normally, the onus lay on Pietro to have a check-up. For a while, he considered it. Twice he made an appointment with a specialist at the Policlinico, and twice he cancelled it. After the first missed appointment, Flavia confronted him: in all the years they had been together, she had never once asked him for anything – never put herself or her desires first. But there was no need for any tests: he was absolutely certain that he was sterile. He couldn't locate a single pulse or vital impulse within him capable of generating new life. Besides, even if he was wrong, and he turned out not to be sterile, what right did they have to bring a child into a union such as theirs? Those words, though unspoken, marked the end of their marriage.

Soon afterwards, Pietro Scala began to put on weight. At first the kilos crept on imperceptibly: he would put on three or four during the year, then lose two during their month in Sardinia. It was only on their return from London in 1992 that his weight gain became grotesque; suddenly, overnight it seemed, he ballooned like a woman following a hysterectomy. His thighs, waist and bottom appeared to be swathed in yards of quilting, while his stomach and breasts grew soft, swollen – androgynous-looking. Like many fat people, the skin on his calves developed mysterious bruises and ulcerations which, thanks to his paunch, he was spared the sight of.

He and Flavia stopped making love entirely; and he would often sleep on the sofa in his study. Eventually, he moved his stuff in, and that became his room.

She left the house early, hoping the hours would pass quicker that way.

Luciana had only just put on the coffee as Lotte finished making up the sofa-bed in the sitting room. It was not even seven, and she was already washed and dressed: all she had to do was brush her hair and put on some make-up. She felt only partly human that day: her neck and shoulders burned as though the skin had been flayed raw; or as though, overnight, her nervous system had been invaded by silicates, blossoming inside her like a profusion of deadly flowers. In the bathroom mirror, her reflection was shiny-eyed through nerves and lack of sleep.

'It's going to rain' said Luciana peering at the courtyard through the dusty green slats of the kitchen blind. On the table, the first Muratti of the day lay unlit beside her tooled leather cigarette-case. Standing behind her at the window, Lotte stared up at the sky; from where she stood, it looked as if it could go either way, but there was no point in arguing: Luciana was morbidly sensitive to changes in the weather, and usually able to predict, with surprising accuracy, how each day would turn out.

'I'd take an umbrella with you,' she advised, as Lotte took her raincoat off the hall stand. Tucking it into her rucksack, she unlocked the door (four twists of the long key, three of the Yale) and walked out on to the landing. The stairs smelled of bleach; and down by the main entrance the Polish woman who washed the floors was hanging her cloth over the bannisters to dry. 'Good morning,' Lotte said to her in English, as she picked her way over wet patches on the marble tiles. The woman and her husband took it in turns to do the hallway; Luciana said they were supporting three children back in Poland with their cleaning jobs.

Most of the shops on Via Stamira still had their blinds down; only the bar, and the mechanic's next door, were open for business. Walking past the workshop, Lotte inhaled the smell of new rubber from the car tyres stacked two rows deep in the doorway: here in Rome, mechanics and petrol stations seemed to spill right out on to the pavement, living additions to the neighbourhood, rather than being tucked away behind impersonal forecourts like they were in London. At the bar, she stopped for a coffee and bought six ATAC tickets: if each ticket lasted seventy-five minutes from the moment it was first punched (allowing for the time she'd spend on foot), that should be enough to keep her on the move till eight o'clock that evening. One thing was certain: she wasn't going home a moment sooner . . .

The idea was to keep moving, keep walking, as though only by devouring those pavements, spooling towards her feet in a never-ending loop, could she hope to assuage the febrile tremor of her body. By the time she reached the post office in Piazza Bologna, the weather had turned; the sky darkened, and gusts of wind were whipping up the branches of the plane trees, causing them to sway eerily above the benches in the square. As she waited at the bus stop, huge drops of rain began to flick onto the pavement, at first singly, then together in a curtain of water which instantly choked up the gutters, causing deep, rippling puddles to form at the edges of the kerb. So quickly did the streets become waterlogged that it was as though a hundred springs lay hidden beneath the roads, all of them synchronised to spurt up at exactly the same moment.

It was only 7.30 in the morning, but the number 310 bus was packed. Most of the passengers appeared to have been caught unawares by the rain; there had been something of an Indian summer over the last few days, and many of the women were still in sandals, while even the ones who did have umbrellas with them managed to look damp about the edges, their thin clothes spattered with raindrops. After punching her ticket in the machine, Lotte pushed her way right up to the front of the bus; there, she stood beside the driver, watching the long, slender windscreen wipers glide towards the centre, then back to the edges of the glass, scything the water into halves like a pair of stage curtains.

It was 28 October, the feast day of San Giuda, Il Taddeo. Who, presciently, as it turned out, happened to be the patron saint of lost causes.

'Give me one good reason why not.'

'I told you before, at La Camillina: because it's not right.'

'Why is it not right?'

'It's not right, for the simple reason that it's wrong.'

'What can be so wrong about wanting us to be together?'

'It's against every law of nature. You're a twenty-one-year-old girl – I'm old enough to be your father. Anyway, you know how the saying goes: mogli e buoi dai paesi tuoi . . .'

'I'm half-Italian. I'd learn soon enough how to cook and do things the Italian way . . .'

'That's not what I meant. I have a wife already; you have your whole life ahead of you – you'll meet someone your own age one day.'

'Tell me that you don't love me.'

'I can't. You know I love you.'

'So you don't fancy me?'

'I do fancy you . . . though for none of the right reasons.'

'And what reasons are they?'

'Because . . . because you remind me of your father.'

'I see. You're gay.'

'Of course I'm not gay. I loved your father because when I was with him I felt like somebody else – like someone I used to be . . .'

'Can you tell me why we made love without a condom if you're planning on leaving me?'

'I'm sterile; there's no need to take precautions.'

'How d'you know you're sterile? Have you been tested?'

'Listen to me, Inglesina mia. I don't have many certainties in my life, but this here is one of them. If ever a man was sterile, that man is me . . . Do you understand? I'm sterile to the core – I'm sterile in every way that God made it possible for a human being to be sterile.'

He'd told her to wait by the Via Marsala exit.

She remembered how the sun was shining that day, and how many of the tourists boarding their coach outside the Hotel Santina were dressed in shorts and sleeveless tops. Already, she felt different from them, in her new linen tunic dress and tan *ballerine* – as though, for the first time in her life, perhaps, they were the foreigners, she the native. *Sono una ragazza italiana . . . una ragazza italiana . . .* She stood watching them as 'Piero' was swallowed up like a rat into a sewer by the teeming crowds around the station, leather bomber jacket hooked defiantly over his thin shoulder.

Now, though, all was dark and gloomy, while the hot damp air inside the station smelled of diesel and burnt rubber. Bangladeshi umbrella-sellers wandered like wraiths amidst the passengers, while a party of school children carrying Invicta rucksacks held hands and sang snatches of songs as they jostled their way towards the platforms. Between a pair of black granite pillars, an old woman squatted on a marble bench: she was wrapped in a pair of matching tartan rugs, one over her head, the other around her shoulders, while her possessions were stacked neatly on the ground beside her. *Even the homeless look aesthetic here*, thought Lotte bleakly.

It was only 8.35 on the station clock, and the day stretched ahead of her, empty as a yawn. Above the newspaper kiosk hung a handwritten sign:
'*I biglietti ATAC sono finiti*'; but this was no concern of hers, as she had been so provident as to BUY SIX TICKETS BEFORE COMMENCING HER JOURNEY. The window of the kiosk was filled with souvenirs: just as when she was a child and Melody would spend all day jabbering annoyingly to her dealer-friends in Portobello, Lotte began making an inventory of the items on the shelves: plaster models of the Colosseum (three sizes), novelty packets of Baci Perugina chocolates; dark green and yellow Modiano playing cards; Kodak film, disposable cameras; decorative coffee spoons in plastic cases; miniature domes with Pinocchio in a snowstorm . . . Beside her, a pair of Brazilian transsexuals in mini-skirts, their faces caked in mocha-coloured foundation, giggled lewdly at the calendars depicting the penises of Rome's statuary.

'I wouldn't mind taking a pair of those *viados* home,' Pietro Scala had said to her that day, as he came to pick her up after her meeting with 'Piero'.

'Which – those ones standing by the shoeshop?'

'Why not? They'd look very decorative in the sitting room.'

She stared at him, appalled and delighted. She didn't think he'd come; not until she saw him walking clumsily towards her in his lightweight checked jacket did she let herself believe it. '*Come stai, Inglesina?*' he said, stooping to kiss her on the cheek. She had to hold her arms to her side to stop herself from throwing them around his middle and holding him tight. *I'm the luckiest girl in the world . . .*

'Where are you taking me?' She felt lit up, provocative.

'Don't ask so many questions.' He flagged down a taxi and opened the passenger door for her. 'Quick – move along, you're holding up the traffic.' Settling down heavily beside her, he craned his neck towards the driver: 'Piazza del Popolo,' he said before leaning back once more in his seat. To Lotte's astonishment, his eyelids soon began to droop; and unless he was a superlative actor, he appeared to have fallen into a deep sleep.

Actually, she couldn't care less: such was her joy at finally seeing him that he could have sat there doing his tax-returns and she wouldn't have minded. As he slept, she took the opportunity of observing his face: there were black smudges beneath his eyes, bruises almost, while tiny skin tags peppered the area towards his cheekbones. His dark hair was glossy and clean-looking; and, unusually for a man of his age, scarcely flecked with grey. A deep bracket of disappointment was scored on each side of his mouth. To her surprise, she realised that he looked like many Italians – not just Al Pacino. He reminded her of a politician from the Republican Party, of Bruno, the little boy in *The Bicycle Thief*, and even, a little, of the drycleaner in Piazza Bologna. He was an Everyman, a prototype, an ambassador for his race: being with him was like having a transfusion of Italianness, as though within that bulky body of his lay a doorway which led to everything she'd ever yearned for. She contemplated hugging him as he slept, whispering in his ear how much she loved him, laying her head on the graph-paper checks of his shirt . . . Driving past Piazza Colonna, she watched a group of men in suits playing football among the tarot-card readers and fortune-tellers seated at low, folding tables beneath the colonnades; while as the taxi made its way slowly up Via del Corso, weaving between tourists, moped riders and elegant ladies on shabby bicycles, Lotte stared out at the shop windows: everywhere she looked, beautiful objects lay artfully displayed: one tiny window, no larger than a closet, was filled entirely with men's shirts (*eat your heart out, Luciana*), another with silk ties and *foulards*. Strangely enough, most of the noses pressed against the glass belonged to men. Some appeared to be on their lunch hour, sauntering out of the bars and *tavole calde* in groups of three or more, ice-cream cones in their hands, all dressed in the regulation dark grey summer-weight suit, blue shirt and tan moccasins. Lotte watched them, and thought: What if one of them awoke this morning, and decided to have a scruffy day, how would his companions react? She giggled, imagining a hastily convened meeting by the water-cooler: *'We'll have to tell Pino there's no way he's coming out to lunch with us dressed like that . . .'*

In some ways it was comical, she didn't deny it, yet still, she thought, Italians seemed touched by gold-dust. That aestheticism, that conformism, came at a price – how could it not? – but at that moment she would have given anything to have been born to that servitude, to have been an actor on that vast, sunlit stage. *I'll marry him*, she thought, *sterile or not – I don't care* . . . They would live in a flat in the *centro storico*; and every morning she would ride over the cobblestones on her bicycle and return with lunch and a *filone* of bread wrapped in brown paper. Propping up her bicycle against the peeling walls of their *palazzo*, she would reach inside her pocket for the key before unlocking the heavy double doors, so that anyone who happened to be walking down the street at that moment would catch a glimpse of their life: a marble courtyard, palm trees in low earthenware pots . . .

The driver was just entering the taxi rank in Piazza del Popolo when Pietro Scala pulled out a 20,000-lire bill from his pocket and handed it to him. 'Keep the change,' he said. As soon as they got out, their place in the cab was taken by a bald, elderly-looking man in a blazer, skin-tight, ironed jeans and check shirt, carrying a sheaf of bags bearing the names of local boutiques. His companion was a young North African girl dressed in a mini-skirt and satin *bustier*, her raven waist-length hair tied in a kind of half-*chignon*, or pineapple, on the top of her head. Lotte watched her pick her way across the cobblestones on a pair of sandals whose straps consisted of bronze snakes wound around the ankle, legionnaire-style, and whose perspex heels were so vertiginously high that her feet appeared to be on tip-toes.

'She must be a great conversationalist,' said Pietro Scala grimly as they walked towards the Egyptian obelisk in the centre of the square. Outside Bar Canova with its yellow damask tablecloths, a young gypsy violinist was playing 'O Sole Mio', while beside him, a small boy in an oversized pin-striped suit, McDonald's cup in one hand, stood laughing as he watched a Jack Russell, which was tethered to one of the potted palm trees around the bar, barking and lunging hopelessly at the pigeons.

Lotte didn't reply; but, later, as they sat on one of the green-painted benches in the gardens of the Pincio, listening to the occasional *thuck* of pine cones hitting the gravel, and the excited cries of teenage girls as they rode up and down the Avenue of Poets on six-seater bicycles, she said: 'They could have been in love, you know.'

'Who could have been in love?'

'That couple we saw getting into the taxi.'

Instantly she realised her mistake; and to prevent him giving her another treatise on *l'ordine naturale delle cose* (and, more importantly, a chance to recall – and perhaps even act upon – his disapproval of older men going with young girls), she quickly changed the subject.

'Ennio used to come here, you know, with his father. Luciana showed me a picture of them standing by that carousel over there.'

But it was too late; the spell was broken. Taking one of her hands into his and squeezing it gently, he smiled at her.

'Only a *romantica donna inglese* could imagine any purity behind such a venal coupling,' he said. Then a shadow crossed his face, and Lotte's heart twisted: *he's going to tell me he has to leave now* . . . Down below the Salita del Pincio, and all over the city, church bells were ringing for the Ave Maria, while the busts lining both sides of the Avenue of Poets were silhouetted in gold. Beneath an ancient ilex tree, *extracomunitari* packed up their wares – wooden trains, whose carriages could be hooked together to spell out a child's name, toy mobile phones, silk vests in cellophane packages – while the owner of the carousel pulled down the metal shutters on his booth.

'I'll walk you to your office, shall I?' she said. *So, afterwards, she wouldn't remember those words having come from his mouth . . .*

On the way back down Via del Corso, they stopped for an *aperitivo* at Bar Alemagna. It was his local, had been for the last twenty years; while he waited to be served, he nodded briefly to several colleagues, all of whom stared at Lotte with barely disguised curiosity. As the elderly white-coated barman placed her Campari down beside a saucer of *salatini*, Pietro Scala looked up at him, and without appearing the slightest bit discomposed, said: 'Arnaldo, meet my cousin. From London.' Equally coolly, as though this were a genuine introduction, she a genuine cousin, the barman replied, '*Piacere, signorina . . . e buona permanenza a Roma.*'

His office was on Via delle Mercede, a small street leading off Piazza San Silvestro.

There was a bus depot in the middle of the square, where ordinarily she would wait to catch the number 61 back to Piazza Bologna. (It was also a kind of meeting place for the unnaturally handsome ATAC drivers, who would sit around their prefab in their sunglasses and crisp blue shirts, drinking coffee, reading magazines and eyeing up passing women as they awaited their slots.) But, as there had been nothing ordinary about that afternoon, instead of putting her on her bus (which, unusually, was about to depart, and with a few empty seats, to boot,), Pietro Scala took her to the doorway of a glove shop. Where he kissed her long and hard, and held her as though his heart, too, had been broken – *had it, though? Had it?* – and once again she breathed the heady oxygenated scent of his skin, a smell which she thought had been lost to her for ever. Then he led her across the square to a side entrance of *La Nazione*, up several flights of stairs which were coated with a kind of black rubber linoleum, through a pair of fire-doors, to a tiny lobby where a plain, middle-aged woman sat at a computer (not Cinzia? Dumpy? Glasses? No make-up?), to the door of his private office.

And locking it behind him, he opened his arms wide.

Around midday, when the rain showed no sign of letting up, Lotte entered La Rinascente in Piazza Colonna. A tiny reckless part of her was contemplating strolling up Via del Corso towards Bar Alemagna, and although she had no intention of indulging herself in this near-suicidal wish, she felt she still ought to be prepared. She imagined entering the bar and, bold as brass, marching up to the elderly barman – *What was his name again? Arnaldo, that was it* – and asking him to inform Dottor Scala that his cousin had returned from London.

In the accessories department she tried on a silk *foulard*, attempting to emulate the effortless way the young girl on the *metropolitana* had worn hers. First, she tried sweeping it over one shoulder, then crossing it in the middle with both ends tucked in, then knotting it to one side à la Penelope Keith, until finally, in desperation, she attempted the cassock style some Asian women in London favoured. But all to no avail; the magic had gone – that flash of instinctive, completely harmonious elegance, which for a brief moment, in her mind, at least, had set her apart from the tourists as she stood waiting for him outside the train station. *I've lost that loving feeling . . .* At the Pupa make-up counter, she tried on some lipstick which, like certain brands of shoe-polish, came in a tube with a curious sponge applicator which you activated by twisting the middle of the tube. But the colour was too harsh for her complexion, and she quickly wiped it off. Somewhere, she remembered reading that the true test of a lipstick was that it should look good on a bare face . . . At the Versace counter, she watched a shabby old woman in a headscarf, instantly recognizable as a time-waster like herself, asking the assistant for a hand-cream called '*Cera di Cupra*', 'because you see in my day, the label was different, and it used to come in a glass jar, not a tube'. Then she wanted to know whether you could still buy booklets containing leaves of rose-scented pressed powder; until finally, she came to the point, and asked to sample the perfume that was displayed on the counter. '*Certo, signora*,' replied the assistant courteously, and she sprayed a generous amount on the old lady's outstretched arm. 'Very pleasant,' she murmured, as though she was contemplating buying it, 'what did you say it was called?' 'Vooman,' replied the assistant, 'by Donatella Versace.'

Of course, when there was a brief lull in the rain, Lotte no more headed towards Piazza San Silvestro than she did back home to Luciana. Instead, she walked up to Piazza Venezia, past the trunk of a beggar – literally, just a torso and a head, limbless as the busts lining the Avenue of Poets – who had been propped up against the wall of the Waxworks Museum on a little home-made cart (by whom? And when would they come back for him? And what if they didn't?), through the narrow streets of the Ghetto and on to Ponte Garibaldi. There, she stood on the parapet looking down at the glassy green waters of the Tiber, boiling and spuming at the sluice-gates near the Isola Tiberina, where patients on day-release from the Fate-benefratelli Hospital wandered the island in their pyjamas, and two trams, crossing the bridge in opposite directions, made the ground rumble beneath her feet.

It began to rain again, just as she was crossing the bridge on to Piazza Gioacchino Belli. She had never been to Trastevere before; she knew her mother used to go and see English films there at the Pasquino cinema in Vicolo del Piede; and that on the day she and Ennio first met in a bookshop, Ennio had taken her to see the frescoes in the church of Santa Maria in Trastevere. Both Melody and Luciana had told her the story of that meeting. There was even a line-drawing of some children playing football against the church wall in Julia's sketchbook which lay at the bottom of her rucksack.

Outside the portico of the church, directly beneath the beautiful mosaics depicting Jesus at Mary's breast, flanked by the figures of the ten wise and foolish virgins, a young gypsy woman sat cross-legged on the ground feeding her baby. Lotte looked down at the child's matted hair, tipped with sparks of gold like the twigs of Silvana's bonfire. Fumbling inside her pocket, she dropped a handful of coins into the outstretched palm. '*Grazie, gentil' signora . . . grazie,*' moaned the woman, as Lotte entered the church.

Almost immediately, her eye was caught by a plain wooden statue of St Joseph bearing aloft the infant Jesus on a red-painted Bible. A small lamp stood on one side of the figure; and on the other, a vase of silk flowers. Folded-up letters of supplication were stuffed in every nook and cranny of the statue, spread out like a carpet beneath Joseph's bare feet, within the folds of his robe, and even high up between the fingers of his outstretched palm. The letters were written on napkins and menus and torn-out pages from diaries: one was even scribbled on a flier from a local disco. 'Cremona, June 1997: Please watch over all our family . . .' 'I pray to you to help my son Massimo win his fight against his demons . . .' 'We love you, Joseph, and petition you to strengthen the bonds of our marriage . . . Matteo and Wanda, Padova . . .' Lotte thought of her mother, and 'Piero's' words in the station restaurant: *she said she'd lit a candle to the Madonna in every church she passed* . . . Like her, Julia had entered a church – maybe even this church – in her hour of need, joining her own petition for grace to that sea of lost causes.

Lotte looked at her watch: in just under three hours, everything would be decided; she would know: one way or the other Pietro Scala would have drawn up a blueprint for the rest of their lives. And no matter how unbearable the outcome, it couldn't be worse than this waiting. Reaching inside her rucksack, she pulled out her mother's notebook, and the four-coloured BIC biro she'd bought at the airport in London. Slowly, she turned the pages of the book, admiring Julia's little line-drawings of everyday Roman scenes – the flower-sellers at Campo dè Fiori, children playing by a fountain in the Ghetto – until she reached the sketch she was looking for, the last picture her mother ever drew: the view from La Camillina, framed by shutters, the place where all their stories began and ended . . . Hesitating for a moment, she ripped out the page, careful to follow the tiny perforations along the margin, then she turned the paper over on to the blank side.

'*Dear Joseph*,' she wrote, '*this is my story, and it was my mother's story too . . .*'

In a dark room on the other side of the river, Pietro Scala lay on a stretcher.

His right arm was attached to a drip, containing a half-litre bottle of 9 per cent glucose-solution which was suspended from a metal frame. His jacket was hanging on a chair beside him, while his shoes lay side by side at the foot of the bed. Through the half-open door, he could hear the ringing of a telephone and the voices of two different secretaries, one Italian, one foreign, who appeared to be taking it in turns to answer it: '*Buona sera, lo studio del Dottor Petilli . . .*'

Peeping above the pocket of his jacket, the signal-light of his mobile winked and flashed beguilingly at him. Without even getting up from his bed, all he had to do was reach over and pull the phone out: the battery was charged, the reception up here near perfect (the first thing he'd checked on entering the room); and if he spoke quietly enough, nobody in the reception area outside need hear his words.

'*Call me,*' she said, '*there's something we need to talk about. If you don't ring – if I haven't heard from you by eight o'clock this evening – then please don't get in touch again . . . ever.*' There was a pause, as though she couldn't quite make up her mind how to ring off after such a drastic ultimatum, until, slightly sheepishly, in a voice which made his heart throb with tenderness, no matter how many times he played it back, she said: '*Goodbye then, from your* Inglesina . . .' According to the log of incoming calls, the message had arrived at 6.00 a.m. that morning. As he sat working at his desk (recently, he'd found it unbearable to stay in bed past dawn) she was somewhere in her grandmother's house, with the telephone in her hand, desperate enough to risk Luciana's fury if discovered.

Flavia, too, had made an early start that morning. When he left for work, the door of her bedroom was wide open, and he noticed the dog's lead was missing from its hook above the mirror. She loved the current dog, Nerina, as she had loved its predecessor, Lady, a stray picked up on a beach in Sardinia. Deprived of any other source of affection (unless you counted her parents, to whom, in spite of the foursomes at *Tresette*, and the holidays spent in their company, she was not close, at least not emotionally), Flavia made do with the dog; she had no choice.

Or rather she did: when the results of the gynaecological tests came back indicating she was fertile – or could be, with the right man – Pietro Scala offered her a way out of their marriage. He understood how much having children meant to her; ever since he had known her, she was the kind of girl who loved babies, and everything associated with their world. Without any experience of her own, she could talk knowledgeably about the best time to start weaning, or the different ways of helping a newborn distinguish between night and day. She had a Chicco loyalty card, which she used lavishly on his nieces and on friends' children, and twice a week she did voluntary work at the Sisters of Mercy orphanage.

Over the years, her somewhat girlish demeanour hardened into an inscrutable cheerfulness: her response to any attempts on his part at broaching the emotional poverty of their marriage was to bounce back at him with a series of rubber-coated platitudes; until over time, he simply stopped approaching the subject. If pushed to do so, he would acknowledge, to himself, at least, that he had ruined Flavia's life; but his line of defence was that, unlike most Italian men, he didn't fool around and in twenty years of marriage had never been unfaithful to his wife. Until, that is, he met Lotte . . .

Pietro Scala groaned. If at that moment he was lying in a darkened room with a three-centimetre-long needle stuck into his hand, it was because of her, Lotte. For the last forty-eight hours to be precise, since they'd made love on the swivel chair in his office), he had turned into one of those men on the brink of leaving his wife. He kept thinking to himself: I could die tomorrow, and all I could show for my time on this earth is a failed marriage and a sore heart. Life had to be worth more than that . . . Lotte loved him and needed him – more than Flavia did – Flavia, who had her parents, and who, in any case, had made something of a virtue of living without love. If he shut his eyes, he could actually see himself doing it: taking her hand, walking out together into the sunshine, turning his back on the dank, empty rooms of his old life – a life where, until now, he and love had never coexisted. But he did love Lotte: only God knew how much he loved her . . . In the midst of this delirium, he decided that his weight, as much if not more than his age, was the main obstacle preventing them being together. (He had no way of fathoming the deep sexual desire his size aroused in Lotte: his body, her bulwark and her storehouse – each ounce of flesh a tiny nibble of Italy.) So, in a highly uncharacteristic move, he approached a colleague from *La Repubblica* who had recently shed a stunning thirty kilos, and asked him the secret of his weight loss. The colleague put him in touch with an ex-GP, a certain Dr Petilli, who ran an unlicensed diet clinic from his flat in Viale Regina Margherita. The regime was simple: no food at all for a month, half a litre per day of fortified glucose administered intravenously, appetite-suppressing tablets morning, noon, and night, unlimited black coffee . . .

Pietro Scala looked around the room: above the weighing scales was a laminated poster showing the WHO-recommended food pyramid, and beside it, an out-of-date calendar from a pharmaceutical company. According to Dr Petilli, if he stuck to the regime, he too could expect to shed thirty kilos by Christmas. That way, he and Lotte could . . . could what? Start a new life together, looking only marginally less grotesque than that couple in Piazza del Popolo? A prisoner of happiness? A middle-aged man with a foolish grin on his face? An uninvited guest, begging-bowl in hand, or the thirteenth fairy at the christening . . .? He stared down at the needle puncturing his plump hand, and an image came into his head of Ennio's last days in the hospital wing of Rebibbia, just before the prison authorities allowed Luciana to take him home. Most of his hair had fallen out, and beneath the regulation gown, his thin arms were covered in haematomas. Then, he too had been attached to a drip, the needle positioned in the exact centre of his home-made tattoo. 'I knew it would come in useful one day,' he muttered through peeling white lips . . . Then he thought of that photograph taken during the hunger-strike at Nuoro, when Ennio weighed forty-eight kilos, less than half of what he himself weighed today. He looked up at the bottle of glucose: drop by drop, his organism was being fed – that fat body of his which only knew the habits of greed and sloth; and which, for longer than he cared to remember, had been so supra-nourished that it was now bearing the weight of two men.

Pietro Scala sat up in bed and looked down once more at his hand. Then, without thinking, he ripped the needle out of his vein and flung it into the sink. Gathering up his jacket and shoes, he walked out of the flat in his socks, past the two receptionists at the desk, down the stairs and on to the street, where he stopped for a moment to lace up his brogues.

Traffic permitting, he'd be home by eight.

Tonight it was the turn of Lily Gruber, the red-headed one.

Dressed in a cute grey trouser suit and a dark blue man's shirt with cufflinks at the wrists, La Gruber, sheaf of papers in one hand, pen in the other, half-leaned, half-sat against the glass-topped studio table; and turning her better profile towards the camera, she uttered the words: '*Buona sera dal TG Uno . . .*'

At which, on cue, Lotto turned to her grandmother and said: 'There's something I have to tell you . . .'

A removals van was parked in the driveway.

All morning, men in green overalls had been loading furniture and packing cases into one of its dropped sides. They were taking away La Guerrini's stuff: her son had sold the flat, and later that day he was driving her to an old people's home near Tivoli.

'You'll have to tell the driver to wait for you outside the gates when you order your taxi,' said Luciana. 'Trust La Guerrini to choose today of all days to do her house clearance.' She packed the last of the frozen steaks into Lotte's suitcase, wrapping them in layers of torn-out sheets from her crossword magazine. 'This is proper Italian beef, mind – no offence, but you don't want to go taking any chances with English meat. Not in your condition, I mean . . .'

Once she'd got over the bitter disappointment of her new kinship to Pietro Scala, Luciana had turned out to be a surprisingly practical *confidante*.

'You're not the first girl to land herself in this kind of mess, and chances are, you won't be the last. You'll manage with the baby, like we all managed.'

Of all the possible outcomes, it had to be this one, thought Lotte. They were a breed unto themselves, the women in her family – genetically wired, it seemed, for single-motherhood. Now it was her turn to be a *ragazza madre*, to take up her place in that endless line of shabby, ill-used women . . . the ones who hadn't managed to get it right – that simple configuration of family life: *Father. Mother. Child.* But it was dangerous to allow herself such thoughts; her pregnancy – what Luciana quaintly termed her *stato interessante* – had turned her into one of those women who find themselves weeping in public. The other day, at the Lion Bookshop in Piazza di Spagna, she'd picked up a Miriam Stoppard pregnancy manual; at the sight of the gummy, prawn-shaped embryo with its snub nose, its cloudy fish-eye, she found it almost impossible to hold back her tears. Everything in the book seemed exquisitely pertinent to her condition: the cross-section of a womb, shaped like a lowering bull's head, curling fallopian tubes for horns (*who would have thought it looked like that?*), the checklist of early symptoms: fatigue (yes); tender breasts (yes); nausea (only on an empty stomach); frequent desire to urinate (yes!); cravings (none); loathings (coffee, cheese, chocolate). The chapter entitled 'Sensual Pregnancy' was full of photographs of couples: there was a man's guide to massaging what looked like every inch of the woman's body; several were of couples just standing there expectantly in the classic, rather soppy 'spoons' position, the man's hands clasped around the woman's belly; while in the birth section there were endless pictures of men – some more *au fait*-looking than others – supporting and holding their partners during the various stages of labour. And this was just the beginning: a foretaste, if you like, of the loneliness which awaited her . . . As she hurried out of the shop, the tears streaming down her cheeks, she thought: *All your life you've done nothing but bemoan the weirdness of your childhood, and now you're all set to pass the baton on to your own child* ... Her body had run away with her, galloping towards its destiny (*it's not my fault, doctor, my body was galloping towards its destiny*); a switch had been flicked on; new life had erupted inside her, and from now on, it was out of her hands.

Blindly, she had stumbled towards the *metro* station at Piazza di Spagna, beaten back at first by the tide of Japanese tourists heading for the designer boutiques in Via Condotti, to the line of payphones beside the ticket machines. At the kiosk, she bought a SIP card for 5,000 lire; and lit up by a kind of reckless fury, she rang his mobile number. *Sono assente*, said the message, *ma lasciate il vostro numero e sarete richiamati*. Leave your number and I'll get back to you. *I'll get back to you* ... Coming from his lips, thought Lotte, that had to be about the biggest untruth ever uttered ... Leave your number, and I'll *never* get back to you, was more like it. Still, she dialled once more (twenty times more, actually, there was no way he'd know it was her), counting the number of rings before the voicemail came on (six), thrilling at the sound of his voice, the worldly, Roman way he had of dragging his vowels, as though no message in the world would ever break through that ennui ... *Because I love you, my little* Inglesina ... his unreadable dark eyes staring towards the kitchen wall of La Camillina –

'What should I say to your philanderer if he calls?'

Lotte's heart quickened. He wasn't going to call – he hadn't until now – so why should he once she'd gone? And yet in spite of herself, a picture from the Miriam Stoppard book flashed into her mind: it was of an older father standing by a Moses basket, on to whose plump, contented-looking features she had mentally superimposed those of Pietro Scala. (In her fantasy, the photograph had been taken in their *centro storico* apartment; and the reason she wasn't in the frame was that she was out on the balcony watering the geraniums, having just returned from a trip to the shops on her shabby bicycle.) 'Nothing. Tell him nothing. Anyway, he won't call, we both know that.'

'You can't know for sure . . . Gilberto waited two years before getting in touch.' Zipping up the last of Lotte's cases, Luciana carried it out to the hall where the other bags stood lined up by the door. Somehow, she thought – *don't ask how* – she'd turned into the heroine of a neo-realist film: *grand-mother in faded housecoat offers grim words of advice; young girl sits at kitchen table and weeps (again)* –

'Listen to me, Lotte. You'll do what you think best when the time comes . . . just concentrate on yourself now, and try and enjoy your pregnancy. You know what they say: a crying mother makes for a crying child . . .' Not unkindly, she took her hand; then, to Lotte's surprise, she pressed something into the palm. It was her fake wedding ring, the one she wore on a chain around her neck.

'Wear it when you go to the hospital: the nurses will treat you like dirt if they know you're not married.'

Half appalled, half touched, Lotte held the ring up to the window. Inside the band there was an inscription engraved in curling script: *'Ti ameró sempre, G.'*

Maybe he really had loved Luciana, she thought: maybe Gilberto's heart, too, had been full of promise that day, almost half a century before, when he stood in a jeweller's shop in a small town in Sicily; and taking the box out of his pocket, had asked the owner to engrave the words of his heart on to a ring: *Ti ameró sempre, G.* Perhaps, like that palm-filled courtyard she had imagined and made hers, Gilberto too had pictured a new life for himself and Luciana in Rome, where the two of them would live together in a flat, their own flat, not the broom-cupboard she was forced to call home: he would return for lunch from his job at the Ministry, where she would be waiting for him in the kitchen, her apron hanging on a hook behind the door . . .

Around one, just before the taxi was due, Lotte went down to the courtyard to see if the removals van was still blocking the gates. As she passed La Guerrini's apartment on the ground floor, she noticed the door was wide open: and there, at the other end of the empty room, she saw a tiny figure sitting by the window on a pile of flat-packed cardboard packing-cases.

'I've been waiting for you all morning. Come in, please.'

Hesitating for a moment, the memory of their recent encounter all too fresh in her mind, Lotte walked across the expanse of marble floor: at least the door was open this time, and, if necessary, she could make a run for it. One whiff of that terrible smell, and there was no saying what might happen . . . Yet, as Lotte approached the window, she realised it wasn't just the flat that looked and smelled different: hands folded demurely on her lap, La Guerrini was dressed in a child-sized red and white FILA tracksuit zipped up to the neck; she smelled of soap and eau de Cologne, and her greying hair was secured neatly to one side with a girlish clip. It was her expression, though, which had changed the most: scrubbed clean of that grubby kabuki mask, her face was tranquil, beatific even, and a happy light shone from her eyes.

'So you're returning to London to have the baby?'

Lotte nodded; how that woman got to be so well informed was a mystery . . . During their last encounter, even though she hadn't worked up the courage to do a pregnancy test yet, La Guerrini had guessed right away about the baby.

'What about you – when are you leaving?'

'Just as soon as those delightful young men outside have finished loading up my things. They'll be depositing them directly at the offices of the Rabbinical Council.'

'I'm sorry?'

'Those art treasures that my Aldo stole . . . I'm returning them to the Hebrews.'

'What made you decide to do that?'

'They were driving me mad . . . I lost my reason because of those objects. All those years I was scared to open the door in case it was one of those poor families come to claim back their things.'

'Why did you wait so long?'

'Ah, *figlia mia*, if only things were that simple . . . here in Italy, we prefer our history to scorch . . . look at your poor father; he was such a good boy, but he got swept up by the excitement of the times . . . just like my Aldo did. I begged him to stay home – it was all hopeless, the Allies were moving in closer with each day, any fool could have seen the end coming – but when that message came from the Duce, to join him in Salò, he couldn't say no . . . right till the end, my Aldo had stars in his eyes . . .'

Maybe there had been stars in her eyes too, thought Lotte. After all, Pietro Scala had never pretended to be a free man . . . For all her disapproval of Julia's infatuation with Ennio, she'd been just as willing to be led by passion, by the excitement of being in Italy, jostling to find her place on that sunlit stage. She wondered how much of it, too, was just a reaction to Ennio's death: *whatever happens, at least I won't be going back empty-handed* . . . 'I'd better go,' she said, 'my taxi will be here soon.'

'Before you leave, I'd like to show you something'. Unzipping the jacket pocket of her tracksuit, La Guerrini pulled out a photograph. It was of an African family seated against a studio backdrop of a waterfall: mother and father in traditional dress, a small child on each side.

'Who are they?'

'They're my adopted family: Camille and Esau, from Zambia. I'm sponsoring them through the Caritas.'

'They look nice . . . What are the children's names?'

Closing her eyes, La Guerrini pressed the photograph to her breast; for a moment, she looked quite mad again. 'Their names are Stella and Richard . . . but in my prayers, they're my little chocolate angels . . .'

9

ENNIO

1. Melody to Luciana

. . . after everything she's been through. Obviously it will take her some time to accept her condition, the last few months haven't been easy, but in my experience, Lotte's more resilient than she appears. To be frank, I was heart-broken when I first found out about the baby: she has her whole life ahead of her still, and we all know what it means to have the responsibility of another human being to look after. I blame myself, partly . . . she was hardly speaking to me when I left for England, and I was worried that she might decide to go it alone . . . Thankfully, things are slowly mending between us. Obviously, it will take time . . . There's a lot she still has to get out of her system, and pregnancy in any case tends to throw up all sorts of hidden emotions from the past . . . At the moment she's keeping fairly active: she swims regularly, and she attends an ante-natal exercise class at the hospital. The midwives say the pregnancy is going well: from her last scan, the baby appears larger than average, although, for now, she's decided not to find out the sex. She's in reasonably good spirits; I think she was glad to return home to familiar surroundings, although she's still not over P.S. – not by any means. I think what upsets her the most is that he doesn't know he's to become a father. I'm still not clear how things went – why she should have left like that without telling him – perhaps you can explain more when you write . . .

. . . I enclose an international money order for annual maintenance of the grave; let me know if it covers everything . . . I hope you are well, and that you will consider coming over here for the birth, if you can take time off from your work . . .

Affectionately yours,

Melody

2. Luciana to Melody

. . . with the usual bronze cheek of the man, now the whole business is to be raked over again I can't even go to the shops without people pointing and making their comments. Thanks to that Scoundrel and his book, Ennio's face is plastered all over the newspapers again, now journalists have started bothering me for pictures of him when he was a little boy I even caught one of them going through the rubbish out the back, it hasn't been that bad since that whole business at La Camillina. I haven't read the book, I've no intention of reading it either. What's past is past . . . Glad that Lotte is doing well in my opinion she's better off managing things on her own without telling that Man, you know how the saying goes: *meglio soli che mal accompagnati* . . . It's not as if he cared about her when she was over here, and who's to say he'd leave his wife even if he did find out about the baby? I don't know the ins and outs of what went on either, she didn't want to talk about it before she left. Please tell her not to overdo it with the swimming, too much jigging about is bad for the baby, she could pick up all sorts of microbes and suchlike from the water . . . The caretaker down at the cemetery wrote to say condensation has got in behind the glass of Julia's frame, he says the photograph is ruined. If you send me another picture, I'll make sure they replace it when I go down for Ennio's name-day. I'll ask the stonemason to fix on a new frame . . . The money order you sent was too much, I'll put the difference towards the frame and next year's annual maintenance . . . I don't know about coming over for the baby, one of my brothers down in Sicily is not well, I might have to go over there for my holidays.

Best wishes to you and Lotte,

Yours,

Luciana Caruso

3. Luciana to Melody

. . . haven't received an answer yet to my last letter, but I know what the postal system is like . . . ought to let you know that that lecher and Cradle-snatcher telephoned me yesterday morning all full of himself, says that Ennio's book is on the bestsellers index now the publisher is talking about translating it into other languages and selling it abroad. Why people from other countries should be interested in reading about the goings-on of a bunch of delinquents I don't know, there's no accounting for some tastes . . . had the nerve to ask about Lotte, I said she was doing fine thank you back in London, then he asks for her address that man has no shame. I said I would let him know in good time if my granddaughter wants to correspond with him.

With affectionate regards,

Luciana Caruso

4. Melody to Luciana

. . . our letters must have crossed paths somewhere over the Channel . . . mine was sent recorded-delivery as it contained a photograph of Julia, a different one from the one in the cemetery, which Lotte chose this time. I passed on the information to her that Pietro Scala had been in touch, and I must admit that her reaction surprised me . . . she went a little quiet, but then she said that she did not want you to give him our address. She didn't mention it for the rest of the day until this evening, whilst we were out walking along the canal near our house, she told me for the first time how things had been between them when she left for London. Apparently, without saying anything to him about the baby, she gave him an ultimatum to get in touch with her; she seems to have spent most of their short affair waiting for him to ring, and I think she had reached the end of her patience. She said it would have clouded the issue if he had known about the baby, and she wanted to be sure he wanted her for herself, not because she was pregnant – 'not just a womb for his child' is how she put it. The fact he didn't call her by the end of that day was enough to convince her that he didn't have serious feelings towards her, at least not serious enough to make him leave his wife. I don't think she took the decision lightly – apparently at one stage, she even contemplated missing the flight . . . She's growing heavier now, but pregnancy agrees with her, and she looks well. Her latest blood tests indicate that she has borderline anaemia, but she's taking supplements which hopefully should bring her iron-count up . . . The baby is moving constantly, and the kicking sometimes keeps her awake at night.

You know, Luciana, these days I'm haunted by the memory of Julia; I look at Lotte, how bewildered she is sometimes by all the changes her body is going through, and it's like a knife to the heart each time I think of how Julia suffered all that alone – nobody to turn to, nobody to unburden herself to. As far as I know, in her short life she'd never come into contact with anybody who was pregnant –

the whole thing must have been completely alien to her. It breaks my heart to know that I am responsible – at least in part – for abandoning her as I did . . . I know her mother's death is weighing on Lotte, too . . . we haven't discussed it, but the other day, out of the blue, she said: 'I suppose, if I die in childbirth, you and Luciana will be too old to look after my baby.' Can you imagine, she's about to become a mother herself, and yet her head is full of such fears? Yesterday we went for a tour of the birthing suite at the hospital: it looks very nice, and not like a hospital at all. All sorts of alternative therapies are available such as a purpose-built pool, aromatherapy, even acupuncture. I'll keep you abreast of how things are going over here . . .

Lotte sends love, as do I,
Melody

5. Luciana to Melody

. . . so tell Lotte not to worry about buying the *corredino* or any of the first things. I've knitted a receiving shawl and a swaddling blanket in cream merino wool, and I'm just finishing off a matinée jacket with matching bonnet and mittens. I'll send them to you nearer the time, she might be superstitious about having baby things in the house before the birth, I was . . . I also sewed a silk vest to put on the baby as soon as it's been cleaned up it's a custom over here, it's meant to bring luck . . . you might tell her about a Sicilian old-wives' cure for anaemia, it's called *la mela inchiodata*. You stick nails inside an apple, leave it overnight, then next morning you pull the nails out and eat the apple . . . it's meant to be full of the iron from the nails. Sure enough, that Scoundrel never rang back for Lotte's address. I must of scared him off, good riddance, I say . . . she's better off having the baby in peace, without getting upset about it all over again, she can get in touch later when the baby's older. Tell her not to dwell on Julia, and you shouldn't blame yourself either, you did the best you could by your daughter like I did with Ennio, in the end it's all in God's hands . . .

With Sincere regards to you and Lotte,
Luciana Caruso

PS The photograph of Julia arrived, she looks beautiful.

6. Melody to Luciana

. . . at my wits' end, Luciana. I've tried reasoning with her, pointing out to her the risks involved, both to her and the baby, but it's as if she's in the grip of an obsession: she will not listen to sense. Her GP also strongly advised her against such a move, but when he told her she just stormed out of the surgery in a fury. I honestly think at this point all we can do is try to accommodate her; the last thing anyone of us wants is for her to face the birth with the odds stacked against her (psychologically, I mean) more than they already are. I telephoned the GP afterwards to apologise for Lotte's outburst, and as a favour, he agreed to write the letter to the airlines, even though strictly speaking she shouldn't be flying any more. Without it, though, we haven't a hope of being allowed to board an aircraft. When I rang one of the midwives from the birthing unit over here to explain the situation, she said that as a rule of thumb it was best to stay clear of private clinics anywhere in the world, which just leaves the public hospitals – are there any local ones you would recommend? And do you think they would agree to take Lotte on at such a late stage? Technically, her baby wouldn't even be considered premature if it were born tomorrow . . . I can't understand it – she seemed to be so happy with the hospital she had chosen here, all the different facilities on offer, and the midwives have gone out of their way to be kind. They'd even sat down and drawn up a birth-plan with her . . . I'll telephone you on Sunday evening to see if you have got anywhere with your enquiries, hoping that in the meantime Lotte will have come to her senses . . .

Thank you for everything, Luciana,
Kindest regards,
Melody

7. Luciana to Melody

. . . the paediatrician I was telling you about on the telephone, the one that was a relative of the Contessa we took Lotte to him to have her vaccinations when she was a baby. He's retired now, he sounded a bit sclerotic, if you ask me, rambling on about going to the midsummer ball at Leonforte, like the Contessa was still alive but then he passed me on to his housekeeper and she said her neighbour's daughter-in-law had her baby at a hospital not far from here called Ospedale San Giacomo – it's just up towards the Colli Portuensi. She agreed to give me the name of the consultant that delivered the baby. When I telephoned him at his *studio*, he said that if Lotte wants to give birth at the San Giacomo she must see him first as a private patient, he would say that, wouldn't he? But at least he said he'd see her, some of those doctors act like they're handing out God's charity if they give you five minutes of their day, and they fleece you for the privilege. So as soon as you let me know the day you're arriving I'll make an appointment with him for the next day, there's no point wasting any more time . . . It's a good thing I never posted the *corredino* to you, I was waiting to buy some tissue paper to wrap it up in, the *cartoleria* in Via Stamira only had coloured paper in stock and I wanted white . . . So you see maybe I'm getting a little bit psychic in my old age . . . I wasn't even surprised when your letter came about Lotte, I remember near the end of my confinement with Ennio I tried to run away from the nuns at Santa Corona it was summertime, there was five of us girls sleeping all together in a tiny attic, ten, if you include the babies, at night-time it was so hot in there the mattresses would be soaking wet with perspiration, and every morning I thought that's it, my waters have broke and the baby's coming . . . They used to send us out in the daytime to wash clothes for local families – imagine having to scrub those big heavy sheets my belly barely fitted over the edge of the sink! One day I said to Assunta, the girl they put me to work with, I'm not standing for it a moment longer – I'm going home. So I walked out of the house, it was the local solicitor's family, down the main road towards the centre of the town, but by the time I reached the bus station Suor' Angelica, that was the Mother Superior, she turned up with Padre Carmelo and they brought me back to Santa Corona . . . Which isn't to say that Lotte's running away from anything, it's just her head or it could be her heart telling her she's got to have her baby in Italy, any fool can tell you there's no arguing with a woman when she's in a *stato interessante*. For all we know that Man might have something to do with her decision, I just pray to God he won't go upsetting her if I'm right and that's why she wants to have the baby over here . . . You don't want to be sleeping in a strange *pensione* when you come, Melody, don't get me wrong, but in Lotte's condition she needs to be in familiar surroundings. The two of you can share my bedroom, I'll sleep on the divan in the sitting room. We'll be a bit tight, but I'm sure we'll rub along fine . . .

With best wishes to you and Lotte,
Luciana Caruso

The Avenue of Poets

I'm writing this because if I don't do it now, it will begin to fade in my memory and all this will be lost for ever. He's sleeping now, I put him down twenty minutes ago, enough time to have a quick shower and get dressed (it's 11.30 in the morning!) and unbelievably he still hasn't woken up . . .

I've never kept a diary until now; partly out of laziness, partly because I always felt that everything to do with my life was so incomplete and unsatisfactory that I'd never have the desire to read back over anything I'd written. Even when I came to Italy the first time round, I still didn't keep a journal – probably, with hindsight, I should have – but that whole period seemed so unreal to me, even as I was actually living through it, that I didn't have the distance to sit down and try to make sense of it on paper.

The funny thing is that all my life I'd believed that if only I could discover the identity of my father, I'd feel complete. And, in a way, when I eventually found out about Ennio and Luciana and the story of my birth it did make me feel complete; but the whole experience was so tied up with Italy, and falling in love with P.S. that it's as if at the end of the day what I was left with was a fantasy identity – someone I hoped I could be, who wasn't really me at all.

But when my son – there, I said it! MY SON! – came into the world, that really did feel like a beginning – a joint beginning, a double birth. I looked at his face and in his features I finally saw myself – not *in* him, but as though I was looking *at* him with a sense of absolute recognition of who I was. Which hopefully doesn't sound too pretentious or confusing. Anyway, enough soul-searching: this account isn't about me, or at least it's not meant to be, and I don't want to waste what little time I have in writing about my own spiritual quests . . .

(A quick break to creep into the room to see if he's still sleeping; he stirred, but touch wood, he doesn't seem to have woken up. We're staying with Luciana for the time being; and she's kindly given us her bedroom.)

He (I'm afraid my darling boy doesn't have a name yet: I have six weeks before I have to register him at the British Embassy) was born twenty-three days ago at the San Giacomo hospital in Rome, at 06.28 a.m. He weighed 3.95 kilos at birth and measured 53 cm in length, with a head circumference of 38.5 cm. (Which makes him practically a genius in my book.)

We had only been back in Rome for five days before I went into labour. I find it difficult to put into words why I felt so strongly that I wanted to have my baby in Italy: it was a combination of different reasons, none of them particularly logical. If I'm honest, part of it was Pietro Scala: while I never actually intended to involve him in the birth (he didn't even know I was pregnant at this stage) I just thought we ought to be in the same country in case I suddenly decided I did want him there. Part of it too was plain superstition; I kept thinking to myself that the only way to exorcise the tragedy of my own birth was by repeating the circumstances of it – as though two wrongs could somehow make a right . . . As I put this down on paper, I realize just how crazy it sounds, and I can see now why poor Melody did everything she could to talk me out of it. Finally, and perhaps most childishly of all, I wanted my baby to be able to say when he grew up: *Yes, I was born in Rome* . . . How sad is that?

Looking back on it, I honestly think I'd gone temporarily insane, in fact there's probably some medical term for what happened to me: I mean, there was a brand-new, well-equipped maternity hospital *around the corner from my house* (offering – no, not offering, *encouraging* – me to have just the kind of natural, active birth I wanted) and instead I chose to go to an unknown general hospital in Rome because I believed it would be *safer*. At some point, Melody stopped trying to talk me out of it and managed to persuade our GP (thank you, Dr Ali!) to write a note saying I was fit to travel, even though I was well past the thirty-six-week cut-off point for even the most no-frills of the budget airlines.

Luciana came to meet us at Ciampino; and I must admit I got a lump in my throat when I saw her standing there at the barrier. In some ways she drove me mad when we lived together for those few weeks in Rome (her non-stop criticisms of P.S. – some of them justified, some of them not – the TV on at full volume all day long, that kind of defeated, bitter way she has of looking at the world) but she was so positive and encouraging when she found out about the baby that it more than made up for it.

The day after we arrived, Luciana took us by taxi to the private practice of the gynaecologist under whose care I was to be at the hospital. (Apparently this is standard procedure in Italy – especially so in my case as I was a foreigner with only ten days to go before my due-date.) Dr Fabiani was a plump, middle-aged man with heavy-lidded Mediterranean eyes whose faintly sardonic demeanour reminded me of . . . you guessed it – Pietro Scala! Each time I come to Italy and see his features reproduced in so many different faces, it makes me feel like I'm in that advert – I forget what for – which takes place in a restaurant, and where every single character – the waiter, all the customers, even the chef – are played by the same actor. Dr Fabiani insisted on addressing me as '*signorina*' for the entire visit, even though (I cringe slightly as I write this) I was wearing Luciana's fake wedding ring. (Mostly to please her, but I suppose a part of me craved the respectability it conferred – at least in Italy, where single mothers are rare.) He took my blood pressure, told me I was seriously overweight – I did put on twenty-two kilos during the pregnancy – and said I was to admit myself into Casualty when I felt myself going into labour. No mention of birth-plans or pain relief, but I set myself up for this . . .

Rome was unbearably hot. Like characters in a Marquez novel, the three of us sat, panting, in the living room of the flat, fanning ourselves with the Thai fans Melody bought from the market in Via Catania: curtains drawn, and not only the shutters, but the panes themselves sealed up against the sun. I kept thinking this was just Luciana being stuffy and unhealthy, until I opened the window and a blast of hot air blew in as if from an oven . . . Actually, the build-up to the birth was a fairly happy time: I felt like an egg – Mrs Potato Head, or a big ripe fruit perched on the edge of the sofa, swollen feet resting on the onyx coffee table, while Melody and Luciana endlessly discussed my condition. If I said I had heartburn, they both agreed it meant the baby would have a full head of hair (true, my little darling was born with a glossy chestnut quiff), but they parted company over their predictions of the sex. Luciana said on the basis of my appearance she thought it was a boy (apparently my looks had improved during the pregnancy, which would have indicated a boy – girls are meant to rob a mother of her beauty); but then she did an old-wives' test on me which involved sitting down cross-legged on the floor and getting up. Because I used my left hand to support myself, she then decided that in fact the baby was a girl. Melody, on the other hand, made me lie on my back on the sofa; then she tied a length of thread around her (genuine) wedding ring and dangled it over my stomach. The ring swung vertically backwards and forwards, which Melody said meant it was a boy. (Whereas round and round would have meant a girl.) The hilarious thing is that the moment he was born, Luciana immediately reverted to her looks theory, denying ever having thought he'd be anything but a boy!

And talking of boys, my little man has just woken up. He's due for a feed, but if I'm not too tired, I'll continue this in the afternoon while Melody takes him to the park . . .

*   *   *

I didn't continue that afternoon, or for another two whole weeks. He's been sleeping so badly these last two nights that I went straight to bed the instant Melody left the flat. Three hours seems to be the minimum amount of consecutive sleep I need to function – anything less, and I feel tearful and barely human. I managed to get almost an hour during his morning nap today, which seems to be the equivalent of at least double that at night. Don't ask me why morning sleep should be so satisfying, but it just is, thankfully. Anyway, to continue with my account . . .

The day it all began, I woke up feeling different. The books talked about the nesting instinct kicking in – this mad desire to get down on your hands and knees and scrub the floor. Perhaps because it wasn't my house, and perhaps because I'm not a particularly domesticated person at the best of times (unless you count that brief housework obsession I had when I first came to stay with Luciana, which was really just a symptom of a kind of generalised obsession with anything *all'italiana*) there were no warning signs. The one thing I do remember feeling though is a kind of fluttery excitement which persisted throughout the day. I'd stopped worrying about the actual danger of the birth the moment I stepped off the plane at Ciampino, though logically I still had everything to worry about: no hospital, no friendly midwives, no birth-plan, and the pain itself was something which thankfully had never dwelled particularly in my mind. (That old chestnut I used to hear second-time mothers at antenatal classes come out with, i.e. that if you knew how bad the pain was going to be you'd never be able to go through with it, is actually true: the pain is *so, so* bad, that I'm getting a kind of anxiety attack just writing about it now.)

In the morning Melody and I went for a walk in Villa Torlonia; we returned in time for lunch (lukewarm *pasta e fagioli*, which sounds revolting, but is actually delicious, especially in summer), then I went to rest on Luciana's bed while my two grandmothers (!) read in the sitting room. The moment I woke up and opened my eyes, I knew it had begun. I remember swinging my legs over the side of the bed, standing up; and the instant my feet touched the marble tiles, I felt a popping sensation and a stream of clear liquid gushed from between my legs on to the floor. The funny thing is that it was so beyond my control that it didn't feel like me doing it at all – more as if someone had just dropped a water-balloon at my feet. The midwives back in London, and all the books I'd read, advised hanging on at home as long as possible: apparently being hospitalised too early would just slow things down. Luckily Luciana and Melody didn't hassle me to go into the San Giacomo; if they were worried, they kept it to themselves, and a kind of party atmosphere prevailed for the remainder of the day. I had a long bath and shaved my legs (the bits of them I could reach, that is), then Luciana put on her glasses and gave me a pedicure by the window. By about five o'clock the contractions were coming fairly regularly, and a part of me – the attention-seeking part of me, I suppose – started to think about going to the hospital: I craved action, results, drama . . . But then I decided to hang on ('This is nothing,' Luciana informed me grimly, 'wait till real labour begins') and instead I went for a walk to Piazza Bologna and back. On my return, we had supper – calf's liver and *purée* – and I suppose it was at around seven o'clock that everything began to speed up. The contractions began to feel unbearable (though Luciana was right – they *were* still nothing compared to what awaited me) and at around 7.30 Luciana telephoned for a taxi. I picked up my bags, one for the labour room, one for the ward; and at about 7.45 we set off for the hospital.

The San Giacomo was a big old building set in its own grounds. Graffiti covered the stone-clad façade, and scary-looking junkies and rough-sleepers huddled in groups around the bar, set apart from the hospital near the main gates. In

Casualty, a grim, Victorian-looking room with enamel sinks and white horizontal tiles right up to the ceiling, a male nurse took my notes and told me to lie down on a stretcher. He pulled a metal screen around the bed, and to my horror, I was shaved, given an enema, and told to put on a backless hospital gown. After that, I was taken by wheelchair to the Labour Ward, Luciana and Melody following me, each carrying one of my bags; then the bags were taken from them and they were told to wait for news in the Visitors' Room next door.

I was then taken to a blue-painted room with streaks of blood on the skirting board, and after around half an hour, a middle-aged midwife came to examine me. Even though my waters had broken several hours before, I was still only four centimetres dilated. Then she left me alone in the room, and I spent the remainder of that night prowling up and down the corridors in my backless gown, waiting to reach the magic ten-centimetre mark. At some point, when I could bear it no longer, I found myself banging on the door of the Midwives' common room where I remember they were watching a Brazilian soap-opera called *Manuela*. After some time, another midwife came out looking very aggrieved. At first she wouldn't believe I was in labour ('You've been here five minutes, and I haven't seen a single contraction') but in the end she agreed to examine me back in my room, the whole time muttering under her breath how the only women left these days who knew how to give birth without making a song and dance about it were Africans and prostitutes. Oh, and gypsies, too, I think she said. '*Ancora quattro centimetri!*' she announced triumphantly, before scuttling off back to her programme.

I haven't written too much about the pain, partly because I can't bear to look back on it, but also because I genuinely don't have the words to describe it. With each contraction, my belly would grow taut, my uterus enveloped and dragged downwards by what felt like a bandage of thorns, as though I had become the plaything of the pain, tossed about by it like a cat tosses an injured bird in its claws, until the contraction subsided and it would temporarily release its hold. Which no doubt sounds highly fanciful; but in a way it was a kind of out-of-body experience (consciously so, to some extent), only instead of visualising something pleasant like they taught us at antenatal class, I just kept seeing these gigantic cartoon claws: unsheathed, gleaming, ready to pounce . . .

Just before dawn, another midwife discovered me slumped over the radiator in the corridor, sobbing. She was a tiny little thing in a mini-skirt, dyed black hair down to her waist and Cleopatra-style makeup – an angel in six-inch heels . . . She said her name was Cleofe; she was from Sardinia, and I think she felt sorry for me because she knew I was a foreigner and a *ragazza madre*. She led me back to the room, and donning gloves and a child-sized white coat, which made her look more like a midwife, but only slightly, as she kept her stiletto sandals on, she examined me (eight centimetres! At last!) and told me we were off: '*Pronte per la partenza*' was how she put it. Even though none of what followed came at all close to the kind of birth I ever thought I'd have, the kind of birth we would sit in a circle and discuss at antenatal classes back in London ('I'll try and keep active for as long as possible', or 'If you rock yourself on a Pezzi ball it's meant to help with the contractions'), the kindly presence of Cleofe made up for it. Almost. *I must be the last woman in Western Europe to give birth with my feet in stirrups*, I thought to myself grimly in a pause between con-tractions. Just before he was born (I'm embarrassed to write this bit, as I know one day my son will be reading the account of his birth), just as I was doing the, ahem . . . shit, which Cleofe triumphantly told me meant the baby would be here soon (so much for the enema, by the way), who should stick his head around the door but Dr Fabiani. '*Tutto bene, signorina?*' he said urbanely, before hurriedly making his exit. I remember thinking to myself: *Luciana paid him 300,000 lire for 'Tutto bene, signorina?'*, then the head crowned: I felt a burning sensation in my vagina, then a kind of bony, knobbly slithering as Cleofe pulled him out . . .

(1 September, and a pinch and a punch for the first day of the month – no returns . . .) I haven't been able to write this account for a few days, as my darling boy has been ill with a cold and a temperature of 37.6 degrees. Melody and Luciana said it wasn't that high for a baby – apparently I had more than 38.5 degrees on several occasions both here with Luciana, and once I was back in England with Melody – but it's easy for them to say that now. . . . I can honestly say that I haven't slept more than about half an hour at a time since he got this cold; he's been in the bed with me, and each time I felt myself drop off, I would wake with a start to check on his breathing. I'm going to try to finish this account off as quickly as possible now, because what I really want to do is start keeping a proper record of his development. He does something new every day; I can actually see him growing and changing before my eyes, even though I'm with him all the time. Yesterday I was changing him on the bed, when he looked into my eyes and gave me the most radiant smile I think I've ever seen on a human face. His whole face lit up, and I got this flash of how he might look when he was a man – devastatingly handsome, as it happens . . . Melody said they always used to say it was just wind when babies that small smiled, but she herself never believed it.

So, back to the birth. Cleofe cleaned him up (I was planning on attaching him to the breast before the cord was cut – another deviation from my birth-plan, but who cares?) and she put Luciana's silk vest on him. The moment she placed him in my arms I felt so much joy well up inside me that it was as though I had been plugged into some great reservoir of human love, the suffering of the last few hours but a distant memory now. I was on such a high that I think I even recall saying to Cleofe that I could have another one right there and then (I didn't know the delivery of the placenta and sixteen stiches still lay ahead of me). When all that was over (almost worse than the birth itself, by the way, especially the stitches), Luciana and Melody were allowed in. They stood beside the transparent plastic crib, both of them weeping, and looked down at my little boy – their joint great-grandson. Finally, Melody wiped her eyes and said he reminded her of Julia when she was a baby, while Luciana, after a long pause, said he was a cross between me and one of her brothers in Sicily. ('Not like his father at all,' she murmured neutrally.)

They made me stay three nights in that hospital, supposedly to rest, but I defy anyone to get any sleep being woken up at all hours of the day and night by a non-stop procession of nurses and orderlies. For me, the worst thing, though, was being separated from my baby. Every four hours he would be delivered to me on a trolley, a kind of giant baby-bus packed with newborns all laid out in a row, just like in the Richard Scarry book Melody used to read me when I was a little girl. I would hear the wheels coming down the corridor, and already I would be sitting up in bed waiting for him. But our enchanted half-hour would be over in an instant; sometimes he would be too sleepy to feed, and I would spend the entire time caressing his cheek or pressing my palm against the silky, unlined soles of his feet; while at others, he would have just latched on to the breast when the trolley would reappear and it was time to hand him back.

Returning to Luciana's flat was like the real beginning of my journey towards motherhood. (Sorry if this sounds corny, but it's truly how it felt.) Luciana set up a canvas travel cot in the corner of her bedroom, what in Italy they call *il lettino della nonna*, which was apparently the very same bed I slept in when I was a baby. On to one of its net sides she had pinned a little coral horn, and on to the other, a blue glass eye to ward against the *malocchio*. In some ways, I suppose, I was privileged: while it was true there was no husband and father beside me to share in my joy, my baby and I could not have been more cherished or better looked after. Luciana made endless saucepans of chicken broth and *passata di verdura* ('You need the *sali minerali* in the vegetables to get your strength back up'); while at sundown, when it was cooler, Melody would take him to Villa Torlonia in the sling I brought from London so I could catch up on my sleep.

The three of us were living through a kind of protracted honeymoon or *baby*moon, I suppose you could call it; Luciana's normally dingy flat looked bright and cheerful filled with the flowers Melody bought from the stall in Piazza Bologna, while the smell of soup and freshly ironed clothes contributed to this sense of order and domestic calm. And at the centre of it all, almost as though this tranquillity were radiating out from him like an aura, lay my baby: a beautiful child in that dusk-filled flat . . . To be honest, I could have stayed there for weeks, months, even, without it ever crossing my mind that at some point I was going to have to make a decision about our future; but it was Melody who gently, one evening, asked me whether I had thought about contacting his father before we returned to London.

Now, when I began this journal, I hadn't yet made up my mind whether I was going to write about Pietro Scala; on some level, I've always been conscious that this account is principally for my son to read when he is an adult – my way, I suppose, of compensating (overcompensating, even) for the complete vacuum of information I grew up with regarding my own birth. For this reason, I have hesitated from going into too much detail about his father; however, on balance, I don't think the story can be complete without mentioning our last meeting. By the same token, I feel I ought at least to touch on my feelings for him leading up to this point.

First of all, why did I leave Rome without telling him – the one thing I can guarantee my son will never stop throwing back in my face (and rightly, so) as he is growing up? *Ci metterei la mano sul fuoco*, as Luciana would say, which roughly translates as: I'm certain enough about that to risk putting my hand in the fire . . . I only have to remember my own anger towards Melody and Luciana to imagine the extent to which, in years to come, he will blame me for depriving him of a father. Why didn't I at least give Pietro Scala the chance to face up to his responsibilities before walking out on him? Well, as it happens, I sort of did give him the chance, in that I presented him with an ultimatum to call me by the end of that day. The fact that he didn't call – even though he knew I had something important to discuss, even though the future of our relationship depended on it – was symptomatic of our entire story. By this stage, I had suffered so much that I suppose I had reached the end of my capacity for suffering; I almost craved the new, clean pain of separation. It seemed the longer I stayed in Rome, the more I was turning into a kind of parody of myself: *la ragazza italiana*, forever aping the locals – anxious, eager to get it right.

Plus I honestly believed Pietro Scala would not be the kind of father I wanted for my child – I could already foresee an endless line of broken promises before he felt ready to assume his responsibilities. (Which I know sounds presumptuous, especially bearing in mind my own total lack of experience in the father department.) If I'm truthful, I suppose I felt, too, that there was no place for a man in my life – especially a married one. I thought things would be easier if I was a single mother right from the start, rather than holding out for him to make a commitment. (Easier for my child, too.)

And besides, I very nearly didn't leave; right at the last moment I almost changed my mind. What actually happened is that I said goodbye to Luciana at Ciampino and went through passport control; then, just as I was collecting my hand-luggage off the X-ray machine, I happened to glance up at one of the airport security guards who was handing me back my change in a plastic dish. Something about his appearance – he was a bit fat, with smooth dark hair and the suggestion of man-breasts beneath his blue cotton shirt – reminded me of Pietro Scala. The lazy way he stood there, one hand tucked into his shirt, squeezing the flesh beneath his armpit as he cracked a joke with his colleague on the machine next to him, was so easy, so sensual – so completely un-English – that I think that's when it really hit me that I was leaving. I remember tears came into my eyes, and I could scarcely get it together enough to gather up my bags from the conveyor belt. Somehow, I made it over to the duty-free shop; and I was just stuffing my boarding pass into the front pocket of my rucksack when there, right at the very bottom, I found a half-used 5,000-lire phone-card – probably left over from that time I'd rung his mobile twenty times after reading the pregnancy book in the Lion Bookshop. There was an orange SIP pay-phone mounted on a pillar right beside the departure gate: nothing was preventing me from calling him at the office, giving him one last chance to make up his mind . . . At this stage I didn't even know if there was any credit left on the card, but I held it in my hand like it was my key out of jail, pressing my thumb down on to the jagged edge where the corner had been snapped off to activate it. It was a sign, I thought: if the card still worked it meant we were destined to be together . . . I waited until our flight was called, watching the passengers with children, who had been allowed through first, filing across the tarmac towards the aircraft. I remember this man was holding an adorable-looking toddler on his shoulders, and that too seemed like a sign. When the departure lounge was empty, and the ground staff were checking through their lists for latecomers, I walked over to the tele-phone and looked at the card. Nobody knew who I was: there was nothing about me which connected me to that Ryanair plane on the tarmac. Turning my back on the gate, I lifted the receiver and fed the card into the slit: *I'll do it*, I remember

thinking, *whatever he says to me, I won't get on that plane . . .*
But, sharp as a retort, the machine spat the card back, and I
heard my name being called over the loudspeaker.

Once I'd returned to England, I was so consumed by the
sense of new life growing inside me that it almost completely
pushed out any residual sadness I had about the way things
ended with Pietro Scala. Which isn't to say I hadn't loved him,
though to this day I'm still uncertain whether 'love' is an
accurate way to describe what I felt for him. Our affair was so
tied up, for me at least, with the shock of finding out about my
father, his subsequent death, and being in Italy for the first
time that I lost all sense of objectivity about Pietro Scala or his
feelings for me. I know (or rather I imagine) that nobody
enters into a love-story feeling objective – surely that's the
whole point – but the multiple shocks I had received in such a
short space of time left me particularly vulnerable to excessive
emotions. Anyway, call it what you will – love, lust, need – my
son was conceived in a moment of true passion, at least on my
part. (Which is as much as I intend to say on the subject.)

It was Melody who telephoned Pietro Scala – yesterday – to
inform him that he was a father. It wasn't cowardice on my
part getting Melody to break the news to him, at least not just
cowardice (after all, I'm still going to have to see him –
tomorrow afternoon, as it happens) but more a desire to
prolong, even for one more day, the fuzzy-edged bliss of early
motherhood. For this reason, I'd been putting off calling him
until the very last moment, and deliberately arranged things so
that the only time we could meet was when I knew I was going
to be pressed for time. (I have an appointment tomorrow at the
consulate to register his birth; besides which, I feel Pietro Scala
should be allowed, if nothing else, to have his say regarding
the choice of name.)

It's 1.35, and time to quickly feed and change him before
setting out on foot for Piazza del Popolo. I told Melody to
inform Pietro Scala that I would be sitting on a certain bench

opposite the Avenue of Poets at 3.00 p.m., which will then leave me two hours to get from the Pincio to the Embassy in Porta Pia for my appointment at 5.00. I'm too nervous to eat lunch; in fact I'm in such turmoil that I'm not sure if I can go through with it. Luckily Melody has offered to accompany me, so that if I do bottle out at the last minute, she can wait for him in my place. Apart from anything else, I don't know what I'm supposed to wear; none of my clothes fit me any more – at least none of the glamorous Italian ones I bought before my pregnancy – so it's going to have to be a forgiving linen shirt and drawstring trousers. Much more importantly, what is my son to wear? (I'm running late, so I'll bring this journal with me and try to do some writing while I'm out. If nothing else, it might help keep the panic at bay . . .)

London, 15 November 2001

Of course I didn't get any writing done that day – what on earth made me think I would? – nor have I made any attempt to bring this journal up to date since then. Just two days after we got back to England, September 11th happened. I don't have the words to describe what it felt like watching those planes ploughing into the two towers. That image was repeated everywhere – on the News, in the newspapers, and even to mark section breaks in TV programmes – almost as if we had to see it that many times to convince us that something so freakish and evil could have really happened. The three of us spent the whole day huddled together in the shop watching Melody's old portable black and white set – I couldn't bear to let her or my baby out of sight, as though more evil lurked just around the corner – as though overnight the world had suddenly become a more dangerous and unpredictable place. (And there was I thinking nothing could get more unpredictable than what I've been through in the last year.) Pretty soon, though, I made a conscious decision to blank out what was happening around me and just concentrate on looking after my baby. I suppose you'd call it a survival instinct. My reasoning was this: the old world order had been destroyed, we were about to be caught in a war of attrition between the West and its enemies, and there was *absolutely nothing I could do to prevent it*. My watching the News wouldn't help any of those poor victims or their families, wouldn't delete the heart-breaking messages of goodbye that people came back to that evening on their ansaphones – and besides, all that crying in front of the TV turned my milk sour. (I know that for a fact, as my poor boy had terrible colic in those days.)

Apart from all this, it feels wonderful to be home. I've had plenty of time to think about things since the last time I wrote in this book, which should go some way towards explaining why I haven't picked it up sooner. From the very outset, I made it clear that I didn't want this account to be about me; and I honestly think if I had started writing before this moment, I couldn't have avoided cramming these pages with my own thoughts and feelings. I keep having this vision of my son, aged eighteen, squirming with discomfort as he is forced to enter into the intimate details of his mother's *stato d'anima* – as if the gory particulars of his birth weren't enough!

So, before describing our meeting in the Avenue of Poets (and to give myself one last chance to decide how I'm going to deal with this next bit), let me bring this account up to date with some of the practical changes which have taken place in our lives since I last wrote.

1) In accordance with Ennio's will, Luciana and I have become financial beneficiaries of the success of the Rebibbia memoirs. Apparently, the profits were always going to be split between P.S. and my father; but as Ennio died before the book's publication, Luciana and I get 25 per cent each of his share. As it has become a bestseller all over Europe and across the Atlantic, this is likely to be quite a considerable sum of money.

2) Luciana plans to use her share to retire to Sicily. She has already bought the cottage where she grew up, and where two of her brothers now live, and is presently negotiating with the Leonforte heirs to buy the property next door. Melody is considering chipping in with the cost of the second cottage, so that she can spend the winter months there.

3) I am using some, but not all, of my share to buy a canalboat moored outside the Dissenters' Chapel in Kensal Green. At present, it is being renovated; but we hope to move in sometime in early spring.

As I write, I have finally arrived at a compromise in my head regarding how I'm to describe my meeting with Pietro Scala. (About time, too, you might say . . .) The obvious thing to do is to write a completely separate account of it *at the back of this book*, so that if now, or in the years to come, I decide I want to rip it out, I can do so without ruining the rest of the journal. (So please turn to ten pages from the end. . . .)

(Ten pages from the end)

It was so sad.

So sad, that as I lie in the dark, feeding you, or listening to the sound of your breath as you sleep beside me on the pillow, I cry when I remember that day. I'm sorry, my darling boy, but that's how it is. I sat by the empty carousel on that hot autumn afternoon, watching your father walk along the gravel path towards me, and this is what I saw: not the lover who just a few months earlier sat beside me on the same green-painted bench and laid down the law about our love (our love, *his* law) – what he called *l'ordine naturale delle cose*, and in doing so broke my heart – but the fat, elderly father in Luciana's photograph, standing beside the very same carousel, his angry-looking boy by his side.

He asked to hold you; so I unstrapped you from the sling

and placed you in his arms. I remember you were wearing this funny white bonnet which made you look like a girl, and a kind of cotton smock which in Italy they call a *coprifascia*. You stirred a little, but amazingly you didn't wake up. I didn't want to think so – I'd hardened my heart long before not to let myself – but a voice in my head whispered: *You see, he doesn't stir because he recognises his father* . . . He looked tired; he'd lost weight and his shirt was crumpled and shabby-looking, or perhaps that's just how I chose to remember it. He asked about the birth, he wanted to know how much you weighed, whether you were thriving, so I told him that you loved your food, and then – almost as though, like me, he'd hardened *his* heart, but still it escaped him – he said: *You see . . . just like his father . . .*

I felt connected to him – how could I not as I watched him hold our child in his arms? – but I couldn't for the life of me imagine we had ever been lovers. It was as though my body refused to dredge up a single erotic memory of that time – that desire which kept me awake at night, or prowling the streets by day in the hope of . . . what? Of bumping into him? Of forcing him at gunpoint to choose between me and his wife? I almost contemplated asking him: *Were we really lovers? Did you ever love me?* But I chose to remain silent. Perhaps I feared his answer . . .

After a while you awoke and began to fret. A little self-consciously, I took you from your father's arms and attached you to my breast. He watched me feed you; then, soon afterwards, he got up and kissed us both goodbye. He said he'd keep in touch, that he hoped to visit us one day in London. When you were older, perhaps. Later, when you'd fed from both breasts, I strapped you back inside the sling and walked through Villa Borghese, past the race-track, towards Porta Pia.

At the consulate, I filled in the forms to register your birth. We named you Ennio.

ACKNOWLEDGEMENTS

My thanks to: Dick Davis, Pat Kavanagh, Alexandra Pringle, Sarah Ballard, Victoria Millar, Romana Canneti, Bettai Manfredi-Simonetti, Ornella Manfredi-Simonetti, Alberto Gentili, Menotti Pergoli and Isotta, Fiammetta and Livio Reichenbach.

A NOTE ON THE AUTHOR

Simonetta Wenkert was born in London in 1965 of
an Italian mother and an Austrian father. After
graduating from Durham University, she translated
A cercar la bella morte (*In Search of a Glorious Death*)
by Carlo Mazzantini, which was shortlisted for the
Independent Foreign Fiction Award. Simonetta has lived
in Athens, Rome and Jerusalem where she worked
as a teacher and translator of film scripts. She currently
lives in London with her husband and three children.
The Sunlit Stage is her first novel.

A NOTE ON THE TYPE

The text of this book is set in Linotype Sabon, named after the type founder, Jacques Sabon. It was designed by Jan Tschichold and jointly developed by Linotype, Monotype and Stempel, in response to a need for a typeface to be available in identical form for mechanical hot metal composition and hand composition using foundry type.

Tschichold based his design for Sabon roman on a fount engraved by Garamond, and Sabon italic on a fount by Granjon. It was first used in 1966 and has proved an enduring modern classic.